# AN IDOL FOR OTHERS

# AN IDOL FOR OTHERS

# GORDON MERRICK

**alyson books**

LOS ANGELES • NEW YORK

MANUFACTURED IN THE UNITED STATES OF AMERICA.


THIS TRADE PAPERBACK IS PUBLISHED BY ALYSON PUBLICATIONS INC.,
P.O. BOX 4371, LOS ANGELES, CALIFORNIA 90078-4371.
DISTRIBUTION IN THE UNITED KINGDOM BY TURNAROUND PUBLISHER SERVICES LTD.,
UNIT 3 OLYMPIA TRADING ESTATE, COBURG ROAD, WOOD GREEN,
LONDON N22 6TZ ENGLAND.

FIRST PUBLISHED IN 1977 BY AVON BOOKS
FIRST ALYSON EDITION: MAY 1998

02 01 00 99 98   10 9 8 7 6 5 4 3 2 1

ISBN 1-55583-295-4
(PREVIOUSLY PUBLISHED WITH ISBN 0-380-00971-4 BY AVON BOOKS.)

LIBRARY OF CONGRESS CATALOGING-IN-PUBLICATION DATA
MERRICK, GORDON.
AN IDOL FOR OTHERS / GORDON MERRICK. -- 1ST ALYSON ED.
I. TITLE.
PS3525.E641313 1998
813'.52--DC21                                98-11230 CIP

FOR LARRY
WITH FAITH IN THE BIG FUTURE

He performed the ritual that permitted him to enter his own house—standing within range of the viewer, speaking the formula that indicated the absence of muggers or gunmen lurking in the background—and passed from the late-May heat of East 75th Street into the air-conditioned citadel of home.

He was immediately caught up in the events of the day. His very executive secretary, Alice, met him in the hall. She had been with him so long that he no longer knew what she looked like.

"Hi, Walter. Did you get it? Are you pleased?"

He held up the small Verdura box he was carrying. "I think she'll like it."

"The boys arrived and have gone out again already," Alice said. "They promised to be on time for lunch. *Time* sent proofs of their cover story, if you want to read about yourself. All the papers have been calling asking for advance copies of tonight's speech."

"That's the committee's business," he said. "Did we get last week's grosses?"

"Yes. A bit better than the week before."

"Real cool, man." He mocked the jargon of the day with impish eyes. He was a tall man with a fine, well-proportioned figure, but the imp still lurked in his face, around the corners of his slightly upslanting eyes, and shaped the curve of his generous mouth. His habitual expression was impishly mocking. Without giving her more than the surface of his attention, he was aware of her hands fluttering about herself in the way she had when she didn't know how he would react to what she was going to say.

"There's a wire of congratulations from the president," she announced.

"You're kidding! Who told that creep about our little cultural activities?" Small things like this occasionally assured him that some part of him still functioned at the old level–independently, irreverently, perhaps even creatively.

"David's waiting upstairs in the library. He brought a friend."

"Did somebody give them something to drink? Tell Clara to join us. And don't let anybody through. We'll go public this evening." He turned from her. There was an elevator, but he rarely used it; he had always been energetic and liked to keep his youthful body on the move. He climbed the stairs, feeling the house close around him. He had been assured that the air-conditioning reproduced the most ideal outdoor atmospheric conditions, so he knew his sense of suffocation my be psychological. Clara's cocoon. Inaccurate. Every piece of fine furniture, every glowing picture, from Bacon to Zadkine, had been coveted more by him than by her.

He turned down a short hall, past some of his splendid possessions, and entered the library. He was immediately dazzled by the first sight of David he had had for almost two years: skin bronzed and burnished to extraordinary apricot tones, hair as golden as ever. David sprang to his feet and rushed to him; they were in each others' arms, hugging and whooping with pleasure.

"God, how wonderful. You made it," Walter exclaimed.

"I'll say. I couldn't have missed your apotheosis as the Grand Old Man. How does it feel?"

"I'd rather be the Boy Wonder."

"You're doing all right."

"You too. You're absolutely gorgeous."

"Still trying to turn my pretty head. How's Clara?"

Even in the exuberance of their greeting, Walter was aware of the guarded note that crept into David's voice at the question, and he

2

closed his mind to its implications. "Fine. She'll be along any minute. She's dying to see you."

They relinquished each other and David turned to include the figure that stood motionless near the empty fireplace. "I've brought Tom. He's just heading back to the Coast. This was the only time I could get you together. I thought you ought to at least meet. Tom Jennings. The great Walter Makin himself."

Walter moved to the stranger and shook hands, offering him a greeting that became perfunctory as he looked at the attractive young man. *Considerably more attractive than most,* he thought. He refused to allow himself to explore the source of the attraction but waved them to chairs, freshened their drinks, and poured himself one. He and David gossiped cheerfully while he dredged up from the back of his mind the few bits of information he knew about Tom Jennings. He had written a successful novel whose title escaped him. David had written about a play Jennings was working on. Something else. Ah, yes. A man he had lived with for a good many years had recently died. The sort of thing only David would dare pass on as being of interest to him.

Walter and David exchanged the questions required by courtesy about their respective wives and children. Then David picked up the day's major event, tonight's award, and gave it a thorough, satiric verbal airing, reeling off Walter's most disastrous failures, quoting vicious criticisms, referring to crises that only they had shared. But despite David's incorrigibly flippant manner, there was a current beneath it of deep affection and admiration.

For the first time since he had been told of the award, Walter felt pride and satisfaction in the recognition of an achievement that had seemed for years only the acting out of a fantasy in which he had somehow been trapped. Would he still feel the excitement of their first triumphs if the break with David hadn't occurred? He glanced at the small package he had left on the bar table and wished Clara would come in. It would be good to present the gift while estrangement was forgotten—or overlaid by a quickened awareness of the solid reality of the work he had done and, in simple justice, of her contribution to it.

3

He felt, while he and David teased and scored off each other, the still attention with which Tom Jennings observed him. He played up to it as a showman giving his audience its money's worth. David's evocation of the past was gratifying, but his sense of timing warned him not to overdo it. Jennings was here for a purpose; he must save time to lend him a professional ear.

"Oh, David," he sighed in a lull in the conversation. "We did have a good time. None of it could've happened without you."

"Nonsense. I was just one of dozens of lovesick slaves ready to lay down their lives for you. I must say I was pretty good at disposing of the competition—up to a point." They smiled at each other, but as the chance remark took on an unwelcome significance, strain crept into their smiles. Walter looked hastily away.

Tom Jennings offered an opportunity to cover the lapse, and Walter seized upon it. "This must be pretty boring for Tom. I'm sorry." He looked at his other guest more directly, but still registered only superficial details. Tom was young, but indefinably so, late 20s or early 30s, and displayed none of the insignia of contemporary youth. He was clean-shaven, his hair curled on his neck above his collar, his clothes would have been regarded as conservative, even by Walter's generation—loafers, slacks, shirt and tie, a comfortable-looking jacket.

"I'm fascinated," Jennings said. "David's talked a lot about you, but it's beautiful to see you together."

The tingle in Walter's veins made him sit up straighter. The deep, quiet voice spoke directly to Walter with a multitude of meanings. Walter realized that while he clowned with David, the young man's stillness was getting through to him, so that now an unknown connection had been made. Involuntarily and undisguisedly, Walter studied the face across from him and saw lightly tanned skin stretched taut over strong bones, eyes arresting for their directness, and a mouth firmly modeled but faintly vulnerable in the curve of the upper lip. He felt the tingle in his veins again as his eyes dropped to the strong, smooth column of neck, then to the hands with extraordinarily long, sinewy fingers spread out on the arms of the chair.

4

"David tells me you've been writing a play," he said, appalled at the inadequacy of the remark. It contained no hint of the recognition of what, almost palpably and in a few seconds, had taken place between them, whatever it was–a pledge of some sort, perhaps simply a pledge of understanding and respect. "Have you finished it?"

"Yes."

"Am I going to be allowed to read it?"

"I'd love to know what you think of it, but I've explained to David that I'd feel foolish submitting it to you in the official sense. It's not on your scale."

"You mean, big, splashy commercial stuff? You don't know how I got started. I haven't always been what I am today. David could tell you some stories." He exchanged a look with David, and they rocked about in their chairs, "Oh, God, do you remember?"

David howled. "It was quite a light in that forest."

Walter returned his attention to Tom. "I wouldn't trust myself anymore to judge you new kids. I know what's bad, but it's that fine line between the passable and the really good where I might fail you. Would that kind of opinion interest you?" Their eyes searched each other.

Tom gave a little nod. "Done. I know I'm good but subject to failure like everybody else." He almost grinned.

It happened. Walter felt it jolt his whole body.

A cheerful boyish voice rang out in a shower room, and a succession of ecstatic moments, unsuspected except by those who had shared them with him, rushed across his memory–Harry's legacy. The secret flaw in a life that presented a perfect surface, the incarnation of a design he had conceived when he was barely emerging from adolescence. Walter Makin, the self-created man.

A secret flaw. He had always conducted himself as if it were a secret, even with Clara–especially with Clara. He hoped she wouldn't come in now. He wanted to sort out the consequences of what had happened and settle on ways to cope with them. He turned to David, feeling as if he had been caught in an unimaginable indiscretion but allowing nothing to show.

5

"I'm glad you brought this guy. Something might come of it." Irresistibly, he turned back to Tom, "You're going back to the Coast soon?"

Tom answered, "Yes, this afternoon."

"Did you bring the play with you?"

Tom's smile broadened. "I don't carry it around with me waiting for somebody to ask for a reading."

"You should. You never know when lightning will strike." They were moving now, moving into each other by their separate routes. The imp was possessing Walter; his eyes markedly slanted upward, his rich laughter flowed from him, a lock of wavy dark chestnut and gray hair fell over his forehead. He was no longer conscious of his charm. He was not attempting a seduction. He didn't have to. Tom's eyes held him directly and beckoned him.

Tom remained still and attentive, but his long fingers stirred in a distant caress, and his deep voice moved to him and embraced him as he said, "You're lucky I don't have it. I'm dying to read it to you."

David ceased to exist.

"There's a lot I'd like to ask you, but you'd probably rather not talk about it until I've read it."

"I don't mind. It's just that there doesn't seem to be much time."

"That's it. We'll have to work things out. What time is it?" It was one of Walter's affectations never to carry a watch, and now it seemed to him that it was ordained for this moment. Tom's consulting his watch was the first small illustration of relationship, of a vast potential for serving each other. He noticed that the backs of his hands and wrists were hairless.

"Almost 12:30," Tom said.

"Good." Walter came to a quick decision. Get him out before Clara turned up. A few minutes alone together would begin the process of exorcising the demon that had suddenly taken possession of him. "I have time to do one last errand before I give myself up to the demands of fame and family. I'm sorry I can't ask you for lunch, but I promised to keep it just us. Can I drop you wherever you're going?"

"I don't want to take you out of your way."

6

"Where do you want to go?"

"Back to the hotel–the Gladwyn."

"Perfect. I'm going within a block of it. The car's right outside." Walter gave his game away with a little chuckle of complicity as he rose. Tom stood and confirmed Walter's impression that they were of almost equal height. It brought their eyes level. He appeared to have a nice body under the unrevealing clothes, trim and spare.

Walter lifted the instrument from its cradle and pushed a button. He was aware of Tom and David drifting toward each other, and he heard them say something about California. He immediately felt a stab of jealousy. Alice answered.

"Tell Mike I'll want him for a little while. I'm coming right down." He tried to remember if there had ever been a hint of Tom's being David's "protégé," in the latter's special meaning of the word. He hung up hastily and turned to observe them. They were chatting easily; the room was once more filled with David's golden dazzle.

"I thought you two might hit it off," David said with his customary exuberance as Walter joined them. "I love you both."

Walter weighed every word for innuendo, but David seemed genuinely pleased that the meeting had gone well. "You don't mind if I leave you alone for a minute, do you, old pal? Clara and the kids will be here any minute. Tell them I'll be right back." He waited while the two shook hands. David made of their farewell a parody of flirtatiousness; Tom thanked him for having arranged the meeting. The urge to put his arm around Tom's shoulders was very nearly uncontrollable. He longed to claim him, however briefly, before the inevitable renunciation. He allowed himself a light touch on his arm as he urged him from the room and down the hall toward the elevator. They weren't likely to run into Clara here.

A door slid open, and they stepped inside, without their eyes meeting. Snugly confined together, Walter's response to the physical presence at his side was so intense that he had difficulty breathing. The descent was mercifully short. They were out of the house and across the burning sidewalk and into the air-conditioned limousine without hav-

7

ing exchanged a glance. Mike closed the door on them and moved around to the driver's seat. Walter gave instructions. "All right, Mike," he concluded, "you can shut us up in our cage." A glass panel slid up, separating front from back. Mike lived with a third-rate prizefighter and was utterly trustworthy.

Walter settled back with a sigh and looked at his fellow passenger. Tom's eyes were already on him. Walter felt the shock jolt through him again as eyes met, held, searched, accepted. Walter was almost hurled forward to hold what was his, but he remained motionless. A cuddle in the back of a car was unthinkable with the impressive young man who was so clearly his own master.

Walter took a deep breath before he spoke. "You know, of course, that I want to spend the rest of my life with you."

Tom laughed, a deep roll of mirth that relieved tension. "I know a lot about you, Mr. Makin. I promise not to believe a word you say."

"Very wise, I'm sure; but it's apt to waste precious time. Let's pretend that I mean it and go on from there."

"It's quite a point to go on from."

"If you know a lot about me, you must know that I don't generally pursue young men, no matter how fascinating. It must be embarrassing for you to have an old gentleman of 50 carrying on like this."

"At 38, I'm still capable of being shy, not embarrassed. Not with you."

"That old?"

"I'd ask the same of you, except everybody knows how old you are. You're having a well-publicized birthday."

"Am I right in believing we've fallen for each other at first sight? Don't bother, I know."

"We both know. The strange thing is that I wanted you to fall for me, even though I know it can lead to absolutely nothing."

"Nothing?"

"Well?"

"Do you really *have* to go flying off this afternoon?"

"I'm not flying. I'm driving."

"Really? Alone?"

Tom chuckled. "I've had an idea I might pick up a companion along the road. You've screwed up that romantic fancy." He put his hand out palm down on the seat between them.

Walter covered it with his own and held it still for a moment. The contact felt so natural that, although it thrilled and touched him, it didn't overturn his mind or unhinge his body as he had thought their first physical intimacy might do. A delicious throb of desire surged up in his groin. He turned Tom's hand over and ran his hand across its breadth and down the long fingers and back so that their hands lay palm to palm and gripped each other, a promise of total union. "That's one small part of you I fell for," Walter said. "I'm queer for hands. That's already more than nothing." Tom's eyes became grave, and Walter saw for the first time that they were guarded. He cleared his throat and hurried to consolidate the promise. "I want to spend my life with you, but we could settle for something more practical–at least for a start. Can't you stick around for a couple of more days?"

"I could, maybe, but I'm not going to. Were you really in a gay bar when you heard you'd been voted Father of the Year?"

Walter winced. "Not exactly, but true enough to let it stand. I grasp your point. You're wrong, of course. My interest in you has absolutely no connection with a pickup in a gay bar."

"I'll accept that, but what *does* it connect with?"

"All the things that matter most in life, I think. If we were in bed together, I'd answer that more fully."

Tom's eyes widened and pain sprang up in them. "Oh, no, Walter. Don't do this. Do you expect me to ask you up to my room now? I probably would if you wanted me to, but I hope you don't."

"As far as I can see, there's nothing about you I don't want, but–well, no, I suppose not. Not like that. There's no time. You've got to stay."

"I can't."

"Stubborn, aren't you?" Humor erased pain and created affection in the looks they exchanged. "All right. I'll follow you to the Coast. I can make it in about a week. After all, it's business. I'll want to discuss the play with you after I've read it."

9

"Now wait. Don't play games with my work. I probably wouldn't see you if you came. Look, Walter, let's say it like it is. As I understand it, you're straight, with a few gay fringes around the edges. I'm queer through and through and always have been. That's all there is to talk about. I don't see how talk will change it."

"Talk won't, but this feels like a good deal more than a fringe. How do you account for that?"

"I don't have to. It's your problem. It's incredible feeling it working between us in spite of David. Nothing could've turned us off. It's one of the most fascinating things that's ever happened to me. Walter Makin, of all people, on the make for me. That doesn't mean I can build a life around it. Frankly, that's all I can let myself think about these days." The grip on their hands tightened.

"I see. What about the companion you thought you might find along the road?"

"It never occurred to me I'd fall in love with him. Remember somebody called Mark? I talked a lot about you with him. I've always known you, Walter."

The car slowed and drew into the curb. They were pulling up in front of the Gladwyn. Walter picked up the speaker. "Go on, Mike. Get caught in a traffic jam for another 15 minutes, will you?" He turned back to Tom. "Who's been talking about me now?"

"Mark—Mark Travere. Don't you remember him?"

"Oh, Jesus. You know Mark?" Memories. This young man had an unerring instinct for loosing the floods of guilt. "It's impossible. That guy was more than 20 years ago."

"Yeah. A long time ago. Not long after you knew him—1950? I run into him every now and then. He gave me my first glimpse of the wicked world. You were it."

"Oh, lord, what was his verdict?"

"Beware of married men who are fatally attractive to boys. I didn't know what he was talking about at the time, but it's fairly obvious now. There's this mad pixie quality about you. Not what you'd expect in a family man of 50. It's ridiculous for me to fall in love with you, and yet..." His voice sank almost to a whisper. "Oh, my God. It's all happening so quickly, and yet nothing's happening. Fifteen minutes. No time to get heavy."

Their grip loosened, and their fingers toyed with each other, intertwining, caressing, playing little games of pursuit and withdrawal. Walter indulged in similar intimacies—the touch of hands, a pat on the behind, a quick evaluation of genitals—with untold hundreds of cooperative youths encountered professionally. It was the heightened awareness of human connection that drew him, something beyond the banality of conventional sexual responses—a perilous exposure and an exaltation of being, part of his creative equipment.

It pleased him to think of it this way, and he disciplined himself to avoid surprises. He had almost believed as he spirited Tom out of the house that he would arrive at indifference by this familiar route. Now he felt himself sinking deeper into an impossible involvement. Could this be the involvement he had promised himself, for all these last long dead years, that he would recognize and accept if it ever happened? Under the circumstances, he didn't know what he could do about it even if it were. He was busy. Tom was leaving.

He wanted to memorize Tom's face. As he did so, he found with delight that there was no single feature that he considered beautiful. He wasn't infatuated with a pretty face. His mouth wasn't the sort that demanded to be kissed, although he dearly wanted to do so. His gray-green eyes were deep-set, which gave them their peculiar penetrating directness, but they didn't melt or swoon as poets had found eyes sometimes did, nor were they shadowed with lashes that brushed the cheeks. His nose was straight. His chin was strong. His hair wasn't quite blond and lay thick and smooth on his well-shaped head, curling slightly around his ears and neck. His fresh skin was stretched over bones with great economy, as if every detail had been carefully calculated and willed with nothing left over or superfluous.

He disengaged his hand and put his arm in back of Tom's shoulders. He moved his other hand across to reclaim the hand he had momentarily relinquished. It was welcomed by caressing fingers. The con-

11

finement of his crossed legs became exquisitely strained. Coming so close to outright possession of the tantalizing body made it seem unnatural and inhuman not to go further, but everything about Tom commanded restraint. "Listen, I want you to tell me exactly what you're going to do when I drop you at the hotel, and then I'll tell you why you shouldn't." Feeling Tom's laughter against him was a revelation; he wanted to hold him forever.

"Well, I've got to make sure my laundry's back. That's pretty exciting. Then I'll have some lunch and pack and check that the car's ready to go. I want to be on the road before the rush."

"Is there any earthly reason why you shouldn't do all those fascinating things tomorrow? You could come to the shindig tonight. You'll have to listen to a lot of people saying what a genius I am, but I don't think I'll make too much of an ass of myself. As soon as it's over, we can split, baby, as they say."

"No, baby. If you think spending the night with me would help you get me out of your system, I'd love to oblige, but I can't. I don't want the knife in any deeper. The way things are now, I'll probably cry all the way to California, but at least you've given me some new ideas about myself. If I went to bed with you and had to say good-bye, it would demolish me. I don't think you understand what you're playing around with. You probably can't. Mark told me everything, you know."

"What happened 20 years ago doesn't necessarily have anything to do with now, but there's no reason to suppose I'm less of a shit." He withdrew his arm and straightened and put both his hands on Tom's. "All right. I'll be out in a week. For God's sake, drive carefully."

"What kind of a car are we in? I ask you now, to cover an awkward moment."

"I haven't the slightest idea. They told me the Rolls-Royce was too conspicuous, and ever since I've been riding around in this beat-up number."

"It's a tough life. I have to keep reminding myself how strange it must be to be Walter Makin. You carry an awful lot of weight around with you, don't you?"

"Yes. A wife, two sons, God knows how many dependents, a house I can't get into, a career I don't seem to know how to stop. I'm no prize, I can assure you. But I can fucking well go to California if I want to. You'd better give me some pertinent addresses and things." He withdrew a slim leather notebook from the breast pocket of his light jacket and poised a gold pencil over a page. Tom told him where he lived. "San Francisco, eh? It's the place I like best in the USA, but of course I'm not allowed to live there. No films. No theater. A wasteland. When do I get the play?"

"David's sending it to you. He'll be back day after tomorrow."

"David. How about David?"

"What about him? Oh, you mean—good lord. *David?* Our very own David Fiedler? Don't be silly. I'm much too old for him. He likes fluffy young things. You must know that. Anyway, it's mostly just talk. He really loves his wife."

"Yes, David's always been an original when it comes to people. I'm bound and chained to mine. Tom—Jesus, I didn't realize what a beautiful name that is. Tom. Thomas. Tom Jennings. Do you suppose I could fall in love with you? That's an absurd question and highly suspect because I honestly don't think I've ever been in love in my life. No matter what you've heard, I swear to God I don't go in for this sort of thing as a rule. Is there nothing I can say to make you stay?"

"No, Mr. Makin. I'm not going to let you demolish me."

"Quite right. I wonder if you're not going to demolish me. No matter. There's really not much left to demolish. If you knew the whole story, you'd stay with me out of simple human compassion."

"Christ, Walter. Don't." Their hands gripped each other until their knuckles went white. Tears brimmed up in Tom's eyes. He grinned. "You see? It's starting."

The car came to a stop in front of the Gladwyn. The two were gazing at each other, both looking spent and distracted. The hotel doorman sprang forward to open the door.

"Just a minute," Walter called in a voice accustomed to command, without taking his eyes off Tom.

13

"This *is* an awkward moment." Tom's grin became shy and touchingly young. "I don't see how I can get out, if you know what I mean. I don't want to show the entire world. I've got to arrange things."

"You too? I should tear your clothes off—the hell with your scruples." Walter felt that he was relinquishing his right of possession as he sat motionless while Tom thrust his hands into his pockets and sat forward on the edge of the seat and shifted about, arranging things. Why should they let anything interfere with their giving each other such easy pleasure? "Doesn't it make a difference if I solemnly swear to come out next week? Wouldn't that prove that I don't just want a night to get you out of my system?'"

"Spending a couple of days in California isn't going to change anything. All that weight." He completed what he was doing but kept a hand in his pocket as he edged around to face Walter. "Forget what I said about not seeing you—I'd love for you to come. At least, I think I will. It all depends on how things go in the next few days. Strangely enough, I think I'm going to be wildly happy."

"How long will the trip take?"

"I allow five days. I've got to be there in six."

"Fine. I'll get there a day or so after you." He squeezed Tom's knee. "Call me collect any time you want."

"I hope I'll be able not to." He put his hand on Walter's. "You know, if we play our cards right, maybe we'll end up just liking each other instead of this other thing."

"It remains to be seen which of us is going to get out of this in one piece. I have a funny feeling it won't be me. You'd better get going before I create a scandal."

Their hands gripped each other again. They exchanged another long, searching look. Tom almost weakened. Wouldn't an hour in bed be better than nothing? No. The thing that had happened between them was too extraordinary to handle in the ordinary way. Maybe Walter would come to California. They might have a fighting chance to make something of it there. He reached for the door as the doorman sprang forward again.

14

Walter watched him go, imprinting on his mind the way he moved, loose and easy, with a hand still in his trouser pocket. He uncrossed his legs and spread them and dropped his hands over his crotch.

"Hey, Mike," he shouted. "Open up." The glass wall separating them descended. "Push buttons, Mike. Open everything."

"It's pretty hot out, Walter."

"Good. Let's roast then. I want to breathe plain polluted air. Home, James."

All the windows slid silently down as the car swung back into traffic. "He's a hell of a fine-looking guy," Mike said over his shoulder.

"You thought so?"

"No question about it. You don't see many beauties like him around this dump."

"That's what I was thinking." Movement created a hot breeze. Walter sat back with his eyes closed and breathed deeply. They would be together again in a week. That thought would get him through today and tomorrow and the next day. After that, it would probably get tougher, but maybe Tom would call and bridge the gap. He should have insisted on his calling. He already felt his absence as an ache of emptiness all through him.

Perhaps it had happened at last. Was he capable of falling in love? He had been emotionally dead for so long that he couldn't believe in it. In a week a trip to California would probably seem a tiresome chore. He could write him, especially if he had something nice to say about his play, perhaps arrange for him to come back to New York later. Time settled everything, even Clara.

*Who do you think you're kidding?* he asked himself. Nothing would ever settle Clara. He had had the choice once, but had handed it over to her. He had made his real choice at the beginning when he had determined never to do anything that might blight his chances to reach the heights. Tonight's award was the payoff; it wouldn't have been conferred on a man with an acknowledged flaw, a flaw that wasn't as secret as he would have liked (Mark had talked) but had never been confirmed by a public scandal.

15

His life was a fantasy, and Clara was trapped in it as surely as he.

His thoughts made him restless and strangely unsure of himself. He opened his eyes and ran a hand over his stomach. Flat. Looking down at himself, he wished Tom knew that he didn't really give a damn—not any more—about show, about all the trappings that made up the public image of Walter Makin, such as his too studied and elaborately tailored pale summer suit. He was suddenly impatient of having wasted so much time on his clothes, taking care not to indulge in any flourishes that might be considered pansyish but incorporating self-designed details that made them distinctive, theatrical, but, most carefully, not effeminate. He wanted to strip down to a pair of jeans and relax—an absurd thought. He didn't own a pair of jeans, and he hadn't relaxed in years. He had rested, embarked on many an elaborate holiday, but not relaxed. A vision came to him of himself and Tom sprawled out beside a mountain stream somewhere in the big country between here and California, a vision of bliss. It clarified everything that had occurred in their few moments of intimacy. He had responded, was still responding to the great reservoir of repose he had sensed in Tom, his calm, serious concern for serious matters, the thrilling contact with down-to-earth reality he seemed to offer. Talk of being in love might be fanciful, but Tom was real.

Jeans and a swift mountain stream. A cliché, but compelling. Tom's straightforward proclamation of his sexual inclinations was very contemporary, so at odds with the way Walter had been brought up that he still couldn't quite adjust to it. His spirit seemed to stretch and soar at the thought of letting himself go. He reminded himself that he was 50 years old, but that didn't quell his body's response. He had once felt like a child, and then he had felt like an adult, and nothing had happened since, no sense of aging, no sharp awareness of time running short—only a sense of time wasted. Something to do with his appearance, perhaps. You're as old as you look?

Mike took the turn into his block, and the reminder of the family gathering awaiting him, abruptly snapping all the imaginary ties with Tom, accomplished what thoughts of age had not.

When he had been allowed back into the house, he started up the stairs but hesitated and turned back for a word with Alice. "Will you call Taylor's? Ask them to send over everything they have by Thomas Jennings. If they don't have them in the shop, get the name of his publisher and call them. There're two or three novels."

"Is that who David was with? What a gorgeous man. Yummy."

"Get yourself under control, Alice. We must concentrate on his literary gifts."

As he mounted the stairs, he adjusted his jacket and drained his mind of all thought except how he would greet his sons—no more kisses. They were drawing back. A handshake, a pat on the shoulder—and no questions about school unless information was volunteered. Nathan and Joel, two names that had struck Clara's fancy for reasons he couldn't remember. An American dynasty of one generation. He sauntered into the library, the impish smile fixed on his lips, and found them in an amiable buzz of conversation. It stopped as they registered his entrance. The boys rose, demonstrating their expensive boarding-school manners. He offered him his predetermined greeting. Sixteen-year-old Joe and 18-year-old Nat, both tall and skinny, both undeniably beautiful in an unfinished sort of way, both intimidating, his progeny, to whom he owed his nomination as Father of the Year, 12 years ago.

"I'm glad your horrible headmaster let you come. Aren't you proud of your daddy?"

"Of course they are, and don't make fun of it," Clara said briskly.

Walter moved on to where Clara sat and leaned over and kissed her on the top of her tinted auburn head. He was swinging into her orbit once more. Whatever she did to him eluded definition. After 30 years, it certainly wasn't sex, although that current could still throw off sparks. Love? A strange sort of love that shriveled him and left him feeling dead. Thinking in her presence of his excitement with Tom made it seem trivial and unworthy of him. She nurtured an image of him that sustained his self-love, an image he had nearly smashed long before it was fixed in the public eye. Only half knowingly, she had stayed his hand, and their life together had been launched on his gratitude to her. Misplaced? Over the years she had been the assurance that he was what the world took him to be—rich, successful, a model father and husband.

The world was almost right on all counts; it was the slight discrepancy between the public image and his private reality that made him feel sometimes that everything had gone disastrously wrong. How had a slight discrepancy turned into such an elaborate hoax? Who was Walter? Who was Clara? Were they prisoners of a spell cast by a dreaming boy? It was probably too late to find out, but whoever he was, he wasn't that popular banality, the victim of the Bitch Goddess Success. Walter Makin would have been an absurdity without success, at any cost. He had never had any doubt about that. Nor had Clara.

Clara looked up at him with her challenging smile. "You seem to have had a busy morning."

"Yes. Secrets. Oh, no, they're not. The major secret is about to be unveiled." He exchanged a private smile with David as he went to the bar table and collected the package he had brought in earlier. "Very well, madam. A small token of esteem." His mind balked at putting in "my."

Clara rose as he returned to her. "Oh, dearest. A present? How divine." She took it, tore off the paper, and opened the box. It contained a large brooch contrived of two gold-and-enamel figures, male and female, lightly draped, holding up a jeweled torch, framed in a proscenium arch surmounted by tiny masks of Comedy and Tragedy. The date, MAY 1970, was unfurled on an enameled banner, and the whole was scattered with baroque pearls and precious stones. "Oh, Walter," Clara gasped, her voice almost girlish with pleasure. "It's superb. Fulco did it? It's the most beautiful thing I've ever seen. It's a Cellini. I can't wear it. We should mount it in a case. Boys! David! Have you ever seen anything so exquisite?"

Walter leaned to her and kissed her lightly on the mouth. "I trust the message is clear. The lady is about the wrest the torch of Enlightenment from the gentleman's hand."

"And bash him over the head with it if he doesn't watch out."

"Precisely." He gave her a little bow, and they laughed into each other's eyes. If there was a hint of animosity in it, it was deeply submerged and overlaid by years of mutual appreciation.

They gathered around and passed the ornament from hand to hand with appropriate exclamations of admiration. Clara could be very appealing when she was pleased, and she was more pleased now than he had seen her for a long time. She had been described so often in newspaper columns as "statuesque" that he supposed he saw her from a different angle than others.

To him, the fire of life burned so hotly in her, her vitality was so aggressively indomitable, that the epithet was inappropriate. True, she was tall. Something about the way she wore her clothes, even the simple day dress she now wore, made her seem robed in majesty. Her surface was of steely serenity. She came up close to him. Holding the extravagant brooch, she looked up at him with her big, ceaselessly probing eyes.

"You must know what this means to me," she said in her flat nononsense tone. "Of course you do, or you wouldn't have thought of it. It's going to make tonight a little bit for me too. Thank you, dearest." A little bit? He knew as well as she did that she had long ago earned the right to be honored as an equal partner.

"The least I could do. Wait till you hear the bits about you in my speech. They'll make you blush like a bride."

She laughed abruptly. "I don't remember even faintly blushing. You did, though."

"Quite proper, Clarry. After all, I was only a child."

They separated and drifted about the room. Walter found himself beside David, while Clara engaged in some discussion with the boys.

"Tom's quite a guy, don't you think, Walter?" David asked, keeping his voice low.

"I do indeed," Walter agreed. He spoke up so as not to sound like a party to conspiracy. "You think he's really good, I gather."

"Absolutely, but I'm not the only one. He made a reputation for himself with *Colson's Dream*."

19

"Yes. I missed it somehow. Oh, lord, I never read anything but scripts. It's a bore."

"Same here. I just happened to know him." His teeth flashed, he tilted his head in his facetiously flirtatious way. "I've tried to stir up interest in him at the studio, but he's made some tough conditions. He can afford to. A guy he lived with for years died not long ago, and now he's rich. I think I mentioned it when I wrote."

Walter felt the hot discomfort of having made a faux pas. He had told Tom to call collect as if he were an unknown kid. He must have found it impudent, but he had sweetly, modestly let it pass. "He said he'd fixed it with you to send me the play."

"Yeah, I have a copy I'll get right off to you as soon as I'm back. You're really interested in him?"

"Of course. You brought him."

David leered cheerfully. "Like Philip?"

"Don't be silly. We were all children then."

"Dear old Walter. You do puzzle me, but I suppose that's because I'm so amoral."

Nat broke away from Clara and slouched over to propose a game of chess with his father after lunch. The buzzer sounded three times to announce the meal.

"Come on, everybody; let's go down," Clara said. "I've had some smoked salmon flown over specially for the Grand Old Man."

"Let's drop that this minute before it gets to be a habit," Walter protested. "Everybody has to be 50 sooner or later."

Emile was waiting to serve them in a white jacket in the stately dining room. Emile and Mathilde, a working butler and a working cook? Or a couple of French character actors he had hired when he had decided to concentrate his creative energies on life rather than art? The luxuriantly planted garden outside was sun-dappled, a fountain glittered in its depths, busy little city birds flitted about in the upper branches and swooped to earth. Walter wished they could open everything and smell and hear the hot damp greenness of it. Did only he feel confined?

20

He joined the others in exclaiming over the smoked salmon, he joked with the boys, he exchanged movie gossip with David, he listened while Clara pointed out the unprecedented significance of the award; never before had all branches in the field of entertainment joined to honor a single individual for outstanding achievement. All the while, Walter was trying to plot Tom's movement. He had long since checked his laundry, probably finished his lunch. He wondered how he would eat–go out to a restaurant or have a sandwich sent up? It was the sort of thing, ridiculously, that he felt he had to know. Now that Walter knew there was money, he should perhaps revise his picture of Tom's traveling light. He might have done a lot of shopping while he was here; he might have a lot to pack. He had said he wanted to leave before the rush hour. Before 5, probably about 4. If he had meant earlier, he would have put it differently–right after lunch or something of that sort. He found that if he could think of him as being still nearby, he could pay more attention to what was being said around him.

Walter left the next course almost untouched. He never ate much at midday, so nobody would find it odd. Emile kept his wineglass full. The wine helped ease the cramped feeling in his arms and chest. For a while Walter felt almost integrated into the group, responding easily, concentrating his charm on the boys, smiling and laughing readily. It wasn't till during a lull, while Emile was clearing away again, that alarm struck.

What if his calculations had been wrong? What if Tom had only one suitcase after all? "Before the rush" could mean anything. It could mean 3. He cursed himself for not carrying a watch, but his highly developed sense of time assured him that it couldn't be past 2:30. There was still time.

For what? To see Tom again? That was all settled. He had his address and telephone number. Once he was back in California, Walter could be with him in a matter of hours if it came to that, although nothing in his experience prepared him to take for granted that he would cross a continent to join a lover; he had never allowed his interest in a young man to become an obsession—except once. His memory of it enclosed some of the most thrilling moments of his life. Others he had tried to overlook in order to go on living with Clara. Perhaps a touch of obsession was needed to awaken him from the deep sleep of his life with Clara.

He managed somehow to remain quiet in his chair while salad and cheese were consumed. As Emile prepared to serve dessert, he slapped the table lightly. "Damn. I promised to call Henry an hour ago. Excuse me. I'll be back."

"Henry? Emile can tell—" Clara began, but Walter was already up and heading out of the room. She sat back, curbing an impulse to follow him. Could he still surprise her after all these years? She doubted it, but she knew all the danger signals of his fascinatingly unpredictable temperament. Leaping up from the table in the middle of a meal was very unlike him. She wondered.

He took the stairs two at a time and rushed to the library telephone. His buzz was answered by a male voice, probably the pretty youth he had been beguiled into hiring a month ago. Jesus. "Call the—no, put me through to the Gladwyn Hotel, please," he directed. He didn't want the young man to know anything about this. There were an unusual number of clicks and pops while Walter fumed—the pretty youth's job hung in the balance—but a voice eventually identified the hotel in a singsong coo. "I want to leave a message for Mr. Jennings, please," Walter said quickly.

"Mr. Jennings?"

"Thomas Jennings. I want to leave a message."

"Just a moment, please. Mr. Jennings? Room 617? I'm sorry, sir. I believe he's already checked out."

Walter's heart stopped. "What do you mean, you believe? Don't you know?"

"One moment, sir. I'll give you the desk."

A man came on the line, cool and efficient. "Mr. Jennings? That's Room 617. Yes, sir, we've got his bill ready. We expect him to check out shortly. I'll put you through."

"No. Wait." Walter was able to breathe freely again. He shifted the instrument from one sweating palm to the other. "Just tell him Walter Makin is coming by the hotel in less than three quarters of an hour. Tell him to wait. It's urgent. Make sure he gets the message right away."

"Certainly, sir. Walter Makin. Before 3:30. Urgent. It's a pleasure, Mr. Makin."

Walter hung up with an audible exhalation of breath, feeling as if he'd narrowly escaped being hit by a truck. He wiped his forehead and palms with a handkerchief and buzzed below again. "Tell Mike to stand by, will you? I'll be going out in a little while."

He stood for a moment to recover his balance. Now that he was reasonably sure of seeing Tom shortly, what exactly did he think he was doing? Even if he were on the verge of falling in love, what then? He could go to California for a week or two, possibly a month, but people often stayed in love for years. What was he supposed to tell Clara? He burst into laughter. He wanted to have some fun with a guy. It was as simple as that. After 30 years of marriage, he should be able to tell her that and get on with it, but he knew he couldn't. Why? Because she wouldn't like it, or because he still didn't like the idea of giving himself away? Both probably. It had taken him a long time to learn that the debt of gratitude he owed her and had acknowledged right from the start could be paid only in deception.

The game must go on. Henry. Who in hell was Henry? The first name that had come into his head. He returned to the party below, all ease and charm once more.

"Who is Henry?" Clara asked as soon as he was seated. "Isn't that who you said you were calling?"

"Yes. You know Henry. I never remember his last name. That man at *The News* who's been helpful. He's been after me to find out if Richard and Elizabeth are going to be there tonight."

"Of course they are. Richard's on the list of speakers."

"Henry heard they might not show. I promised to get the inside dope from Roger."

"Did you?"

"I checked earlier. They're all set."

"Who in the world do you ask for when you call *The News?*"

Walter laughed. Now that he was getting in deep, he felt as expectant and exhilarated as he had that night 30 years ago when she had saved him from wrecking his life. "You may well wonder. I just ask for the city desk. Everybody there knows Henry."

"I must say I'd never forgive those two if they didn't turn up. They owe you a lot."

"They might forget their debt of gratitude, but they wouldn't miss the chance to shine at a high-class cultural event, poor loves." Walter glanced at David and caught a quizzical look in his eye. He slitted his up-tilting eyes at him in a sort of wink.

The boys were finishing extravagant cake and ice-cream confections. When they started scraping their plates, Clara rose. "That will do. It's likely you'll get another meal tonight."

They went upstairs to the living room, where Emile brought them coffee. The spacious room, the twin of the dining room, overlooked the garden and was ablaze with paintings. It was further enriched by a casual and heterogeneous collection of 18th- and early 19th-century furniture, mostly French and English. The room was done in cool pale shades of beige and green and blue, with a few touches of gold—a stage drawing room, designed by Walter. An antique ivory chess set was laid out on a game table in front of a window, and Nat tried to draw his father to it.

"A little later, old son," Walter countered. "Chess is for the long late-afternoon hours. I want to discuss something with David."

The boys slumped with magazines into the sofa. Clara was going through the morning papers on another. Walter and David stood at the table where coffee had been served. The room was spacious enough for privacy. Walter turned his back on the others and faced David.

"You're going to have to stand in for me, pal. I'm going to disappear for a while. When I'm missed, act mysterious. Drop hints about my having to arrange something special, for her tonight. There'll *be* something special, so you can play it up all you like."

24

David's eyes and teeth flashed at him. He tilted back his golden head. "I thought so. I have an idea we're in for some surprises."

"I don't know what you're talking about, but I'll leave you to your wicked thoughts." Walter chortled with laughter. He was feeling keyed-up and pleased with himself. He touched David's arm and slipped unobtrusively from the room.

He ran upstairs to his bedroom and went to the bath to freshen up. He didn't look at himself. He was afraid that what he saw would strike him as ridiculous–a mature man distraught with desire for another man almost young enough to be his son. He went to the bedroom telephone and sent word to Mike that he was on his way. The bedside clock told him it was just 3. He was on time. He went down the hall and took the elevator again to avoid unwelcome encounters. "Back to the Gladwyn, hunh?" Mike said after he had settled into the back of the car.

"Right, Mike."

"That's sure where I'd be if I were you," Mike said.

"All right, Mike, try to keep your mind above your belt," Walter said, then told himself to remember this good advice. "When you drop me, you can take off. I think I'm still capable of finding a taxi."

"Let the doorman get one for you. You don't want to be wandering around the streets. You don't know what it's like."

"I appreciate your solicitude, Mike."

"I'm not sure I know what you're talking about, Walter; but it sure sounds classy."

Walter unfastened his tie, pulled it off, and folded it away into a pocket. He slipped off his jacket and put it over his arm. He unbuttoned his shirt, exposing the froth of hair on his chest and turned back his cuffs. Better. He was no longer a magazine illustration of the impeccable Walter Makin. If things went the way he intended, the less there was to take off the better. When Mike pulled up in front of the hotel, he leaned forward. "This is strictly between ourselves, Mike. If anybody asks, say you left me at the corner of 53rd and Lexington. You have no idea where I was going." Did he have any idea himself? He felt his old

25

exhibitionistic urge to strip. Would that be enough to make Tom his? He suspected that it would take time, and time was lacking. Tom was determined to leave. Why not leave with him? He had been waiting for years to do something outrageous. At least, so it seemed to him now. He had a chance at last to break loose with a hell of a yell. He would give a great deal to see Clara's face if she discovered that she had been left to accept the award for him. Clear out. Disappear for a week. The imp came strikingly to the fore, a wickedly gleeful imp. Anything might happen.

The doorman was waiting. Walter nodded as he emerged from the car and was amused to note the rapid play of reactions on the man's face—recognition, an impulse to participate in glee, the disciplined return to duty, his hand touching his cap. Walter crossed the sidewalk and swept across the hotel lobby to the elevators without having himself announced. Tom was expecting him. Tom must have known he would come.

As he stepped into an elevator, thoughts of Harry were with him, offering highly suspect guidance. Perhaps he was about to find out at last who Walter Makin was, although he had an uneasy suspicion that the deeper he probed, the less he would find. His life wasn't a detective story in reverse, leading back to the scene of the crime. No crime had been committed, unless sins of omission could be so severely categorized. So much had happened at the beginning that there had been no time for second thoughts or self-doubts. Besides, Clara had no use for such weakness. Clara had almost known how to make him forgive the unforgivable. Magic. She had her own. The point of magic was that it evaporated if too closely scrutinized. He thought of Tom's eyes and wondered if he should let the elevator carry him down again.

Harry was the beginning. Before Harry, Walter had been a cautious, brilliant, studious youth, tall and gangling, with the face of an androgynous woodland sprite. He was a year ahead of himself at school so that he was younger than his classmates and was shy and awkward with them. He had no friends. He was at the head of the class, but the only unusual thing he knew about himself was his infatuation with the theater. He kept it to himself because he had been taught to suppress manifestations of individuality.

Walter was an only child. His father was a dentist, and his mother was a loud, harsh, passionate woman. When he was old enough to start talking about a career, he decided to say that he was going to be an architect as a safe compromise to conceal his secret aspirations. The inhabitants of the world he knew barely took into account the existence of the theater, certainly not as an acceptable field for a normal, healthy man.

Harry was his god, the star athlete of the second-rate private prep school they both attended in Morristown, New Jersey. He had the head of Adonis and a body to match, which Walter tried not to look at when they were all naked in the shower room after compulsory games.

He couldn't understand why he had chosen Harry to worship. They had nothing in common. Sports bored Walter; Harry wouldn't know anything about the theater or books. He probably wouldn't even be able to discuss a movie. This was only a supposition since they had never exchanged more than a few words at a time.

In their senior year the range of Walter's reading widened, including a grueling attack on Proust; and for the first time he began to consciously question the values and attitudes that he had been taught to cherish. There was a great deal more to life than was contained in Morristown. He had nobody with whom to share his dreams; but even if he had, he would never have dared express the revolutionary thoughts that were stirring in him.

Harry inexplicably remained his god. Walter supposed he represented some childish schoolboy idea, a vision of what he had been taught he ought to be but had no intention of becoming. As school drew to a close, Walter began to feel that whatever he felt about him, he must end it. When he masturbated, the image of his fantasy partner always dissolved into Harry's at the moment of climax. He never quite admitted to himself that this happened; but deep in the back of his mind, he knew that it involved something odd and forbidden. He was barely 16, and he told himself he sure needed to get himself a girl.

He knew his worship of Harry couldn't have anything to do with sex. He had read and heard things that he didn't understand, but he was aware of perversions and criminal sexual acts that he shrank from even imagining. These acts could have nothing to do with him or anybody he knew.

Still, his thoughts of Harry bothered him to the point that he began to take advantage of his position as editor of the school paper to skip athletics as often as possible to avoid the shower room. On other days he rubbed himself down with a towel and went home without a shower.

One spring afternoon, with only a month of school remaining, Walter was sweating over the dummy of the paper in the cubbyhole assigned to him as an editorial office when he decided he had to cool off. It was mid afternoon. He knew the shower room would be deserted for another hour, so he decided to take a shower. He was surprised to encounter Harry in the hall near the library as he went down through the building, but he only nodded and hurried on. Even such a brief brush with his god made his heart race and sweat break out on his body. He found the lockers in ghostly silence, as he expected. His sense of privacy was so complete that as the rush of water soothed his body and filled it with sensual cravings, soaping himself became a dangerous temptation to give himself an erection. The soap leaped from his hand, and he froze at the sound of the worshiped voice directly behind him.

"Hey, I hoped I'd find you in here," Harry shouted cheerfully above the sound of water. Paralysis passed, and Walter was able to glance over his shoulder to see Harry advancing on him, divinely naked. He immediately hated his own body. Except for the fact that he was a shade taller than Harry, he considered himself a physical nonentity. He managed to blurt out a greeting and turned back to scramble for the soap.

"Can I share?" It was customary to share when the showers were full, but it was surely unusual under the present circumstances. Walter made a sound that bore no resemblance to speech. "I've been wanting to talk to you," Harry added. He seemed to fill the stall.

The lurch in Walter's groin struck him with panic at what might happen. He had been feeling sexy before Harry turned up. It had nothing to do with anybody in particular. Now Harry was touching him all over. He bumped him with his chest and belly when he moved in to soak himself. When he took the soap, he seemed to make a point of their hands meeting. His arms and elbows were everywhere.

"What's up?" Walter asked as soon as he could trust himself to speak.

"Well, it's just that we never seem to get together. I figured we ought to be friends. After all, we're the two top guys in the class. I'm the body, and you're the brain. Actually, if my brain was as good as your body, I'd be a lot better off."

"You must think you're a half-wit." To Walter, getting out a whole sentence, especially in a teasing vein, was a major achievement.

"I'm not kidding. You've got great shoulders." Harry put his hands on them, and Walter felt the lurch in his groin again. He wished Harry would leave him alone. He wasn't used to being touched. Harry's eyes surveyed him. He rocked him playfully back and forth with his hands.

Walter fought an appalling impulse to press himself to his god, feel all of his body against him. "How come you're not out at practice today?" he blurted.

Harry slid his hands down his arms and rested them lightly on his hips. He grinned. "I gave my ankle a turn. I'm supposed to take a day or two off. You know, you ought to try to get out more often. All you need is to fill out a bit here and there. I bet if you worked out with me for a month or two, I could turn you into a real athlete."

"That'll be the day."

"I'll bet you're hung too." Harry flicked Walter's cock once, twice, with the back and front of his hand. Walter felt as if he had leaped 12 feet in the air. When he came to earth, his cheeks were burning. Harry chuckled. "What's the matter? Don't you like to be touched there?"

"No. I mean, I don't care...I was only..."

"That was just a love tap. I like to see how guys are hung. It seems I'm bigger than average. You look as if you're big too."

"I don't know." Perhaps this was the way the athletes talked and acted together. It was all jolly and straightforward. If he could strike that note, he might be able to get by without disgracing himself. "I don't see how there could be any comparison. You've got the most beautiful body I've ever seen."

"Hey, listen, what are you doing after?"

"I don't know. I thought I–"

"Well, how about it? Wouldn't you like to find out? Why not come home with me? We'll have some fun."

Walter felt the muscles of his face going rigid. Rigidity was spreading down into his groin. His brain seemed disconnected from his eyes. He found himself staring at Harry without seeing him. "Yes, sure," he managed. "If you–"

"Great. Boy, you really are hung. I thought so. If we don't look out, we'll be able to compare right here. Come on. We'd better go before we give the whole school a show." Harry stepped into the center of the shower and ran his hands over his body, displacing great bursts of spray. "Meet you at the door in five minutes," he shouted and was gone.

Walter turned the cold water on so hard that it hurt, and he waited. As soon as dared, he turned it off and made a rush for his towel and covered himself. Safe at last, he hurried to his locker. He wouldn't allow his imagination to dwell on what Harry had in mind.

It turned out that Harry had things in mind that went far beyond anything Walter's imagination could have conceived. His hero obviously didn't fear being branded a sexual outcast.

The last month of school passed in a trance of terror and delight, of resisting and indulging Harry's vice, of awakened sexuality, of heartbreak and the discovery that he could be loved. At the end of the month, he escaped from Harry to the seashore, where his parents had a small summer cottage.

He felt driven to pursue the girls at the seashore. Despite his total lack of experience with girls, the outdoor life and the scanty summer clothes made it easy to get at them. It became quickly apparent that pursuit was hardly necessary. Nobody fled from him, perhaps because of the sexual confidence acquired from Harry and the fact that his body, developed in the gym for a month under Harry's tutelage, was beginning to be almost impressive.

Still, there was the problem of virginity, and, in the few cases where that didn't apply, there was the problem of pregnancy. The obvious solution to the latter was rubbers, which some of the boys made a point of carrying, but Walter found he couldn't use them. His cock had enjoyed such perfect freedom with Harry that it had apparently developed a pathological resistance to being shrouded. When he tried to put one of those things on, it lay down and died. He practiced on himself to no avail. What felt like the most invincible erection collapsed in seconds at the contact of a rubber.

He lay naked or almost naked with a dozen girls that summer, but none of them aroused in him the intensity of feeling he had known with Harry. He supposed it was understandable. They fussed and withheld themselves instead of surrendering gratefully to his ecstasies as Harry had. At least, technically he was no longer a virgin. It seemed a small reward for so much effort, but he had established to his own

31

satisfaction that he was firmly girl-oriented, which was what he wanted to be.

He had won a scholarship at Rutgers, and, abandoning dreams of Princeton or Harvard, he went there in the fall. He immediately discovered that this was where life would begin. He was lost in a big ugly town. He was free to make what he liked of himself. The notion of being self-created acquired a hold on his imagination. Nothing in his background contributed to what he dreamed of becoming. He would create his future out of himself and his own tastes and capabilities. The sexual adventure that had recently occupied him so intensely faded into the background, part of boyhood that he had had to get out of his system. There were many more important matters that required his attention—such as how to launch the brilliant career that Harry somehow had made him feel lay within his reach. It was simply a matter of proclaiming his goals to himself and the world and allowing nothing to stand in the way of achieving them. Something had happened with Harry that made him understand that.

Harry had also demonstrated to him the precarious control he had over his hitherto unexplored emotions and how dangerously off-balance he could be thrown by them. He was determined not to go Harry's way sexually, to avoid the outcast's brand, but above all he had resolved to steer clear of all emotional attachments. His ambitions would require the concentration of all his energies.

W alter was late for the theater. Debby had insisted on making love after supper. His presence at the performance wasn't essential, and she knew it. It was the last night of the week's run, and there was nothing more he could do with the performance, but he had found that his amateur actors took their work more seriously if they knew he was there.

Debby had been his girl since he had returned to Rutgers for his junior year a couple of months ago. She was a local girl who had been active in the little theater and was a great convenience to him because she liked to prepare food for him and he was able to add the money she thus saved him to his Broadway theater fund. The fund was supplied primarily by his buying books at the college bookstore, which charged them to his parents, and selling them secondhand. Debby's culinary generosity was good for an extra balcony seat every few weeks.

She was also the first girl who offered him complete sexual freedom. The virginity problem didn't exist, and she took the pregnancy problem lightly. As a consequence, he had learned a great deal about the female body, some of which he would have found distasteful without a strong effort of will. He had a girl, and she was beginning to become a burden. He didn't like being late for the theater.

Fortunately, Debby lived not far from the community hall where the New Brunswick Buskers put on half a dozen plays every season. He walked rapidly through quiet streets toward it, a tall, graceful figure with a notably fine physique and an elfin child's face. That a Rutgers undergraduate should be its director was an anomaly and quite unofficial. It had started the year before when the regular director, with whom Walter had struck up a friendship, had been suddenly called away. For lack of anybody better, Walter filled in for him. The committee was still talking about finding a replacement while Walter did the shows, an arrangement he felt sure would continue as long as he chose. For the first time in memory, people were coming to the theater for enjoyment rather than because somebody's uncle was starring in the cast.

At college, he continued to take architectural courses, but only because he found they could be applied to theatrical design. He was taking every drama course offered, but this was more literature than theater. He read extensively on his own. He studied the early years of the Theatre Guild in New York, knew the theories of Gordon Craig, was familiar with the work and doctrines of the great Europeans, Stanislavsky, Copeau, Dullin. As he covered the last hundred feet to the hall, it became his theater in which he had total artistic control over sets, texts, music, casting, everything. It was a unique personal creation. He added a few years to his age—he was perhaps 27. Now that he was in fact 18 at last, he could think of himself as "practically 19." It seemed like a long time to wait.

He arrived as the show broke for intermission. The audience was streaming into the lobby. A member of the committee waved to him across the crowd and beckoned him over. "Hi there, Walter. It's going pretty well. There's somebody here who wants to meet you. David Fiedler. Walter Makin, our boy genius."

Walter turned to the stranger and was momentarily blinded. Eyes and teeth flashed at him, a hand glittering with gold exerted a warm pressure on his own.

"Andy Carlson told me to say hello if I ran into you," David said in a voice that seemed to bubble with high spirits. "Nick here is an old friend. I came to see your show. It's one of the best amateur jobs I've ever seen."

"Thanks." Walter made connections. Andy Carlson was one of the queer young men he had met in New York. This blinding apparition appeared to be in his mid 20s but spoke with the authority of vast experience. His dazzling blue eyes were slightly protuberant. All his coloring was vivid. His cheeks were peaches, his lips as red as Harry's. He was shorter than Walter, and his body was compact, but something about his peachy skin and the smooth modeling of his features suggested a full, rounded physical opulence.

"I'd like to talk to you later," David said, making it sound as if it would be fun. "You may be just the guy I'm looking for."

"David's the manager of the Steelman School of Dramatic Art," the man called Nick interjected, while the other two studied each other with humor and approval. David's eyes were loaded with messages that got though clearly to Walter.

"There's a bar around the corner," Walter said. "We could have a drink after the show."

"Are you allowed in bars? You look 12."

"Yes, I've always looked older than my age. Actually, I'm ten."

David laughed. "OK. You win. I'll buy you a drink, and we'll talk. Unfortunately, it'll have to be quick."

The audience was moving back into the auditorium. David gave him another flirtatious look before he was led away.

Walter remained bemused in the lobby. Did Fiedler want to recruit him for his school, or was he interested in his person? The Richard Steelman School was well-known, with famous names on its roster of teachers. In the summer, in addition to offering training to paying students, it operated a theater on Long Island that was more star-studded than the general run of summer theaters. He had said he was looking for somebody. That could imply a job. Walter began to get tense with anticipation. He hoped there wouldn't be sexual hurdles. Life must be so simple for the guys who casually jumped in and out of bed with each other. Girls had a way of complicating matters. If Debby had had her way, he wouldn't have been here to meet this Fiedler character. A job. He would play him along until he saw what was up.

35

He was pleased to see that David was alone when he saw him after the show. They went to the bar around the corner and ordered whisky and took the drinks to a booth where they could talk in private.

"First of all, what is a gorgeous thing like you doing in this dump?" David began, rolling his eyes outrageously.

Walter laughed. "Learning things. It's beginning to seem like a waste of time."

"You mustn't let it. I'm all in favor of education. You did some very canny things with that little show. It wasn't the usual imitation Broadway hack job. I like the way you handled your actors so they didn't get a chance to show how bad they were."

"You noticed that?" Walter warmed to him. "I'm working out some theories about actors. The star system's all wrong. Have you seen the Gielgud *Hamlet*? There's a star for you. He acted all over the place, but he was a lousy Hamlet. The whole production was lousy. I'd like to get my hands on it with some plain competent professionals."

David gave him a quick, shrewd glance. "I take it you plan to go into the theater seriously."

"Yes, I don't quite see how to go about it yet. So much of it seems to be luck." David's interest in him was obvious. This was the first time he had talked to somebody who was in a position to help him. He had to play his cards carefully.

David leered. "I don't think it'll have much to do with luck in your case. I'm not making a pass at you, because I haven't got time. I have to catch the train back to town in less than an hour. We better stick to business. You've heard of the Steelman School?"

"Sure."

"I more or less run it, especially in summer. I need an assistant to take the load off my weary shoulders. I'm supposed to make the apprentices feel they're getting their money's worth by working their young asses off. I direct the shows that we don't bring in from outside. I seduce the girls and some of the boys. Does that sound interesting?"

"The boys would be safe, as far as I'm concerned," Walter said with a knowing smile. He was being offered a job. He mustn't get flustered by the sophisticated trimmings. He wasn't used to such open unortho-dox references to sex.

"That sounds rather narrow-minded," David said with a toss of his golden head, "but I'm sure it'll add to the moral tone of the joint. I'm primarily interested in talent and ability, but I do like pretty faces around me. It's rare that you find it all in one gorgeous package."

"When do you want him—this assistant?" Walter managed to throw it in casually, but his heart beat with excitement.

"Not till summer. I might add that I'm not offering any pay. In your case, if it really makes a big difference to you, I'd be willing to give you a pittance out of my own pocket. You won't have to sleep with me if you're able to resist, but I like my assistant to at least *look* bedable. It gives people something to talk about. I know what a hard worker you are, and I know talent when I see it. Are you temperamental? Do you take orders easily?"

"I don't know. Nobody around here gives me orders. I know more than they do."

"I'm sure you do, but so do I. I'll be your boss, and I like things done my way. You're not really the assistant type. I might go so far as to say you're slightly awe-inspiring. Will it work?"

"I know I still have a lot to learn, if that helps."

"It should. You'll have to come up and talk to Dick Steelman, but that's just to make him feel that he's *my* boss. When you come to town, I'll ply you with champagne. No boys, eh? We shall see. How about an-other quick one before I run for my train?"

They had another quick one and talked about Walter's qualifications in a flurry of David's blatant sexual references.

Walking back to his room, Walter felt as if a whirlwind had swept though his life. David created such an intoxicating air of fun and ex-citement around him that the job seemed more part of a game than the enormous break it promised to be. It had been dangled before him so gaily that its importance was easy to overlook. In fact, it would bring him close to the big time, offer him invaluable contacts, give him an opportunity to seriously gauge what hopes he could permit himself in the fascinating world he had chosen for himself. David was a tonic he had been thirsting for.

The interview with Steelman would take place after the first of the year. Letters were exchanged in due course, and a date was fixed. He wasn't nervous about the interview; David had made it clear that it was no more than a formality. David invited him to spend the night with him—the interview was set for late afternoon—but Walter made an excuse about school work. He had a drink with David afterward, and his job was confirmed. He returned to school in a state of high euphoria. He was practically a professional. David insisted on paying him $12 a week.

After that, David made a habit of sending him theater tickets, and Walter stopped swindling his parents. He also picked a quarrel with Debby and unloaded that burden. He was approaching real life. Debby had been left behind. David held the key to the future. They began to see each other regularly in the city. He was barely five years older than Walter and had been working since he was 17. He owed his start in large part to Richard Steelman's infatuation with him. He had recently earned a college degree through part-time attendance at Columbia. His ambitions were purely commercial, with none of Walter's high artistic and intellectual aspirations, but he listened to Walter and seemed to take him seriously. Genuine affection flourished between them.

The sexual jokes continued, but Walter had discovered a nice quality in David that made him feel sure that even if he made a serious pass and was turned down, there would be no unpleasantness.

As the scholastic year ended, Walter went home for a brief stay to repack his bags; and before his mother's loud lamentations had stopped ringing in his ears, he found himself getting off a train on Long Island.

David was there to meet him in, appropriately, a station wagon. He was in full blaze, a glow of sun already on him, a gold chain around his neck added to the gold Walter was familiar with. His summer shirt and slacks revealed more of his body than Walter had seen before—a smooth, luxurious body, very sexy—even to Walter's cautious eyes. His nose jutted, and his full, formless mouth was spread in a blinding smile. Getting into the car beside him stirred sexual associations in Walter that made his face burn and his mouth go dry with shame. Damn Harry.

"I have you in my clutches at last," David exulted good-naturedly. "You'll be amazed to learn that the only place I could find to put you is with me. We have separate rooms for appearance's sake. We'll see how long we stay in them."

The theater was in East Cove, near East Hampton. David had been lent a great cottage on a large estate. The two drove through the burning early summer afternoon, turned into a drive lined with great trees and flowering shrubbery, then took another turn and stopped in front of a small frame house. "There. How's that for a love nest?" David demanded.

"Marvelous. There's just us here?"

"Curiously enough, that's the way it turned out. Tomorrow it's noses to the grindstone. Tonight I'm laying on a full-scale seduction scene. I'm taking you to dinner. There'll be candlelight and wine. I'll gaze hypnotically into your violet eyes. We'll see who doesn't like boys after that."

They laughed together as they took possession of the house. There was a living room, separate bedrooms, and a bath. Within minutes Walter felt as if he had never lived anywhere else, or with anyone else. They had drinks outside on the edge of the lawn. He drank rarely, but he liked the worldly feeling of holding a glass.

"There's a pool down there." David indicated where the lawn sloped away to a clump of trees and a low roof. "We can use it. The Peabodys aren't here. Somebody comes and fiddles around with it in the evening. Otherwise, we have the place to ourselves. Nobody will hear your screams of protest when I have my way with you."

The seduction scene proceeded as scheduled, with the result David seemed to expect: They slept soundly in their respective rooms.

They were at the theater promptly the next morning. It was a handsomely converted barn set in trees. Behind it, discreetly removed from it, was a long derelict-looking building that was the dormitory and eating hall for the apprentices. The first show was coming as a touring package and was rehearsing in New York; none of the small resident company of actors was here yet. Walter was to take charge of the apprentices and get them organized.

He found them gathered in casual groupings in back of the theater. He called out names and tried to fix them to faces. Jerry, Bill, Malcolm, Philip, Betty, Anne, Helen, Clara, Jo, Marilyn. He realized that most of them were older than he.

They seemed amateurish—scrubbed, fresh-faced, patently the offspring of well-to-do parents. David had told him that one of the girls was a special case; she paid, but had spoken a line on Broadway and was a member of Equity. Clara Something? David had told him so many things.

He assigned them chores and took part in some of them himself. He knew how to build and paint sets and made himself useful to Oscar, the young designer. Walter's attention was quickly caught by a tall girl with a regal bearing and arresting auburn hair. Her features were regular, her body graceful but not the sort to attract stares, and yet something about her set her apart from the others, who were merely pretty in a conventional way. He had told her to load handbills into the station wagon, and he watched her passing back and forth from the theater to the car. When this had happened several times, he put down his paintbrush and stood in front of her.

"Are you Clara?" he asked.

She looked him over before answering. "I'm Clara Washburn," she said, her head lifted.

Walter suppressed a smile. The name struck a chord in his mind, but he didn't immediately identify it. "I probably should've had one of the boys carry those," he said. "Is there anything you'd like to do? How are you with a paintbrush?"

Her eyes challenged him and turned mocking. "I don't have to do what you tell me, you know. I'm just helping out until I start rehearsing. You're David Fiedler's new boy."

"Yes, his assistant." Walter hoped he had said it in a way that concealed his indignation at the way she had phrased the statement. Was she suggesting that he was "bedable"? Had David already encouraged talk? He still feared the brand.

Clara uttered abrupt but not unfriendly laughter. "You're living with him in that ghastly cottage of the Peabodys. They offered it to me, but I preferred something more convenient. I suppose you weren't given much choice."

"I like it," Walter asserted. This girl demanded attack. He felt a hard masculinity in her that he was immediately determined to dominate. "Aren't you staying over there in the dormitory?"

"Good heavens, no. I'm practically a member of the company. I've found a madly quaint little apartment over a garage, only ten minutes' walk on the sea."

"You walk on the sea? Sorry. That wasn't worthy of me. When are you going to ask me over?"

"Oh, you're one of those boys, all he-man and bluster." She looked at him, with more challenge than mockery in her eyes now. "I'll wait and see how much you count around here. If it looks as if it would annoy David, I might ask you soon."

"You don't like David?"

"I adore him. He just makes me feel competitive. I don't see why he should have all the fun."

"That's fair enough. We could do something about it. Why don't you have dinner with me as soon as I find out what my schedule is?"

She looked at him and said: "I do believe he might be civilized. How un-American. And those eyes. They're violet, aren't they? I hadn't realized fauns have violet eyes, but what else could they be? Quite promising." Her abrupt laughter rang out. He urged her to join him with a paintbrush, but she maintained that she had never been able to make paint stay in one place and went back to loading handbills.

He had never met a girl like her but felt he had got through the exchange in good array. He wasn't sure that *attractive* was a word that would be applied to her, but she engaged his interest more com-

41

pellingly than most people. Arresting. Spoiled. Difficult. She was all those things, and yet he liked her. The urge to dominate her remained in him. She challenged. He accepted the challenge. His impish smile played around his lips as he went back to work.

He stopped in mid stroke. Good lord. Could she be one of *those* Washburns? If so, he really was breaking into the great world. The Washburns owned most of one of the big cities of what he thought of as the West. Cleveland, was it? But their importance went far beyond that. Washburns had been founding museums, organizing scientific expeditions, sponsoring symphony orchestras and opera companies for several generations and not only in the city of their origin, wherever that was, but in New York as well. If she were one of those Washburns, she *was* the great world.

He watched for opportunities to make small contacts with her during the day, searching out the center of her appeal, her attraction, whatever it could be called. Her mouth was lively in a way he had never seen before. He found himself watching it to see what it was going to do next, although it did nothing that mouths don't generally do. It spoke, it widened with laughter. It looked all the time as if it were about to gobble something up. There was something about the way the determined chin joined the neck that made him want to touch it. This was her only vulnerable area; the rest of her seemed unapproachable and inviolable as a priestess, or a queen.

One of the boy apprentices—Malcolm? Philip?—brought him the keys to the station wagon. "David says he'd like you to distribute the handbills so you can get to know the town. He says to take one of us to help. How about me?"

"Thanks. We'll see." He suspected that most if not all the boys were queer—or gay, Harry's word—and had no intention of playing favorites with them. He gave a final swipe of the brush and went looking for Clara. He found her backstage with some other girls cleaning up the dressing rooms. He asked her to join him for the handbill job.

She made an impatient sound in her throat. "Oh, it's all so boring. Think of something exciting and glamorous for us to do. I'll be waiting."

He took one of the other girls. By the end of the day, his amateurs had accomplished more than he had expected, and he had begun to feel like the leader of a team. David emerged, and they went across to the dining hall for an early supper with the others, but removed from them at the staff and company table. Clara had left.

"How's it going, doll?" David inquired. "I have the impression that you're not just a pretty face. You seem to've got everything organized very quickly."

"The kids work better than I thought they would at first. They're such a decorative lot."

"A photograph comes with every application. I don't supervise the selection for nothing." David leered.

"What about Clara? Is she one of the Washburns?"

"The Snow Queen? I'll say. An only daughter, the crown princess. She's one of Steelman's prize acquisitions. If she gives you any difficulties, roll over and wag your tail. Dick has designs on the Washburns."

"I'm more likely to spank her. It's what she needs."

"If you think she'll go for the rough stuff, don't hesitate. This is her second summer. We don't want her to get bored."

They went back to David's office and worked another couple of hours. Walter was able to make useful suggestions about various administrative details. Already he knew he could run the theater as well as David.

There was little time for personal relations, but Walter had a spare moment. He was more intrigued than attracted by her; if he could shatter her regal manner, that might change. The fact that she was a Washburn didn't count against her. She had connections that might prove useful. If nothing else, he wanted to make enough of an impression on her so that they would go on seeing each other when they left in the fall. They never had time for a real conversation. He hoped for a free evening so that he could make a firm dinner invitation, but almost a week had passed before he caught her as she was leaving for the evening. He suggested walking her home. David could struggle along without him for half an hour.

43

She gave him a long, reflective look. Her mouth worked. "You look so ridiculously young. Rather overgrown, of course, but a perfect baby. It makes it difficult to take you seriously as a suitor."

"Is that what I am?"

"Well, aren't you? You're paying quite a lot of attention to me. Did David tell you to?"

"David doesn't want you to get bored. I think I'd probably bore you as a suitor."

She uttered her abrupt laughter. "You're really very clever."

He had scored. He didn't expect her to let him go to bed with her, and he wasn't sure he wanted to if she did. She was too formidable for him to think of her easily in those terms. He wanted to meet her challenge, best her, establish his mastery. Nobody had ever made him feel like this. He didn't see how he could do it without going to bed with her.

She moved majestically into step beside him. In repose, her features might have been too perfect and symmetrical to be interesting, but they were never in repose. Her eyes mocked and challenged, her mouth looked as if it were about to do something startling, the place where her chin and neck met invited a tender caress.

"I suppose you know all about me," she said as they turned into the street toward the ocean. "Who are you? I don't even know what your father does."

"He's a dentist," he said.

She missed a step, caught off-guard. "A dentist!" She uttered a hoot of laughter that ended in a gurgle of delight. "How divine. To think I'm with a dentist's son. I can't wait to write my parents. They'll probably want me to come home at once. Oh, dear, why couldn't you be black too? Or Jewish maybe? They'd like that."

Walter smiled at her, not minding in the least. His father existed only because everybody had to have one. "What's yours?"

"Mine? Oh nothing. He runs things."

"And what about you? Are you going to be an actress?"

She looked at him as if he'd lost his mind. "I *am* an actress. I don't know whether I'll go on being one. I'll be quite rich someday. I might want to put money in the theater. Anyway, I like it here once the season gets started. I like theater people, and I adore the theater. You don't want to be an actor, do you?"

"No, everything else. I want to have a theater of my own. When are you going to be rich? You might come in handy."

"It won't start for ten years. That's when I get the first slice."

"That's too bad. I can't wait that long."

"You still have another year of college, haven't you?"

"Yeah. It's a bore."

"I shouldn't be wasting my time on you. I like people to be established, doing things."

Just when they were getting to be friends, she hit him below the belt.

"Are you established?" he demanded.

"Of course. I had a part on Broadway this winter. It lasted only three nights, but that wasn't my fault."

"Do you live with your parents?"

"What difference does that make? It happens to be more convenient for me. They're not there all the time. It's the same as having my own place."

"Sure, without the bother of having to work for your living. Then you'll marry a rich guy and stop even pretending to be an actress. Why should I waste my time with you?"

Harsh laughter broke from her. "Oh, good—at least you don't take me lying down. I told you I wanted you to be exciting. I'm beginning to think you might manage it. Your eyes help. In this light, you're Pan. Is he the one with the tail? I hope not."

"I never can keep those people straight. Dionysus is the one I'd like to be. He got the theater going. He didn't have a tail."

"Fancy a dentist's son wanting to be god of the theater. That's truly exciting."

"Really? You don't think it's silly?"

"I think anybody who doesn't want to be a god is silly."

"That sounds like Washburn talk."

"What do you know about it? I hate the Washburns."

45

She said it with such passion that he was startled and thrilled by her. She had somehow entered into an alliance with him. *Attractive* was too weak a word for her. She was magnificent. He couldn't imagine her letting herself be seduced, but he definitely wanted to try. He thought of Debby, pleading for love. He couldn't see Clara playing that scene. He could imagine her taking him if it struck her fancy and promptly dismissing him. He chuckled. "We'll have to have a referee if we see a lot of each other," he said.

They walked a few more minutes until dunes and a glimpse of the darkening sea appeared before them. The sun had already set behind them. There was a big house at the end of the street, and behind it a two-floor garage with outdoor stairs leading to the upper floor.

"Do you want a drink?" she asked. "You do drink, don't you?"

"Sure, but I don't have time now. I've got to get back. Let me see where you live, and then I'll run."

She preceded him up the outside stairs, her narrow shoulders carried proudly. They were about to be alone and in private together. It was a step in the right direction. She ushered him into a living room with big windows overlooking the ocean, furnished casually with outdoor things.

"My palatial abode," she announced. "I have some whisky. Do you want some?"

"I shouldn't take the time." He looked into her eyes and found no hint of the response he had learned to detect. He had to kiss her if only to prove that he wasn't a child. He stepped to her and put his arms around her and touched her closed determined mouth with his tongue. She didn't pull away but did nothing to encourage him. She was so tall and felt so slim and flat in his arms that it was like holding a boy. He had never held a more unresponsive body, but she was flesh and blood, and she excited him. He tightened his embrace and kissed an eye in a way he had found usually produced some reaction, but in this case it failed. He drew back.

She looked at him squarely. "Why do you keep your arms around me? You don't want to neck, do you? I think kissing is absolutely hope-

46

less. It either means nothing, or it should lead to a great deal more. Of course, you're a raving beauty, so you're probably used to everybody falling for you. It'll take more than a stroll in the gloaming to make me fall for you." Her laughter mocked herself.

He released her and moved away, still unexpectedly tingling with the feel of her. He wasn't upset or embarrassed by her indifference. Girls liked to play hard to get. The sexual note had been struck, and she had become more than a Washburn. She was a desirable girl. He turned back to her. "I agree with you about kissing. I don't kiss a girl unless I want a great deal more. I guess we've got that point clear."

"I'll keep it in mind. You're really very sweet in spite of your devilish look. Your mouth feels lovely. I hate girls who tease. I won't make any bones about it if I discover I want a great deal more."

She spoke almost gently. Her voice was an instrument of attack, but it contained infinite modulations once the ear was attuned. He looked at her throat as she spoke—a lively throat, capable of emitting venom, or honey. He wanted to put his arms around her again, but she had closed the door on that for this evening. If she had given in a little, there was still a long way to go. She made it seem worth a determined campaign.

They went to the door together, and he held her hand while he said good night. Their eyes met and briefly he saw the kindling of sexual interest in hers, but he pulled away and left her. The first step in the campaign was to make her understand that she couldn't make all the rules.

A few days later the actors arrived; the opening night went off smoothly, and the theater took over their lives even more completely than before. Everything they had been doing acquired an importance that lifted it above drudgery. There were rehearsals all day and performances at night. The apprentices demonstrated that Walter had welded them into a highly effective unit. The girls no longer acted as if they hoped for personal attention. There were no more suggestive undertones emanating from the boys—with one exception, Philip, who continued to eye him insistently. He countered by treating him more coldly than the others, to no avail. He felt Philip's eyes on his whenever they were in each other's proximity. He was a romantic-looking youth with a sweep of silvery blond hair, enormous eyes, an exquisitely modeled mouth, and a breathtaking long sculpted line of chin and neck. He had a willowy body all pared down to the bone except for the delectable curve of his behind. Thoughts of Harry came unwillingly to mind. Unlike the others, Philip never wore blue jeans but always dressed eccentrically in white, which was impractical for work but made him easy to locate. Not that he would have had to search for him if he had wanted to find him. Philip was always near, and his eyes were always on him with a persistence that began to nag at him.

He found occasion to mention Philip's name to David and had to smile his way through an extravagant parody of David's having uncovered an unnatural passion. He couldn't resist mentioning him to Clara and heard him dismissed as "that silly little faggot." He had never heard the word used that way, but he understood what it meant.

He saw the white figure passing one morning when he was getting out of the station wagon. He had just collected a batch of tickets from the printer, and he checked an impulse to avoid him. There was nothing to run away from. He could face the kid and make it clear that his attentions were unwanted. He waited and watched Philip alter his course to move to him as if he were a magnet. When he reached him, Walter allowed their eyes to meet and hold to administer a rebuff. He felt his eyes widen as they sank into depths of undisguised desire. His breath caught, and there was a hollowness in the pit of his stomach and a humming in his head. He struggled to the surface, feeling as if he would gladly drown in the great pools of Philip's eyes, and turned away, his heart pounding. He managed to give instructions about the tickets and waited until the boy left before he could breathe again.

After that, there was no point in trying to hide it. Their eyes met constantly, either near or from afar, and held for long seconds in a contact as explicit as an act of love. They exchanged only the routine words necessary for work while their eyes dedicated themselves to each other. He cursed Harry. Without Harry's initiation, he would not know what pleasure he was being offered, wouldn't believe what his response implied. This was worse than Harry, because he knew now where temptation might lead him. His innocence with Harry had provided no basis for rational judgment until after it had happened.

When he looked at Philip, his ears echoed with a boyish shout and the rush of water. Abhorrent, disgusting—perhaps only pathetic—memories stirred wild passions in him that he was determined never to experience again. Feared he would never experience again? Hoped he would never experience again? Harry waiting for him at the locker-room door, looking damp still from the shower, his clothes a haphazard cover, as if they would fall off at a touch. He obviously hadn't bothered to put on underpants. His cock was thrust, bold and naked, into the sheath of his trousers. He carried a jacket over his arm.

Somehow, Walter was in Harry's car, sitting in a car that was carrying them away. He was leaving school with Harry. He was living in a dream. They hadn't even left the school grounds when Harry reached across him and fiddled with the handle of the door and dropped his hand and drew it lingeringly across Walter's lap and chuckled. "I guess we're ready to compare, all right."

That was the tone—easy, cheerful, straightforward. It made everything perfectly natural. He had felt as if his life depended on concealing his erection, but Harry had found it and apparently approved. In another moment, without his knowing how it had happened, Harry's fly was open, and he was holding the hard column of flesh that lifted from it. He told himself that there must be limits to what was permitted, but in spite of himself, his fingers began to move along it. It was Harry, and he held it, the instrument of a god.

Intimacy. That was what made his heart beat so fast. He had attained intimacy with another human being. With Harry. With his god. He became aware of the pleasure he was giving him and began to handle the bold flesh more freely. As if it were his own.

Harry instructed him. "Put your arm around my shoulder. Yeah." He unbuttoned his shirt down to the unbuttoned trousers and pushed clothing aside. He laughed. "I'd like to feel your hands all over me. Go ahead. Act as if I were a girl."

It was a game. There was no need for restraint. He forced laughter but found that his hands had desires that weren't merely playful. They roamed the worshiped body, learning for the first time the feel of physical beauty. He told himself a girl would feel better, but he didn't believe it. He realized with horror that he wanted to have sex with a boy. He wanted them to be completely together. He couldn't imagine Harry reciprocating, but at least he seemed to like what Walter was doing.

"Yeah. Go on, Walt," he murmured. "Gee. I'll bet you really know how to make love." Harry turned, and their eyes met. Walter's first instinct was to hide his head, but Harry's eyes seemed to melt into his before he turned back to the road. Walter was left with his heart in his throat. Currents of passion that terrified him seemed suddenly to swirl around them. He became desperately aware of the difference in their ages. He knew Harry was almost two years older. He hoped he wasn't getting into something that was over his depth. For an instant he had felt as if they were about to kiss. Of course that was beyond all permitted limits, but Harry's look had been somehow girlish. Walter's eyes swept over the powerful athlete's body. Harry was the school hero. There was nothing peculiar or feminine about him. He ran his hand the length of his cock and began to stroke it rapidly. Perhaps it was best to get this over with. He had heard of guys' jerking each other off. There was nothing very special about that.

Harry dropped a hand on his and held it still. "Hey. Don't. Wait till we're home. Boy, you've got me really worked up. I want you to do it. Really do it. The real way. You know what I mean?"

"Sure." Nobody ever admitted to ignorance about sex.

"I've been looking at you a lot recently. I'm sure you've got a big one. I can't wait to get you out of those pants."

Walter didn't dare speak so freely, but he supposed it must be perfectly normal to express an interest in another guy's body. He was beginning to feel possessive about the superb body he was fondling. He wanted to kiss it all over. He was obviously out of his mind.

They turned into a driveway and stopped near an opulent old frame house set under trees in an ample lawn.

"We're in luck," Harry said, pulling his clothes together. "Nobody home. Come on." Out of the car, he raced for the open front door, shirttails flying. Walter ran after him. Harry held the screen door open for him and hustled him upstairs and across a hall into a room. He was naked once more almost before he had locked the door behind them. His prodigious erection was a proud permanent fixture. As he reached for Walter their eyes met again, and Walter caught the odd look. It was unmistakably girlish this time. All Harry's features had softened, and his eyes were filled with a yearning, yielding desire. A shiver ran down Walter's spine. He knew with a shock of scandalized delight that Harry wouldn't draw the line at kissing.

In another moment they were in each other's arms, and Harry's mouth was open on his. Harry's tongue thrust between his lips. He opened his mouth and lost all control over his response. For a moment he thought he would go wild with excitement and desire. His clothes were unfastened and torn from him. Hands closed on his sex and moved over it eagerly, measuring and assessing it. Harry drew back and looked down. His lips were parted in a strange, bewitching smile.

"What did I tell you?" His voice crooned strangely. "It's big, all right. Just what I hoped. Look at us. We're practically the same."

Walter saw that it was true. He had supposed all guys were the same until he had seen Harry. The cock he had held in the car had seemed colossal, but his own looked just as big. For the first time he felt a twinge of pride in his body.

Harry dropped down in front of him and lifted first one foot and then the other to disentangle him from socks and trousers. As he did so, he allowed Walter's cock to play over his face, seeking its touch. Walter uttered a succession of little cries as he saw and felt it touch an eye, slide along a check, brush through the hair over an ear.

When Harry had finished stripping him, he ran his hands over his thighs and closed them over his cock. He held it and put it in his mouth. Walter cried out. His hips jerked convulsively. The moist velvet of the mouth raised goose bumps all over his body. His head swam. His knees almost buckled. Harry relinquished him and stood. Walter

51

steeled himself to look at him as if nothing had happened. It was inconceivable; his god, the school hero, was a cocksucker, a pansy, a pervert. He was everything a vile boy could be. He waited for all of him to rise up in outrage and call a halt to this disgraceful episode.

"I love sucking guys off," Harry said. He was casual and cheerful, the familiar Harry, radiating health and wholesomeness. "I bet I'm better at it than anyone you know, but with you I want it the real way first. That's what you want, isn't it? I'll get the stuff."

Walter was trapped by the assumption that he was experienced. He couldn't tell Harry that he didn't know what he was talking about, that he had never dreamed that people actually performed these acts. Harry swung away toward the bathroom, and Walter's eyes roamed over the broad shoulders, down the tapering back, clung to the powerful curve of the buttocks. He felt his sex growing so rigid that it seemed as if it would break. He wanted whatever Harry was planning. There was something about this he hadn't understood. It was quite simply impossible for a star athlete to be a fairy.

Standing alone with a hard-on made him shy of his body, and he moved toward the bathroom. Harry emerged, a towel over his shoulder, carrying something in his hand. Walter hurried to meet him, instinctively hiding himself against him. Harry put an arm around him and looked at him and chuckled as he put his open mouth once more on Walter's in the extraordinary way Walter assumed he had invented. His lips were soft and yielding. His darting tongue created an even greater intimacy than their nakedness. Walter flung his arms around him and held him. The surrender he felt in Harry's body unleashed a great surge of power and passion in him. Once more he lost all control over his responses.

Harry breathed rapidly as he drew back and looked up at Walter from beseeching eyes. "Gosh, Walt. I guess we really go for each other. Come on. I'm ready for you." He led Walter to the bed. He pulled back covers and spread a towel on the sheet and sat on it. Walter started to drop down beside him, but Harry held him in front of him. He squeezed some ointment from a tube into his palm and began to apply it to Walter's leaping cock. His mouth was open, and his gaze was spellbound. "Boy. It's a real honey. This is going to be something."

Walter thought it was wrong for Harry to be so interested in his cock, but he couldn't dislike it. Harry's hands both soothed and aroused him. He hadn't known that his body was capable of such complete pleasure. Was this the "real way"? A cry was wrung from him.

"Wait," Harry cried.

His legs were knocked out from under him. He found himself spread-eagled on Harry's back.

Harry's powerful hands took charge of him, and his cock slipped into moist, warm confinement. Harry's hips worked, and he felt himself more deeply engaged. It took him an instant to understand what he was doing, and then he struggled to extricate himself, but Harry's hands clasped the back of his thighs and pulled him in closer. He made a deep, sliding plunge, and their bodies slammed up against each other. They were both gasping and shouting. He was seized by a frenzy of taking his pleasure, of taking possession. His mind was no longer operating; nature dictated his body's movements.

He experienced a moment of soaring, triumphant power, and then he felt himself flying apart, his life spurting from him in great jets, drained, shattered, still wrung by the gigantic ejaculation. Harry's body heaved under him, and their shouts mingled in throes of their shared orgasms.

Walter lay on top of him, taking great gasping gulps of air, and waited for coherent thought to impose some order on the chaos within him. He was damned, doomed. He had performed an act so hideous that he would never be able to face himself in the world, but the sense of soaring power remained. His god had offered him his beautiful body. It was his. He had taken it. His cock was still inside it, establishing his possession of it.

"God, Walt, you're huge. I've never felt anything like it. You can really fuck."

The four-letter word sent a chill through him. He knew at last what fucking was. He had fucked Harry. There was nothing queer about

53

fucking. He had done nothing very different from what he might have done with a girl. It was Harry who was damned, Harry who liked to suck guys' cocks and be fucked by them. It was obviously nothing new for him. Now Harry was his. His cock lengthened and hardened, and Harry moaned with pleasure. He had a big cock. Harry had never felt anything like it. He began to drive it into him again, suddenly determined that Harry would never want another. He had taken his first step toward youthful heartbreak. His whole being was dedicated to satisfying the glorious body that he had worshiped from afar. Harry's ecstatic shouts were as thrilling to him as the orgasms they heralded.

"Gosh, Walt," Harry gasped. "We're in love with each other. I knew it. It's the first time for me. Fuck me, honey. You're really it."

Later Harry insisted, "You're gay, honey. We're right together. You'll find out."

"I know I'm not," Walter said as he prepared to take his friend in the way that had become as natural to him as breathing. "Even if I could be, I wouldn't let myself. I'm going to be famous. I couldn't go running around after guys."

Harry had been an exception. Sex had turned a schoolboy crush into an agony as intense as any love affair he had ever read about. It couldn't happen with anybody else. Three years had passed and confirmed this conviction. There were girls, not boys. Why was he letting Philip get under his skin with his insistent inviting eyes, his frail poetic appeal, his undeveloped body? If he let himself look at the boy enough, he would find something repellent in him, something repellent in the thought of wanting him. It was Clara's fault. He should have picked one of the girls who was ready for sex. Celibacy didn't suit him. Being a suitor and paying court didn't suit him. Of course, decent girls didn't go in much for sex, with rare exceptions like Debby. Maybe that was the trouble; maybe he was oversexed and shouldn't expect decent girls to pay any attention to him.

At every opportunity, his eyes lingered on the hollow of Philip's cheeks, on the tilt of his nose, on the way his hair fell around his exquisite ears. The more he looked, the more angelic beauty he discovered. His determination not to make an overt move remained unshaken. Gossip flew around the small community. Trivial scandal was always brewing. He had no intention of being the subject of what could be a major one.

He shared with Clara what little spare time they both had, assuring himself that the progress they were making toward a more relaxed relationship was all the satisfaction his emotional life required. She seemed less inclined to make a test of every moment with him. She might yet give in, to the extent of letting him kiss her and hold her in a restrained form of lovemaking.

The fourth play of the season was to be another prepackaged touring production; and during the week before it arrived, there was a slight slackening off of the pressures of work. Walter was having a cigarette outside the theater during a break in the rehearsal he was running for David when Philip joined him. Their eyes met as usual in an exchange of promise and surmise.

"I'd like to talk to you some time, Mr....uh...Walter," Philip said. His expression was habitually grave, and he was economical in his movements. He had no nervous mannerisms; he made an impression of cool composure.

"Sure, about anything in particular?"

"That depends on you."

"Well, I don't know what that means, but I'd like to find out. It looks as if we might have a little time off in the next couple of days. We'll look out for each other. I have to get back inside now." Their voices bore no relationship to what their eyes were saying. They held for another moment. Walter flicked away his cigarette and returned to the rehearsal with his heart pounding.

He couldn't concentrate on work. Philip was taking charge. He had to prepare himself for the confrontation the boy was seeking. He felt on the verge of a dreaded revelation about himself, and he rejected it without even defining it in his mind. He couldn't be what it seemed he might be. What about Debby? What about his attraction to Clara? Perhaps the memory of Harry made him think he wanted more than he did. The thought of being swallowed up into the grotesque, hermetic all-male community he had observed in New York terrified him. The brand. He was safe from Philip so long as he didn't let himself get caught alone with him.

He lay in bed that night unable to sleep, memories flooding his mind despite the long discipline of keeping them locked away from his consciousness, astonishingly vivid memories, still capable, to his dismay, of giving him an erection. He lay on his back with his cock heavy on his belly and felt Harry's body against him, heard the sigh of delight in his voice as Walter took him: "Yeah, honey. You're the best ever. Do it, honey."

The only friend of his boyhood. His hero, endowed with a physical splendor that might have overturned anybody's normal controls. That had been the point, the excuse and justification. He had been an innocent, a pushover. His response to Philip was a sex-starved aberration. Physically, he was a mere stripling; it would be like going to bed with a child. Philip offered nothing that he wanted except perhaps a brief meeting of lips to acknowledge the connection that they had made with their eyes.

Walter tossed restlessly in bed, listening to David's heavy breathing in the next room. His erection plagued him. He was tempted to take it next door and see what David would do with it. Playing around with David would be a more sensible solution than an entanglement with Philip that threatened to engage his emotions. It obviously couldn't be primarily physical. Emotional entanglements were to be avoided at all costs. That was the wonderful thing about Clara. For the first time, he could imagine being friends with a girl. There was sexual attraction, of course; but she had a character as strong as a man's. He couldn't imagine anything happening between them that would give rise to the torments he had childishly allowed to get out of hand with Harry. If only she would yield a little further, acknowledge him as a man who could be important to her, she would give him the direction that would free him from these other cravings. He didn't have to be lying here alone. His hand inched up onto his belly, and he satisfied his body's needs, thoughts of Philip overlapping with memories of Harry, and was finally able to sleep.

David left the house at the usual early hour the next morning after asking Walter to stay at home to check some accounts that needed attention. "I'll pop back later when I see how things are going. You'll probably have to take rehearsal later on. I can't postpone that Baldwin business any longer."

More and more, Walter was becoming the director in all but name. It meant that he had to work to David's overall concepts, but he was hoping that this restriction would soon be lifted. He went to work on the accounts at David's desk in the living room.

He had been at it for some time when he heard the car in the drive and the honk of the horn summoning him. He went to the door and saw Philip getting out of the car. His heart leaped, and he took care not to look at the visitor as he went out.

David remained behind the wheel. He seemed to be bursting with inner glee. He rolled his eyes and tossed his head. "I gave this lad a lift. He wanted to see you, and I thought you'd have time for him. I let the poor actors out of their cages. The rehearsal call is for 3. You'll have to take it. I'm off. I'll be driving all over the countryside till this evening. Try to have fun without me."

Walter and Philip stood transfixed, their eyes summoning each other. "Was it all right to come?" Philip asked finally. "I asked David where you were, and he insisted on bringing me out."

"Sure. Fine. Come in." His voice sounded casual. He hoped it would stay that way. If they could talk together casually, perhaps they would be able to look at each other without making it an invitation to bed. They went into the stillness of the living room. Walter felt suddenly as if it were pressing in on them, pressing them to each other, forcing an embrace. He moved hastily to the desk, heart and mind racing. "Look, I still have a bit of work to do," he said, staring at the accounts without seeing them. "Why don't you go down to the pool? There's some trunks in the shower room. Get some sun. I'll be down in no time." He went to the screen door that opened onto the lawn and stepped out and held

57

it open for Philip without looking at him. He kept space between them and pointed down at the clump of trees. "It's right down there. You don't have to worry about meeting people. Nobody else uses it."

"You won't be long?"

"No, 15 minutes at the most." His eyes dropped to the coveted bottom as Philip turned and started across the lawn. He forced himself back into the house. He breathed deeply and ran his fingers through his hair. At least he had gotten him out. He had room to think coherently. He was in a rage with David for playing this trick on him. He was probably laughing his head off, wondering if he would succumb. He hadn't yet. He had created difficulties for himself and forced a postponement. If Philip put on the trunks, he would be able to look at all of him and dispel the mystery of his body.

He was in no state for dealing with accounts. He ran upstairs and stripped and went to the bathroom and hitched a towel around himself. He looked down and saw that he jutted out conspicuously under it. He rearranged it so that the folds hung down the middle and concealed him more effectively. He found himself staring at David's suntan oil. If—no, but Philip was so fair that he should probably have some. He took it and went slowly downstairs. Should be revise the script and start over from the beginning? Should he get dressed and go call Philip back and talk to him sensibly in the living room? With the bed waiting just above? No. They couldn't go on like this indefinitely. The opportunity had been offered him to resolve the issue. Being outdoors was a safeguard. He would see him naked and trust in the satisfaction of his eyes, even touch him and know that he couldn't really want a boy.

He went out and crossed the lawn and descended the slope to the pool. Philip was nowhere in sight. A yew hedge enclosed a small area at the side of the bathhouse. He went stealthily to the break in it and found him. He was lying on his stomach on a towel, his head cradled on his arms, the enticing behind encased in brief trunks. He sprang forward silently and pulled off the towel. When he reached him, he held it in front of him and dropped down on it and flung an arm across

58

the slight shoulders. "Alone at last," he said melodramatically, taking refuge in a joke.

Philip's head jerked up, his great eyes wide as if he had been asleep. "You scared me."

Walter realized he'd gone too far. The sudden intimacy committed him. Its effect was immediate. He had to shift to make room for what had happened beneath him. He wouldn't be able to get up until the boy left. "You scare me all the time," he said, his eyes on the mouth only a few inches from his, on the delicate nose, on the fine arch of the brows. "You're more beautiful than a host of angels."

Philip craned his neck slightly and darted his eyes down over him. "You're naked," he murmured, as if dazed with wonder.

"Sure, we don't have to bother with clothes down here." He kept his hand motionless on the shoulder, still able to hope that his excitement might subside when he got used to having the boy close and almost naked beside him.

"Can't anybody see us?"

"Not here, you picked the perfect place."

Philip eased over so that he was propped on one elbow. The movement dislodged Walter's hand but somehow created no more space between them. They still touched all the length of them. Walter slid his hand down to the narrow waist, establishing the right to hold him without turning it into a sexual advance.

"I'm pretty smart," Philip said.

"That depends. Are you sure we're both thinking the same thing?"

"After the way we've been looking at each other? I don't know why you've waited so long."

"Waited? Anyway, why should it be up to me?"

"It is, of course. You're god around here."

"All the more reason to wait, whatever it is you think I'm waiting for. What did you want to talk to me about?"

"This."

"I see." Philip obviously wasn't going to let him evade it with meaningless words. "Aren't you a bit young to know what you're doing?"

"Older than you, I found out. Old enough to know I'm in love with you. Well, everybody is. You can take your pick, boys or girls. You look at me as if you're in love with me, but I don't want to get my hopes up. We're going to make love, aren't we?"

"Are we?" Walter was amazed at the ease and tranquillity with which people announced they were in love. Harry. Debby. Anyway, guys couldn't fall in love with each other. He was sure of that much. Doubting that Philip knew what he was talking about, he tried to tell him what he felt. "I want to look at your face until I know everything about it. I want to know what you feel like. I suppose that's sort of making love." There was an appeal in Philip's face, perhaps in male faces generally, that he had never found in a girl's—a poetry, a mysterious vulnerability. Even Harry, who was hardly poetic, had had a guileless, happy sweetness in his face that approached poetry and was uniquely male. Girls were so down-to earth and knowing. He allowed his hand to move back along the top of the trunks. Philip's eyes closed, and he let himself go so that his head dropped against Walter's shoulder. He made a small sound like a sob. Walter thought of Clara and wondered if she would ever be capable of such sweet, moving surrender. Philip's hand worked its way down between them along his side. Walter felt his body giving way to its touch, lifting to allow it to find what it was seeking. He clamped his stomach to the ground.

"Please. Take me somewhere we can…" Philip's urgent murmur broke off. His mouth was open on Walter's skin.

"I don't know what…" He too found it difficult to finish a sentence. "You scare me. You make me feel that if I…if we let it happen, I'd never be able to let you go."

"That's all right with me."

Soft lips moved against him thrillingly. He had all that he had imagined he wanted. He held him. He felt his lips against him. He had praised his beauty. If he wasn't what he was determined not to be, desire should be assuaged. He wished the trunks would vanish but forbade himself to remove them. He made a further effort at control. He found that he was still clutching the bottle of oil. "Here," he said

60

breathlessly, forcing another postponement. "I brought you some sun-tan stuff. You're getting pink. Let me put some on you." He moved Philip's head so that he was lying out flat and poured oil on his shoulders and began to stroke it slowly into him. Philip's hand crept along Walter's side still trying to work its way under him. Walter had to keep his muscles taut to prevent it from reaching its goal.

He watched the movement of his own hand as he caressed shoulders and back and learned the feel of the slight body. Philip's profile was turned to him, the eyes closed, the pale hair in touching disarray, his lips slightly parted as he uttered his small sounds. His beauty was angelic in its fragile purity. Walter felt a great wrench in his chest, and his throat tightened. Was he fighting his true nature? He wanted all that Philip offered him.

His hand moved down the small of the back. Philip tucked his thumbs under the top of the trunks and lifted his hips and pushed. The gentle curve of buttocks was uncovered. "If you're naked, I don't see why I shouldn't be," he said. "Put that stuff all over me, it feels so good—your hand making love to me."

Walter seized the trunks and pulled them down to the knees and up over the jack-knifed legs and tossed them away. He forgot control at the sight of the slender body now completely naked and exposed to his will. He spilled more oil into his hand and ran it down between the buttocks. Philip's muscles worked as Harry's had. He moved his fingers caressingly into him and slipped his other arm under Philip's head and drew him closer so that their bodies turned and closed to each other.

Philip cried out as their mouths met, teeth clashed. Another cry was strangled in his throat as his hand closed on its goal. Walter blindly reached for more oil and drew back from the hand that was stroking him and spread it on himself. He relinquished the hungry mouth. Philip dropped his head and flattened himself against the ground, trembling from head to foot and making little whimpering sounds.

Walter took him, slowly until he was in full possession of him, and then with joyful abandon as he rushed headlong back into the realm of forbidden pleasure.

61

He brought Philip to a sobbing climax and collapsed onto him in the triumph of orgasm. He waited long enough so that he could slip from him easily and gave him a little hug. "I'm going to take a shower."

He stood under the bathhouse shower and hoped Philip wouldn't join him immediately. There was so much to absorb and bring into focus. Did he know himself now beyond any shadow of doubt? If he was one of the damned, he would have to come to terms with it somehow. Was it possible, after all, to fall in love with a boy? Harry had insisted that it was, but they had been schoolboys. The things he did now became part of real life and the future. If he gave in to it, he would have to abandon his campaign to win Clara. He would have to renounce his ambitions; he couldn't be in the public eye with the risk of discovery hanging over him. He would be an outcast. For love?

Harry had insisted that they were in love and in the next breath had told him about another boy he had his eye on.

"There's a kid in the class below us—have you noticed him?— Callaghan, a cute blond with a terrific body. Hey. How about it? We could bring him home and have some fun, all three of us."

Walter was shocked and made him promise not to have anything to do with the boy. He would never forget the afternoon he had come out of the school building just in time to see Harry driving away with Callaghan's golden head at his side. He didn't know how he had got home. He had wept. He had torn his hair. He had ripped a pillowcase to shreds. He had smashed the watch Harry had given him and resolved never to wear one again. As he recovered, he had felt steel entering his soul and had welcomed it as a sign of growing up. Never again would he allow himself to become so deeply attached to another human being, especially male. Men together couldn't know anything about being in love. The fireworks of the physical side of it could be stupendous but were bound to be short-lived. Was he going to forget the lesson of the most crucial experience of his life and allow himself to be deflected from the course he had set for himself?

Philip appeared in the bathhouse door and approached the shower. Walter's eyes roamed over the willowy body from the shapely feet to the appropriately slim and delicate sex, up to the celestial head, and felt no resistance to him but a surge of pride in his possession of him. He held his arms out to him and watched his pace quicken until he had pressed himself to Walter's dripping body. Their eyes met with acknowledgment of what had happened.

"God, Walter," he murmured, again in a daze of wonder. "I knew it had to happen, but it's hard to believe it really has. I've been waiting and wondering when you'd let it."

Walter drew him closer and took his mouth in his. He handled him gently. He turned him and soaped his back and his delicious behind. He felt almost paternal toward him. "We better get back to the house while our luck holds. That was pretty crazy."

"I'll say. I wouldn't have cared if the whole town had been peering over the hedge. It was heaven."

Walter ran his hands over him, extending his possession of him while he rinsed away soap. His hair was so pale that the down on his arms and legs was almost invisible. He turned off the water and put his arms around him as they crossed to the towels. He saw with pride that his handling of the slight body had begun to arouse it again. Power. Power to give pleasure. Power to bind another being to him. Had he a lust for conquest, regardless of gender, a craving for deep total connection with those who stirred his imagination? It was probably related to the drive he felt in the theater as he molded his actors into an expression of himself and exulted as the audience swayed to his will. Sexual drive. Creative drive. If it were all mixed up together, he wasn't simply a pervert but needed both sexes to express himself fully.

They dried themselves, standing close to each other, their eyes meeting and moving on to learn each other's bodies and returning with messages of delight and discovery.

Philip put his hand on Walter's cock again. "I want to look at it the next time it's hard. It's beginning, isn't it?"

"It's been beginning ever since you came in here. You don't suppose it's like that all the time, do you? It's a bit soon for it to go any further."

"I've got so much less that it happens in no time. Especially when I'm with you."

"So I notice. I like that. Come on. Wrap a towel around yourself. You can carry your clothes."

They trotted up the lawn and reentered the living room. Walter put a hand on Philip's shoulder and looked into his eyes with proprietary tenderness. They were strangers, yet in an hour Philip had become precious to him. He was prepared to admire everything he did, find ways to please him. It wasn't just sex, but the craving to get behind people's facades and learn what they really were. The quickest way to total intimacy he had found was in the meeting of bodies. Was there another way he would discover? He didn't want to make love to him again until he could make love to the person called Philip, not just his body, but the fact of having known his body made the person called Philip accessible. "How about eating something and getting that out of the way?" he suggested. "I have till 2:30. What about you? Are you supposed to be doing anything?"

"David let everybody go till 3. Do you suppose he did it for us? I mean, everybody knows about you and David. I was amazed when he actually seemed to want to hand me over to you."

Walter tried to exempt Philip from his indignation. "What does everybody know about me and David?"

"Well, you live together, don't you?"

"Sure. We share the same house. That's all there is to it. You thought we were having an affair, and you still wanted this to happen with us?"

"Well, of course, if you wanted it. It wasn't up to me. How amazing." The angelic head lifted, emphasizing the thrilling line of chin and neck. "That's absolutely wonderful. I've been wondering how we were going to go on from here. He won't mind me being with you?"

"Why should he? It's none of his business. That's the way we're going to keep it." He gave his shoulder a pat and moved thoughtfully toward the kitchen.

Philip followed him. "I don't understand. If that meant anything, won't you want us to be together?"

"Here? Of course not." Walter began to get things out of the icebox.

"How else can we be together? If there's nothing going on between you and David, he couldn't mind. He's already doing it with Bill."

"Not here, he isn't." Walter distractedly started to make sandwiches. "If people talk about me and David, what would it be like if there's really something going on?"

"You mean with us? They'll talk anyway. They can't say anything bad. I mean, they're all doing it themselves. They'll be wildly envious, but that can't hurt us. What're you afraid of?"

Walter stiffened, a knife poised in midair. "I'm not afraid of anything. You're not going to tell anybody, are you?"

"Not if you don't want me to, but they'll know. It'll probably show, whether I like it or not. Everybody will see how happy I am. No matter how hard we pretend, they'll see we're lovers. If that's what we're going to be."

It was impossible. It would always be impossible. Walter felt threatened by the crushing weight of anonymous condemnation. The brand. He couldn't face it. He hurriedly finished the sandwiches and poured glasses of milk. He motioned to Philip to take his and went into the small dining room and sat. Philip sat beside him. Walter avoided looking at him. "We'd better talk about this," he began uncomfortably. "It's obvious you can't stay here. Is that what you were talking about? Sort of moving in?"

"I would if you wanted me to," Philip said. "I don't know what this means to you. It can't be just sex. Half a dozen of the kids are a lot more sexy than I am."

Walter put a hand out to where Philip's was resting on the table and held it. "I hadn't noticed. I haven't noticed anybody but you. That's the trouble."

"It's a bit new for me too. I've been sort of in love before, but not like this. It happened the minute I saw you. I want to live with you."

Walter lowered his head over his sandwich and took a bite. Philip's cultivated voice touched Walter's ears with music. It made everything he said sound intelligent. Humor seemed to lurk beneath his impassive surface. Walter sensed in him a delicacy of spirit that matched his physique. An illusion? He was talking to a homosexual about entering into a homosexual liaison. Was he prepared to go so far? He had been kept awake half the night just wondering if he would let himself go to bed with the boy. Now that he had, nothing was resolved. He didn't understand the rules or know even if there were any. His experience with Harry suggested that there weren't any. In any case, there had never been any question of living with Harry. They had talked about fixing it so they could go to college together, but they had already been committed to different schools. They had been kids, with kids' incomprehensions about tomorrow.

He pressed the hand he held and raised his head and looked at Philip. His pale hair floated around his head after the vigorous toweling he had given it. The hollows of his cheeks made him look touchingly undernourished. His enormous eyes offered himself. Walter hadn't even known what color they were. More gray than blue, he noted. Walter's throat tightened with a rush of tangled emotions. "I just don't know," he said. "Don't expect me to be in love with you. I don't mean I'm not fascinated by you. I obviously am. But then what? We're too busy ever to be alone together. I can't let you actually live here. I guess we could fix it so it would seem natural for you to stay here sometimes. Maybe I should talk to David about it. How does he manage with Bill?"

"They go down to the beach during performances. It's different for them. I happen to know what Bill likes. Anyway, it's just sex."

"What if it's just sex with me?"

"All right. But you act as if you'll want it to happen again."

"You all seem to know so much about each other."

"Well, naturally. You're the only mystery man. What about Clara? Are you really interested in her, or is she a blind?"

"A blind?"

"You know—to make people think you like girls."

"I do like girls. There's been only one guy—over three years ago. Now you."

He gripped his hand and pulled him up with him as he stood. Towels dropped from them. Philip looked down at him and ran a hand lightly along him. He looked up with a smile of angelic purity and innocence.

"No wonder you're god around here. We've all been guessing about this. They'd love to know. I promise not to tell," he added carefully.

Walter ran his hand through his pale hair and dropped it to his smooth flat chest. His other hand moved over his behind. "You do fascinate me. You're so slim and elegant. Even your cock is elegant. Mine looks indecent next to it. It seems almost indecent to want you the way I do."

Philip laughed lightly. "I'd like to go to bed so you can be as indecent as you like. There's nothing elegant about where I want you."

Philip's body vanished into his light embrace, responding to his slightest pressure, so that he felt in total control of it.

Philip closed his eyes. "Oh, darling. I'm about to come just feeling your hands on me. Oh, please. Not yet. Let me go for a minute."

Walter withdrew his hands, and Philip dropped down onto a chair and pulled him close. Walter saw his mouth opening to receive him, and a shiver ran down his spine–an angel in thrall to the beast. He had always refused to perform this act with Harry. Was that all that separated him from the queers?

It another moment Philip rose and kissed a nipple and looked up at him. "I'd gladly go on, but I want so much what you did before. I'll do anything you want."

Walter put his arms around him and bent to kiss the exquisite mouth. "Let's go upstairs where I can have all of you." They stretched out on Walter's narrow bed, and he gathered Philip to him with a long, voluptuous sigh of contentment. He didn't have to be alone here again. Philip would make no demands. He simply wanted to be taken. David would have no objections.

He made a mental note to get something to replace the suntan oil while he prepared them for union. Philip lay in an inertia of surrender, making his small sounds of pleasure. What would Clara think if the "silly little faggot" moved in with him? Exactly what they would all think. Impossible.

Walter made love to him with tenderness and care. He felt none of the self-absorbed aggression he remembered with Harry. It had been a contest in which he had been barely a match for his voracious partner. His body moved on Philip's in deep, gentle communication. He was the guardian, the protector. Was homosexual lovemaking so different from any other? He had to know and know what he was risking. He could still isolate it from life for a little while, but life had a way of taking charge. Philip had already gained a dangerous hold on him.

"It's good, baby," he said when he lay at rest, dwindling but still joined to his boy. The endearment came easily, and he offered it gladly. He wanted to give whatever he could find in himself to give. "It's wonderful. I hate not knowing when we can be together again."

"I can't imagine not being with you all the time. Nobody's ever made love to me like that. If that's just sex, I've never known anything about sex."

"Don't let it get too important to you. Not yet. I just don't know. Can we have beautiful times like this together without my hurting you?"

"You can't hurt me unless we discover we mean something to each other. If I can be important to you, I'm willing to be hurt. I worship you, but maybe I better stop saying so. Just let me be your love."

There was an undercurrent of melancholy in him that Walter had detected earlier. He was finding the person called Philip. He wanted to make him happy. Could Philip understand that without thinking it was more? His hands moved over him with caressing possessiveness. He took his mouth with his and kissed him until Philip was whimpering, and he had begun to stir in him again. He drew back gently. "We've got to go. You see what I mean? We're together all the time, but God knows how we'll ever be alone together."

"If you want me, there'll be ways."

Walter withdrew from him and sprang up. There was no shower in the little old-fashioned bathroom so washing was a nuisance. This was the part of it he had never been quite able to accept. Philip took his turn in the bathroom, and Walter remade the bed and put towels away so there would be no traces left for David to see. They dressed and went downstairs together. Walter stopped at the door and held the white-clad body close against him. Philip's chin lifted. His great eyes looked up with peaceful adoration.

"You know, these last few weeks when we've been looking at each other all the time," Walter said, "I knew we might go to bed together, but I didn't think about what it would be like. I never thought of really liking you."

"Just another little faggot? I know. Do you like me, darling?"

"Very much."

"That's the best thing you could've told me."

The kissed lightly on the lips, and Walter let them out of the house. They walked together to the theater, but when they were within a few minutes of it, Walter sent Philip on ahead. It took a concentrated afternoon's work to make him feel at ease once more in the familiar surroundings and confident that he wasn't marked by the brand.

He frequently walked Clara home after the show, and he made a point of doing so that night, knowing that there would be no loving arms waiting to hold him when they arrived. As they were leaving the theater, he caught sight of a solitary figure in white loitering under the trees and felt as if Clara were tearing him away from something precious and necessary to him. When they reached the garage, he hesitated, considering another attempt at softening her with kisses, but she showed no signs of being receptive, and he let her close her door firmly on him.

He ran most of the way back to the theater. The figure in white had vanished. David was waiting to drive him home.

He spent another hot, restless night. He no longer thought of Harry. The feel of Philip's body was imprinted on his hands and arms and torso, and he wanted him. He hadn't expected it to happen again, but it had, and there was no point denying himself. He was still young, younger than Philip. When he was Philip's age, he would have found a girl he really cared about and who cared about him, and he could start thinking about marriage. Meanwhile, he didn't have to go around telling everybody he'd turned queer overnight. It was a question of caution and discretion. This was the last night he would let Clara come between him and the boy he wanted.

The next day was a scorcher. They were all streaming with sweat by the time the morning's work started. Walter gave Philip assignments that kept them in frequent contact. When their eyes met, they held with desire. They no longer questioned. At a break in rehearsals, Walter gave him a look that summoned him and went outside. Philip followed, and Walter committed what seemed to him the enormous indiscretion of walking with him a few yards out under the trees.

"I almost went mad wanting you last night," he said quietly.

"Did you? I'm glad. So did I. Do you want me tonight?"

"Yes. Is it all right if you come out for an hour or so and don't stay all night? We could go down by the pool. Even David needn't know."

"I like what happens down by the pool. People saw me leaving with David yesterday. They all think he's had me. Bill is livid. I just looked mysterious." They laughed softly together.

"Don't get far away from me. I can't work if I don't see you around."

"Oh, darling. What an incredible thing to tell me. Maybe you're falling in love with me."

"We'll talk tonight, baby." He forced himself to turn from the elegant figure in white and congratulated himself for not having touched him. He felt as if the whole company were watching him.

As the day wore on, he grew dissatisfied with his arrangements. He didn't want to send Philip away alone as if his body were a convenience. He wanted to keep him all night. The possibility that David might hear them at the pool made it more reasonable for him to know. He encountered David in his shirtsleeves in front of the theater before the show.

"I've got to put on a tie and jacket," David complained. "We all ought to be in swimming trunks."

"Hey, why don't we drive down to the beach after? We might be able to cool off. The pool's getting like soup."

"A proposition, at last. Fine."

"If we drive a little way out of town, we wouldn't have to wear anything."

"Better and better. An indecent proposition."

"How about taking Philip with us?" Walter suggested, steeling himself for a barrage of gleeful innuendo. "We had a good talk yesterday. I like him."

"A threesome. Why not," David agreed briskly, for once even sparing him a leer. "He's a toothsome morsel. We'll dance in the moonlight at the edge of the sea, our lovely young limbs intertwined."

Despite the facetiousness, the image stuck in Walter's mind. It was there when he found Philip at his usher's post and told him of the plan. His reserved expression brightened.

"With David? You suggested bringing me? That's marvelous. Have you told him?"

"Not yet. I'm sure he'll approve."

Walter spun out a fantasy during the evening, the details vague but involving kisses exchanged, all three of them lying naked together, ending at home with David giving his blessing as Walter took Philip to his bed. Walter would have an adult affair with a boy and find out what if offered. He sensed a world of fraternity and comradeship opening to welcome him. He already felt a weight lifting at the thought of sharing his secret with David. If he was headed for a crisis of decision, a turning point, he might as well meet it and get it over with.

The three of them gathered at the station wagon right after the performance. Walter felt a trifle self-conscious, but their being three made it irreproachable. He put Philip in the middle and sat with his arm along his shoulders with a hand just brushing his chest. He felt Philip's eyes on him, and he gave him a secret hug. David started the car.

As he did so, Walter's eye was caught by a flurry of movement under the trees off to his right, the blur of something light moving.

In another moment he saw it was Clara, advancing on them like doom. Why didn't David get moving? He didn't want her to catch him with the "little faggot." He felt his mouth going dry, and a tremor shook

71

his hand as he moved his arm up on the back of the seat away from Philip. He thought of getting out to head her off, but it was too late. She was approaching rapidly. In a moment he could feel her breath on him, and she put her hand on the window frame of the car. David flicked on the light, and her face sprang up close to him, her mouth set but with a small quiver in her chin. She ignored the others' existence; her attention was fixed on him.

"Where are you going?" she demanded in the flat, level tones of barely controlled fury.

"We're going for a swim." He tried not to cringe from her. Nothing had occurred between them to prepare him for this, nothing that could be interpreted as having established claims on each other. It hadn't occurred to him to protest when she seemed to be getting very friendly with a couple of the actors. He wanted to get away from her. "Let's go, David," he urged.

"If you go with them, I'll kill you," she said, her voice hard and flat.

"Oh, God, another nut," David said wearily. "We do get our share of them. Do you think you'd better stay with her, Walter?"

"He doesn't need your advice, David." Her voice began to lose pitch and develop little quavers and breaks. "He can make up his own mind."

"But we're just going for a swim," he repeated. "What is all this? You're welcome to come, but we don't have suits. We want to cool off."

"If you go with them, I'll–" she began.

David cut in. "Maybe we'd better drop it, Walter. I don't know what it's all about, but I gather the lady disapproves of your taking a dip in the ocean. It's a bit eccentric, but I don't think we want to make a major issue of it."

"Well, I do," Walter said. "Come on, David. We're going for a swim. Let's go."

"Now, let's not be hasty. Remember Steelman. He wouldn't want us to make each other unhappy. I think you'd better get out and soothe her shattered nerves. After all, you can't blame her. You might've drowned."

"Don't you move just because he tells you to," Clara commanded him. "You can make up your mind for yourself."

"Now, listen…" He wanted to go for a swim. He wanted his fantasy to unfold. Philip's hand was hidden on the seat between them. Fingers moved against him in a desperate plea for him to stay. He glanced at David, who gestured with his head toward Clara and turned off the motor. He wouldn't mind so much if they didn't go without him. He released a resentful sigh and opened the door and let himself out, sliding his arm caressingly along Philip's shoulders to reassert his possession of him.

Clara turned on her heel and strode off. He trailed angrily after her. In a moment they were out of range of the car's lights. He heard a motor start up, the grinding of gears, and sound fading. Had they gone off together? He hadn't heard a door slam. He couldn't blame David for taking what he could get. He didn't know Philip was his. Philip was in love with him. He wouldn't give himself to David.

He moved forward and fell into step with Clara. He was so preoccupied that he didn't wonder immediately why he was following her. "Where are we going?" he asked absently.

"I'm going home. You can walk with me if you want."

"Thanks. You'd better explain why you carried on like that. I don't understand it."

"It just makes me mad, that's all, to see what David's trying to do to you," she said.

He blushed and was glad for the dark. "You must be out of your mind. David isn't trying to do anything to me."

"Really? Then it's your little faggot, is it? I thought you made a big point about liking girls. If you're queer, just say so. Lots of men in the theater are. I just can't stand you letting him act as if he owned you."

"I don't know what you're talking about."

"God, you're dumb."

"You mean David? All his talk about…well, you know, all his joking about himself and all that. It's just a joke."

"Ha, ha, ha." She uttered the monosyllables hollowly, and then inexplicably she really laughed. She doubled over as she walked, then straightened and threw her head back. "Some joke. Are you queer?"

"You mean...certainly not." He blushed again. He still found it difficult to believe that she or any girl could know about such things, let
alone talk about them.

"Well, then, I made a big fool of myself, didn't I?" She laughed again,
full-throated and not remotely apologetic.

At least she seemed to accept his denial. It emboldened him to attack. "You'd better apologize to both of them. You're really impossible,
screaming your head off and making all sorts of dirty suggestions
about David and that kid and then laughing uproariously as if it were
a big joke."

"I can be awful, can't I? Nobody else seems to mind. I'll apologize if
you think I should."

He wasn't inclined to be appeased by her sudden docility. By now
the three of them would have been naked together–floating, touching,
and playing together in intimate comradeship in the sea. As it was, he
was still sweating, locked in conflict once more with Clara. It was impossible to remain indifferent to her. She strode along as if she didn't
care whether he was there or not. He felt like tripping her. The thought
of her in a heap at his feet pleased him enormously. The thought of
helping her up evoked different emotions–tenderness and the excitement of holding her.

"How come you turned up just when you did?" he asked.

"I was watching you. I waited until I was sure you were going off
somewhere together. I was spying on you. There. Something else
awful." She sounded quite delighted with herself.

"I suppose I should be flattered you took the trouble."

She turned her head quickly to him. He knew they were looking
into each other's eyes, although he couldn't really see hers; her face
was all shadow and odd highlights. "There's nothing flattering about
it." Whatever was happening in her eyes, her voice made no concessions to him. "I did it to thwart David. If there's nothing to thwart, it
was a waste of time."

Just as his walking home with her was a waste of time, he thought
bitterly. They walked the last few hundred yards in silence. Fireflies

74

winked in the shrubbery. The still, hot air throbbed with the song of frogs. He wondered if she would ask him in and whether he would accept if she did. Why bother? She had ruined his evening. If he tried to kiss her, she would laugh at him. She could never be a comrade.

When they reached the short drive leading to the garage, she stopped and faced him. Again he knew that their eyes were meeting, but he still couldn't see into hers.

"If you're so keen on a swim, why don't we have one?" she asked. "It *is* hot."

"I told you—I don't have anything to wear."

"That shouldn't make any difference. David isn't the only one who'd like to look at a beautiful naked man."

"I thought you said you weren't a tease?" He was so angry that he didn't stop to wonder if she meant it. "I do like girls. You better believe me. If we were naked together, I'd—well, things would happen. I can promise you that."

"You mean, you'd stand up all lovely and hard with desire? I'm dying to see a man like that. Girls are curious too, you know. We talk about the most scandalous things. I have a wicked friend who says that some men are like stallions and others are so small that you can hardly feel it. Which are you?"

"Come for a swim," he said curtly, waiting for the blow of her iron fist. "You'll find out for yourself." He knew there was a trick in it. She was the last person in the world to romp around naked on a beach.

There was a brief silence while he could feel, rather than see, her look deepening. Her voice had softened when she spoke. "I told you I'd let you know if I wanted more. I do. I want everything. And don't think I'm a loose woman. As it happens, I'm a virgin."

He didn't know how long it took for his ears to communicate her words to his brain. He found himself standing in front of her, stupefied. He seized her and drew her a few feet into the drive in an ineffective attempt at finding privacy and took her in his arms. She clung to him and thrust her hips up against his and swayed against him. When they broke apart for breath, there was a thrill of laughter in her voice.

75

"You feel like a stallion. Come along. I won't be a second. I might as well simplify matters for myself."

"What about—you know, babies and so forth."

"We're going for a swim first, aren't we? Anyway, you don't have to worry. My mother practically invented Margaret Sanger."

He didn't know what she was talking about, but he accepted her assurance. It was to be expected that the Washburns weren't subject to the natural laws of procreation.

She found explanations demeaning; she had no intention of explaining that some games invented by naughty cousins one summer years ago at Cap Ferrat had left her with only a theoretical maidenhead, that her mother had approved of her being one of Mrs. Sanger's guinea pigs. She led him up the exterior stairs and stopped at the door. "If you come in, we may never get to the beach. Wait here. We'll come right back. I promise. I'm not a tease."

He stood at the door, scarcely knowing how he had got there. All the events of the evening were wiped from his consciousness. Everything began with this moment. His mind struggled to encompass the impossible: Clara Washburn was going to give herself to him. The momentous fact enclosed him and cut him off from all other experience. In what seemed like seconds, she was back, wearing toweling cut into a robe of a sort he had never seen before. She handed him a towel and left the door open and the lights on and swept him down the stairs with her. He saw that her feet were bare except for the thongs of sandals.

They quickly reached the end of the road and were climbing dunes. They laughed and giggled together as they stumbled and fell against each other in loose sand. They reached firmer footing, and Clara set off along the sea. Small breakers rolled in toward them. The uneven segment of moon lit the beach more brightly than it had the town and drained her hair of color. Her hair was as dark as the hollows of her face, and she looked like a ghost in her robe.

"Right along here," she said. "The houses stop in a minute. Oh, do you feel it? It's almost cool."

76

He put his arm around her waist as the going got easy and ran the other hand through the opening of her robe and found the infinitely soft skin of her breasts, punctuated with nipples that grew hard under his touch. He loosened the tie of her robe as he ran his hand down over the slight swell of belly and ruffled the pubic curls.

"Oh, Walter, dearest, wait," she begged breathlessly. "I'll faint. You don't want to have to carry me."

The endearment seemed to shatter his ears. He caught the first note in the surrender he had so often dreamed of. He lifted his hand and held first one breast and then the other in its hollow and felt the soft weight of them as they moved with her movement. They walked another few minutes, and then she stopped and moved in against him and lifted her head.

"This is far enough," she said.

He ran his hands over her bare shoulders under the robe and pushed it from her. Their mouths opened to each other again, and his hands flew over her, and he let her feel his nails on her until she was shivering and making sounds of protest. He drew back and surveyed her as his fingers tore at buttons and cloth.

Her breasts looked fuller than he had expected, young and firm and proud. Her hips were ripe without being wide, and her long legs gave graceful support to the slight curve of belly. He threw clothes from him and stooped to disentangle his feet and stepped free and stood before her, his hands at his sides. His eyes bored into hers, intent and searching for signs of misgivings or withdrawal. She met his look for a moment, and then her eyes wavered and fell. Her lips parted with a quick intake of breath.

"Aren't we beautiful?" she said with a touch of wonder. "Adam and Eve." She raised a hand and ran her fingertips over his chest and down along the muscular concavity of his abdomen and held them trembling near his pubic hair. "Will anything terrible happen if I touch it? Is it very depraved of me to want to?"

"Not that I know of. I want to touch all of you. Nothing terrible will happen."

"I was afraid I might make you come."

He laughed, finally relaxed and carefree. The straightforward expression coming from her lips transformed her. Why had he allowed her to bully him into thinking of her as a sort of sanctified presence he must approach with awe? She was a girl who wanted her first man. He had the power to make it thrilling for her. "You'd have to touch me a lot for that to happen." He moved her hand down to his cock and left his hand with hers to share what she was feeling. Her fingers moved timidly the length of it and grew more confident as they encircled it and moved back and touched his balls. He dropped his hand and left her in possession as it leaped up to her.

"It's marvelous," she said. "It's so alive. If this were mine, I'd want to use it all the time. What makes it so hard?"

"You."

"That's not very scientific. Never mind. You can tell me all about it later. I want to know lots of things. You are a stallion. Are some boys even bigger?"

"I don't know. I suppose so."

"I doubt it. I always get the biggest and best for myself. I'm trying to imagine it later. It's going to enter me and take me." She spoke thoughtfully, weighing each word. She had never liked the idea of allowing any mere male to violate her body in that way; it seemed to put the woman in such a subservient position. Now, looking at this vigorous part of his beautiful body, she realized that she would be taking him while she was being taken. She felt an unexpected satisfying equality.

"Right here, if we don't watch out," he said. He lifted a hand to her breasts and felt the velvet skin with the backs of his fingers.

"I'll probably want it here some other night," she said. "For the first time, I suppose we should have all the comforts of home."

He drew her closer and bent and took a nipple in his mouth. She cried out. "Oh, darling. Is it going to be like this? Your body feels so glorious against mine."

He straightened and smiled at her. "I have a feeling this is going to be quite a night. We'd better have that swim."

He put an arm around her waist, and she didn't relinquish him as they went down to the ocean's edge. Pride dictated that he should remain erect; he didn't want her to see him in repose until he had had her. The shock of cold water was daunting, but he counteracted its effect by staying close to her, enclosing her between his legs, brushing her breasts with his arms as they moved to keep afloat. They laughed into each other's eyes as he thrust himself between her legs.

They staggered and struggled from the sea and went running up the beach hand in hand to clothes and towels.

"What bliss," she exclaimed as they toweled themselves. Her hair hung in wet strands around her shoulders. She looked very young and defenseless. She put on her robe without bothering to fasten the tie and pushed her hair back. "I can't take my eyes off you. You're so magnificent. I won't ever let you wear clothes." She was experiencing shock after pleasurable shock, amazed by him. He had caught her attention from the first by the strong feminine streak she had sensed in him. There was nothing effeminate about him, like the apprentice boys, Philip and his type, even David slightly. He moved with manly grace, his gestures were firm and incisive. It was his personality that she found arrestingly feminine, his response to beauty, his intuitions about people, his lack of sexual aggression. He was stubborn like a woman. Men had always humored her and made allowances for her or tried to reason with her as if she were a child. Walter met her head on—man to man or woman to woman, often illogically, but always with understanding.

Suddenly she found herself dissolving in a purely feminine way before his masculinity. His body was superbly compelling, beautiful in a way a woman's body could be beautiful, but powerful. If, in taking her, he demanded submission, she was prepared to be his woman.

He hopped his way into trousers, trying to fill them with sand, and started to push himself into them.

She stopped him with a hand. "Don't fasten it in. I want to see it strutting out in front of you when you walk. You can hide it when we get near the house."

He carried the rest of his clothes and held his pants up, and she stroked him avidly, tantalizingly as they headed for home. He had no difficulty staying erect. They made a dash from dunes to garage, the lights of her apartment guiding them. She closed the door on them, and he dropped his clothes onto a chair and stepped out of his trousers. He scuffed sand off his feet as he went to her. She let her robe fall from her, and he folded her into his arms and took her mouth. When their breathing became difficult, she dropped her head back and looked up at him, her eyes flooded with improbable surrender. It had happened. He had conquered her at last.

"I'm glad we had a little time on the beach to get used to it. This is a pretty important moment for a girl. I feel as if we belong to each other."

Clara led Walter back to the bedroom. Her virginity proved to be less of a problem than he had been led to expect. Once the problem was disposed of, he took her gently, reveling in release after the strain of his long erection. He gave her an orgasm quite quickly, and he was fairly sure that she came again with him. He took all her body with his hands and mouth. He summoned up his varied experience and taught her things that made her laugh and shout obscenities and call his name. Her eyes were spellbound, and she moved in drugged obedience to the directions of his hands. Her body shuddered with repeated orgasms. They lay side by side for a brief respite and spoke at last.

"Nobody told me it was like this," she said. "Does everybody do the things we've done?"

"I guess so. It'd be pretty difficult to invent something new."

"I've always thought that gentlemen had cocks and stuck them into ladies and fucked them. It isn't like that at all. It's utter magic. Have you had dozens of girls?"

"No, only a few. Only one who wasn't worried about babies, like you. I don't understand that."

"It's quite simple. I have a gadget. I'll show you tomorrow if you want. It's not absolutely foolproof, but when you're inside me I'd be perfectly willing to have a three-headed monster to keep you there. Oh, darling. Has anybody ever told you what it's like? I know it's bigger than anybody else's. Girls have told me things. It's not at all like what you do to me."

"Tell me what I do to you."

"Oh, you're so magnificent. When you put your cock into me, you make me something that belongs to you. I couldn't stop you even if I wanted to. I cease to exist except to be filled by you. It's the bliss of…of giving everything, myself, everything, giving all of myself to you and your magnificent cock taking what belongs to it. I've always thought jealousy sounded utterly idiotic. I still do, but that doesn't mean I'm not going to be jealous. I couldn't stand you doing this with anybody else. Do you think you'll want to?"

"Well, I can't think of anybody offhand, but you never know." He chuckled.

"Just you try. I want to stay in bed with you for the rest of my life. Would you like that?"

"I'll say. We're going to live together. I'll move in here. We'll do everything together from now on." As he spoke, he heard Philip's voice in his ear. The moment in the car seemed an age ago. He must have been mad to think that sex with a boy could offer the limitless fulfillment of a girl like Clara. He wanted to get rid of the gadget and make children with her. The guilt and secrecy he had been living with for the last few days was replaced by a heady freedom to declare himself openly. He sat up on one elbow and leaned over her impetuously. "Hey, I've just thought of something. I'm not going back to college. How could I now? We'll go to New York together. How about getting married?" He let out a howl of laughter. So much for being damned. He was as normal as he had always known he was.

"You're beautiful and mad," Clara said with a dreaming voice of love but with the light of challenge immediately rekindled in her eyes. "We can't possibly get married—not for years and years. I've got to marry a man who is somebody, a man who can handle my family. You have no idea what it's like."

"Don't worry. I'm going to be somebody—maybe sooner than you think. What do our families matter, anyway? We'll be together."

"Ha, ha, ha," she intoned hollowly. "Dentist's son. You have a lot to learn about families. Let's just talk about being together."

"You mean, you'll live with me without being married?"

"Well, maybe not exactly live with you, but it could amount to the same thing. I'll certainly go to bed with you. Good heavens, yes. Do you really mean you're going to quit college? Can you? Wouldn't you have to make a living?"

"Sure, I'll find something in the theater. Nothing very interesting at first, but I'll manage. David will help me."

"Oh, David. I'm sure I know more important people than he does."

He was counting on that. Her being a Washburn made it much easier for him to think about leaving college. Her being a Washburn meant a great deal to him. He was a child of the Great Depression and dreamed of a world where money was never mentioned. One of the things about Harry that had held him after he had become adept at their sexual practices was the fact that Harry's family lived on a higher economic level than the Makins. It was a stunning relief from the parsimony of home. Harry introduced him to a world of country clubs and swimming pools and tennis courts. Harry had his own car and a lavish wardrobe. Harry took him to dinner at a restaurant and spent over $6 on the meal; Walter had been trained always to order the $1.50 special when he at out with his parents. Harry showered him with gifts of his own clothing and a gold wristwatch that he insisted was a spare he rarely used. Walter had smashed it, but even as he did so, he was aware of the pleasure of indulging in such wanton extravagance.

The affluence with which Harry had been surrounded confirmed Walter's already half-formulated determination to escape his background, just as Harry's casual sexual rebellion helped Walter to see his own rebellion in clearer perspective. There was nothing very wicked about choosing his own career and developing his own talents. Going into the theater might be unconventional, but it was hardly depraved. If Harry had been a revelation, what mightn't be expected of a Washburn?

"Tell me how we'll live together if we don't get married," Walter demanded, letting his eyes gloat on her and deciding that a naked Washburn was already very much in a naked Makin's power.

"It's no problem while we're here. The people around here who know my family aren't apt to hear any theater gossip. If you come to New York, you'll have to have some place to live. I'll be able to spend the night with you quite often."

"Yes, I see. Well, we'll find out. I think we'll probably have to get married. I'm not going to have any secrets about us, especially with your family. If they mean anything to you, they're going to know about me."

"Listen to him." She hooted with laughter. "I suppose I can't blame you for getting bossy after the way I've been carrying on with you. Anyway, my family doesn't mean a thing to me. I'm much more interested in dentists' sons who make good. That's what I'm waiting for."

"We'll do it together, Clarry." He felt her attack still, blunted but a force to be reckoned with. The challenge would always be there, but now he knew how to meet it and win. His hand wandered over her breasts and thighs, and he dropped his head and tasted her lips with his tongue.

She pulled back from him. "Do you suppose we'll have to go through all the business of being in love?" she asked. "It sounds so boring."

"Oh, Clarry, lots of people are in love. It doesn't sound big enough for me. We're made for each other. Don't you feel it? Everything fits together so perfectly that there's no way to say it. We had to find each other. That's the way it should be."

"You do say lovely things. You may be right, but we're both such babies. Parental consent and all that nonsense. You're even younger than I am. It's too dreadful. Why couldn't you be a tycoon going gray at the temples?"

"If I've got the biggest cock in the world and it keeps getting hard for you, I don't think you should ask for more."

"Now that I know what you look like all hard and enormous and waving about, perhaps I can do without the graying temples. You know what I'd like now? I'd like to take a bath with you. I want to feel new and shiny, if not virginal, and start all over again."

"Wonderful."

So much had happened to her that she craved a moment of removal to absorb it. He had taken her but had taken nothing *from* her; he had given himself in return. He had led them across frontiers of male and female so that she scarcely knew now what the difference was. He had conquered her by making her feel more greatly herself. She needed him as she might need a magnifying mirror to keep these new enlarged dimensions in focus. He seemed to fix the direction of her life. She had never expected it to be with a man. Men, maybe, never one man.

As the night progressed, Walter was beginning to see all around the momentous experiences. Clara was his. It was immense and incredible, but it was only a stone cast into a pool from which the ripples spread to infinity. Sexually she offered him an enthralled submission, an unrestrained participation that hitherto he had associated with his two male lovers. Beyond that, she was an arresting personality who commanded his complete attention. There could never be anything slack between them; she kept him on his toes, keyed to his highest pitch, striving. Now that he could think about the earlier events of the night, he knew that if she hadn't stopped him he might already be committed to a half-life of secret perversion. She had confirmed in him all that he thought he knew of himself. She had brought him to a place where he could launch himself into the world without limitations on himself. Deep within him was planted a gratitude that bound him to her. If he felt none of the sloppy sentimentality that he associated with being "in love," he assumed that they were stronger, more clear-headed, better balanced than ordinary mortals.

They didn't sleep. They bathed and performed new wonders with each other's bodies. They became absorbed in the smallest discoveries they made about each other. Clara found a mole on his neck.

"Why haven't I noticed that before? Dear mole." She kissed it. "I'm so glad I found it. Without it, you'd be perfect. That doesn't do for a man."

"I bet I'll find one on you somewhere."

"I doubt it, but I don't want you to stop looking."

They bathed again and had drinks and gave each other orgasms with their mouths. "How extraordinary," Clara commented. "I'm really beginning to feel I know you. This way is amazing. You pose rather a problem, but I loved it. I hope I did it nicely."

"Very."

The room turned gray. "You're not sleepy?" Walter asked.

"No. Good-bye, beautiful night. Hello, glorious day. I'd like to ride a horse or sail a boat, making love to you all the time, of course." She switched off the light and moved him up over her. "I must be old-fashioned. Every now and then I want you pumping away on top of me the way I thought ladies and gentlemen always did. Please. Once more, to make me feel like your wife and not some fancy girl you picked up. Then I'll fix us some breakfast."

Walter obliged. When they got out of bed, Clara put on a silk dressing gown. Walter started to wrap a towel around himself, but she pulled it away. "If I'm going to have a man around the house, I want to look at him. I'd look like an awful slut sitting around with nothing on, but you–is it all right to say 'hard-on'? You look so neat when you haven't got a hard-on, like the statues little girls weren't supposed to look at when we were taken to museums. I don't understand where it all goes."

They talked nonsense and laughed and ate an enormous breakfast and took turns in the bathroom. Walter was still naked when he emerged from it and found her, naked and immaculate, studying herself in front of a long mirror on the back of the closet door. She glanced at him over her shoulder with bold eyes. "You've made me feel so madly desirable. I wanted to see if I'd been transformed overnight."

"You're beautiful, Clarry," he said, going to her. "You've got the loveliest body I've ever seen. Those long legs, your beautiful breasts, everything." They stood side by side looking at each other in the mirror.

"We do make a handsome couple. You're not looking quite as neat as you did."

"I know. It's ridiculous. I haven't kept count, but it seems to me we've done pretty well for one night. Now look at me."

"How lovely." She reached for him and stroked him knowledgeably. "Oh, yes, we're going to have to do something about this. That's the point of being naked, so I can see when you want me. Come lie in our sinful sheets. I want to watch you getting big. That's something I haven't done. Try not to let it happen too quickly. I want to see how it works."

She stretched him out on his back and curled up at his hip and continued to stroke him as he lengthened and filled out and hardened. When she had completed her feat, she held him upright and stroked him rapidly until he reached down and pulled her up to him.

"It's miraculous," she said. "I want to watch it all, from the beginning right to the end."

"Sure," he said, "but right now I want you to be my wife before we face the day."

They walked together to the theater, and he felt the freedom burgeoning in him as he realized that there was no more need for a furtive entrance. They went in hand in hand, but being reminded of Philip caused a pang of what he regarded as unreasonable guilt at the thought of encountering him. He had nothing to feel guilty about. He had warned Philip that he liked girls. He had refused to be drawn into a declaration of love. He gave her hand a squeeze in front of the theater. "See you at lunch. I've got to go check in with David." He found him in his office.

"Well." David greeted him with a cheerful leer and tilt of his golden head. "It took you quite a time to calm the lady down."

"Yeah." Walter grinned at him. "I was furious with her for dragging me away, but it all worked out fine."

"So now you are a man. Congratulations."

"What about you?" If David gave a hint of something having happened with Philip, he could confront the boy with it and absolve himself of having encouraged false hopes, if that was what he had done.

"Me?" David looked blank.

Walter's grin became suggestive. "Didn't you have your swim with Philip?"

"Oh, that. I had the impression it was more your swim than mine. Philip seemed to think so too. He wouldn't go with me. Ah, well, he's a bit pale and poetic for my robust tastes. I prefer girls to boy-girls. I gathered he's sworn eternal fidelity to you."

Walter's grin vanished, and he felt a blush mounting to his cheeks. "What do you mean? He couldn't have said anything like that."

David's leer became gleeful. "Not exactly, but it was inferred. You know me. I love to draw scandalous conclusions. Much to my regret, I have a feeling your secret is safe with your lovelorn lad."

"Really, David. You're impossible." He dismissed the subject as airily as he could and hurried on. "If you want to know a real secret, I'm going to marry Clara."

David's eyes bulged. He looked suitably awed. "Well, well, well, do you mean it?"

"Sure. I don't know exactly how or when, but it's all agreed. What do you think of that?"

"My mind is boggling. You're tougher than I thought. Don't forget. There's a Washburn around every tree."

"I can manage them."

"Spoken like a true member of the master race. We Fiedlers are easily intimidated."

Walter laughed, exulting in his triumph and in making it public. "She's marvelous. You just have to stand up to her. I raised hell with her last night. She's going to apologize to you."

"Clara? Apologize? Love conquers all."

"I guess maybe it does. Hey, listen. I'm going to quit school. Do you think I can make a living in the theater?"

"Of course not. Nobody can." David sobered and studied him for an unusually thoughtful moment. "Have you definitely made up your mind?"

"I think so. Well, of course I have. How else could Clara and I—I've been meaning to ask your advice for some time."

"OK. I haven't told you this because I didn't want to influence you one way or the other. After all, getting a degree is important for most people, but maybe not for you. Steelman's been very impressed by your work. The theater's never operated so well. He's ready to give you a job at the school, part-time, sort of carrying on as my assistant. He mentioned $20 a week, I think. You could get by. If you win the hand of the fair Clara, you'll have him on his knees before you. We'll have to find you a cheap room somewhere. You're still welcome to share with me if you want."

Walter stared at him incredulously, unable to take it in, feeling that so much good fortune couldn't befall him in such a short time. "You're going to have to say it all over again. My God, David, why haven't you told me? Life is too good to believe."

"Enjoy it while it lasts. There's more, while we're at it. I've told you about all the groups I've worked with over the years. The Bronx is crawling with them—Elks, Hadassah, the Church of the Holy Lamb. I don't know what. They all want to put on what they call theatricals for fun and profit. I haven't time for them anymore, but they still ask me. I could turn them over to you. They'll drive you mad, but they're good training, and they pay. With the school and a bit of luck, you should average over $50 a week. I've decided to give you the last two shows to direct on your own, with your name in the program and everything. It'll give you something to talk about when you're trying to impress a church board. You can branch out from there." He rose and went to Walter and put a hand on his shoulder. "I hope you know what you're doing with Clara."

Walter flung his arms around him and hugged him and kissed him on the mouth. "I've wanted to do that for a long time. I love you, David." He was overflowing with love and gratitude.

David stood for a moment with his eyes closed. "Fine. Now I'm your slave for life." He opened his eyes, and his face sprang to life with playfulness and his sense of fun. "You don't have any idea what you do to people, do you?"

"How do you mean?"

"Never mind. Just stay the simple, unspoiled monster we know and love. There's a lot to be said against your getting married too soon. To tell the truth, I brought Philip out the other day because I thought you might want to broaden your experience. Versatility. It counts in this business. You never know who might hold the key to the big break. You've got to roll with the punches. Anyway, I don't understand why some guys make such a fuss about having their cocks sucked. It's very pleasant, and you can always close your eyes and think about somebody else if you don't like who's doing it. Those are my words of wisdom for today. We've got to get to work."

Walter was aware of Philip's hovering near him from time to time during the day. Their eyes met once, and he nodded and smiled. He took Clara into town for a quick dinner, bursting to share with her David's promises and assurances. The day had given her time to reassemble her imposing facade, and she seemed less impressed than he had hoped.

She had a job backstage that week, and he delivered her to the stage door. He was walking around to the front when he found Philip barring his way. He was immediately impassive and on guard.

Philip moved close to him. "What's the matter?" he demanded in a low voice, his enormous eyes beseeching.

"Nothing."

"Please. You've got to tell me, no matter how bad it is. You look at me as if you'd never seen me before."

"I'm sorry. Listen, Philip, we've got to pretend it never happened. I loved it, but I told you it probably couldn't make sense for me. For a few days I thought it might, but something important happened between me and Clara. I'd appreciate your keeping quiet about us."

"I see. Well, at least it's not with another guy."

Philip's eyes looked dangerously close to tears. Briefly, remembering the way his body felt in his arms, Walter wanted to hold him again, but he shut out the thought. He was finished with childish games. He allowed himself to touch the boy's arm lightly and went on his way. He felt no pull to turn back to him.

The past was tidily swept up and disposed of. He was keenly conscious of it during the evening as he took stock of the momentous past 24 hours. College was the past. He had work that would make it possible to defy his parents, who were the past too. He had found the love of his life and an introduction to circles beyond his wildest ambitions. The sense of being launched stayed with him. Going home with Clara after the show was a step into the future.

"Shall we go for a swim again?" she suggested when they reached the garage. "I'd like you to have me out of doors. It sounds wicked and dangerous." She put on her robe and gathered up towels, and they returned to the scene of their initiation.

They got very little sleep for the rest of the summer. Walter didn't move in with her. He kept most of his things at David's in case anybody turned up who shouldn't find out about their arrangement. He found that he had to conquer her nightly; it barely lasted through the following day. There was never a moment when he could take her for granted. It was the way he had expected it to be, and he thrived on it. It was a constant affirmation of his powers for he always ultimately triumphed over her. When he wielded his scepter, she obeyed.

She slowly unfolded the full extent of her impressive connections. Cousin George Wharton owned a Broadway theater. Uncle Perry ran some sort of organization that handed out grants to writers and esoteric theater groups, among others. Cousin Herbert Blair was an intimate of Roosevelt's and was currently one of the heads of the WPA Theatre project that was doing exciting work on the fringes of Broadway. To Walter, every name was a stepping-stone to his own success, but if he suggested that one or another might be useful, she dismissed them all grandly as "my tiresome family."

The seat of Washburn power was, in fact, Cleveland; but the family covered the country like a growth and spilled over into Europe. There were headlines that summer announcing ominous events across the sea, but they stirred little interest at the theater. Walter was more aware of them because Clara kept wondering what would happen to Cousin This or Aunt That if war actually came.

It did, but Walter was so absorbed in directing the last play of the season that he gave it little thought. Clara was playing a small part in it, one of several she had been given during the summer at Steelman's insistence. Walter was surprised at how uninteresting she was as an actress. She looked splendid, but her personality didn't come across. He was glad she had no ambitions in that direction. It made him uneasy for her to display any weakness.

The war was pushed further into the back of all their minds by the approaching move to New York. David had learned of a one-room apartment in his building that Walter could afford if David's estimate of his income proved accurate. He had been in correspondence with his mother, whose letters were filled with prophecies of doom but who had agreed to gather up his possessions from Rutgers and home, including some essential furniture, and send them to David's address.

The final performance was performed, and there was a party afterwards for all the theater's personnel, including the apprentices. Most of them were to disperse the next day. David had offered to drive Walter and Clara to the city the day after. The party was boisterous and mildly drunken, and Walter was the center of much admiring attention for his success with the last two shows. He stayed close to Clara but was aware of Philip's circling close to them during the evening. When he went out to have a pee under the trees, Philip stepped out of the shadows as he was headed back to the party. He stopped and let him approach. He and Clara were so firmly established as a couple in everybody's minds that he wasn't nervous at being seen with the boy.

"I gather I wouldn't have had to take that job at Rutgers," Philip said, his great eyes glowing in the dark.

"No, we'll all be in the city together. I'll be watching to see how you make out."

"I'll be OK. I know it probably doesn't make much difference to you, but I wanted to tell you I don't feel bad about anything. I'm still in love with you. You wanted me for a little while. I'm glad it happened. That's a lot better than nothing."

"Thanks for saying so. I didn't want to hurt you."

91

"You couldn't." Philip looked down. "Will you kiss me good-bye? It would mean a lot to me."

Walter glanced around them and decided it was dark enough. "Of course." He drew him closer and kissed his lips. He intended it as a chaste embrace, but suddenly their mouths were open to each other, their bodies writhed and clung, passionately locked. The feel of the body in his arms seemed a familiar need, deeply experienced. In seconds he recovered control. He broke away and glanced hastily around him. He saw nobody, but how could he be sure in the dark?

"Jesus," he muttered. "I'm sorry. "It…it couldn't work here. Do you understand? Maybe in the city—we'll keep in touch."

"It's a nice idea. Thanks. For everything. I'll never forget it."

"Aren't you coming back to the party?"

"Later, maybe. After that, I'd better wander around for a while."

"OK. See you." He gave his hand a squeeze and hurried away, badly shaken, eager to feel Clara more at the center of his life.

He spent a large part of the next day with David tidying up loose ends. There was a great bustle of departure back and forth between the theater and the dormitory. When he was helping David load files and office equipment into the station wagon, he heard somebody call a question about Philip and an answer being that he hadn't slept there the night before. He wondered, with a twinge of unwelcome jealousy. The vow of fidelity discarded?

The next morning Walter and David drove back to the garage to get Clara, who appeared transformed, wearing a smart suit, a wide-brimmed hat, a strand of pearls, and gloves. For a moment he had the impression that she was dressed up in her mother's clothes, but then he decided she looked exactly right, the way Clara Washburn would have to look in the city, expensive and distinguished. He must do something about his clothes as soon as he had some money. He owned only a few well-worn slacks and jackets and one all-purpose suit. They loaded her luggage into the station wagon and set off in high spirits.

Clara had begun to unbend with David. Walter was with the two people he cared for most in the world, and he felt as if his happiness would burst its seams. When it occurred to him that, but for Clara, he would probably be heading back for Rutgers now, he threw back his head and laughed with glee.

The three of them waited at David's apartment for Walter's things to be delivered and spent the rest of the afternoon helping him to get settled in his tiny new home. Eventually David fixed an hour for Walter to meet him at the Steelman School the next morning and left them. Clara immediately proposed inaugurating the new bed.

"Later I want you to come home with me and spend the night so I can feel full of you wherever I am." When they had undressed, she made him stand in front of her while her eyes dropped to his midriff. She put her hands on his shoulders and moved her breasts and belly against him. "Mmm. You feel good."

He had never expected a girl to be so outspokenly fascinated with his body; she was turning him into a confirmed exhibitionist. He loved hers; but it was the one thing about her he could take for granted and use for their mutual pleasure. He had found no part of it that displeased him. Even the musky smell between her legs, a smell that had made him cringe in the past, was light and clean and agreeable.

"My winter lover has a lovely cock, every bit as nice as my summer lover's." She looked up at him with laughter in her eyes. "There's something extravagant about it, the way I want everything to be. Oh, darling, do let's be extravagant. I don't mean money. Everything."

Later Clara took Walter to her family's Park Avenue apartment but made it clear that she was doing so only because there was no chance of his being seen.

The Washburn establishment wasn't what Walter had expected. It was a big duplex with rooms filled with handsome old furniture arranged for comfort rather than display, some of it rather shabby. There was nothing lavish or decorated about it. The pictures on the walls ran to dark portraits and romantic landscapes. It all looked as if it had been there a long time.

"Is this where you grew up?" he asked, standing in the big crowded living room, trying to learn what it could tell him about her and what

93

promises it held for him. He wouldn't mind the place becoming a sort of home for him in the city.

"Heavens, no. I've spent most of the last few years here. Before, it was Cleveland and London and Paris, even Switzerland." Clara made a little face. "I told you I had this place practically to myself."

"Cozy for you. How much time actually do you allow your parents to share it with you?"

"Oh, they're usually here about four or five months of the winter."

"That's quite a slice of the winter. Now listen, I don't insist on getting married as long as your gadget does it's job; but you're going to live with me. I'm not going to be your backstreet boy while you stay up at the castle. You can work it out any way you like so long as you keep that in mind."

She laughed abruptly; her eyes were at their most dangerous. "You look about 15 when you get all bossy and masterful. As it happens, I've already decided. I'm going to keep a complete change of clothes at your place. If–"

"Our place."

"All right, baby, our place. You'd be more convincing if you took your clothes off."

He realized with a shock that she meant it. "Honestly, Clarry," he said indignantly. "I'm not a strip artist. I'm talking about something important."

She approached him and hung on his arm and laughed up at him. "So am I." She straightened and adopted a more tractable manner. "If you let me finish, you'd see it's going to be all right. If I have to come home at dawn sometimes, that's my lookout. You see, we're not exactly cramped for space here. I come and go without anybody noticing. If I keep up the impression of living here, nobody'll be any the wiser."

"I don't see why it wouldn't be simpler to tell them about me and get married or at least tell them we're going to."

"I've told you. I'm not going to marry a nobody. You're going to have a brilliant career, but it takes time. We're young. If we let them get their hooks in us now, they'll turn you into a Washburn. I won't have it. I want to be Clara Makin."

"That's easy. All we have to do is go down to City Hall."

"At 19 and 20? Try it."

"That's true. I keep forgetting. I don't feel like 19. Are you sure all this hasn't something to do with my being a dentist's son?"

"Of course it has. It makes it all the easier for them to turn you into a Washburn."

"You must think I'm awfully impressionable. What's being a Washburn like?"

"You'll find out." Her laughter was grimly minatory. "It's not like me, I can assure you."

Walter persisted. "I can't quite see it in practical terms. What can they do to me?"

"They'd take you over. Don't you understand? They'd hate your being a dentist's son, and you're not even going to be a college graduate. But at least you're white and Christian, so they'd think there might be some hope for you. They'd offer you the world on a platter, and you wouldn't be able to resist. Why should you?"

"Why, indeed? I'd love somebody to offer me the world on a platter."

"Uhh." It was a growl of exasperation in her throat. "Look around you. Do you see anything here that interests or stimulates you? The Washburns are patrons of the arts? Ha. They're patrons of what they know and think is safe. You're supposed to rescue me from the castle. Get moving."

Walter threw back his head and laughed. "You're wonderful, Clarry. I think I'm beginning to understand you. The big difference between us is that I'd like to have a crack at the Washburns to see if I couldn't beat them at their own game."

"Fat chance. They're not at all going to fall in love with you just because I did."

He held her and kissed her until he could feel her wanting him. He stepped back and put his arm around her waist. "Come on. Show me the rest of the place."

She leaned back on his arm and looked at him teasingly. "I will if you show me the rest of you. I'd love to see you naked here where we all sit around primly in the evening."

He withdrew his arm hastily. "Don't be indecent, Clarry."

"I mean it. I'd love you to take me here on the floor in front of all of them. This room would never depress me again."

"You're mad. What if the maid found us?"

"She won't, but she'd run like a hare if she did. A naked man! I dare you. I dare you to take me."

Their eyes met. Clara's blazed with challenge and mocked Walter for his hesitation. She was making the point that she didn't belong here any more than he did. He shrugged off his jacket, keeping his eyes on hers. She kicked off shoes and laughed.

Once he had started to strip, he threw off his clothes happily, with no trace of self-consciousness. She was definitely turning him into an exhibitionist. He had never felt so naked in his life as in this heavily furnished citadel of Washburn power. He stood there waiting for her, and she surveyed him triumphantly as she disposed of her panties and her bra.

"Lovely. Lovely," she crowed. "Pan conquers Park Avenue. Now watch, everybody. Clara Washburn is going to be fucked by a beautiful dentist's son."

He took her on the floor as she wished. She had never responded with more passionate abandon. He wished that in doing so she didn't shut him out so firmly from the Washburn world.

He kept his appointment with David the next morning at the extensive premises of the Steelman School just off Sutton Place. David led him into his office distractedly and closed the door. He looked haggard and pale.

"I just had some ghastly news," he explained. "The police called from the Cove. Philip has hanged himself."

"Philip?"

"Philip. Philip Vreeland. They found him hanging in the middle of the stage."

"Philip? Has done what?"

"I know. I can't get it through my head either."

Walter sank into a chair. His mouth opened as if he were going to shout, but no sound came. He bowed his head and ground his fists into his eyes. His shoulders heaved once. He dropped his hands and sat staring at the floor, trying to block out memory, shutting his mind to a vision of angelic beauty.

"I'm sorry, Walter. Maybe I should have broken it to you some other way. I didn't know—"

Tears sprang into Walter's eyes, and he dashed them away with the back of his hand. He shook his head and looked up. David was sitting opposite him on the other side of his desk. There was a knot in Walter's throat. He tried to swallow it. "I don't believe it. Tell me."

"There's not much to tell. He'd apparently been living in the dorm since everybody left—well, at least for the last day or so. They found his things there, and a window had been forced. The condition of his— well, you know. They say he did it some time last night."

A tremor of fear flicked through Walter. "Why? Did he leave a…a note or anything?"

"Nothing's been found. It made the police suspicious at first, but they're convinced now it must be suicide. Who knows? I hardly knew him. I told you I had nothing to do with him. He always seemed a bit odd. God knows, he was as queer as they come. Unhappy in love, I suppose."

"No." The denial burst from Walter before he could stop it. He lowered his eyes and shook his head again. "I talked to him for a minute during the party. Outside. He thought he was in love with me. He stopped me outside, and he made a point about not being upset with the way things had turned out. No regrets. That sort of thing. He asked me to kiss him good-bye, and I did, you know…well, why not? I—" He raised his eyes and looked at David. "I was nice to him, David. I swear to God I was."

"I'm sure you were. Poor kid. It seems his face was marked as if he might've been hit. Not hard. The police say it could've been caused by almost anything, a fall or something. There was no sign of real violence. It's a straight case of suicide."

Briefly, in his relief at knowing that Philip hadn't involved him, all Walter could think of was his own nearly disastrous weakness. Never again. He had known nothing good could come of such temptations. He felt the slim boy's body in his arms and fought back tears again. "He didn't sleep at the dorm Saturday night," he said, trying to make it clear that he was no more than a helpless bystander. "I heard some of the kids talking about it. Maybe the tried to pick somebody up and got into trouble." He ran a knuckle under his eyes, wiping away the remains of tears. "God, David, this thing of being queer is horrible. If somebody took a swing at him, it could've been the last straw, his whole life going down the drain." Now that shock was passing, Walter felt only a vague sadness for waste and extinguished beauty. They were all too young for tragedy; Philip's act was an incongruity. His gratitude to Clara dug deeper into him. He had come so close… "We don't have to tell Clara about this, do we?" he asked.

"I don't see why we should, but it's the sort of thing that's apt to get around. Do you care?"

"It's not important. "It's just—well, she's had ideas about you. About me too, as a matter of fact. He was with us that night. It's nothing I can put my finger on. I just don't want to talk about it anymore with her. I'm not sure I'd be able to."

"Yes, well, I'm certainly going to try to keep it quiet. I've asked the police to be discreet. We have influence."

They looked at each other searchingly, confronting each other for the first time without the lift of gaiety. "We'd better talk about things," Walter said finally. "I mean really talk. No kidding around."

"I don't feel like kidding around."

"I don't know how queer you are, David. I'm not, but I understand things I've maybe pretended not to. I know something might've happened with us if you hadn't turned it into a big joke."

"And why do you suppose I did that? I don't believe in guys falling in love with each other. That's the way I was headed."

"Maybe me too. What about guys playing around with each other? Don't you think it's time to cut it out?"

"I've been wondering. I've never been faced with a suicide before. It makes you wonder about a lot of things, but it can't turn me completely straight. I'm double-gaited. If a girl wants me, fine, but not many make it simple. The boys are there. I like playing around with them. I never go near a guy who doesn't make it clear that he's ready and willing and is entering into it in the spirit of good clean fun. I've given myself till 30; then I'll find the right girl and get married. You know us Jewish boys. We're big on family. Meanwhile, I don't think I'm doing myself or anybody else any harm. God rest Philip, poor kid."

"You make it sound reasonable, but it scares me. Maybe I'm thinking about myself. I guess I'm afraid it might not be for laughs. What would've happened if I'd fallen in love with you?"

"We've probably fallen in and out of love with each other several times. Fortunately, we haven't done it at the same time. If I found myself in bed with you, I'd laugh my head off for the sheer madness of it, and nothing would happen." David's teeth flashed. He had talked himself back into reasonably good spirits.

A cloud still darkened Walter's. He went over the boy's last words to assure himself that they exonerated him of responsibility. The knot continued to form in his throat. He wanted to be with Clara, he wanted to feel her in his arms to obliterate the memory of a boy who had smiled like an angel in a dream. Clara left no room for dreams.

He was glad when David turned to business. He set up working hours for Walter and made wicked comments about the other personnel of the school. He had a list of groups that might be in the market for Walter's directorial talents. Walter was about to be launched, if not quite on the dazzling career that awaited him, at least on the mysterious process of making a living.

David proved as good as his word. Little more than a week had passed when he was engaged as director for one of the little theater groups. It was the first of many. He spent the winter traveling to the farthest corners of the city, casting his spell on clerks, secretaries, and insurance salesmen to produce what Clara referred to, disrespectfully, as his church sociables. As the long gray months stretched out before him, he couldn't always pretend to himself that life was as thrilling as he had dreamed it would be. He was pushing 20, and he was still dabbling in amateur theatricals. His faith in his destiny dimmed. How would people who counted find out what he had to offer? Walter agonized over whether he was following the right course, but David insisted that he was gaining more valuable experience than he could in some menial backstage job on Broadway, no matter how professional.

"You're a genius, old pal," David assured him during one of his spells of discouragement. "We all know that now. You're bound to get impatient. Let me be your trainer for another year or so; then you can give with the fireworks."

His insistence that Clara live with him proved academic. He was too busy. He couldn't expect her to wait for him in the little apartment till midnight or later. She frequently went to bed with him during the day when he had some spare time; on special occasions she spent the night. Her clothes were there as a symbol of a shared life. It had worked out as she had predicted. The Washburns remained a closed book. He couldn't make a very strong case for getting married, even though he wanted to if only because marrying Clara Washburn would be more exciting than anything else he was doing.

Light dawned just before Easter. David had been dropping small hints, but Walter assumed that they had been intended to keep his spirits up. As it turned out, David had been working up to a dramatic effect.

The summer theater was to be reorganized. David would devote his time to production and administration. Walter was offered the job as director at $60 a week. Not only a big professional break, but riches as well. Even with the offer singing in his ears, Walter was able to retain sufficient sangfroid to bargain. It wouldn't be a theater of his own, but he wanted to make it as nearly his as circumstances permitted.

"If I'm the director, I'll be totally in charge of casting. Right?" he demanded.

David tossed his gold head. "I told Steelman if we gave you an inch, you'd end up in China. Right. With my approval."

They looked at each other and laughed. "Fine," Walter agreed. "You're a pushover. I also want a say in the play we do."

David vibrated with delight. "What else? Do you want to hand-print the programs? You know the policy. You can give me a list of what you have in mind."

What was left of the winter flashed past in an exciting flurry of planning and casting and selecting plays. Clara enrolled as an apprentice again to satisfy her family that she had a good reason for returning to East Cove, but she was firm in her decision to do nothing but assist Walter. She and David had swapped houses, on the grounds that the Peabody cottage was more suitable for a pair. Memories briefly troubled Walter, but he knew that the ghost was a dim pale spirit, saddening but almost forgotten. Walter was too busy for ghosts.

Walter sat out on the edge of the lawn of the Peabody cottage and studied the envelope with a lingering trace of incredulity. It was addressed to him as Director, East Cove Summer Theatre. Accurate, but still unbelievable. He enjoyed so much looking at the address that he postponed opening the letter. Clara joined him with their predinner drinks and sat beside him.

"Who's it from?" she asked.

"I don't recognize the handwriting. It looks personal. I doubt if it's a million-dollar contract, probably one of my church-sociable crowd."

The second production of the season was already in rehearsal, but nobody had yet approached him about a job for the fall. If he were a genius, what were they all waiting for? He tore the letter open and looked at the bottom of the single sheet within it. It was signed Johnny Bainbridge. He remembered the name but couldn't put a face to it. Johnny had been a classmate at Rutgers, and they had seen a lot of each other in their freshman year. He had been passionate about politics and wanted to be a writer. He had talked about going to Spain to join the Lincoln Brigade. When Walter didn't see him around at the start of their sophomore year, he assumed he had gone and gave him no further thought.

The letter was terse. Johnny Bainbridge wanted to come see him. He didn't say why, only that "I have something you might be able to give me some advice about." It could be a disease. Something to do with the theater? He had grown accustomed in the last few months to his contemporaries coming to him for advice; word was spreading in the tiny confines of the theater district that he was on the way up and might be a valuable contact. He couldn't imagine how Johnny could have heard of him. He shrugged and handed the letter to Clara.

"Who is Johnny Bainbridge?" she asked when she had read it. She listened to Walter's sketchy memories of his former friend. "He wanted to be a writer? He must've written a play."

"I can't imagine Johnny doing anything so frivolous." They laughed and chatted about the proposed visit.

They were finally living together, openly and on a 24-hour basis. It felt more daring than Walter had realized it would, not at all the way it had been with Debby, who had been as obscure as he. There were Washburn connections all around them. The Peabodys must know. Walter was certain word would eventually reach Clara's parents. He lived in expectation of a fine old blowup. It wasn't quite the way he would have chosen to make his entrance into the family, but he supposed it would precipitate their marriage. Clara would be 21 in a matter of weeks; then the Washburns would be powerless to make any real trouble. After that, he had only to wait nine years until the terms of some relative's will would make his wife a rich woman. He expected to be so rich himself by then that it would make no difference.

He wrote to Johnny to explain that his only free time was after the performance, suggesting that he come out for the night. Having somebody stay with them would be like inviting a witness to their irregular situation. At this rate they would soon feel so married that they might forget the detail of a ceremony. Johnny replied, announcing his arrival for the following afternoon.

Walter met him at the station between rehearsal and performance. He hoped he would recognize him. He did, but only after a double take during which he tried to digest the fact that a classmate of his could look so old and worn. He was as slight as he remembered, all skin and bones, and his plain features looked ravaged. Four years were immediately erased as they shook hands and a relationship was re-created in which Johnny was the leader. Johnny cared about things, not nec-

103

essarily things that Walter cared about; but his concern carried conviction and aroused curiosity. It was a quality that had made him conspicuous among his callow aimless contemporaries. Walter had been drawn and was drawn again by what he felt as hard, unbending integrity. His own effusive welcome seemed false and theatrical, and he began to tone down his manner to suit his audience.

"Tell me all about yourself," Walter said when he had started up the car and they were on their way home. "How in the world did you manage to find me?"

"Professor Collins told me you were out here. I wasn't sure you'd remember me, but you were the only person I could think of who would know something about the theater."

"I'd never have guessed you were interested. Are you thinking of writing for the theater?"

"I might. What I want to talk to you about is a play I've translated from the French. It was a success in Paris just before the war started. It was written by a friend of mine. We hoped to get it done here, but I don't know how to go about it."

Walter was proud to be able to display considerable professional knowledge in discussing the problem. He asked about rights. He explained technicalities of production and told him what he could expect of various producers.

"Of course, the author's a Communist," Johnny pointed out. "So am I. We wouldn't be interested in anybody who's just looking for a commercial success."

Walter felt vistas opening that made his life seem humdrum. Johnny was a Communist. He had seen war. He was a strikingly dramatic figure. "Have you brought the play with you?" he asked eagerly.

"Yes. You don't sound as if you have much time, but if you could glance through it, you might be able to tell me if it has a chance. I'm completely out of touch with everything here. I just got back a month ago. It wasn't easy."

"I'll find time to read it. I don't have to stay till the end of the show tonight. I'll get Clara to read it too." He explained who Clara was and about their life together. He was ahead of Johnny there. He parked the car in the front of the cottage, delighted to produce this evidence of his unconventional past. Clara sometimes talked as if he hadn't existed before he met her.

They found her sitting outside on the edge of the lawn. Walter performed introductions and explained the purpose of Johnny's visit. Clara rose decisively, as tall as Johnny and more splendidly regal than ever besides his worn, gaunt figure.

"You two have drinks. You must have a lot to talk about. I'll start the play right now. I should be able to read most of it before we eat."

Johnny gave Clara the play, and he and Walter sat out on the lawn with their drinks. Walter pressed him to tell about his experiences and Johnny did so—Spain, wounds, hospitals, the suspense story of getting out of Europe. Clara appeared at the screen door in the gathering dusk, tears glittering in her eyes.

"It's tremendous," she said in a voice that throbbed uncharacteristically with emotion. She looked at Walter. "You've go to do it."

Walter laughed. "I'm glad that's settled. Let's go."

"I haven't finished the last act, but I'm sure it can't go wrong. It's beautiful" She came out and joined them. "This Michel Leclos. Who is he? What else has he done?"

"He's published quite a lot of poetry. He had another play that's interesting and very well-written, but he's not satisfied with it. He was working on a new one when I last saw him. God knows where he is now. He's probably gone underground."

"When you say you're a Communist, do you mean you have a party card?" Walter asked.

"How else can you be a Communist?" Johnny looked at him coolly.

"Is there anything communistic about the play?" Clara asked. "It didn't seem so to me. It's so moving."

"Michel's an artist. He doesn't believe in the Russian theory of social realism, but the implications are there."

"I'd rather you wouldn't talk any more about it till I've read it," Walter said.

105

"You're right," Clara agreed. "You're going to be mad about it."

They ate one of Clara's haphazard meals and talked some more about Johnny's European years. Clara treated him with more deference than Walter had known was in her. Later the three drove to the theater, and Walter and Clara performed several chores while Johnny watched the play from the rear of the theater. After an hour or so, they returned to the cottage, and Walter took the play up to the bedroom to read.

He was impressed from the opening pages. It wasn't a tract, as he had feared. It was dramatic, moving, original. It was sufficiently experimental in form to allow him great freedom as a director. He knew immediately that he could turn it into an exciting production, but he was uncertain of its chances for success. This didn't bother him, but he knew it would matter to any prospective producer. And if a producer were willing to take a chance on the play, would he also be willing to entrust it to an untested director? It was highly unlikely. He finished it and went down to join the others, afire with ambition to do it and unhappily aware that there was little hope he would be allowed to.

"It's good," he announced, putting the script on his desk as if it were already his. He turned to expectant faces. "You've done a hell of a job, Johnny. It reads beautifully. I'd give anything to do it. It's a director's dream. That's the trouble. I don't think a straight commercial producer would touch it. If you move on to the serious producers who're willing to gamble on something good, I'd be out."

"You've got to do it," Clara asserted. "It's the chance of a lifetime. Take an option on it and worry about a producer later."

Walter laughed. "Even if we pretend I have the money, it wouldn't be fair to Johnny. He wants his play done."

"He wants it done right," Clara insisted. "Nobody could do it like you could."

"I don't understand any of this," Johnny said. "The producer's the guy who has the money. Right?"

"Or gets it from somebody else."

"And you think a big producer might want to do it?"

"It's a possibility. You certainly ought to try them."

"No, he shouldn't," Clara protested. "Johnny doesn't want his play ruined."

"What's your idea?" Johnny asked her.

"I want Walter to take an option on it. He has to. That means he'll have the rights to it for—six months would be fair. We wouldn't let anybody do it unless they hire him to direct it."

"Why wouldn't it be better for me to find a producer with no strings attached?"

"It won't make any difference to you. We'd pay you, naturally."

"I haven't any money, Clarry." Walter pointed out.

"I have $500. That's as much as anybody else would pay."

"Five hundred dollars would come in very handy," Johnny said. "I'm broke."

"There you are. It might take months before you found somebody else who'd take it."

Walter watched them striking a bargain, exhilarated and incredulous. Living with an heiress might pay off, after all. Clara was marvelous. "Why didn't you tell me you had $500?" he said. "I might've retired."

"I wouldn't spend it for just anything."

"You know perfectly well what's going to happen, Clarry. If we find a producer, he'll refuse to hire somebody who's never done a show on Broadway."

"If producers go on saying that, I don't see how you ever expect to get started."

"I sometimes wonder myself. But that's not Johnny's problem. I'm not sure we have the right to tie him up for six months."

"Don't worry about me. I'm willing to wait. I need the money."

"You're sure? The amount is fair. Nobody would give you more. Do you understand about the option? It has nothing to do with your final contract. The money's yours. I'll talk to David about the right sort of paper to draw up."

"What's David got to do with it?" Clara demanded.

**107**

"Everything. You know that, Clarry. If we expect anything to come of this, we'll need his help." He paused and fixed her with his eyes. "Of course, there's another possibility. If you'd introduce me to a few key members of your family, we might think about producing it ourselves. It's the sort of play Uncle Perry's outfit might put up money for." He watched her expression closing him out and knew there was still a point beyond which she refused to play heiress.

"No," she said flatly. "This is what I've been waiting for. Afterward you can spit in their eyes. Besides, they wouldn't have anything to do with a play by a Communist."

"They wouldn't have to know." He turned to Johnny. "Is Michel what's-his-name a well-known Communist?"

"He hasn't held any positions in the party, if that's what you mean. Everybody in Paris knows who he is."

"I doubt if anybody here would bother to find out. What about it, Clarry? Was that a final no?"

"Yes, you've got to have a free hand. If they did anything to spoil it, I'd never forgive myself."

"OK. I'll talk it over with David. I doubt if we can do anything, but we can sure as hell try."

The next morning David was consulted about the option, and he gave them the address of Steelman's lawyer, who could draw up the necessary paper. Johnny sat with him during the morning rehearsal. Walter took him outside for a cigarette during a brief break.

"You're amazing," Johnny said in his flat, unadorned way. "You still look like a kid, but you turned into a man in there. You certainly give the impression you know what you're doing."

"I do, Johnny. It's the one thing I do know."

They smoked while Johnny watched with brooding eyes the decorative apprentices going about their chores. "It's hard to believe that kids can still look like that when the rest of the world is being torn to pieces. Who's that one?"

Walter laughed. "You're human, after all, Johnny. That's our own Hedy Lamarr. Her name is Sophie Hofritz, in case you want to have it

108

engraved on your heart. She's every bit as dumb as she is beautiful, which helps. Otherwise, I'm afraid we'd all have torn her clothes off the first week." The season had got under way with the usual flirtations and small scandals and gossip. Walter had so successfully switched off his antenna that he had no idea if any of the boys entertained amorous thoughts about him. Sophie was impossible to ignore. She was the embodiment of every man's fantasy girl. Her breasts were ripe fruit, as were her buttocks. She had pansy eyes, her nose tilted bewitchingly, her mouth was a rosebud. They watched as she paraded her sublime curves past them.

"I don't see how you concentrate with stuff like that around," Johnny said.

Walter chuckled. "You get used to it, more or less."

Walter drove him to the train at the midday break. They had settled all the details they could deal with for the time being. Johnny had two more copies of the play that he promised to send. They had settled the terms of the option, and instructions were to be sent to the lawyer, along with Clara's check. Nothing more could be done, except by correspondence, until the end of the summer season.

The play was a dazzling gift from Clara. In the first days that followed, it was something he thought about the last thing at night and filled him with excitement the minute he woke up. He gave it to David to read. David returned it one morning in the theater lobby.

"It's the best play I've ever read," he said. "Do you happen to have $25,000 on you? We could set fire to it right now and save you a lot of trouble."

"You don't think it has a chance?"

"Sure it does. It's antiwar. It's un-American. It will appeal to people of intelligence and taste. That ought to pretty nearly fill, oh, about one house."

"You don't know how I'll direct it. I'd make it a real sock in the eye. Do you think there's any hope we could produce it?"

"This is a free country. Anybody can become a producer. The trick is to find the money."

"Damn it. I know it's insane, but I think we might make a mark with this, even if it didn't run."

"Who is the 'we' you've turned into?"

"You and me, of course. We'd produce it together."

"Ah, well. I suppose we're not too old to dream. What does Clara think of the idea?"

"What should she think? It's the most natural thing in the world, isn't it?"

"I wonder. When she talks about all the fabulous things you're going to do, she makes it sound very much like a one-man show. Have you talked to her about raising money?"

"A bit. She won't let me contact her family, if that's what you're thinking."

"Somehow that's the first thought that comes to mind. So there you are. You're just a poor boy with a play. I'm afraid it's a lost cause."

"I know. Still, I wish you'd try to think of somebody who might be interested. I'm going to send the script to a couple of big people just to see what happens. If you have time, I wish you'd work a sort of rough budget. You know more about Broadway costs than I do. If by some wild chance something happens, I can count on–" Sophie Hofritz passed in front of the theater. They both watched her until she was out of sight.

"Where were we?" David asked. They looked at each other and laughed.

"I want to be sure I can count on you, that's all. I can't do anything without you."

"Oh, I always do everything you say. You know that. It's the one flaw in my character. I love working with you, but to be perfectly frank, Clara intimidates me. If you think you can keep her under control, I'm your boy."

"Thanks, old pal. I know the whole thing is ridiculous, but we've got to start somewhere. As long as we're here, actually running a theater, we're in a position of strength. People know who we are. They're coming out from New York to see us."

"That's because word is spreading that you're hot."

Walter beamed. "You mean that somebody might eventually offer me a job?"

"It could happen, maybe in the next ten or 15 years."

"Thank you for those kind words. You give me courage to go on."

They went about the day's business. After that, they had frequent brief conversations about the play, such as: "I've been thinking about Greg Boland for the lead." Greg Boland had been a junior member of the company the year before and had played a few good parts. "What do you think?"

"The last I heard," David said, "he was about to sign up with some movie company."

"Then why not try to get some money out of them? They back shows sometimes, don't they? He'd be more valuable to them if he made a splash on Broadway."

"Now you're talking. That's not a dumb idea. I'll look into it."

Or:

"I've got the set all worked out. I've made some sketches. It could be built for next to nothing."

"You've got to hire a union designer. It's one of the rules."

"Fine," Walter replied. "We can put Oscar's name on the program. He'd do what I tell him."

"I knew it. You'll be hand-printing the programs yet."

Walter sent the script to a few carefully selected producers, and a month passed with no replies, although he had used the theater letterhead, with his name on it as director, to give his cover letter some professional standing. He began to resent Clara for her gift. If she were so determined for him to do the play, why wouldn't she go all the way and help with the financing? Not knowing what she might accomplish was maddening. Lacking proof to the contrary, he was soon convinced that she had only to say a word for money to come pouring in.

With half the season gone, autumn loomed. He stood on the threshold of the big breakthrough; to retreat, to be forced to resume the church sociables would be a crushing defeat, perhaps a final surrender to the treadmill. Clara was responsible. She had trapped him somehow, robbed him of something. What was it? He didn't know. She was blocking the free flow of his energies, forcing him to make his own way but at the same time reserving the right to tell him how to do it. They had been together a full year, and she still refused to acknowledge his existence, except in the tiny community here. He was beginning to feel like the skeleton in the Washburn closet. It was insulting. At the same time he couldn't even look at Sophie without feeling guilty.

He began to look at Sophie a great deal. She had a studied come-hither look for every male, but he liked it when it was directed at him. It made his trousers feel pleasantly tight. She had only to speak for the sensation to pass. Her voice was a childish piping, the twittering of birds. Why should he care what she said or sounded like? She was a unique and wondrous physical creation, meant to be looked at and enjoyed. He felt sure that if it weren't for Clara, he would have enjoyed every inch of her by now.

He met her looks with looks of his own, amused but insinuating, and knew that she wasn't letting them pass unheeded. He encountered her one day in cramped quarters backstage. Instead of edging around each other, they moved in closer. The beautiful face lifted as if she expected to be kissed. Their eyes met with acquiescence. Walter shifted so that she could feel the tightness of his trousers. She swayed her hips lightly against it. He lifted a hand and moved it slowly over her breasts and instantly resolved to have her.

"Do you want to see them?" she piped. "Boys always do."

"I'm like most boys."

"Why haven't you ever asked me for a date? I don't live in the dorm, you know. Mummy and Daddy have a house here. I'd love you to come by some night after the show."

"And you could show me these?"

"You're such a cute boy, I might."

"It's a bit difficult to manage. We'll see. I'd better stop doing this, or I'll undress you right here." And undress himself. That was an aspect of it that excited him as much as the prospect of seeing her naked. The exhibitionism Clara had cultivated in him was a drive that demanded fresh outlet. He wanted to show himself off to her.

"Oh, you're wicked," she twittered. "I might be a little wicked too. I do like you."

His hand lingered another moment on the sublime flesh. "In that case, we'd better get together," he said. "I'll see what I can fix."

It was ridiculous to feel guilty. She was a beautiful girl, and she had practically offered herself to him. He and Clara were presumably going to get married, but it was her fault that they weren't married yet. He still had the right to have some fun. He liked girls. If you liked girls, it was in the plural, not just one. There was no reason to feel furtive or guilty about it, as if Sophie were a boy.

He found a moment alone with David later in the day. "Do you have any handy excuses for why I should spend an hour or so with you after the show some night?" he asked with a meaningful smile.

"This is so sudden. An hour or so with me? I take it the point of the excuse is that you'll be with someone else. Let's see. Mrs. Wilton is coming to the theater tomorrow night. She's commanded me to have a drink at her place after. We could say she'd commanded you too. Is that the sort of thing you have in mind?"

"It might do." Mrs. Wilton was an important patroness of the theater. Clara avoided her because Mrs. Wilton knew her family. "There's no reason on earth for Mrs. Wilton to tell anyone I wasn't there. Yes, that should work. Fine. Spread the word."

He kept an eye out for Sophie, and when he saw her he had a final struggle with his qualms before saying the word. He was taking risks with what he saw as the crucial fact of his life–his eventual marriage to Clara. But wasn't Clara taking risks by keeping him waiting indefinitely? He couldn't be expected to have only one girl for the rest of his life. He told Sophie he could come see her the following night.

She lifted her pansy eyes and looked at him with lovely mindless delight. "Oh, that will be nice."

"It'll be our secret, won't it?"

"Oh, yes. I'd like having a secret with you."

Clara accepted his story with no great show of interest. David had apparently already told her about Mrs. Wilton's invitation. The lie came out easily; nothing he did with Sophie could have anything to do with Clara. "I'll only be about an hour," he said. What difference did an hour make in a lifetime?

He drove away from the theater with David after the show the next night, and in a few minutes David dropped him near Sophie's house. Her parents were out. She made the point that she expected them to be late. She couldn't think of any reason why they shouldn't go up to her room. When he began to undress without preliminaries, she was a maiden in distress. But when he continued, she was out of her clothes before he was. She had nothing on but shoes and a dress. He was enthralled by the perfection of her beautifully rounded body. She squealed over his. She put up a pretty resistance to his entering her without safeguards; but he knew how to overcome resistance with his hands and mouth, and when he was ready, he drove easily into her while she explained that she had never allowed a boy to do it without wearing a rubber thing. She agreed that it was nicer this way. He exulted as her body shuddered with repeated orgasms. Before he was through, she had forgotten resistance and caution and was begging him to have his orgasm inside her. He remained until the last perilous second and tore himself from her in a paroxysm of slightly frustrated pleasure.

Being joined to her body, all open to his naked thrust, had revived his procreative fire. He had known it only with Debby, and it had made him briefly think he loved her although he had always suspected that she was so free with her body because she knew she couldn't have children for some reason. Walking back to the Peabody cottage, he realized that he had probably just had the most straightforwardly masculine experience of his life, since it had been devoid of any intellectual or emotional contact. He, as a male, had wanted a beautiful female—as simple as that. He had always known he wanted girls, but Clara's assumption that she was the girl of his life had made him suppress his response to others. If he didn't let himself desire a girl, how

**114**

could he be sure that he did? Living with Clara effectively protected him from the brand, but he was sure that boys were no longer a threat after the terrifying lesson of Philip, even though he had found it prudent to keep his distance from attractive boys whose tastes were suspect. After tonight, he felt he could be as friendly as he liked with any boy, no matter how attractive, without any risk to himself. Sophie made him think of other girls at the theater, girls who had caught his eye without his being aware of it, but he doubted if many of them could match her uncomplicated lust.

Clara was waiting for him. She didn't press him with questions about Mrs. Wilton. He assured himself that nothing had changed while being aware that something had. He felt recharged with vitality. He was in a better temper with her than he had been for the last couple of weeks. She hadn't hemmed him in. He could strip with all the girls at the theater, but he didn't want to slip from the tether, whose constraint had become essential to him. He had to show Clara that he still needed her. He needed to need her for life to evolve in the way he had chosen.

When he took her up to bed, he was very aware of the gadget cutting him off from complete access to her body. He wanted to be married and start having children. That would be the ultimate fulfillment. The excitement of knowing that he had come within seconds of filling Sophie's body with his life had made him feel like a god.

The next day, David showed him a letter from the film company that had signed Greg Boland. It was cautious but didn't flatly reject the idea of financing the play. Walter spent the rest of the day in a state of high euphoria. Clara had been right; they could beat the world together. The little interlude with Sophie was so unimportant that it might not have happened. Then he received a letter from Johnny the following day saying that he had heard Michel Leclos had been killed and was trying to find out whether his rights would be affected.

Walter was plunged into gloom. This was an omen; he would never do the play. Clara was somehow to blame. With the might of the Washburns behind them, it would have been only a small stumbling block.

International strings would have been pulled. Without them, or similar powerful backing, he might as well give up. The only success he could count on was in bed. His thoughts turned once more to Sophie.

He was glad when Clara decided to stay home that night to write the family lawyer about French inheritance laws. His plans were immediately made. He attended most performances because he learned a lot from audience reactions, but it wasn't required. When he reached the theater, he conferred with David and was lent the keys to the garage apartment. As soon as the performance started, he caught up with Sophie as she was leaving the theater and murmured brief instructions. He went back and watched the play for a few minutes so they wouldn't be seen leaving together.

He enjoyed taking his clothes off for her again. She was chattily enthusiastic about his body, and he was pleased to find it responding so vigorously to a girl who meant nothing to him beyond her physical perfection. The only moments he found genuinely exciting were when they were joined in a natural state and he could indulge in thoughts of filling her with child. Again, he remained within her until it was almost too late, while she begged him to go on to the end. They stayed for an hour and then returned to the theater, separately for the last 50 yards; and he watched the second half of the performance.

The following week Clara received voluminous replies from her lawyers and stayed at home for two nights in a row to attend to her correspondence. On each occasion Walter took advantage of David's and Sophie's hospitality. It was an escape, a momentary relaxation of his growing restlessness as time passed and hopes of a production faded. Maybe Clara was right. Maybe they shouldn't rush into marriage. David had always insisted it was a mistake. Sophie meant nothing, but at least she offered him a further exercise of his masculinity. On the second night, David came rushing up to him as he reentered the theater.

"Thank God, you're here," he said, keeping his voice down. "You may be in trouble. Clara's been here."

Walter's face froze. "Really? Why?"

"No particular reason, as far as I can tell. Checking up on you, maybe. I did what I could. I told her you'd been around all evening. I said I'd seen you here just a minute before she turned up."

"Thanks, old pal. When was she here?"

"She left about ten minutes ago. She wasn't here long. Less than half an hour."

"I see." His mind worked rapidly, setting up a line of defense. "As far as she knows, I could've come back right after she left and been gone only 20 minutes or so. Is that it?"

"That's the way we could make it look in court."

He curbed an impulse to follow her home immediately; it would only make him look guilty. He would go through the rest of the evening in an ordinary way and give himself plenty of time to prepare for an interrogation. "OK, so I went for a walk for 15 or 20 minutes," he told David. "She said nothing about wanting to see me for any particular reason? I mean, she didn't say she wanted me to come right home?"

"Not a word. She carried it off very well, but I don't think she liked not finding you."

"This is ridiculous. I'm barely 20, and I'm already behaving like an old married man." He gave David's back a pat and went in to watch the end of the play.

He walked home and found her waiting, tight-lipped. She was sitting in the living room and didn't move when he entered.

"I hear you came to the theater," he greeted her. "Anything up?"

"You'd know more about that than I."

"I mean, was there something you wanted to see me about?"

"Yes. I wanted to see why you're so anxious for me to stay home these days."

"I thought you had things to do that were more important than hanging around the theater."

"You too, apparently. What happened to your sacred duty to watch every performance?"

There was no doubt that this was to be a serious confrontation. He concentrated his guards to parry her attack; but in the back of his

117

mind, his observer's eye remained alert. This was a classic scene of drama, the wronged wife, the guilty husband; and he wanted to record it all and see how the drama was expressed in gesture and intonation. "I got bored tonight all of a sudden. I walked down to the beach and back. It seems we just missed. David says you left a couple of minutes before I came back."

"David! How convenient. That little Sophie wasn't there either."

He met her eye easily. There was an attacking edge in her voice, but he kept his light and disengaged. "What do you mean?"

"That's a simple English declarative sentence. Perhaps you'd prefer to make it a French farce. *Sophie n'était pas là non plus.*"

A nice touch; he noted it. "You took a head count of all the apprentices, and Sophie was the only one who wasn't there?"

"The only girl. Curious coincidence department."

"Not really. You know she doesn't live there. I guess she goes home when she hasn't anything to do."

"And you follow her? Or does dear David let you use his place for a quick fuck? Anything for his beloved Walter. He was flustered. I can tell you that. I almost went down there to find out but decided not to lower myself. I suppose I should expect this sort of thing. You're such a baby."

So much for the garage; he couldn't risk using it again. He must never forget that her mind was as agile as his. "So I'm supposed to have had a quick fuck with Sophie, as you so elegantly put it. What do I do now? Utter an impassioned denial?"

"I don't care what you do. You can have your Sophie, if you have such primitive tastes. What I can't stand is your thinking you can make a fool of me."

He sat down and wondered why he had moved at that particular moment. He looked as her and wished he could take her at her word. It would be so much simpler to tell her the unimportant truth and continue to have his plaything when convenient and without subterfuge. He smiled at her and put all his conscious charm into it. "Nobody can make a fool out of you, Clarry. Considering our sex life, do you honestly think I need anyone else?"

118

"I don't know. You and your goddamned cock. People fall for you. I understand that. I understand something else too. I don't care what you may think, girls are the same as men. If you start playing around, so will I. You're not the only attractive man in the world."

He sat forward, stung. She wouldn't dream of giving herself to another man. He hated himself for having made her say it. Once said, it was the sort of thing that could grow into a possibility. "You know perfectly well, Clarry, you're the only girl I want to spend the rest of my life with."

Her throat worked, but she was not so easily disarmed. She fixed him with challenging eyes. "Thanks, but we're not talking about the rest of your life. Were you with Sophie this evening?"

"Of course not," he said, his voice still convincing but his eyes meeting hers with greater difficulty.

"If you're lying, you'll be sorry. You know I can find out. I've already decided to ask Mrs. Wilton about last week."

He sprang up and turned his back on her, no longer able to face her. A show of anger was the only way out. "I won't have this, Clarry. What's it all about? Why have you got Sophie on the brain?"

"Because I've seen her put her hand on your cock, that's why."

He started to speak but couldn't. He forgot to feign anger, as all that he counted on most in life seemed to crumble from under him. How could he expect her to love him if she had seen what she said she'd seen? He knew how much infidelity hurt. It had almost driven him crazy, and he had sworn never to be so affected again. The awful fact was that she might have seen Sophie touch him. They had exchanged secret caresses around the theater, no more than playful; but when described in words they sounded squalid. He turned back to her without looking at her and dropped into his chair and put his head in his hands and kneaded his forehead. "All right. I didn't go to Mrs. Wilton's," he admitted, steeling himself for the end of his life with her and of all the ambitions he had centered on her.

"I see. You were with Sophie. You could count on David to cover for you." She made a contemptuous sound in the back of her throat. David

**119**

was the enemy. She didn't care about Sophie. David, encouraging and protecting all of Walter's weaknesses. She had never quite believed in the innocence of his interest in the pale poetic blond last year. The ambivalence of his lovemaking was a source of wonder and discovery, his infinite tenderness, his narcissistic pleasure in her infatuation with his body, his rare bursts of male aggressiveness. She had learned that it was an essential element to the magic she required in life and which he provided in such abundant measure. What could little Sophie, or any ordinary girl, understand of such things? It took a tough, masculine intelligence like hers to know them and cater to them. She knew the enemy. "Did he let you use his place?" she demanded.

"No. Certainly not. I...we... She doesn't have a gadget like yours. We haven't really been to bed together in the real sense of the word. She just–I don't want to talk about it."

"I'm fascinated." Her voice was cold and implacable. "Does she just suck your cock?"

"Don't be disgusting."

"If it's disgusting, why do you let it happen? I like to suck your cock. What's disgusting about that?"

"What we do has nothing to do with anybody else." He dropped his hands and looked at her again, amazed that she was still speaking to him. She filled him with a sudden poignant awareness of how inconceivable life would be without her. He wanted to beg her forgiveness, but to do so would cause dislocation between them, like a picture set crooked in its frame. He had conquered her and asserted his domination of her. To retreat from that position might end this misery, but it would also end his hold over her. He knew instinctively that she wanted him triumphant in all circumstances. "It's *not* the same for men as it is for girls." he declared. "If I get a hard-on–Sophie has the kind of looks that do that to men–if she sees it and does something about it, what am I supposed to do?"

"I don't know, and I don't much care. If you have a hard-on and she opens your pants and does whatever she does do, well, that's that. But even you wouldn't let it happen in front of the whole theater. You have to plan. You have to find a place to go. You have to invent stories about Mrs. Wilton. What about that?"

"I didn't invent anything. Mrs. Wilton did invite me for a drink that night. You can ask her if you want. I made an excuse at the last minute."

"And went sneaking off somewhere with Sophie."

"I didn't sneak. She asked me to come by her house. How could I expect anything to happen there, with her parents and everything? Before I had time to think, she'd taken me to her room and pulled her dress off. She has a beautiful body. That's all there is to it."

"And you didn't really go to bed with her?"

"No, you know how I hate those things men are supposed to have for every occasion."

"You simply romped around the room with no clothes on."

"You can put it that way if you like." Real anger was coming to his rescue. She was making him look ridiculous, but the heavens hadn't fallen. He had done something wrong, but if she could practically make a joke out of it, it couldn't be as wrong as he had thought. "You wouldn't be in a state if I looked at a picture of a beautiful naked girl. The museums are full of them."

She uttered her harsh abrupt laughter. "Really. You're such a child. The next thing I know you'll be masturbating." Her voice suddenly lashed him. "Pictures of naked girls can't touch you and suck your cock and make you come."

"All right, Clarry. It was stupid and wrong." The unexpected constriction of his throat made his voice a growl. She was hurt. He hadn't realized how much hurting her would hurt him. What he had done with Sophie had nothing to do with Clara, but her finding out had a great deal to do with her. Was that the point of fidelity? He wanted to erase the last week and find words to prove to her that it hadn't happened. "You've got to realize it wasn't a great plot the way you make it sound. Not many girls are so open about wanting boys, as she calls them. She's a nymphomaniac. She's so dumb that she hardly seemed real to me. She is beautiful. I can't help paying attention to beautiful people, but that has nothing to do with sex. Or not much. At least, it shouldn't. I know that. Nobody exists for me the way you do. That must be obvious to you."

"What's obvious is what we're talking about. If you think other girls wanting you will drive me mad with desire to keep you, you're wrong. If you're easy to get, I don't want you."

"I'm not. You know that."

"The thought of your letting that little whore play with your body makes me sick. I'm not sure I do want you." She stared at him with cold appraisal, but the thrust of her attack had softened.

He dared offer her a small conciliatory smile. "Don't say things like that, Clarry, even if you're angry. It's wrong. We need each other."

"Do we? Even if we need others too?"

He rose and dropped on a knee beside her and held her arms. "We haven't talked much about being faithful, and I didn't feel any of the things I feel with you, so I thought it didn't matter. I know now."

She studied him for another moment, and the belligerence died in her eyes. "If you looked at her like that, I'll kill you."

"I didn't. I couldn't. I love you. I looked at her the way I'd look at any beautiful object. That's what she is. Maybe you should stop wearing that thing." Thinking of taking her without it immediately aroused him. "I know it couldn't have happened if we were making children together. That's what it is with us—love making life. It makes playing around with bodies seem idiotic."

The one commonplace streak she had found in him was his attitude to marriage and family. She was determined to root it out. She threw off his hands and rose. "Children! I'm not going to have children for years. If that's what you need to keep you away from little teenage whores, find yourself a nice placid earth mother. We have a lot to do before we think about children. What if you have to go to war? Do you think I'm going to sit at home dandling a baby on my knee?"

He rose and looked at her proud back and laughed. She was splendid. The crisis was past, but she wasn't one to cover it over with healing tenderness. Her battle continued on all fronts.

"Come here, Clarry," he said.

"Children," she repeated indignantly, turning to him, "when you still can't get a job on Broadway. I'm beginning to think I'd better let you see Uncle Perry, after all."

He couldn't believe his ears. He stared at her. This was the greatest triumph of all. He must have given her a real scare if she were ready to sacrifice her precious principles. He sprang forward to her and took her hands, making no attempt to disguise the light of victory in his eyes. "And the others, Clarry?" he demanded.

"If you think you can go to them without its being an admission of defeat."

"Defeat? I'm not defeated. Don't you realize what I've accomplished in a year? This production we've been talking about—it'd be impossible for anyone else. Everybody needs help when they're launching something like this. We'll wait and see what Johnny finds out and if we can get a firm reply from the movie people, and then we'll talk about it. I don't want the Washburns unless I need them. Except one." He drew her to him and kissed her.

She permitted a meeting of lips and then pulled away.

"I'm not sure I'm ready to be pawed by you yet," she said. "It's fairly obvious, but you haven't actually told me if you were with her this evening."

He was briefly thrown off-balance before he realized that, in fact, he hadn't. There was no need for further confessions, since there was no way for her to know. "No, I told you. Last week."

She looked at him and burst into mocking laughter, mocking both of them. "I don't suppose it matters. You're the most attractive man I've met so far. I might as well enjoy you while I still want you."

He put an arm around her and headed for the stairs. He felt like a full-fledged grownup at last and wise beyond his years. It had been a small domestic drama, but it was his first, and he had survived it. He had somehow plucked triumph from what he had feared would be ruins. The production had moved an enormous step closer to reality. Once it was all set, he would insist on becoming a father. He was bursting with optimism and vitality.

Optimism proved to be justified. The first good news came from Johnny Bainbridge. He had heard from a friend of Michel Leclos to say that the latter had left his papers in order before he had dropped out of sight, including a document that secured Johnny's rights in his English translation in the event of Leclos's death, or disappearance. This confirmed the agreement Johnny already had. They could go ahead. Clara sent a copy of the play to her uncle Perry with a cautious cover letter in which Walter wasn't mentioned. She knew people who were interested in producing the play and wanted to know if it qualified for a grant.

Within a couple of days, David had another letter from the film company. When he called Walter into his office to show it to him, there was an explosion of joy. The company had offered to put up a third of the production costs against a majority interest in various rights.

When Walter's exuberance had subsided somewhat, David began to point out all the objections to the offer, but Walter wouldn't listen to him. "Fix it any way you like, sweetheart. Just get the money. As far as I'm concerned, we're in business."

"Sure. We just have another $18,000 or $20,000 to dig up."

"Chicken feed. Now that there's film interest, people will be showering us with money."

"Maybe if we shake them right. I'll make some calls and send out some letters. There's some people here who might be possibilities, the Kennicutts. Rich. I've heard they've invested in a couple of shows. You know them? You'd probably recognize them if you saw them. They come to the theater a lot."

Clara's eyes widened with triumph when he passed on the news. "What did I tell you? We don't need my dismal family."

David sidled into the row from which Walter was conducting rehearsals the next morning and eased himself down beside him. "I talked to those people I mentioned–the Kennicutts–last night," David whispered.

"Hold it," Walter called to the actors on the stage. "Take it again from Amy's entrance." He had found it difficult to concentrate on rehearsals yesterday. If David had more news, good or bad, he didn't see how he could go on working. He turned to his partner and saw that it wasn't bad.

"She just called," David continued in a whisper. "She wants to see you. I suspect she has the hots for you. Anyway, she wants to talk to you—alone. I arranged for you to go for a drink at noon. I'll take over here if you're not finished." He explained the way to the Kennicutt estate and left him in a state of agitation.

He had forgotten to ask David, but he assumed "she" was Mrs. Kennicutt. This was their first chance of raising money on a direct personal basis, and he was going to have to sell the idea on his own. He knew how reproachful he would be if David failed under similar circumstances. He had to succeed. He wondered if he were dressed appropriately. He had on his most casual working clothes, shirt and trousers and frayed espadrilles. He didn't know anything about the lady. He didn't even know how old she was. If she had the hots for him, as David put it, he could imagine an interview strewn with pitfalls.

He found the Kennicutt house without difficulty after driving along an extensive stone wall. He passed through a stone gateway and drove up through tree-shaded lawns to a massive ivy-clad stone structure. It was the most imposing mansion he had ever entered. He was admitted by a butler in a white jacket and conducted through a wide hall and across an enormous living room. He should have gone home to dress. David's remark about the hots was obviously a joke. He pictured a little old lady in black to match the house. He was ushered out onto a terrace.

"Mrs. Kennicutt is waiting for you out at the pool, sir," the butler said, indicating a low building with a tall yew hedge extending in front of it across a wide expanse of lawn. He rejected the little old lady as he made his way to it and was at a loss for a replacement. The building turned its back on him. He found a break in the thick hedge at its side and saw a pool stretching before him, completely enclosed by yew. He turned a corner and came out onto a sort of paved patio covered by an overhanging roof. He gathered the impression of a luxurious outdoor living room filled with white furniture and greenery before he focused his attention on the woman, wearing sunglasses and a beach robe, who strode to meet him. She removed the glasses as she approached, and he instantly recognized a regular patron of the theater. He had been impressed by her enormous chic. There were few signs of it now. The voluminous robe was closed demurely to her neck. Her brown hair hung straight, combed out but still damp from pool or shower. She wore no makeup, except perhaps a little lipstick.

She looked him straight in the eye and extended a hand. "I'm Fay Kennicutt. I know very well who you are. How nice of you to come."

He offered his hand, and she took possession of it with both of hers. They smiled at each other. Her eyes and the pressure of her hands told him immediately what she had in mind. He wouldn't have needed David's forewarning. "It's nice of you to ask me," he said agreeably while he tried to decide how to cope with her. She was athletic-looking, flat, and slightly angular. She was almost plain, but whatever it was that saved her from being so made her intriguing instead, even alluring at moments. Her most distinctive feature was a wide, slightly comic mouth. She was far from young–a bit past 30, he guessed–but there was a gleam of wicked self-aware humor in her eyes that he liked. Searching for an actress to cast in her part, he settled on Katharine Hepburn. She didn't look like Hepburn, but she was the same type. She even had a distinctively quirky voice.

"I've seen you so often at the theater that I feel we're old friends," she said. "You're doing brilliant work. The season's never been so good."

"Thanks. I've noticed you too. You were there last Thursday."

She looked impressed, as if he had made a move in her game that she had thought beyond his powers. "How clever of you to remember. It's very flattering, even a bit surprising. Rumor has it that you chaps at the theater aren't much interested in women."

She said it in a pally, man-to-man way, but Walter flushed with indignation. He wasn't going to be forced into anything just to allay her suspicions. "It would be pretty easy to disprove that rumor," he said, looking at her pointedly.

"Oh, I was sure there'd be exceptions. Let's have a drink." She moved in beside him, still holding his hand, and crooked their arms so she could hug his against her. It was an astonishing assumption of instant intimacy. She directed them across the patio toward a cabinet laden with bottles on the opposite side. "I was terribly excited when David suggested we might be partners. Of course, he's a super salesman. I gather you're the guiding light. I thought if I talked to you, I'd get a more complete picture. I have the feeling that anything you're interested in would be more than just a business proposition."

*Whatever that may mean,* he thought. She was very disarming. The way she handled him made it easy to feel that they were indeed old friends, even old lovers. He was wary of her assumptions. If he got launched on his pitch for the production and, as was inevitable, got carried away by his enthusiasm only to find that her interest hinged on the sexual question, he would find himself committed to a sort of barter that he would rather not face. He could imagine hating her for making it a condition and hating himself for giving in. If it were going to happen, he wanted it to happen quickly, on his own terms, so that he could retain the upper hand. Once sex was disposed of, one way or the other, they could talk seriously.

She unlinked their arms when they reached the cabinet and turned to him. He saw that crossing the patio had somehow caused the top of her robe to fall open, revealing the gentle curve of small naked breasts. He fixed his eyes on them so that she could have no doubt where he was looking. She toyed with the lapel of the robe with one hand without pulling it closed. She disengaged her other hand from his and lifted it to brush hair back from her forehead. This caused a new disposition of the folds of the robe so that one breast was almost completely exposed, and he caught a glimpse of the nipple.

She dropped her hand to his arm, and her fingers moved slightly against it as she subtly urged him closer. He was amazed that she could touch him in a way that made him feel that they were accustomed to holding each other. He knew she wanted to be taken in his arms, but she was obviously naked under the robe, and he wasn't sure he would like touching her naked body. It was much older than any he had known. If he was to perform for her adequately, it would have to happen on some surge of excitement, without preliminaries. He felt her eyes on his face, but he continued to gaze at her ill-concealed breasts. They were pretty, and her showing them gave him a pleasant proprietary feeling but didn't excite him.

"What do you drink?" she asked. Her voice had slipped down a tone or two and was charmingly husky. "I think I'll have a pink gin."

"Fine with me." He lifted his eyes and met hers with a detached smile. Her expression was amused and relaxed, but her fingers tensed on his arm.

"I hope you'll forgive the informality," she said, looking at the bottles as if she didn't know what to do with them. "I spend most of the day out here. I love the privacy. I've trained the servants not to come near unless I call. I can swim without anything on."

He seized on the cue. "Does that apply to old friends too?"

"You're one of the exceptions, are you?" she said playfully. "Feel free, darling. I have the impression you would anyway, with or without my permission."

He was to play the dominating male, he noted, she the helpless female. "Well, we have important things to discuss." He unbuttoned his shirt and pulled it off. "I want to put you in a receptive mood."

She removed her hand from his arm and placed it flat on his chest. Her eyes ran over his shoulders appreciatively. "Very handsome. You've already put me in a receptive mood. Are you really going to take everything off?"

He had found his line and was eager now to pursue it. "Sure. Don't you want me to?" He kicked off his espadrilles and put his hands on the top of his trousers.

"Oh, I want you to very much. It's never happened to me quite like this before. Not many men could carry if off with such aplomb."

"Did you want the big seduction scene?"

"It's usual, but this has a certain abrupt charm. You look so young. I thought I might intimidate you."

He chortled. "Not remotely," he said as he peeled off his trousers and shorts with the effect that stripping for a new audience seemed to have on him. He straightened and stood boldly naked before her, erect, hands on hips to make a masterful show of himself.

"Bully for you, darling. This is so sudden and so forth, but it's lovely for you to make it so startlingly clear what you want." Her eyes roamed over him with gratifying rapacity. She trailed a hand across his chest and down his abdomen and held his erection. "My word. What an exception. I've heard of men like you. It's high time I saw one. It's a bit alarming and utterly irresistible. Had you planned to put anything on it?"

"No."

"Good. We'll do it for real. It's a bit risky, but I expect we're not in a mood to worry about that." She dropped her robe, moving with confidence in the attraction of her thin, stylish body.

He took her on a wide chaise longue beside the pool. He had a sense of its being a milestone. He was using his body to achieve his goal. *Whoring* was a good enough word for it. He was fucking her for $10,000. Her pleasure appeared to be intense; every cry and moan he elicited from her slim, wiry body was money in the bank. It was agreeable to assert his authority over her, but his mind was full of assurances for Clara that this time it really didn't touch them. Doing it for real made him think of the "real way." If it weren't for Clara, he might be so sunk in vice by now that he wouldn't be able to get it up for any woman, let alone a woman who hadn't particularly attracted him. Taking her made her attractive or made him attractive to himself. She howled rapturously as he got a tight grip on her and bit her and drove himself into her. It was thrilling to know that his body could reduce such a chic and stylish lady to helpless animal paroxysms of lust. His orgasm was an ecstasy of self-satisfaction.

"Now," he said while he lay on her and remained big within her, "shall we talk about that play?"

"I love the way you do business." They laughed with amicable understanding. "Did I make it disgracefully obvious that I wanted you?"

129

"It was pretty clear. It's nice being wanted. I knew I was going to fuck you almost from the moment I arrived." He used the plain word to plainly mark the limits of his involvement.

"It's really quite extraordinary. We're total strangers, and now this. You've fucked me. I've wanted you to fuck me for weeks. It was getting to be quite an obsession. I must say, you've surpassed my wildest expectations."

"If we stay like this for a little while, I'll do it again."

"I'm deliciously aware of that possibility. You make your presence felt, darling, to put it mildly. Did you fuck me so that I'd put money in the play?"

"Of course. But I wanted to do it before we talked. This way, you've had me even if you turn the play down. You can't say I'm a complete whore." Her face being so close to his reduced it to the light in her eyes, which made communication seem so direct that duplicity was impossible. He opened her mouth with his tongue, and their lips scarcely touched as she put her tongue out to play with his. She moved her hands over his back and buttocks and down between his thigh and pulled him into her.

"I don't think you need worry about being turned down. I'll talk to my husband tomorrow night. You can count on me. I'll manage it. If you come see me day after tomorrow, I'll tell you about it." She laughed with a lilt of satisfaction. "I seem to be saying the right things. It feels awfully hard again."

"It's getting there. Don't you want to hear more about what you're putting your money in?"

"I have what I'm putting my money in. If you were a whore, I'd gladly pay for this. When I want a man, nothing else counts. I doesn't happen all that often, and now I'm afraid you've spoiled me for most men. Your body—I could tell you a lot about that, but you've probably heard it all before. I hate to state the obvious. Sublime. It's just a hunch, but I wouldn't be surprised if you're going to be the father of a child." Her breath caught, and the light in her eyes burned brighter. "I *have* said the right thing. Is it as exciting as all that, darling?"

"God, yes. I'm going to fuck you again just to make sure, whether you want one or not."

"Please do, darling. I'm afraid it can't be rape when the lady's so willing. I'd love to be raped by you. Yes, darling, you're definitely going to be a father. Do you fuck lots of girls?"

"As many as possible," he said so she wouldn't get any ideas about exclusive rights.

"Of course. No woman could hope to keep you all to herself. You make me feel more thoroughly fucked than I've ever imagined being. It's such fun doing business with you. My God, you're not a child. When you—if I'd know it was like this, I'd have had your pants off at the theater weeks ago. Rape me."

He performed satisfactorily a second time. It was a milestone, another turning point. He was attractive to women and could satisfy them, not just puppyish nymphomaniacs like Sophie, but smart, mature, rich women like Fay Kennicutt who could be useful to him. He could begin to take his sexual nature for granted. There was no further point in a Sophie, whom he had warned off in any case. He wanted to be faithful to Clara, but he could see now that professional considerations might dictate a little latitude. He supposed he could have teased Fay along until she had spoken to her husband, but he wanted an ardent advocate, not just a go-between.

Sipping the drink he had been offered almost an hour earlier, taking in the luxurious surroundings, feeling at ease and replete, he suddenly saw the future in the everyday terms of now, rather than as an unlikely triumphant pageant that would start someday, like a play, with the abrupt rise of a curtain. His career had already started, catching him unaware. Difficult though it was to take in, he had perhaps acquired his first backer. He smiled up at her and toasted her over the rim of his glass. She stood close to him once more in her robe, idly toying with his hair, which was wet from the swim they had had together. He sat on the end of a chaise longue wrapped in a towel.

"When you smile so devilishly, you open up vistas of unspeakable delight," she said with a ripple of irony. "You're enchanting. I'm quite absurdly infatuated with you, as if you were my first man. I should think it would be quite pleasant for you. I don't go in for heavy affairs—just jolly good sport when the occasion arises."

She massaged his neck and shoulders. She was handling him again with friendly familiarity, which assumed a great deal but was no longer bothersome to him. It was almost asexual, almost as if she were mothering him, or perhaps it was more sisterly. He arched his neck and uttered chortling laughter. "If you wanted me, I don't see why you waited for the fairly faint chance that I'd come to see you about backing a play."

"Oh, I knew it would happen sooner or later, and I don't mean that to sound as if I thought you were madly attracted to me or even knew of my existence. The nice thing for a woman, if she's not conspicuously deformed, is that most men will take her if she offers herself. You're all such pushovers. That's why no woman can expect a man to be faithful."

"Really?"

"You say that as if there's somebody you feel you should be faithful to. Clara Washburn? I've heard. She's superb and so young and much more attractive than me, but look what happened. You want me to help you, of course, but that couldn't make you feel sexy."

"If you knew about Clara, you didn't mean what you said about my not being interested in girls."

"Of course not. You? A fairy? Good heavens, no. That was just to start the ball rolling." She touched his neck with the tip of her index finger. "A mole." Her expression suddenly clouded, and she snatched her hand away. "How stupid. It's because I knew somebody who—I get these psychic flashes. I really must stop." She strode across the patio and came back with two lighted cigarettes, putting one between his lips. She put a finger on his neck again. "That mole if frightfully sexy."

"It's my conspicuous deformity." He took a puff of the cigarette. It happened again: They had touched; he had partaken of an essence and made another primary contact with the elusive reality outside him. He rose. "I've got to leave. We're not strangers anymore, are we?"

132

"I've never really felt like a stranger with you, darling. You're young enough to make me wish you were my son, and you're man enough, if you'll forgive the understatement, to make me wish you were the father of my son. For a woman, that's a devastating combination. I've always thought Oedipus was what it's all about."

He looked at her as she moved in close to him and hung on his arm. "You're an amazing lady. I think you'll like the play. Is there anything more I should tell you about our production plans so you can convince your husband? The main thing is that we know the play's a risk, but we don't intend to stop there. David and I want to produce in a big way. Anybody who starts out with us is apt to see some exciting developments—and make money too."

She smiled up at him and hugged his arm. "I've never known anybody who seemed so certain of being a success. I'll take bets on you any day, darling." She went with him to the cabinet, where he had discarded all his clothes. He dropped the towel, and she ran her hands over him while he put on his shirt. "Hurry up and get this out of my sight, darling, before I disgrace myself. It's feeling so thrillingly heavy." She giggled as he pulled on his shorts and trousers and she helped tuck him in.

She put her arm around his waist and matched his stride as she accompanied him to the edge of the paving. She released him and took a step back from him. "My word. It's thrilling to feel you move and know what you look like under those clothes. I'm as dazzled as a schoolgirl. Is Clara Washburn sensible about sharing you?"

"No."

"Very well. I'll keep it a deep, dark secret. Run along, darling. I'll expect you day after tomorrow."

He left her, barely restraining a whoop of joy as he crossed the lawn. He was bubbling with excitement when he reported a tentative success to Clara and David, although there was little of substance he could tell them to substantiate this claim, and he was obliged to invent some dialogue. His thoughts were so firmly fixed on money that he could even talk to Clara without being self-conscious about Fay Kennicutt's charm and friendliness, implying that she was too old to be considered physically attractive.

By evening he had worked himself into such a pitch of suspense that he wondered if he should try to see her again before the fateful talk with her husband. Was he counting too much on his sex appeal? Should he take her David's budget and show her how much they could make if the play were only a moderate success? David had told him that neither of the Kennicutts had wanted to read it on the grounds that they couldn't judge it without seeing it performed. The more he thought about this, the more alarming he found it. It didn't sound like Fay. Had he already served his purpose? He was too nervous to contemplate taking her again, so he decided to let it ride and struggled though the next day in alternating gloom and euphoria.

Clara and David, full of advice and encouragement, accompanied him to the car when the hour finally came for his appointment. The butler directed him to the pool once more. Fay strode to meet him as she had two days before, again in a robe, but a lighter one that revealed more of her trim figure. He had almost forgotten what she looked like.

"It went very well, darling," she announced immediately. "It seems he's been looking forward to taking another flyer on Broadway, as he calls it. He wants to see you and David on Sunday. You'll have to go over all the facts and figures, but he's definitely interested."

"Wonderful," Walter said, determined to act as if he took interest for granted. Until they had it all on paper, she still played a key role. He looked at her to reacquaint himself with the woman he had possessed. Except for the wide mouth, which amused him, her features were pleasing without being distinctive. Her skin looked slightly tight, as if it were on the verge of cracking with signs of age. Her hair was dry today and hung straight with a metallic sheen to slightly rolled ends. She looked smart and competent and healthy.

"I really must be more efficient about drinks this time," she said, linking their arms and leading him across the patio. She handled him with neither more nor less familiarity than she had from the moment they had met.

"Has he given you any idea how much he's thinking of putting up?" he asked, trying not to sound overeager.

"He talked about $5,000 at first. I tried to talk him up to ten, but I think it's finally up to you and David to swing the deal."

"If he makes it ten, our worries would be just about over. I'm counting on you to soften him up for the kill."

"I'll keep working on him, darling."

When they reached the bar cabinet, he noticed that her robe had remained closed. He was feeling more reticent physically than he had the other day. He had resolved to permit himself no further intimacies if her husband's reply had been negative. He wasn't even sure, now that there was no novelty in stripping for her, that he would be capable of the necessary response. He watched her as she dealt with bottles and glasses and ice and tried to get some feeling of her expectations.

She turned to him with a flash of her expansive smile and gave him a glass. "That's one of my specialties. We'll drink to the meeting on Sunday." She spread her hand out flat on his hipbone and eased closer to him and looked up at him. "I'm still dazzled. I love so your being here and being able to touch you that I don't really need anything else unless you do. If you're feeling faithful to your girl, I'll quite understand."

"To be perfectly truthful, I've wondered. You don't think it might turn into a heavy affair if we go on?"

"No heavier than it is now. We can't go on pretending that I have to see you to discuss the play, so we may not have another chance to be alone anyway. I'll give you some pointers on how to handle Freddy, and then I'll be out of it. You don't need my help anymore."

Her graceful withdrawal aroused him to pursuit. The fact that he had had her made it almost necessary that he should have her again. The thought of the pleasure stirred him further. He didn't have to worry about being impotent with her. Reassured on that score, he wanted to demonstrate it to her. "You're not going to get rid of me as easily as that," he said. He parted the folds of her robe and stroked her breasts. Her nipples were hard.

135

"I do believe you're going to fuck me again, darling. How lovely. I want you to, of course, but I want other things too. If all goes well on Sunday, I'd love for you and Clara and David to invite me to dinner. I want us all to be friends." She began to unbutton his shirt while he wondered what it would be like seeing her with Clara. He decided she could carry it off with style. She moved closer to him and kissed his chest. "Such a handsome young man. Can I keep on undressing you, darling?"

"Please do." Her hands on him consolidated his erection so that it was straining for release when she lifted it from its confinement. "My word. I haven't had a chance to see it like that since before we became so well acquainted. No wonder I'm dazzled." She let go of him so that he could finish getting out of his clothes and dropped her robe and went to a chaise longue to stretch out. She reached for him as he lowered himself over her and uttered a long moan of pleasure while he entered her. "So good, darling. I did want to feel that again. You can't imagine how good it feels. Now we can get on with our business of making a child."

"Is that a joke, or do you mean it? Do you really think I might make you pregnant?"

"Why not? We're certainly doing things that frequently have that result. I should think the way you're built would make it even more likely. There's very little of me you haven't fucked. Oh, darling, it gets so hard when we talk about children. It feels as if it's determined to give me one."

"And you want it?"

"Why not? I have the usual two—one is six, and the other eight. They'll be just about grown when this one is ten. That should keep me young longer."

"How come you haven't had any more with your husband?"

"We decided not to. I always wear my diaphragm when he does it. I'll tell him I forgot it one night."

"Well, then, let's do it for real." As he began his rhythmic thrust into her, he felt the thrill of what was surely one of life's big moments. He

136

was fucking a woman to give her a child. He had come into full possession of his manhood. He had been so preoccupied with business the other day that he had scarcely known what he was doing.

When they were done, he lingered briefly for her to give him her pointers about her husband and fix the date for 11:30 Sunday morning. He had stayed just long enough for it to seem reasonable for her not to have disposed of the business by telephone, but not so long that Clara would be bound to leap to conclusions.

He and David dressed for the Sunday meeting in jackets and white flannels. The Kennicutts received them in the great living room; Fay dressed with the extraordinary chic Walter remembered. She was a conquest to be proud of. Her husband turned out to be a heavy, phlegmatic man. David called him Fred and seemed at ease with him and immediately took charge. Following Fay's advice, he rattled off figures with authority. He had armed himself with businesslike-looking lists of costs, which he thrust at Fred, who looked at them and nodded and grunted. They had agreed that Walter would describe the sort of production he had in mind, and he did so vividly and dramatically, looking into Fay's dazzled eyes through most of it. Fred seemed upset that there were to be no stars, and Walter elaborated on his concept of an ensemble acting company, with references to the great European companies. It sounded impressive.

"You fellows seem to know what you're doing," Fred agreed. "It's a gamble, but I'm prepared to put up $5,000."

Walter found the definitive words so exhilarating that he was ready to throw his arms around Fred and let it go at that; but, still following Fay's advice, David leaped in with persuasive arguments for putting up more. The Kennicutts should have an interest at least equal to the movie company's, and so forth. Fay offered to put in some money of her own. Fred appeared not to like this and with a grunt upped his offer to $7,000. He was clearly determined to stick there. David grandly offered to give him a week to think it over before he negotiated the remaining backers' shares. The butler appeared. Fay ordered champagne. David continued to talk business with Fred. Walter and Fay

137

rose and wandered around the room, sipping wine, while Fay pretended to show him her possessions.

"You're absolutely stunning all dressed up," she said, standing in front of a handsome desk. "The more you have on, the more I want to take it all off. Are you pleased?"

"I'll say. Thanks. You're pretty stunning yourself."

"I know how to wear clothes." She laughed. "That may well come as a surprise to you, darling. Am I going to get that dinner invitation?"

"Absolutely, as soon as I see how we can fit it in."

"I know you're frightfully busy, and Clara and all. You probably won't be able to come see me again; but if you do have the opportunity and feel like it, you know I'll be in a receptive mood."

"It'll be difficult. We'll see."

"Maybe it'll be easier when we're back in the city. By then I'll probably be all nice and pregnant for you."

"Fabulous."

"Is it getting hard?"

"Yes."

"How lovely. I know what it looks like. Fancy my knowing that! It's an incredible new fact of life." She linked their arms and leaned against him, and they wandered back to the other two.

He and David were subdued as they drove away. "It's getting so close. I don't think I could stand it if anything went wrong now," Walter said.

"Yeah. It's so different from what I imagined. I thought someday I'd be sitting in an office peddling some cheap little comedy to a bunch of guys smoking cigars and one of the guys would say, 'OK, I'm in for 15 grand,' or whatever guys like that say; and I'd put on my cheap little comedy and make a million dollars. Now look at us—sipping champagne and discussing art and about to lose our shirts. You've got class, honey. I would never've dared approach the Kennicutts if you weren't there to front for us. That may've seemed easy to you, but I happen to know they're tough. You must've played your cards right. Don't stop. We may need more from them, and I've a feeling the lady will get it for us."

"I wonder. I told her ten was what we were aiming at."

"Didn't you notice what happened when he started to loosen up? She offered to put up her own money, and he didn't like it. She must've known he wouldn't like it. You can't blame her for wanting to keep her hand on the tiller, if I can put it that way. She knows now you may hesitate to withdraw it."

Walter chuckled. "Really, David. You're impossible. Do you have to be a whore to get along in this business?"

"It helps, honey, it helps. I told you I'd turn you loose when the time came. Well, it's coming. Just don't forget my little lessons."

They drove to the Peabody cottage, where Clara was to give them a quick lunch before the afternoon rehearsal. She appeared at the door before David had stopped the car.

"Is this the famous producer, Walter Makin?" she asked as he approached. She stood tall and serene, her auburn hair burnished by the sun, a serene highness. There was neither mockery nor challenge in her eyes; they glowed with pride and confidence.

"We've taken another step in the right direction," he announced with quiet satisfaction. The place under her chin that made him feel protective was looking particularly vulnerable. He touched it and kissed her mouth lightly.

Her lips worked for an instant as if she were about to speak, and then she burst into abrupt laughter. All her face became animated. "Words almost failed me. Well, that's that. We're definitely going to do it." She put a hand on David's shoulder and herded them into the house. "Lunch is ready. Come on. I even have a bottle of wine. I knew this was going to be a celebration."

"We're going to be winos before we even start casting," David said.

Clara led them through the house and out the back. She had instituted picnics on the lawn. It gave a festive air to her plain fare. They sat on a blanket, and she passed out sandwiches and poured wine and asked questions about the meeting.

"Yes, it's really going to happen," she asserted when they had told her all about it. "The movie money has never seemed quite real to me.

Having people in it makes all the difference. Does she intend to go on summoning you for little discussions of your plans?"

"Of course not," Walter assured her. "As a matter of fact, she told me last time she'd be out of it from then on. I have the impression it's definitely his show. Wouldn't you say so, David?"

David ducked his head and bulged his eyes comically before turning a straight face to Clara. "Absolutely. When she tried to put in her two bits, he slapped her down."

"She wants to have dinner with all three of us. I think she's lonely."

"Poor thing." Clara shrugged. She didn't regard Fay Kennicutt as a threat. She was practically middle-aged, a mother, and there had never been any gossip about her. Still, there could always be a first time. "It's pretty fishy her insisting on seeing you alone—twice."

"Oh, Clarry—" Walter began.

"I know exactly why," David cut in smoothly. "They think I'm a smart operator. She was supposed to sound Walter out to see if there was anything phony about the setup. I told Walter. It may have looked easy, but they don't part with their money for anything that isn't strictly respectable. Walter did it for us—and possibly the rumor of a Washburn in the background."

"Amateurs. They're climbers, rather." Clara shrugged again. "Dinner with the three of us. Typical."

"Time!" Walter exclaimed, blessing David for taking care of the subject so neatly. "We hardly have time to eat ourselves, let alone have people for dinner. If we get any more involved in this production, the season here is going to fall apart."

"We're really hardly more than halfway making it," Clara pointed out. "I know the rest of the money will turn up somewhere, but you're right, dearest. Time is going to be a problem. We can't do any more from out here. What about it, David? Do you expect to hear from any of the people you've contacted?"

"If I don't in another few days, it won't look too promising."

"Well, there's always my family, if Walter really wants to tackle them, but none of them will be around until after Labor Day. Before we get in any deeper, don't you think we should talk more about some sort of business deal between us?"

"We needn't waste time on that," Walter said. "We'll just split everything fifty-fifty–if there's anything to split."

Clara started to speak, but David was ahead of her. "I still haven't taught you much about business, have I, old pal? For one thing, you'll have your salary and percentage as director. It's in the budget, if you'd bother to look. As for the production setup, I've been thinking. You found the play. Clara's put up the option money. What if we form a company with three equal partners? We'll split the producer's fee and percentage three ways."

"You're nuts," Walter said, dismissing the suggestion without even looking at Clara. "You're the producer. We probably shouldn't have any share at all."

"Fine," David said with a toss of his golden head. "Clara and I will be partners. If you're very nice, we might give you a job."

Clara crowed with laughter and took David's hand. "You're being awfully nice, darling."

"Try to keep the note of incredulity out of your voice. I'm making complete sense. I suspect you'll handle the business just as well as I once you learn the ropes. Pool old Walter's hopeless; but we want him to have control, so we'll have to pretend he's worthy of being our partner. I don't want to quit the school until we see things go, so I won't even be working full-time. Later, if we go on and you two get married, we may decide I should have a bigger share."

"I certainly wouldn't want my name connected with it," Clara said. "I think it should be 'Walter Makin presents' and then a line about "A Walter Makin–David Fiedler Production.' How about that?"

"I like it. It's better than Metro-Goldwyn-Mayer."

"Listen to us," Walter said jovially. "We sound like a bunch of big businessmen."

"That's what I'm going to be, sweetheart. Don't be fooled by my pretty face." Gold flashed in the sun as David lifted his hand to smooth his hair. "Now listen, partners. We've got four more weeks here. At least I have. I have to stay till we shut down. You two could leave right after the last show opens–three weeks from tomorrow, or the next day. Money comes first, but we have a lot of other things to do–casting, getting a set built, finding a theater–that's going to be a big problem, but the movie people will help there–and that's only the beginning. If we pretend it's just one more church sociable, we might not lose our heads. The movie people want us to open in November at the latest so they can count on getting Greg out to Hollywood next spring. If we don't get the money in the next month or six weeks, we're going to be in trouble. We can't sign actors until we post the bond with Equity."

"I'm not worried about that. Walter and I have made lists that we could cast the play five times over."

"OK. I'll call Steelman's lawyer and get him to turn us into a company. We'll get everything legal and official and open a bank account so we can get our hands on what we've collected so far. It's enough to give us a nice vacation in South America if anything goes wrong. Cheers."

They drained the remains of the wine and sat for a moment in deep thought. Clara felt vaguely cheated. She had wondered how she could propose some arrangement similar to David's without making it sound as if she were trying to get rid of him. Now that he had made the suggestion himself, she suspected that he had scored on her in some way. It was too good to be true. Once she had a firmer grasp of the details, she would be in control. "I might go up before either of you," she announced. "I could go tomorrow. I'm not needed here."

"Oh, yes, you are," Walter said as they all picked themselves up off the blanket.

"Thank you, dearest." She looked at him with a secret smile. "You're looking quite adorable in your rumpled finery and all covered with crumbs." Walter and Clara laughed together as she brushed them off.

"You two may have forgotten, but we're due at the theater," David reminded them from outside the closed circle they instantly created.

The next major event was a letter from Uncle Perry. He was deeply interested in the play and wanted to discuss it with Clara's friends.

Clara warned against overoptimism; Uncle Perry's foundation doled out grants in very small sums. There was no question of both David's and Walter's being absent from the theater at the same time. Clara was against David's going alone.

"Frankly, Uncle Perry won't like dealing with a Jew," she told them.

"In that case, I won't be dealing with Uncle Perry," Walter said.

"What've I been telling you? Did I ever suggest it was fun dealing with my family?"

Whoring apparently assumed various guises. It was settled that Clara and he would drive up into the city one evening after rehearsals so that he could make a 10 o'clock appointment the next morning and return in time for afternoon rehearsals. He almost forgot the dinner he had promised Fay Kennicutt. He called her and arranged it for the day after the New York trip.

"Just you, or your husband too?" he asked.

"Oh, no. I thought you knew. Freddy's rarely here during the week." She said it in a way that made it clear she would like the company. Walter felt guilty and defensive; there was no time for Fay.

His first exposure to Clara's family connections made him eager for more. The meeting took place in surroundings he was beginning to take for granted—rich, imposing, confidently old-fashioned. Uncle Perry's committee had approved a grant of $1,000 for the production of *A Light in the Forest*. Clara's uncle was so enthusiastic about the play that he hoped it wasn't too late to invest in it himself. He was a tall, thin authoritative man, and Walter graciously admitted that his offer of $5,000 would be very helpful while he successfully suppressed a fit of the giggles. He supposed he must learn to take himself more seriously.

"I suppose you're even more impressive than I realize," Clara commented when they were on their way back to East Cove. "I don't mind Perry so much. He's connected with the foundation, and he's not a complete philistine—only about three quarters. We're so nearly there now. If only David would come up with a few thousand dollars. I don't want this to turn into a Washburn circus. It's all yours. You don't need their kind of help."

"Well, Perry isn't helping in that sense. He was stunned by the play."

"Yes, but it won't be like that with the others. I'll have to introduce you, and it'll immediately become a family affair."

"I guess I understand what you mean. Anyway, David still thinks there's a chance the Kennicutts will put up more."

The dinner with Fay went so well that he hadn't a moment's embarrassment seeing her with Clara. They seemed to like each other. Fay was delighted with the new recruit to the backer's list. It was an easy, friendly occasion. David stopped him in front of the theater the next morning.

"I think we've reached a moment of decision," he said. "If we had $4,000 more, we could get rolling. Without it, we can't really do anything. Do we wait another couple of weeks until people are back in town and we run the risk of getting squeezed for time, or do we strike while the iron is hot?"

"I don't get it. Is it up to me?"

David rolled his eyes. "I think it is. Once more into the breach, old pal, if you'll forgive a classic reference. I've just talked to Fay. She asked me last night to call. She says if she has another talk with you, she thinks you can help her find the right thing to say to Fred so he'll fork up the rest of the dough."

"Oh, God, I can't. You know what Clara would think, especially after last night. She'd want to know why Fay can't talk to all of us."

"It's a thought that might occur to anybody. We could say I'm going with you, and I could drop you and wait around somewhere while you say your magic words and pick you up later. But I have a better idea. I have things I'd like Clara to take care of in the city. I'm going to ask her to go up tomorrow or the next day. She'll need two or three days to get everything done. You see what I mean? It's entirely up to you."

"Oh, damn." Walter sighed. He thought of Clara's determination to keep the Washburns out of it. If, as she said, the production was all his, he supposed he should be ready to dedicate himself to it totally, body as well as soul. He and David looked at each with complicity. "It's a dirty trick, but if you're sure it'll work, I guess we better do it."

"All you have to do is more of whatever you've done already. If you will go around making us all fall in love with you, you have to take the consequences."

Clara took the train the next day, very self-important with the errands David had entrusted to her. When she was gone, Walter called Fay and proposed coming to see her after the show that evening. He explained that Clara would be away for a day or two.

"Will you spend the night with me, darling?" she asked.

"Is that possible?"

"Oh, yes, darling. How thrilling. Don't ring the bell, or anything. I'll be watching for you. You can't make it sooner?"

"No, I have to watch the show." He had learned his lesson. He would scrupulously follow routine in case Clara had spies. Nobody would know where he went after the show. Fortunately, the Peabodys hadn't put a telephone into the cottage, so there was no way of Clara's trying to reach him. He resented Fay for forcing him to take all these details into consideration until he realized that she wasn't forcing anything. It was David's idea, and he was carrying it out.

The massive nail-studded door of the Kennicutt mansion opened magically as he approached it. Fay stood beside it to let him in and closed it behind him and took possession of him in her usual familiar way, slipping her arm under his and drawing him close. She was at her most chic, made-up, carefully coiffed, wearing a dressing gown of such style and so beautifully cut that it almost could have passed as an evening dress except that she was clearly naked under it.

"What a marvelous idea, darling," she said, keeping her voice low. "I thought you might pop in at noon like before. Let's go up. There's nobody about, but still…" She directed him toward baronial stairs and started up. "I suppose David gave you the impression that I was making a condition of seeing you before I'd talk to Freddy again. I put it like that in case you needed an excuse to come. I have every intention of speaking to Freddy anyway. When he hears Perry Washburn is in with us, there'll be no problem. Wasn't I good the other night?"

"You were perfect."

**145**

"I wanted you to see what a well-behaved mistress I can be. That's important if I'm to be the mother of your child."

"Now that you mention it, I suppose it is. When will you know?"

"In a few weeks, I should think. I'm awfully vague about exactly how those things work." They mounted to a wide hall and followed it to an open door at the end and entered a big room that was handsomely furnished as bedroom and living room. There was nothing conspicuously feminine about it except for a very feminine dressing table. Masses of flowers were everywhere. She closed the door, locked it, and turned to him.

"There, darling," she said, resuming her normal voice. She put her hands under his jacket on his chest and moved her fingers against his shirt. "I feel very sinful having you here, waiting to get into a real bed with you, waking up with a beautiful naked man beside me. I hope we make it as sinful as possible. Here, let me have your jacket." He slipped it off, and she took it to a closet and hung it up. "Sit here," she said, leading him to a big armchair. "Do you want a drink? Have a glass of champagne with me." She went to a desk where there was a tray of glasses and bottles. An open bottle of wine was in an ice bucket.

He was tired, and her solicitude made him pleasantly drowsy. Thinking of her as the potential mother of his child made him confident of his abilities as a lover. She had as good as said that their money worries were over, but he was here to make sure. She returned to him with two glasses and perched on the arm of his chair.

"Nobody's ever taken such good care of me," he said, lazily taking a sip of his win.

"That's because you're such a lovely son and lover. Pardon me, Mr. Lawrence." She drank off half her wine and put the glass on the table at his side. She ran a hand over his hair. "I'm still absurdly infatuated. I hadn't intended to be. When I've wanted a man in the past, once or twice was sufficient. I wonder why it isn't like that with you. I've wondered quite a lot about it. Your looks, of course, and the way you're built. I probably shouldn't admit it, but that's a big part of it." She laughed as she unfastened his tie. "A big part, indeed. If I'd known

146

other men somewhat similar, perhaps I wouldn't be so thrilled by it. I know I can't have it often, but will you go on letting me have it from time to time?" She unbuttoned his collar and put both her hands around his neck.

He covered them with his hands and chuckled. "What a peculiar conversation. I told you I'm not a complete whore. I want you to put more money in the show, but I'm honestly more interested in you as the mother of my child. If that happens, I'll want to see you probably more often than I'll be able to."

"Then that's settled—show and child. I do like to do what you tell me to." She unbuttoned his shirt and moved her hand lingeringly over his chest and into his armpits and down to the waistband of his trousers. "What a beautiful package for me to unwrap." She unbuckled his belt and opened his fly and spread her hand out flat on his belly. He shifted in the chair to make himself more available to her. She moved her hand down into his trousers and found his hard flesh and drew it out. It swung up against his belly. "My word. I've never seen anything so outrageously sexy. A great beautiful boy, all undone and half naked, and that, rearing up out of your pants."

He put down his glass and gave her hand a pat and leaned forward and unfastened his shoes. He pulled off his socks and shed clothes as he rose. She stood and let her dressing gown fall open as she moved in close to him. Her hands were on him, and she followed them with her eyes.

"When I see you naked and all ready to take me, I can hardly believe my luck. I want to do all sorts of disgraceful things with this. Put it in me quickly, darling. I don't want to let it become too much of an obsession."

He was asleep almost before his orgasm had ended. He awoke to find her eyes on him, and he moved in over her again. As he did so, he was aware somewhere in his half-waking mind of how restful sex was when it was simple and natural. Clara made a point of washing a great deal. If only she'd agree to have children.

"Good morning, darling," Fay said against his ear.

147

"Is it morning?"

"Very early. I've been waiting for it to be in me again. I know it awfully well now. I've been looking at it all night. It stays so hard. Did you know that?"

"All night?"

"Yes, when you were all sprawled out on your back so I could play with it to my heart's content."

"I think I'll be able to get back tonight if you want."

"Please do, darling. And you and David can see Freddy again on Sunday, and you'll have all the money you need for your show."

"You're a very well-behaved mistress."

During the next two days, he felt at times as if Fay were his comfortable, motherly wife, making a family, and Clara his mistress, fierce and passionate. When she returned, full of all she had accomplished in the city, she didn't seem surprised to find that financing for the production had been completed.

"I knew when Fay had dinner with us that she'd talk her husband into putting up more," she said. "Money attracts money. You see? You don't need Washburns. You're going to be rich and famous and successful all on your own."

By the time Fred confirmed Fay's promise, Walter was starting rehearsals for the last play of the season; he and Clara would be gone in a week. David had an uncle with a novelties business who had spare office space in the theater district. The rent was minimal, and they took it sight unseen. Makin-Fiedler Productions had acquired a geographical identity. David arranged for a telephone to be put in and ordered stationery printed.

David saw them off at the station. They were all conscious that a chapter of their lives was ending. Walter would probably never work here again. Even if *A Light in the Forest* were a total disaster, his status would have changed. Perhaps he would find a summer theater of his own to run.

As soon as they had disposed of their luggage, they moved into the office like children taking over a toy shop. It was a grubby cubicle in a building on West 47th Street. There was room for one desk, a couple of chairs, and a filing cabinet full of somebody's papers. The one window revealed a blank wall a few feet away. The door was partially obstructed by a water cooler. The telephone was there. Several large bundles of stationery had been delivered.

"It's so absolutely, marvelously awful," Clara said with glee. "I hope you're making notes for your autobiography, dearest. This is just right for a sensational debut." She picked up the telephone and called the *Times* drama editor and announced the imminent production of a distinguished French play by a newly formed company. "There," she said, settling down behind the desk with a brisk executive air. "That'll bring every actor in town to our doorstep."

She called Johnny Bainbridge, and he soon joined them, a sobering presence—but looking a little less worn than he had two months earlier. He accepted the news that they actually hoped to have the play in rehearsal within three weeks with satisfaction but expressed no astonishment at what seemed to Walter and Clara an almost incredible achievement. They worked out a schedule of interviews with the actors Walter had already selected so that Johnny could pass on them.

"What if I don't like them?" Johnny asked.

"Then we'll have to find others," Walter said. Writers would be treated with respect in his theater of the future. "Except Greg Boland. He's tied in with the movie money."

"I never expected to be a power in the theater," Johnny said with a crinkling of humor around his eyes.

"You'd better accept Walter's judgment unless you feel very strongly," Clara advised him. "We've gone over them very carefully."

They spent the rest of the week seeing actors they had summoned and dozens who were drawn by Clara's announcement. Walter wanted to talk to all of them as part of his mission to discover new talent, but he soon learned that it took too much time, and Clara put a sign on the door saying, NO CASTING.

David had given them a list of things he wanted them to do, such as hiring a rehearsal hall and having actors' copies of the play typed, and

Walter stuck to it. He hated spending any of the money they had so miraculously raised; he felt lost without David's experience and guidance. Clara wanted to branch out on their own and fix dates and commit funds without consultation with their partner. He firmly restrained her. She presided serenely over the office from behind the battered desk. The telephone rang constantly. The film company's press department was lining up behind the production. He and Johnny were in demand for interviews.

David arrived at last, teeth flashing, gold glittering. Walter breathed a sigh of relief. "Thank God you're here, old pal. Take over. I've been working on designs for the set. You can get Oscar in, and I'll go over them with him. The cast is penciled in. Johnny's pleased. You should draw up a contract for him. We're about ready to go."

"Except we don't have a theater."

"We have four weeks of rehearsals to find a theater."

"No, you wanted the regular three weeks of rehearsals, plus an extra week in the theater with the set. That's the way it's budgeted. Three weeks to find a theater."

"True."

"I wonder…" Clara began. Her eyes explored the air in front of her, in the way she had, without focusing on anything in particular. She looked out at the world rather than into herself when she was thinking. They hung on her words, but none emerged.

"Generally speaking, you don't go into rehearsal if you don't have a theater," David elaborated. Clara had allowed him to take her place behind the desk in honor of his arrival. The cramped quarters gave everything that was said great weight. They breathed into each other's faces.

"Let's not worry," Clara said finally. "Walter's ready to start. I don't think we should keep him waiting."

"The thing about Clara is that she understands genius," Walter said.

They decided to start rehearsals in ten days. Being able to make such decisions lent an air of fantasy to the whole enterprise. The first rehearsal returned Walter to the familiar atmosphere of his church sociables. He sat at a table flanked by Johnny and Clara, facing the actors in a row of folding chairs, with Greg Boland in the middle as befitted the leading man. He was lean and loosely knit with the right combination of intellectuality and rough-hewn appeal that Walter wanted for the part. He let the actors read through the play without interruptions while he checked his heavily annotated script and scribbled additional comments. He sensed excitement stirring in the bare, drab hall. The company burst into applause for Johnny at the end.

"It looks all right, Johnny," Walter said.

"It's thrilling," Clara asserted.

Johnny shrugged. "It's good," he agreed.

From then on, Walter was so absorbed in the play that the only time that existed for him was the time he was creating within its dramatic framework. He was quickly satisfied that he and Clara had chosen the actors well. Greg Boland seemed to rely rather heavily on charm, but Walter was confident that Greg could dig below the surface once he knew his lines. Walter refused to listen to Clara when she came to him with production problems. "Work it out with David" was his standard rejoinder. He was aware that they were constantly conferring together. They told him they had found a theater and that the budget seemed to be holding up to the pressure of a number of small, unexpected expenses. He was more interested in getting Jill Cummings, the lead actress, to remember a "but" she kept leaving out of one of her big speeches.

After two weeks he was ready for the first full-length run-through. Everything was going smoothly—but not too smoothly, he hoped. He knew the theatrical superstition about chaos being the prelude to success. There was nothing chaotic about the run-through. If it had been a routine Broadway success of the sort he was used to directing, it would have been almost ready to open. He had created tension but not impact. Several of the key performances, including Greg's, lacked resonance. It was exciting where it should have been searing.

He knew where the trouble lay. The play was too long. He had stressed pace at the expense of emotional values. He had never been

**151**

in a position to edit a text to suit himself and hesitated to suggest cutting to Johnny for fear of disrupting the harmony with which they had worked. Johnny and Clara waited for him while he went over his notes with the actors. He joined them and suggested they all go have a drink.

"Well, how did it go?" Walter asked after the three of them were installed in a booth in the back of a small theatrical bar in the neighborhood.

"It's going to be brilliant," Clara announced stoutly.

He looked at Johnny, who made an almost imperceptible movement with his shoulders. "It's hard to say with all the interruptions. This is the first time I've sat through a play in rehearsal. In Paris it seemed to go a little faster, but that might have something to do with the language. Of course, it was new to me then."

Walter took a swallow of his drink. "How about trying some cuts, Johnny?" he suggested, digging in for a storm.

Johnny looked at him impassively. "Where?"

"Well, that whole section after the big scene with the mother, for instance. It doesn't go anywhere. I know it has some lovely writing in it. That's why I haven't suggested it sooner."

"Can't you speed it up, dearest?" Clara asked.

"You know better than that, Clarry. Pace has nothing to do with speed. The pacing is very tight already. There're several places where I'd like to open it up. I know I could get more from Greg. I'm talking about adding maybe ten minutes to the playing time when I should be cutting by at least 15. How about it, Johnny?"

"You're aware, of course, that's where the whole point of the play is established," Johnny pointed out.

"That may be what's the matter with it. You're stating something that doesn't need to be stated. The play makes its point for itself."

"You can't compromise with a thing like this," Clara challenged him. She continued to treat Johnny with special deference. "You're worrying about theatrical effects when it's a question of ideology."

"I'm interested in the theater, Clarry, not in politics."

"But that's what Johnny keeps telling you. The theater is politics. Everything is politics."

"In that case we have nothing to worry about. I'll concentrate on theatrical effects, and they'll turn out to be politics."

"Very funny, but you still don't want to rob the play of its whole meaning."

Johnny studied her disinterestedly. He didn't even make the concession of being grateful for her support. He turned to Walter. "You might have something," he said. "I can see that the passage with Leonard might be extraneous, even though it's one of my favorite things in the play."

"Same here, but we've got to think of it as a whole. How about it? Will you perform the operation, or shall I?"

"You better. That way I can holler if I don't like it."

Clara made an impatient sound in the back of her throat. "Really, Johnny. I thought you'd fight for what you believe in. Why does everybody let him have his own way?"

Johnny smiled faintly. "I guess because there's no excuse for him unless he's right. We'll soon find out."

Walter stayed up most of the night to make the cuts he had indicated and others he had been considering since the beginning. He didn't have to rehearse the changes to know that he was making the play more manageable for himself, more conventional, and much more accessible to a Broadway audience. He felt sure that by simplifying the dramatic line and gaining time for it to grow from within, the play would develop the impact that it lacked. He had made it so completely his own that he felt no compunction toward the author. Success counted far more than literary experimentation. He didn't call another run-through during the last week in the rehearsal hall, so Johnny wasn't able to assess the effect of the cuts.

The first day in the theater where the set was in place provided a taste of the chaos that was generally considered lucky. Walter had provided himself the luxury of an extra week of rehearsal to be followed by a week of public previews in place of an expensive out-of-town try-out, so he didn't feel rushed and flung himself cheerfully into the avalanche of work.

The set was lit; clothes were checked and adjusted. Props created problems that had to be solved. The three partners were all over the theater at once, backstage, down front, in the box office, up in the balcony. They ate whenever something came to hand. Walter never knew what time it was, and at one point Clara told him that he hadn't left the theater for over 36 hours. As order reemerged, rehearsals became a succession of complete performances.

"I don't quite know how you've done it, but you've almost turned it into an American play," Johnny commented when he'd seen his first uninterrupted run-through. "It may be less impressive–less distinguished, maybe?–but I feel more part of it somehow. I guess I'm an American after all."

Walter was delighted at the success with which he had molded the company into a sensitively integrated ensemble. The actors were playing off each other, constantly enriching and expanding the dramatic values of the text. Only Greg Boland remained slightly mechanical, an actor in the center of a living organism. Walter knew that there was more in him and decided not to push him until he saw him in front of an audience. Some actors were incapable of opening up without the stimulus of a public. He wasn't completely satisfied with his set either, but he had theories about a bare stage that he didn't dare put into practice yet.

He was briefly annoyed one evening when he found the curtain down until he remembered that it was the night of the first public preview. Since everybody would be there on cut-rate tickets or free passes, he regarded them as a nuisance. He knew, though, that their presence would completely alter the performance, so he attempted to anesthetize himself to the shocks the evening was bound to bring.

He thought it went well. The actors overplayed, as was to be expected; there were disconcerting shifts of emphasis here and there; but there were no technical hitches, and he was surprised at the lethargy of the applause at the end.

"People who come to these things never know how to react," Clara said, standing at the back of the theater. "They need the critics to tell them what to think."

When he went backstage to go over his notes, he was lavish in his praise of the actors and crew to counteract the feeling of letdown in the air. Morale was as important now as lines or light cues. He was tempted to cancel the next day's rehearsal as a demonstration of his confidence but was aware of the delicate balance between the benefits of rest and the near-paralysis that could ensue from a relaxation of tensions.

During the following night's performance, he concentrated on the audience. It was restless at the beginning, doubtless resentful of having been lured to an unknown play with unknown actors that apparently wasn't even going to be funny. The play slowly got a grip on the house. He was beginning to look forward to the final curtain and an expression of the enthusiasm that he felt building up when the spell began to dissolve.

He had keyed down the final scene. Coming after the violence of the earlier scenes, it had the aching desolation of the aftermath of a particularly devastating storm. It wasn't coming off. He felt all his body tensing as he fought through every word of Greg's long bitter final speeches. "Come on, come on," he kept muttering to himself. It seemed so nearly right. Just the slightest additional pressure of intensity, a shadow of a stress, and Greg would have them. He felt as if they were engaged together in a struggle to tame some willfully stubborn dumb animal. They failed. The curtain descended once more to lethargic applause.

He hurried backstage distributing the elixir of enthusiasm that the audience had withheld. He asked Greg to stay and sent the others away with a valiant display of optimism. He told Clara to go home and to make sure the girl who had been hanging around Greg went too.

"Are you ready to make a night of this?" he asked when Greg had changed and removed his makeup and they were alone together on the stage in the light of the bare bulb overhead.

Greg studied a long bony forefinger, held straight and horizontal before his eyes. "What seems to be the trouble?" he asked without taking his eyes off it.

"The last scene. The audience isn't getting it. We'd better go over it. How does it feel to you?"

"All right. You're not going to cut it?" he demanded, voicing the actor's dread of losing any of his lines.

"No, it's not that. This is a tough play for a Broadway audience. They're probably expecting more of a punch. We may be playing it too fine for them."

"I'm playing the play the way I feel it," Greg said. "You told me you wanted it that way."

"You're doing a brilliant job, Greg," he soothed him. "Everybody agrees about that. I want to do everything possible to make this a real showcase for you."

His moody face brightened considerably. "All right, fella, let's get going." He made a vaudevillian one-two feint at Walter.

They started to walk through the scene, Walter close beside the actor, throwing him cues and murmuring suggestions. "No self-pity. Make it stronger than we had it before. More of a protest…" "There. Where the old woman interrupts you. I'll have her make it bigger, almost a scream. Now start building…" "That's it. Now hit it. 'If some die.' You're accusing all mankind. Really lay it on…" "Good. Now break it right off. Beat. Beat. Beat. Beat. Hold it as long as you like. You'll have to time it with the audience. Then way down. As if you can hardly believe your own ears. 'I can still say it. Blah-blah-blah.'"

Walter kept it an exercise in technique, trying to pump passion into a scene that had been written for chilling irony, making a statement out of a question mark. Greg was a naturally reticent actor. Walter had to explore him to find the spring of passion.

"This isn't the way I see it at all," Greg said petulantly at one point.

"Don't worry. We'll run through it once more and then try some other things." They walked through it again. "OK. Keep all that in mind and let's just talk it–for each other."

They moved about the stage and conversed together about love and betrayal and renunciation in Johnny Bainbridge's words. The fact that they were speaking into each other's eyes gave a new intensity to Greg's interpretation. At one moment he put a hand on Walter's shoulder. It was an actor's gesture, but Walter felt a sexual current in it. The slight shock it caused him was followed by the sudden realization that he was at last using the ambivalent communication system he had been holding in reserve. Men and women, boys and girls–he could guide them to express the truth, his truth, whatever it was, which he could imagine emerging only in some dramatic situation. He wasn't attracted to Greg. He had black Irish good looks but was probably hairy. In back his trousers fell in an almost straight line from belt to heels. Walter knew he had been married once and was about to get married again. Still, he might have a hidden twist that could be exploited.

They came to the long pause Walter had suggested before the curtain line. Greg's eyes searched his; Walter's met them encouragingly. Greg barely breathed the final words with an upward inflection, like the question that was implied in the whole play.

"Great," Walter burst out. "Great, kiddo. If you can put it all together somehow, you'll have them cheering in the aisles." He hugged him and could feel that Greg liked it. "That's enough for tonight. Let's go have a drink somewhere before the sun comes up."

They found a nearly deserted bar and settled into a booth. Walter deployed all his powers of seduction. He flattered the actor, he laughed at his jokes, he let his eyes linger admiringly in Greg's. All the exhaustion of the last few days had vanished. He was excited, not by his quarry but by the potentialities of the situation.

"I'm a bad influence," he said after they had both had several drinks. "I should've sent you to bed hours ago."

"It's been a big evening. How about if I go back to your place with you and get a couple hours' sleep?"

"We probably better break it up. We're apt to keep each other awake all night."

157

"Yeah, I guess you're right. Hey, I didn't mean any queer stuff. You know that, don't you? I'm not queer, for God's sake." His speech was getting heavy with drink.

"Of course not," Walter said lightly.

They parted in the street, and Walter went on his way with a revitalized spring in his step. Later the same day, back at the theater for rehearsals, he pursued his conquest of Greg. An odd relationship was developing between them, hunter and hunted. Walter stalked him. Greg shied from him with fear and fascination. Walter felt himself breaking through layer after layer of reserve as he wore him down. He didn't quite know what he expected to happen; he suspected only that in Greg's state of tension and fatigue, an unfamiliar sexual goad might prove explosive. He wanted to throw him off-balance so that his full emotional range would be exposed.

He encouraged him to play the last scene in the high-pitched, theatrical way they had worked out the night before and geared the other actors into it. It brought Johnny and Clara running.

"What in hell does Boland think he's doing?" Johnny demanded at the end of the morning run-through. "If he's going to play it like this, I'd better add a line about his just having escaped from a nut house."

Walter chuckled. "Don't worry. It's only an experiment. Greg's a good actor. He can't play against the grain like that for long. Something's gonna give."

Clara was more vehement. "I never thought he'd be the new Olivier, but I didn't think you'd let him ruin the play."

"He won't. I think I'm on to something. If it doesn't work by the end of the week, I'll put everything back the way it was."

Greg's performance at the night's preview frequently made Walter flinch, but it was breaking out of the mold of charm in which it had been set. He caught reverberations of the real feeling he had evoked when they had worked alone together. There was no slump in audience interest, and the curtain fell to more robust applause than they had had so far. He went backstage radiating confidence and encountered an air of bewilderment. The actors were gratified by their recep-

158

tion but doubtless were wondering what they had done to deserve it. He told everybody they were great and asked Greg to stay again. Wearing him down physically was part of his plan.

They went through the scene repeatedly as they had the night before, but Walter wasn't interested in interpretation now. He interrupted constantly, he cajoled, he harassed, he seduced with praise. Greg looked at him like a beaten dog that wanted only a pat on the head from its master. Walter stayed close to him and provoked physical contact and felt the sexual current growing stronger. As tension mounted between them, he made greater demands on Greg's vocal resources; and hostility flared in him. For a moment, he thought Greg might hit him. He called a halt finally and took him out again for drinks.

"If it's going to go on like this," Greg said after they had had a few, "we might as well live together until opening night."

Walter knew it might not have been intended, but it came across as a rather wistful proposition. "It's an idea, but we'd probably end by killing each other." Walter went into reverse. He dropped his seductive wiles and became listless and weary. "Come on. Drink up. We better get away from each other for a few hours." There was hurt and reproach and puzzlement in Greg's eyes when they parted.

The next day Greg approached him repeatedly on one pretext or another. Walter adopted a calculatedly curt manner. It was his turn to be wooed, and he made it clear it would have to be done from the stage. "We'll have a talk after I've seen your performance tonight," he said.

The curtain hadn't been up long before Walter felt like letting an exultant shout. All the play had filled out and come alive at last. Greg was playing with a new blaze of energy and bravado. The listless preview audience was caught and held. There was an excited babble in the lobby during the intermission. For the first time Walter allowed himself to wonder if they might have a hit. Everything continued to go beautifully, although he could see that nerves were beginning to tell on Greg.

As he started into the last scene, Walter knew a crucial moment was coming up. He froze to attention and gripped the rail in the back of the house. Greg had discarded all the histrionics they had worked out together and returned to Walter's original muted interpretation but was underpinning it with tense, agonized longing. His voice and body were gripped by a paroxysm of repressed revolt. It was a daring approach and utterly right, but required iron control. Walter sensed Greg's slipping. He held his breath, wondering if he would make it to the end. His timing grew erratic. He stumbled over his lines. Walter was able to breathe again as he reached the final pause before the curtain line. Greg turned to face the audience. Its silence was dense with expectation. The pause stretched to infinity, and still he held the house in his grip. His mouth opened. Walter prayed for deliverance. No words came. His eyes went blank and staring, the spell was broken, and he sank to his knees, a man collapsing in public. The curtain dropped like a knife and didn't rise. Walter raced for the backstage pass door, leaving the audience in a tumult of confusion from which arose a scattering of applause.

He found Greg stretched out flat on the stage, his eyes closed, surrounded by the cast. He pushed people aside and bent over him. "Come on, kiddo," he said gently. "Everything's perfect now."

Greg let out a howl and began to writhe about the floor.

"Leave him alone." Clara spoke from behind him. "He's not worth bothering about."

He glanced back at her and gave her a warning look. He took hold of Greg's arm and started to pull him up. Greg's body contracted, and he rolled away and staggered up and headed for the wings. Walter caught up with him and put an arm around him. He let his body go against him. "Sweet dreams, everybody," Walter called over his shoulder. "Rehearsal as usual in the morning."

He dragged Greg to his dressing room and eased him into a chair. He slumped over the dressing table and began to beat it with his fists. Jars and tubes danced and rattled on its surface.

"Get out of here, goddamn it," he shouted. "I've had enough. Let Holloway play the part. I'm through."

"Don't be a fool, kiddo. You're going to bring the house down on opening night."

"I won't be there, I tell you." He continued to beat on the table. "Play the part yourself. You've hounded me and hounded me until I don't know what I'm doing. You goddamned son of a bitch. Get out of here." He suddenly lifted his head and froze as if he had heard a voice calling him. He delivered the curtain line in a roar of full-throated despair, completing his performance. Walter felt his scalp tingling, electrified. Greg hung his head over his fists and spoke in a strangled voice. "That's the way I was going to do it. Then everything stopped. I thought you might not like it. I couldn't–" He slid forward, scattering makeup across the table, and burst into loud, harsh sobs.

Walter watched him for a moment, exulting. There would be no more reticence now. He had succeeded in unleashing a torrent of emotion. He was sure that Greg, as any good actor, should, had been observing himself even during his wildest outbursts. He was adding a new register to his equipment that Walter would be able to tap at will. He moved in over him and began to stroke his head and neck and shoulders. He was glad that he could handle a man lovingly. "Everything's fine now, kiddo. There's nothing more to worry about," he soothed him.

Greg's sobs slowly subsided. He lifted his head slightly and swayed it back and forth and managed to speak. "Why did you do this to me? Why do you want to destroy me?" He dropped his head again as he was shaken by a fresh outburst of sobbing.

Walter gripped his shoulders and waited. When he was quieter, he pulled him up against him. "Destroy you? Don't you realize what you did tonight? You were magnificent. If those damn fools backstage had brought the curtain down slowly, you'd have had a standing ovation. You didn't need the last line. All you need is to get a final grip on it, and you'll be the sensation of the season."

He dropped his head back against Walter's abdomen and shook it slowly. "No, I'm through. You don't expect me to work again tonight?"

"Of course not. We've got plenty of time. You'll get it set tomorrow."

"I suppose you hate me. Why did you pull back today? I thought we were in this together?"

161

"We are. I just wanted to give you a chance to work it out on your own. Boy, did you ever. I couldn't have done that for you." He reached over and stuck his fingers into a pot of cold cream and dabbed it on Greg's face and rubbed it into his makeup. Greg's body was shaken by a long shuddering sigh, and he opened his eyes. "You mean it? It was really good?"

Their eyes met in the mirror. "It was more than good. It was great. Better than anything I ever hoped for."

Greg's breath caught, and silent tears spilled from his eyes. Walter reached for a stained towel and began to remove the mess from his face. Greg was his instrument; he had mastered him. Handling him and ministering to him aroused him agreeably. "There. That's most of it." He wiped his hands and tossed the towel back onto the dressing table and rested his hands on Greg's shoulders. "How about it? Are you ready to change and get out of here?"

Greg's hands shot up and gripped Walter's. "Oh, Christ, Walter. I'm sorry. You'll stay with me tonight, won't you? You've got to. I'm scared to death. I've never been so close to cracking up. I know you can get me through it."

"You're damn right I will. Come back to my place. I'll give you a drink and put you to bed, and we'll get a decent night's sleep."

"You know I'm not after you, don't you?"

"I don't think it much matters." He laughed and stepped closer and moved his crotch against Greg's shoulder. "You feel what's happening there? So what? We've created something together. Thinking about what a fabulous performance you're going to give makes me a little hard for some reason. I don't care if you know it."

He took him home and opened the foldout bed and put the bedclothes on it and told Greg to get into it while he mixed them drinks. He brought the drinks back and stretched out on top of the covers and reassured him at greater length about the insignificance of the night's disaster. He was determined to untangle his nerves and restore his confidence so that the breakdown would be forgotten in the morning. Greg dissolved into tears once more and clutched his hand. It was evident that a further step was required. Walter took his clothes off and got into bed and gathered him into his arms. He kissed his eyes until the weeping stopped. The sexual encounter was brief, quickly terminated by Greg's orgasm. After that, they slept.

It marked the end of Walter's creative involvement in the production. The next day he began to grasp at thoughts that had nothing to do with the production. He remembered hearing Clara and David's discussing the allocation of first-night seats, and it occurred to him that Fay was probably back in the city. When he had the opportunity, he dropped a nickel in the phone backstage and called her number and gave his name. In a moment she was greeting him with friendly warmth. She had been back in town less than a week and was looking forward to the opening night.

"I was just going over arrangements for the party. You won't be a flop, will you, darling? I do want the party to be gay."

"What party is that?"

"The first-night party. We're giving it. Didn't Clara tell you?"

"Oh, maybe she did. I haven't listened to anything anybody's said for weeks."

"I hope you're listening now, darling. I have some rather nice news. Our production is all set to appear in about eight months."

His mind ground into action, circled the words, fixed on their meaning. "You're kidding," he shouted. He let out a whoop of laughter. "You mean it? It's really going to happen? Oh, God, I wish I could see you."

Fay laughed softly. "In view of the way paternity affects you, I wish I could see you, darling. It's nice knowing the little dear has such a beautiful father."

"We've got to get together as soon as possible. Next week when all the fuss is over, I want to hear all about it."

Fay laughed again. "You're a darling boy. I don't see what more I can tell you, but I'd gladly reenact the way it happened in case you haven't quite got the hang of it."

They laughed together, and she wished him luck and promised to arrange a meeting for the following week. He encountered Greg in the corridor, and they winked at each other as they passed. Finished business. The passions he had unleashed were all harnessed and working productively.

The final preview ended with what was as close to an ovation as could be expected from an audience of freeloaders. Clara hugged Walter, and Johnny gave him a restrained pat on the back while they watched the curtain calls from the back of the theater.

"It's a bloody miracle," Johnny said. "I was sure he was going to kill the show."

"What did you do to him, dearest?" Clara inquired, her eyes glowing with pride. "You've turned him into a great actor. I'm rather sorry to see him wasted on Hollywood."

"I've just been made an honorary member of the Svengali Society," Walter said.

He was faced with the three dangerous days of waiting for the opening night. It was plenty of time for the performance to fall apart, but he didn't know what he could do to prevent it. It had been planned this way from the beginning, but he knew now that it had been a major blunder. Once actors were accustomed to an audience, it was like depriving them of air to make them work in an empty theater. He gave them a day off. The day after that he brought a stack of plays to the theater and had them all do readings as different as possible from the parts they were playing. It was an experiment in using a permanent company. They all enjoyed themselves. After that there was nothing to do but put them through a final run-through to make sure they hadn't forgotten their lines and hope for the best.

Faced with an opening night in a few hours, Walter supposed he must be nervous, but it manifested itself in lethargy. There was too much at stake to think about it. Since the rewards of success were incalculable, he preferred to dwell on the possibility of failure, which would leave him no worse off than he had been before. "Let's get away from here for a while, Clarry," he said, standing onstage and taking a last look around the deserted theater. "I can't believe it's all going to be decided so soon. It seems only yesterday Johnny brought us the play."

164

They picked up coffee and sandwiches and went to the office a couple of blocks away. David wasn't there. Clara went over some recent bills. Walter sprawled as comfortably as he could in a straight chair and tried not to think. There was no reason for their being there, but he couldn't think of anywhere else to go. He hadn't made love to Clara for more than a week, and this wasn't the time to resume. He heard fire sirens screaming through the streets.

"It would be interesting if the theater burned down," he commented idly.

David called ten minutes later to tell them that that was what had happened. He threw down the telephone and lunged for the door without stopping to tell Clara. She came sweeping after him. When they reached the scene of the disaster, it was all over. The fire had been confined to the stage and backstage area, but the auditorium was a shambles. The set was gone. The costumes were gone. David, who had been there though it all, greeted them with a hopeless shrug.

"Didn't I say something once about setting fire to $25,000? Well, here you are," he said with none of his usual bounce. "It was quite a light in that forest."

Walter looked at him and burst out laughing. He leaned against the wall in the lobby and shook with helpless laughter. Clara joined in. The contagion spread to David, and the three of them stood in the lobby, rocking and clutching their sides in a hysteria of shattered nerves. A man in a waterproof coat and hip boots and a fireman's helmet slogged past. He glanced at them disapprovingly and shook his head. After a few moments they managed to get themselves under control.

"We'd better have a little chat," Walter said to David. His shock and dismay were tempered by curiosity. What in the world would they do now? He supposed there was a proper procedure to follow. If it involved delays, collecting insurance, raising more money, it struck him as dreary. He already had an idea of what he wanted to do. His lethargy was gone. "Come on. Let's go back to the office." He set a fast pace as the three of them strode off down the street.

They shut themselves in the office, with Clara's presiding behind the littered desk. There was complete silence. Walter righted an over-turned coffee carton and took a quick breath to repress another wave of laughter.

"Well," David began. "We'll have to postpone for two weeks, maybe three. We're going to need more money. The set's covered, of course; but it'll take money to keep the company together and all the rest. This is an item I didn't include in the budget."

"I don't want to put more money in it," Walter said.

"We've got to. We've done damn well so far. Even if we have to throw in another $10,000, it'll still be cheap."

"I don't want to." He could feel Clara's eyes boring into him. She knew he was about to spring something on them.

"There's no alternative, old pal. I don't get it. What do you think we can do?"

"Well..." He threw his head back and laughed. "Oh, for God's sake, let's stop being so goddamned grown-up and solemn. We're young. And what does youth do? It laughs in the face of adversity."

"So I'm laughing. Then what?"

Walter sprang up and took a turn around the confined quarters. He faced them. "Why shouldn't we just go ahead and *do* the goddamned play?"

"How do you mean?"

"I mean, just get up on a stage and *do* it."

"Now, wait a minute, honey. You saw the theater. There's no stage to get up on."

"Call Al Finebaum, or whatever his name is. Ask him if he can give us a theater for tonight."

"For *tonight*?" David's voice broke with disbelief. "There's no pro-duction. We don't even have a backdrop."

"The hell with a backdrop. I've never liked that damn set anyway. Call Al. *Make* him give us a theater. Let's have a little fun, for God's sake. Everybody takes this business too damned seriously." He looked at Clara. She smiled.

"If Al's no help, there's always Cousin George." She had never found him more thrilling. This was the way she wanted life to be–innovative and unpredictable. If she had been given a free hand, she couldn't have invented anybody so elegantly mischievous while at the same time sublimely young and awesomely authoritative *and* so physically irresistible.

They sprang into action. David and Clara took turns on the telephone. They were offered a theater for ten days. "Take it," Walter ordered. If they had a hit, there would be no trouble finding another. They called the city desks of the papers and suggested coverage of the story. They managed to contact all the members of the cast and gave them instructions. Signs were rushed to the burned-out theater to announce the change. Making one feverish call after another, they generated an excitement between them that they imagined must be spreading throughout the theatrical district. An event was being created. When they had done everything they could think of doing, they sat back and looked at each other and laughed excitedly.

"This may be the flop of the century, but at least it'll be a resounding flop," Walter said.

Somehow he found time to rush home and put on the dinner jacket Clara had insisted he must buy for the occasion. He hurried to the new theater, where David was waiting for him with the stage manager and backstage crew. He devised a simplified light plot. He paced the stage and confronted the problems created by not having a set and worked out solutions on the spot. At David's insistence he went out to the stage door and met several reporters and photographers. Much was made of the fact that he was not yet 21. Together they dreamed up the story of the parade up Broadway, Walter and David at the head of their cast, which landed on the front page of several papers the next day and which gave the impression that the fire had occurred just before curtain time.

He spent what little time remained working with the actors on the changes imposed by the bare stage. They were fired by his excitement at improvising, at creating theater out of a vacuum. At about 8 o'clock, somebody suggested that it was time to lower the curtain, but on the spur of the moment he decided to leave it up while the audience was arriving. He went on coaching the actors. Eventually he heard the house filling up behind him. By this time, he had reached a sort of delirium of nerves and excitement in which all his perceptions were vividly heightened while he remained outside events and moved in a dream. He gave directions in a voice that couldn't be heard across the footlights, but the audience remained quiet, straining to hear, and he knew he was achieving his purpose of winning its participation before the play began. He enlarged his movements and dramatized the role of the director in the theater, as if he were the conductor of a symphony orchestra. He beckoned actors to him and moved with them about the stage. A pattern emerged, a sort of mime of the play to come. Only the creak and clatter of seats being occupied by latecomers broke the almost religious concentration of the house. When David gave him a signal from the wings that it was time to begin, he closed his eyes in an instant of unformulated prayer. When he opened them he turned slowly to face the auditorium and lifted his hands. The hush in the theater became more intense.

"Ladies and gentlemen, because of circumstances beyond our control," he paused, making the most of it, "tonight belongs to a writer and to the actors who know his words."

It brought the house down. He saw David in the wings hugging the stage manager and joining the applause. The curtain descended, and he hurried off into the arms of Johnny Bainbridge.

"I hope I never have to go through anything like this again, but Jesus–" Johnny actually choked with emotion.

When Walter looked back, the curtain had risen, and the play had begun.

It worked. The actors responded to the challenge and gave a better performance than Walter had thought possible. The play emerged strongly in this novel treatment. Before half an hour had passed, he knew he was having a triumph. He hid in a bar during the intermission. Greg took over in the second half and turned into a star before the

168

spellbound audience's eyes. The curtain fell to stunned silence and then the thunder of applause. There were shouts of "Bravo!" There were calls for the author.

Walter bowed his head, tears spilling from his eyes. This was Broadway, and he had done it. He choked with pride and gratitude and the wonder of being him. Clara moved in beside him. He fought for control and lifted his head. His throat was blocked with an aching knot.

"It's...so...damn...good." He barely got the words out one by one.

"Oh, my dearest. It's you; you're wonderful." She stood before him, head held high, more majestic than ever. "This is what you can do. I'm so proud I've left you free to do it. No wife, no family—just you, and the world to conquer."

He was famous overnight, so he soon felt as if he always had been. He had the impression of being rich because so many of his new friends were, but it took more than another year before any substantial sums accumulated. He was too busy to spend them. Success permitted him to do the work he had been waiting to do, and he flung himself into it. He followed his first success with two more, one a fantastical musical in which he experimented with masks and novel scenic effects. He was the Boy Wonder, whose touch turned everything to gold. His name became a trademark for high, but not solemn, quality. He contributed a lighthearted touch to everything he did. He taught Broadway that Chekhov could be a comedy smash. His fourth and fifth productions didn't break his winning streak. When he was preparing his sixth, he saw a chance of striking it really rich. By becoming his own backer with the money that had been piling up, he would with luck be in a position at last to set up the permanent company in his own theater that had always been his dream. David urged caution, but Clara encouraged him. The play ran less than a week and wiped him out.

He discovered that events compressed time. Three years passed in a flash during which he had kept a step ahead of the draft. The unfamiliar feel of failure seemed to dictate a change in pace. He bowed to circumstances and accepted a commission and entered the entertainment branch of the Army.

The only nonprofessional event of any significance during that period had been his marriage to Clara. It occurred just after his 21st
birthday. To his surprise, Clara allowed her family to turn it into a
major Washburn event. He had always imagined they'd run off to City
Hall in a spare moment. The press had a field day. By now he was accustomed to publicity, but his grand marriage into the overwhelming-
ly grand family put him on a level far above any run-of-the-mill Broadway celebrity. Despite Clara's strictures, he got along easily with the
Washburns, and they seemed to welcome him. They couldn't turn him
into a Washburn, but he didn't despise the official connection.

Clara found a small apartment on West Tenth Street with two big
high-ceilinged rooms and moved them into it. It wasn't the sort of place
he intended to live in eventually–there was no room for children–but
he was too busy to make a fuss about housing. The low rent proved a
blessing when he went off to the Army.

Walter's new Charvet dressing gown rustled as he sat opposite Clara and poured himself some coffee. She was deep in the morning papers. He had been back in residence for such a short time that it was still a novelty to join her for a leisurely breakfast in the living room overlooking Tenth Street. She made an impatient sound in her throat and handed him a neatly folded paper. She went through them with businesslike efficiency, never letting them get rumpled or disordered.

"What?" he asked.

"The McClaren column."

His eyes ran down it and were caught by the paragraph.

> What Golden Boy of Broadway was slapped the other night by a famous Movie Queen at the Garden Room for his oh-so-friendly attentions to her husband? Clue: Rumor has it that he was given his pinkie ring by his producing partner, sometimes known as the Boy Wonder. Whoops, my dears.

Walter's cheeks were burning before he had finished the short item. This was the fourth or fifth such reference to appear in the column since he had been out of the Army. He hated it. All Broadway would be tittering; he and David had practically been called queers again in public. There was no doubt about the identity of the Boy Wonder. He glanced across the room at the six framed posters of his Broadway pro-

**171**

ductions. His name was in bigger print on each successive one; on the last it was almost top-heavy with the pride that goes before a fall. There hadn't been much talk about the Boy Wonder for the last year. Now that he was about the resume his career, he didn't need this sort of talk.

"Damn it," he burst out. "I wish he'd go further so I could sue him."

"I shouldn't think that would help, dearest," Clara said serenely. "More publicity. Considering the number of certified faggots there are in this business, you'd suppose they'd find somebody else to pick on. I know we can't do without our precious David, but he does strike an unfortunate note."

Walter, feeling threatened, pushed the paper from him. It reduced him to angry irrational fear of discovery. There was nothing to discover. His fidelity to Clara probably made a lot of girls think that Walter Makin wasn't interested in the opposite sex, since fidelity was the last thing that was expected of anybody. His intermittent but long-standing affair with Fay, who had a special status in his mind as the mother of his child, didn't affect his reputation since nobody knew about it. In the absence of any hard gossip about him, the brand he had always feared remained poised over him.

He wished David didn't look so flamboyant. They weren't returning to regular commercial production. He had laid the groundwork for his permanent theater, not completely on his own as he had once imagined but as a major cooperative venture; and he needed the help of all the cultural forces he could activate. The break provided by the Army had been useful to him. He had made important business and political contacts. He had had time to consolidate his thoughts about what he wanted the theater to be. He had his talent lined up. His acting company was assembled on paper. He had several brilliant designers and musicians, and he was encouraging a handful of young writers with option money. He had taken a long lease on a theater. Theatre Today was to be as close to a national theater as the country would permit. He intended to do five or six productions a year in repertory with the emphasis on contemporary native drama, but including classics and whatever new writers he could find in postwar Europe.

He was dealing with state and federal arts councils, theater developments funds, theater wings and theater leagues in an effort to win tax concessions, public subsidy, and massive private financing. Uncle Perry was helpful, but a hint of scandal–he stared at the offensive newspaper that to him carried much more than a hint–could wreck his plans. Girls wouldn't matter, but anything perverted would be disastrous.

"It seems to me there's been an awful lot of harping on this whole queer thing since I've been back," he complained. "There was nothing like this before."

"That's just it–you've been away." Her discreet campaign was just beginning to take effect. "David's been in the limelight without you, and he hasn't always been very tactful. We know him and love him, of course, but some people are shocked by him. He forces this new friend of his down everybody's throat."

"So I hear. I suppose I could talk to him about it. But it seems like butting in on something that's none of my business." He admired David for leading his own life in the limelight. The lack of privacy imposed by celebrity had alarmed him at first, and he had thanked his stars that he had nothing to hide. The stories he had heard about blackmail made the dangers clear. His marriage to Clara had provided a splendid insulation from gossip, if there had been anything to gossip about. The press had even treated him as something of a hero when, after the years of dodging the draft (Washburn strings had been pulled), he had finally accepted his commission (more Washburn strings). He and Clara were the darlings of the glossy magazines. They dressed and lived picturesquely and were always good for a picture spread; they were already scheduled to be the subjects of a piece about his doffing his uniform for *Harper's Bazaar.*

Her mouth assumed a series of expressions while she studied the air between them. "I don't suppose anything David does can really hurt you." She dismissed the subject and looked at him with her gloating smile. "You're scrumptious in that dressing gown. We must have you photographed in it. It's so divinely decadent after all your military

173

austerity. Have you thought any more about what we'll live on for the next year?"

"David seems to think we'll be all right. He says I can go on salary as soon as the charter is approved by the unions, or something of the sort. I don't quite understand it."

"Oh, I understand that. It's not the way I'd handle it, that's all." Her hair was piled on top of her head so that her neck looked long and imperious. "He can't get used to the idea that this isn't a money-making proposition. You should be treated as an expense, like the office. David's the only person who should get a salary, as business administrator."

"That sounds like sense. Have you talked it over with him?"

"Not in detail, I wanted to wait till you'd settled in again. We'll have to spend a day at the office soon and go over it all. We're going to be quite poor."

"We'll be too busy to notice. I hope you don't mind."

"It's lovely to have you back, dearest." Her laughter began and ended on a single note. "I've been so *bored* all these months." She was glad they were going to be poor for a while. After their wedding in the Gothic castle in Cleveland and his first total exposure to her family, she had detected signs of his becoming "sensible" about money. Her father talked to him about investments. Walter wanted to move into a proper establishment uptown, possibly on Park Avenue, with servants. She had clung to the place on Tenth Street as tangible evidence that they belonged to bohemia. She was delighted when all the money had vanished in the last production. It was something that would never have happened to a Washburn.

He rose and moved around behind her so that he could touch her under the chin. "I've got to get going. I don't suppose many people who really matter read that bastard McClaren." He glanced at the paper and withdrew his hand. "I've got that lunch on Wall Street. I'll spend the rest of the afternoon at the office. What about you?"

"Odds and ends. Don't forget the Brewster dinner."

"Black tie?"

"Of course, dearest. The war's over." She watched him go and then picked up the offensive column again. Life had begun again and promised to be more exciting than ever. Things were going her way. She reminded herself to call her father and ask him to keep the pressure on McClaren's publisher but to take care how Walter's name was linked with David's.

At Walter's lunch two influential Wall Street men who figured in his plans referred to the McClaren column and wondered if it were true what they said about theater people. From the way they spoke, Walter wasn't sure they had identified him as the Boy Wonder, but he found it very unpleasant. As much as he disliked doing it, he must talk to David.

"Is the Golden Boy there?" he asked Alice as soon as he reached the office. Alice was his secretary, but doubled as receptionist when they didn't have a show in production.

"He's been here all day, unlike some people I know."

They had long ago graduated to a glittering suite in Rockefeller Center. Walter went along the corridor to David's room and entered. David was on the phone and rolled his eyes in greeting as he continued to talk. He hung up. "Hello, Wonder," he said.

"Hi, Goldie." Walter sat on David's desk. "I suppose you saw McClaren's column this morning."

"Yeah. Not a word of it truth, of course. Lana was drunk and socked her husband, not me. I don't know why he's after me. We've always been very friendly. How did the lunch go?"

"OK. The column was mentioned. I don't like it, old pal."

David looked at him in silence, and his expression clouded. "I see. We're going to have to have a heart-to-heart, are we? Well, what am I supposed to do about it?"

"There's an easy answer to that. Cut out boys. I suggested it before."

"So you did." There was a hard little glint to David's prominent eyes. "If you were me, how would you react if I said that to you?"

The corners of Walter's mouth twitched. "Tell you to go screw yourself, I should think."

David laughed. "You're all right, old pal. I keep expecting you to turn into a shit, but if you haven't by now, I guess you won't. So let's have a heart-to-heart." He rose and perched on the desk beside Walter. "I know it's important. If McClaren goes on pushing this thing, I could become a liability. I know that."

"What happened to your plan to stop playing around and find yourself a nice little wife when you were 30?"

"I have a month still." David's laughter turned a trifle rueful. "I'm ready to get married now. Paul's made me realize that. I've never lived with anybody before–it's fun–but I can't very well marry him, so I guess some nice little Jewish girl is about to get lucky."

"Well, that settles that. That's great, David." Walter was delighted to drop the subject. There were so many more important things to talk about, but he made a point of telling Clara that David was thinking about marriage as they dressed for dinner that evening. She made no comment but listened with a cryptic little smile.

They were leading a hectic social life in celebration of his return to civilian life so that their sex life had been diverted into odd hours. He was making love to her late the next morning when it occurred to him that it was time for her period. He asked her about it.

She looked at him thoughtfully. "You were so lovely just now that I'd forgotten about it myself. I guess I'm a day or two late."

His heart stopped. His head swam. For a moment he couldn't breathe. It was going to happen. Clara was going to have a child. He had given Clara a baby. It was the ultimate consecration, far more binding than the dim ceremony that had been performed over them in Cleveland. They would be truly married after that.

Success had made every attractive girl and boy in the theater available to him. He had resisted all but the most transient temptations–doubling up with young officers in war-crowded hotels had led to a few lapses–but why be obliged to resist temptation at all? Parenthood would make such encounters seem grotesque. So much for McClaren. There would be no more risk of gossip, the pretty youths would no longer dare offer themselves with their eyes if he were a father.

He was careful not to press her with questions while the next few days passed in a blaze of anticipation, underlaid, enriched, made almost heartbreaking by a great unfamiliar aching tenderness for her. Was this finally what falling in love was like?

"I went to the doctor today," she announced one evening while they were getting dressed for another dinner.

"Why? Is something wrong?" he asked innocently, reminding himself not to leap in the air with excitement.

"You know perfectly well what's wrong. I'm going to see him again tomorrow, but it's practically sure. Damn, damn, damn."

He knew it would be tactless to shout with joy, but he couldn't keep himself from going up behind her and perching with her in front of her dressing table and putting his arms around her. He immediately wanted her. "I gather you're not entirely pleased, Clarry, but don't mind too much. We're going to have children eventually. Why not start now?"

She made a growling sound in her throat and tried to shake him off. "If you put on a Doting Daddy act, I'll scream. It couldn't happen at a worse time."

Adapting to her mood, he pretended to commiserate with her. "That's true, I suppose. Nine months. Theatre Today will be just about ready to open. What do you suppose went wrong?" Nothing, he assured fate so as not to put a jinx on the child. Everything was wonderfully right.

"I've always known that gadget isn't foolproof. That's why I've always been so careful to wash. It must've happened as soon as you got back. I got a bit carried away the first few days."

"It's wonderful, Clarry," he burst out and hastily modified his tone. "I mean, once you get used to the idea, you'll probably begin to like it. You'll be able to work all through the important time while we're getting everything set up. Once we're running, there'll be plenty of money again. We can get a bigger place and somebody to help with the baby. If it's happened, it's happened. We might as well think of all that's wonderful about it."

His hand was opening her dressing gown, and she pushed it away.

"Who said it's happened? I've heard that if you jump up and down a lot you can cause a miscarriage. I'm going to talk to the doctor tomorrow and—"

"For God's sake, Clarry, don't say things like that. You could do something terrible to yourself." He quickly slipped his hand under her dressing gown and moved it back to unfasten her bra.

"What are you doing, dearest? We're supposed to be dressing for dinner."

"We've got time."

"Stop it. You'll rip something."

"Then take everything off. I want to look at you." He rose and pulled her up with him. He had on only trousers and a shirt and removed them quickly while she did as she was told. She stood before him and allowed him to admire her. "You're really beautiful, Clarry," he murmured, awed at the thought of her carrying their life within her. Being successful and famous seemed trivial compared to this.

Her eyes mocked him. "I suppose you're going to tell me that maternity has filled me with an unearthly glow."

"I might. It changes the way I look at you." He moved to her until their bodies were lightly touching here and there. "I love you, Clarry. You're more exciting than ever."

She glanced down at his growing sex. "We can't. I haven't put that thing back in."

"So much the better. If you're pregnant already, I can't make you pregnant again. I'm going to do it for real for the first time."

"Oh, no, you're not." Her eyes turned hard with defiance. "Seeing your cock standing up so grandly infuriates me. Don't you realize what you've done to me?"

He laughed and took her hand and put it on his sex and moved it back and forth. "Feel it. It can batter down walls of rubber. If it were yours, I'd gladly have your babies."

"I'm in no mood for phallic worship. I want to get dressed."

"No, you don't." He flung his arms around her and pulled her to him and took her mouth with his. He felt her breath quicken. He moved insinuatingly against her resistant body. He loved to feel her giving in to him. He drew back and took her hand and pulled her across the room to the bed and threw off the cover. "I've wanted to fuck you for years with nothing in the way. No obstructions. Just you."

She jerked her hand away and started back toward her dressing table. "You can run around naked all your life if you so choose. I'm going to get dressed."

"Oh, no. I've always wanted to rape someone." He made a rush for her and grabbed and dragged her back to the bed. They were both laughing, but there was a spark of real struggle in it, and her laughter was dangerous. He threw her down and flung himself on top of her.

She looked up into slanting eyes and the impish smile, and her heart raced. She felt him sliding into her and filling her, and sounds of delight and pleasure were wrung from her. She felt all of herself opening to him. She couldn't control her body's surrender. All the more reason why she must cling to detachment and common sense when there were important decisions to make.

"Oh, Clarry. Feel that. We're joined. We're one. I know it's all imagination, but it seems so different when you don't have anything there. It's like having you for the first time." After all these years, incredibly, it *was* the first time in a real sense, more tremendous with his wife than it could have been with Fay or Debby or little what's-her-name.

"You do feel more inside me than usual." She pulled him to her with her arms and legs, clinging to him. She didn't know if other men could be so thrilling and still felt no inclination to find out.

"God, my cock feels so good there. It seems unfair for you not to know what it's like."

"You don't know what it's like having a beautiful cock inside you. I wouldn't trade places for anything." She wondered why she hadn't gone mad with jealousy and desire while he was away. Knowing how highly sexed he was, and how irresistible, she knew he was bound to have had bedmates. He was hers again now. She flung her arms out on the bed and let him move freely on her. "Show me how long it is, dearest," she requested.

They both giggled as he drew slowly back from her and slid into her again. Her body was shaken by sobbing laughter when the demonstration was completed. "That still makes me come. You're so good to me, dearest. Have you always made your girls come as often as I do?"

"My girls, indeed. You won't let me have any."

"No, it's horribly selfish of me not to want anybody else to have this much fun."

"Isn't it better without the rubber wall?"

"If you say so, dearest. I'm not sure there're degrees of bliss. I adore it, with or without the gadget."

They were late for dinner but were forgiven. Everybody indulged the Makins. When he got home the next evening, he found a note from her. She had used a pad from the office.

Memo to:   Walter Makin
From:      Clara Ditto
Re:        Child

The doctor wants me to have an overnight checkup, so I'm going to a hospital. I'll call in the morning. The Lunts are delighted to have you as an extra man. See you tomorrow. You're my dearest love.

Mrs. Ditto

He smiled and dropped the paper into the wastebasket. Typical. She would scratch his eyes out if he absented himself so casually without even telling her where he was.

He wandered around the much-photographed room looking at the things in it. It was filled with odd or beautiful objects that he had picked up in the first heady flush of having money to spend—fans, boxes, statuettes, porcelain birds and animals, candlesticks. The walls were crowded with pictures and mirrors and the posters of his shows. The furniture was eclectic, including draped tables and a big Louis XV settee of doubtful authenticity. The marble fireplace worked. He liked the place, but it wasn't big enough for a baby. There was only this room and the bedroom and a sort of passage they had turned into a dining room. When they gave a dinner party, Clara ordered the food from a restaurant near Washington Square.

He wondered how soon they could afford to move. They still had four years to go before she got her first millions. Everything depended on the theater. A baby couldn't take up much room the first year. They could keep him in the dining room. After that, the theater should be well established, and they would know where they stood. And by then there might be a baby brother on the way. Now that it had happened at last, he wanted more than one—two boys and a girl would be a nice mixture—and he wanted the sort of place he had been dreaming of before he lost all their money. Servants. A first-class cook, so they could give the kind of small grand dinner parties he liked to go to. The children would be beautifully brought up by what the Washburns called a nanny. The children. Clara was going to have a baby. He beamed at the room as he went to the bedroom to dress for dinner.

She called when he was beginning to wake up the next morning. She sounded brisk and chipper. "I'm just waiting to see the doctor, and then I'll be home. Do you have to go out?"

"Not till 12:30."

"Oh, I'll be there long before that."

He heard her key in the lock as he was finishing his breakfast coffee. She dropped a small overnight bag by the door and sang out. "Here I am," and swept majestically to the middle of the room, pulling off her gloves. It was an electrifying entrance, and he watched it with appreciation. If she were capable of reproducing it on a stage, he could make her a star. She wore one of her big swooping hats and a smart suit. He saw her falter slightly, and she moved more slowly to him as he rose to greet her. She sagged into a chair but immediately straightened and pulled off her hat with a flourish and looked up at him as if she expected to be given a prize.

"Well, it's all taken care of," she announced.

"What is?"

"Why, my condition, as they say."

"Everything's all right? You're definitely having a baby?" He sat opposite her and reached across the table for her hand.

She ignored him. Her mouth opened to emit a bark of derision. "Don't be silly, dearest. I couldn't possibly."

"I don't understand." He didn't want to understand. His stomach was beginning to know with protest. "It was a false alarm? Tell me about it. Where were you last night?"

"I told you. In a divine little private hospital near Beekman Place. There was nothing to it. Once I was sure, we arranged it all in no time."

"Please, Clarry–" He had trouble with his voice. He closed his eyes and bowed his head and felt all the excitement and anticipation wither away and die in him. He lifted his head and forced himself to look at her. "Am I following you correctly? You've done something to it? A– an abortion?"

"Technically, I suppose. When you do it so early, I'm not even sure that's the right term for it. It really wasn't much more than an elaborate douche. I feel a bit pulled about, but the doctor says I'll be as good as new in a couple of days, practically virginal."

He looked at her and knew for the first time that he could hate her. He wanted to spring at her and beat her. He was restrained by the fact that she obviously wasn't well. "You had no right to–" His voice was flat and expressionless. "You're my wife. I'm your husband. You can't make decisions on your own that affect both of us."

"Exactly. We didn't plan on having children yet. It was an accident. If it had happened after day before yesterday…" She looked into his eyes and made a purring sound. "I let you have your way then, didn't I?" She knew she was playing with dynamite, but she would not give in to his silly sentimentality about babies. She had an obligation to him to keep him from being distracted from his main goal. She leaned toward him, and her manner softened. "I know you did your best to act pleased about the little accident, but you didn't fool me. You said yourself it would mean moving and finding somebody to take care of it and all the rest of it. We haven't time for that now. I can't be laid up just when you need me most. We still have plenty of time for a family later."

182

He stared at her as sterility seemed to become the condition of their lives. The creature they had made with love was gone. It took time for it to sink in. She had murdered love. Did she think she was so important to him that she could replace one of a man's most basic urges? Why had they got married? "I don't understand it." He forced words from the depths of outrage and desolation. "How did you arrange it? It's illegal. You let some doctor pull your body about, as you put it. I could have him put in jail. He must know that. How did you get him to do it?"

"Now, dearest, don't be melodramatic. It happens all the time. Naturally, reputable doctors have to be careful. Daddy was able to say the right word—"

His eyes suddenly blazed at her. "Your father?" he demanded. "He let you do this without speaking to me?" He sprang up, and his chair toppled with a thud. "Goddamn it, Clarry, how long is this going to go on? When are we going to do things for each other, with each other? Why is it always conflict? What are we always struggling for?"

She lifted her chin imperiously, and her eyes blazed back at him. "Plenty, and you know it. I'm not Mrs. Mouse, and you wouldn't want me if I were. What would you be if you hadn't found me? Darling David would still be looking after you. You'd be an arty faggot director without the guts to walk down the street with a boyfriend, let alone found a theater. Why are you so desperate to have children? Are you still trying to prove you're a he-man?"

"I don't need you to prove that," he shouted, giving vent at last to his rage and bereavement. "I've got a child. I just thought it would be nice to have one with you."

Silence left the words echoing around the room. Walter was breathing heavily. They stared at each other while Clara rose slowly. Her lips quivered and set firmly, and a smile lurked in their corners. Just when she feared she had overplayed her game, he delivered himself into her hands. "In that case, why all the fuss? I can understand a man wanting to produce evidence of his procreative powers—after all, he can't know what it's like to have a child. If you've done it, that should take care of your primitive little urges." She picked up her hat and gloves

**183**

and flipped them about in her hands. "Are you the father of Fay Kennicutt's little boy?" She looked at him calmly with the lurking smile.

There was another silence. He had recovered his control, but he wasn't sorry he had said it. The only thing he was sorry about was that she didn't appear to be hurt by it. "You can think anything you like," he said, trying to goad her further.

"It always struck me that little Gerald belonged in the Funny Coincidence Department. Born nine months after the Kennicutts agreed to put money in *The Forest*. I must arrange to see him sometime. I'm sure I'll be mad about Gerald." She approached him with a slight unsteadiness in her walk. There was no tenderness in his eyes, but she didn't flinch from them. She preferred his anger now to his soft, reproachful side. "Why don't you admit you're glad I did it? We've got to keep the decks cleared for action. You know that as well as I do."

How could he get at her, short of walking out and never coming back? "Maybe you're right, Clara," he said coldly. "Maybe the decks need clearing. I'll start with your father. If he thinks he can make my decisions for me, I'd better set him straight."

Her laughter rang with steel. "Hooray," she crowed. "Clear him out. You're the one who's wanted to be chummy with my family. I admit they're useful. If we're going to be chums, why not make the most of them? Daddy always knows exactly what to do, especially when it comes to getting around the law."

Walter turned abruptly and looked at the ornate Empire clock on the mantelpiece. "I'll go right away. I want to hear from his own lips what he was thinking. I'll take care of you later."

Clara laughed again. "It's about time you took charge. While you're at it, why not clear out David too?"

He swung back to her. "What's David got to do with it?"

"You say you want us to do things together," her voice rang out, defying him. "How can we if David's always there to hold your hand? Conflict! For years I've accepted and even tried to love a man who's in love with my husband. Don't you suppose that might cause a little conflict?"

"Don't be stupid, Clara. We got that straight right at the start. He's not in love with me and never has been."

"No, and he's never been to bed with a boy either. It's all just a joke. He's certainly not interested in the most important thing that's happening in the American theater. All he cares about is being with you. It's getting to be a public scandal, but you'd let everything go rather than lose David."

"I've had enough of this, Clara." His fists were once more ready to strike. "You said yourself we shouldn't pay any attention to that newspaper crap."

"I've told you, I've tried to love him. It isn't easy. You expect me to sit at home and have babies while David takes over your whole professional life. Well, I won't have it. He's not good enough for you. Everything I've done has always been for you. Everything *is* you. You're the biggest force the theater has had since God know when. It could be a little bit for us if you'd let it be. We don't need David anymore, and he agrees. I'd be begging you to give me babies if you'd recognize your own importance and take charge and not let him drag you down."

"Goddamn you. Why didn't you say any of this two days ago?" he raged, stunned that she would bring David into it to mitigate her own guilt.

"Because I'm not a blackmailer," she cried, her head lifting. "The baby's gone. You can suit yourself. I'm not going to try the usual female tricks on you." She let her body slump and turned from him, but not before he had had time to see the tears coaxed from her eyes.

He looked at her back and wondered what she thought she was accomplishing. She had taken from him the one gift she alone was capable of offering him, the promise of which had filled his love for her with more warmth and joy than he had ever known with her. Were they so completely out of touch? He could make another child, but the sterility of her attitude repelled him. She was prepared to barter for something so precious as parenthood. She would give him a child if he would get rid of David. If he stayed here another minute, he would begin to hate her. Perhaps her father could tell how she had been

185

brought to commit this outrage. "I suppose you should be taking it easy," he said with such indifference that it sounded almost contemptuous. "Give me ten minutes in the bathroom, and you'll have the place to yourself till this evening."

She waited until he was out of the room and then dropped into a chair. She knew she was bleeding again. The pain was intense, but she couldn't let him know. She must treat what she'd done as trivial, not worth serious attention. When she had allowed time enough for him to dress, she pulled herself to her feet and adopted her most serene manner and forced herself to move across the room, plumping a pillow, adjusting a flower in a vase. He would see there was nothing the matter with her.

He emerged looking stunning in a shirt he had designed for himself with a softly rolled Byronic collar and a dark suit of cashmere so fine that it molded to every line of his splendid body. The effect was elegant but somehow theatrical, as if he wished to mark his distance from the Washburns.

"Heavens, dearest," she said. "You still look much too young to be able to be a father. I've been thinking about your little bombshell. Gerald. I think I've taken it very well, but remember what I told you once before. I don't believe in the double standard. If that's the way you want it, I could let myself be interested in other men."

"Don't be cheap, Clara," he snapped. He hadn't begun to punish her. She remained peculiarly invulnerable. What did she think she had up her sleeve? "Anyway, I didn't mention Gerald. That's your idea."

She watched him leave. The door clicked behind him, and she dropped into a chair and released a sob and beat on its upholstered arms with her fists. Real tears streamed down her cheeks. It was fine for women like Fay, leading utterly empty and meaningless lives, to take their pleasures where they found them without worrying about the consequences. She was married to a genius, and she was responsible for guiding him around the pitfalls into which his weaknesses would lead him. Why did he suppose she had let her insides be torn up? For fun? He must know she wanted children as much as he did.

But she wanted other things too. She had bet her life on him. So far she was a winner, but she had the right to see that the return matched the outlay. She hadn't intended to go so far about David, but she felt circumstances finally permitted it. Walter was just climbing back from his failure, launching the project that would take the definitive measure of his genius. She had the right to a full partnership in the endeavor. David had outlived his usefulness, if he had ever had any beyond catering to Walter's soft, ambiguous side.

She took a deep breath and shook her hair back and pulled herself to her feet. She dragged herself into the bedroom and began to get out of her clothes, preparing herself to cope with the bloody swab she was supposed to replace.

Walter pushed the bell beside his in-laws' familiar front door, hoping that behind it he would learn the truth and find it possible for him to forgive Clara. Driving uptown in the taxi, he had tried to pin down her motives but had remained at a loss. Apparently her old jealousy of David had been revived during his absence, but would she risk wrecking their marriage to vie with David for power? Her father must have encouraged her for some reason. It was inexplicable, but he had to know.

The door was opened by an aged but surprisingly affable butler. "Good morning, Peters," Walter said and entered the massive dimness of the Washburn apartment.

"Welcome, Mr. Walter. Nobody told me to expect you, sir."

Since Walter rarely bothered with a coat or hat and wore neither now, there was nothing to detain him at the door. "I just dropped in for a minute. Is Mr. Washburn in his study?"

"Let's see."

Walter followed the butler down the corridor to a partly open door. Peters knocked and opened it farther. "It's Mr. Walter to see you, sir."

"Oh, yes, of course," a voice called from within. "Come in, my boy."

Peters stepped back, and Walter entered a heavily furnished room with books lining the walls. His father-in-law was seated beside an empty fireplace with a book in his hand. He looked up and settled his glasses on his nose. "Good morning. I don't suppose I have to get up for a young sprout like you. Sit down. Some sherry?"

Walter sat on the other side of the fireplace while Mr. Washburn gave the butler instructions. Walter looked him over, settling on his line of attack. He was a tall man and looked it even sitting down. In spite of his conservatively expensive clothes, he had a weathered look that Walter thought of as Western. He was bald, but his fringe of hair was spikey and untamed, suggesting the cowlick that Walter had seen in old photographs of him. Unlike the East Coast elite, he had no urbane aristocratic stamp. Walter would have cast him as a rich rancher rather than one of the city's cultural leaders. They exchanged a look that made Mr. Washburn close his book and put it on a table beside him. They were served sherry. "That's all, Peters. Close the door behind you."

"Well, Aleck, I guess you know why I'm here," Walter began.

"I wasn't surprised to see you. I'm told everything went very well."

"There's just one thing I want to know. Did Clara make it clear that she was acting without my permission?"

"She made it clear she didn't want you to know anything about it till it was done."

"Then why did you help her arrange it?"

"I don't think I follow you, Walter. Clara's my daughter. She's headstrong. I know she was capable of going ahead, with or without my help. I didn't want her to fall into the hands of some quack. That seems a natural reaction."

"But you don't agree I had the right to have a say in the matter?"

Aleck Washburn shifted his big body and looked at the ceiling. "I don't meddle in marriages, Walter. How was I to know the child was yours? Just because she said so? Have you thought about that?"

"No." He was so taken aback by the suggestion that for a moment he couldn't think of anything to say. "Did you have any reason to doubt it?"

"Frankly, no. Why should she lie to me about it? I just want you to see my position. Your manner is bordering on the offensive. I'm not accustomed to being called to account for my actions. You think I should

188

have consulted with you rather than help Clara carry out a decision she'd already made?"

"That's exactly my point."

"It might be a point worth considering if this were an ordinary marriage, but it isn't. Since you've raised the question, I'm sure you want me to speak frankly. You must know that we've never entirely approved of you as Clara's husband. You came from nowhere, but because you were a talented young man and you were both of age, we were obliged to close our eyes to your obvious disadvantages. For the time being, that is. We aren't obliged to keep them closed forever."

Walter's shock was so great that he didn't know whether to get up and walk out or burst into tears of wounded pride. He did neither. He sat briefly numbed by outrage. He had come from nowhere? It was the view he took of himself; but when a Washburn said it, it didn't sound the same. He thought of his parents. His mother had refused to come to his wedding ("We've never known people like that, and we don't want to start now"), and he had been grateful for her tact. He suddenly hated himself for having given way so readily. He should have insisted on their coming and forced the Washburns to acknowledge the Makins as their peers. He wasn't a snob. He had simply never felt that his background was relevant.

He sat back carefully as if sudden movement might break some balance in him. He wanted to hear everything his father-in-law had to say. "Would you like to tell me about my obvious disadvantages?" His voice was dark with intimations of a gathering storm.

"I don't think we need to belabor it. Your attitude to life is dangerously individualistic. I value the restraints of tradition. There are things about you that are–shall we say?–suspect. I don't suppose you'll deny that your partner is a…what we used to call a 'nelly boy.' It's an unsavory association for a man with a wife, especially now that it's getting into the papers."

His anger was given a simple focus. "My partner is my oldest friend. He's also a close friend of Clara's. I haven't seen his name in the paper except in connection with our professional activities."

"His name. Exactly. Friends of mine who know Broadway better than I do have explained the innuendoes that have been appearing about him recently."

"Very helpful of them, I'm sure. There's still something I don't understand. He was my best man at the wedding. He's been around ever since. Now all of a sudden he seems to have something to do with Clara's having an abortion. Can you explain that?"

Washburn removed his glasses and held them to the light. He replaced them and turned them on Walter. "I'm a man of the world, my boy. I'm afraid one runs into this sort of thing more often than one used to. Not long ago my cousin Myrtle had the wool pulled over her eyes by one of these fellows. She married him, and less than a week after the wedding she caught him—maybe I should say, 'it'—in bed with the chauffeur. He got out of town in short order, I can tell you that. And we didn't have any trouble recovering the settlement Myrtle had been damn fool enough to make on him. I don't know many reasons why a healthy woman would want to get rid of a legitimate child—insanity in the family, maybe? Or if she finds out her husband is a pervert? Wouldn't you say that could be a reason?"

Walter's fists were clenched. This was a day for hitting Washburns. The muscles of his jaws clamped his teeth together. A sick woman and an old man. He forced himself to relax. "By God, Aleck, I know you're an older man and all that, but watch it. I'm beginning to want to knock those glasses off your self-satisfied face."

"I'd be glad to waive the age difference. I think I can still take care of you, young fellow. You're cocky for a man who hasn't got much more than a dime to his name. I guess it must make you feel good to know that Clara's the sole heiress to one of the country's great fortunes. We take a keen interest in who *her* heir is going to be. So far, I'm not completely comfortable with the thought of your being in a position of such privilege and responsibility."

"Goddamn you, Aleck! Have you forgotten who I am? I've accomplished more in five years than you ever will, even if you live to be 100, which I sincerely doubt."

Washburn favored him with a forbidding smile. "You're in no position to judge my accomplishments, Walter, however meager they may be. You're still on the fringes. You're getting ready to move into areas of real power, and you're counting on the backing of some of the most influential men in the country—Ben Williams, Herb Altenthrope, Chris Morgenham—I know them all, and I know their attitude toward lilies. That sort is getting to be as much of a threat to this country as the commies. They're all in cahoots, if you ask me. Now these men aren't going to let the closest thing this country's ever had to a national theater fall into the wrong hands. I admire your ambition, but if you turn out to be a flash in the pan, Clara's apt to get disenchanted quickly. There's when the differences in your background will begin to count. If your marriage breaks up, I wouldn't want children to give you a hold on the family. Of course, when we got through with you, your rights would be nil, but why ask for complications? You understand my thinking?"

His anger grew and became exultant. He no longer had to keep up pretenses of courtesy or respect. "Thanks for making it so clear. You don't give a damn about people. You actually see yourself as the head of a goddamned dynasty. You wanted Clara to have an abortion."

"She wanted it, and it certainly seemed the sensible thing to do at this time."

Walter leaped up, hoping that his father-in-law wouldn't see that he was trembling. His movements were awkward with stress. He shoved his hands into his pockets to brace himself. "I ought to make a charge against you and that doctor for conspiracy. You've committed a crime. How would you like to go to jail, Aleck?" His voice was louder than he had intended and was rough with anger. He tried to match his adversary's composure. "I'll make allowances for you this time. Just don't forget that my lack of background makes me quite indifferent to the traditions you probably think count more than decent feelings."

"You'll learn eventually that feelings don't stand much chance against tradition. For one thing, Washburns don't go to jail."

"That worries you, does it?" Walter managed his most devilish smile, feeling that he had finally scored. "It should. But I won't give you

191

a chance to make any more dangerous mistakes. I'm going to forbid Clara to see you again. Has she known how you feel about me?"

"We're no barbarians. We've tried to put a good face on it. I made it clear that I approved her decision yesterday." Washburn rose, and Walter poised himself in case the older man had decided to "take care" of him. He longed for an attack. His lust to counterattack was almost obscene. He wanted to snatch the glasses off and beat his face to a pulp. Clara's husband was a pervert, a lily? He wanted to make her father grovel at his feet and retract his words. He backed away from his enemy, the thoughts of revenge too sweet to trust himself within reach of him.

"You're declaring war, are you, young fellow?" Washburn said, oblivious of the violence he had so nearly unleashed. "You shouldn't have been so careless with your money. You'll need a lot of it if you're going to take me on."

"I'm not going to take you on. I'm leaving you off." He loaded his words with disdain. If he couldn't hit an old man, he could at least mortally insult him. "You play no part in my plans for the future, Aleck. I don't think there'll be much of a war. Don't forget, the heir to the dynasty is going to be called Makin. I'll teach him to despise you and everything you stand for as thoroughly as I do." He didn't wait to enjoy the effect of his words. He made for the door in good order, although his heart was pounding and his stomach churning. His trembling became more pronounced as he strode down the corridor. He was aware of Peters holding the door open for him and of their exchanging routine words of farewell. Then he was in a hotel bar a block away with the better part of a double whisky inside him.

Once he had calmed down, he wasn't greatly alarmed by the interview. He didn't think Aleck could, or would, hurt him; the Washburns' sense of family would compel him to keep the rift out of sight. It simply marked the end of Walter's thinking of himself as in any way a Washburn, the end of regarding Clara as specially privileged. She was a girl who happened to be his wife. It was time he taught her a lesson. How dare she make a crack about his being an arty faggot? Had she said something to her father that made him feel free to refer to his partner as a "nelly boy"? What about McClaren? Why all the queer references all of a sudden? He wasn't going to put up with it. In a few more years she would have several million dollars of her own (he was looking forward to them more than he had expected), but meanwhile, if he wanted children, she would damn well have them. She would show decent respect for his partner, who also happened to be his dearest friend. When she was rich, he might consider a new set of rules.

He reminded himself that he was due for lunch soon with one of the influential men Aleck had mentioned and ordered another drink. He was aware that a youngish man standing near him at the bar was trying to pick him up. This didn't happen often outside the theater district. He looked at himself in the mirror behind the bar to see if he could spot anything that suggested he was an easy mark, a "lily." His clothes were original but not extreme. He wasn't remotely pretty. If he was attractive-looking, it was in a slightly odd but wholly masculine way. He hadn't adopted any of the camp jargon that was current in the theater, so there was no risk of his saying something that would give people the wrong idea. He looked ridiculously young, but since he was only 25, there was nothing he could do about that.

The scene with Aleck hit him in the bladder. He felt as if he were bursting. He took a hasty swallow of his fresh drink and left it on the bar and went to the men's room. He was standing relieving himself when he heard the door open behind him and realized that his move might be interpreted as an invitation. He was jostled slightly as somebody moved in close beside him at the urinal. It was the young man from the bar. He was good-looking in an all-American way, slightly reminiscent of Harry and about the age that Harry would be now, with a curious quality of slightly worn glamour as if he were used to people paying attention to him. All this Walter had noted at the bar without really looking at him.

Walter kept his eyes front and shifted his hands slightly to conceal himself. His time in the Army had taught him to take this sort of thing in stride. In a world of young men, uprooted, in uniform, on the move, unorthodox sexual advances were commonplace. His neighbor put a hand on his hip and nudged him with his elbow. Walter's eyes strayed involuntarily. He tried to pull them away, but they were held by the size of the organ that was being displayed. The hand on it fondled it discreetly, making it lengthen astonishingly. When it looked as if it were getting out of control, it was somehow returned to cover.

"I'm staying here," the young man said quietly. "Would you like to come up to my room?"

Walter was prepared to be indignant but found that he wasn't. Perhaps his wife's and his father-in-law's practically calling him a faggot had exhausted his indignation. His wife had murdered his child; she had reduced their lovemaking to an act as empty as anything he might do with a man. He had always wondered if the stories he'd heard about 12 and 14 inches were possible. His neighbor's curiously glamorous air, however worn, attracted and intrigued him. He had half an hour to kill. "Why not?" he said.

"I'll meet you at the elevators."

Walter heard the door open and close while he was fastening himself up. He remembered things he had been told about blackmailers. Never fall for a setup. If anybody had reason to expect him at this bar at this hour there might be cause for caution. He had turned into the first bar he had come to, scarcely knowing where he was. The young man was apparently as intent on discretion as Walter should be. They wouldn't be seen leaving here, or the bar, together. This was a first-class hotel room, not a hangout for hustlers. He returned to the bar and swallowed down his drink and paid and took the door leading to the lobby. The young man was waiting for him without appearing to do so, and they rode up silently in an elevator.

In another few moments a hotel room door closed behind them, and they were undressing. Walter found that his exhibitionism remained a dependable stimulant. He was simultaneously naked and erect when his companion darted past him to a bureau. He turned back with a camera in his hands. Walter heard a click before he could duck behind a chair.

194

"Hey, what the hell are you doing?" he demanded.

The young man laughed. "Don't worry. I'll develop it myself. You're the new star of my collection."

Walter postponed deciding what to do about a stranger's having such a photograph while he took in the anatomical phenomenon on display before him. The young man's pleasing body was dwarfed by the instrument that was slowly lifting before it. Inch was added to inch, but it had yet to achieve full erection. It seemed to Walter too big for any practical purposes, but it was an extraordinary spectacle, a monument to the male organ.

They met in the middle of the room, in preliminary exploration of each other. His partner's erection became staggeringly complete when he touched it. Walter felt a sense of achievement in having produced such a monumental response. As his eyes grew accustomed to it, he guessed that it was probably about a foot long, but ordinary terms of measurement didn't seem to apply. A foot of rope was nothing. A foot of cock looked bigger than the body to which it belonged. His own was modest by comparison.

When they lay together in bed, Walter couldn't deny that he was enjoying himself. Although it was no longer something he would seek, he still felt a special edge of excitement in being like this with a man. By being outside the norm, it seemed to entail a more than normal exposure of being. He suddenly felt closer to this stranger than he did to some of his closest friends. He looked into his eyes and saw old wounds in them and a spark of fear in their depths. He would make it his business to erase that look for a little while. Their bodies reveled together. His partner's body was trim, supple, well-proportioned except for the phenomenon that swung against him like a truncheon while its owner did avidly expert things with his mouth.

When Walter looked at him again, his hair was awry with his exertions. His eyes were peacefully intent with pleasure. Years had fallen away. Walter's memory was jolted with a shock of recognition.

"My God," he exclaimed. "You're Frank Farley, aren't you?"

"Didn't you recognize me before?"

195

"I knew there was something." Walter remembered an extraordinarily beautiful youth who had appeared in a few films when he was at college and had soon dropped from view. Now that he knew, he could see the beauty still lingering beneath the coarsening of time. "My goodness. You gave me some very peculiar dreams when I was a kid. Had I but known. Not in my wildest imagination—" He reached for the monument, and they laughed together. Time had run out. He let Frank bring them both to climax. When it was done, he pulled himself out of bed and headed for his clothes.

"I've got to get going," he said, starting to dress. He had to get the photograph and wondered how to go about it. He was aware of Frank Farley's moving about the room while he put his socks on. Farley came and stood close to him, combed, wearing a dressing gown, looking his age again.

"When are we going to see each other again," Frank asked.

"I don't know. I'm awfully busy." Walter hoped it didn't sound too dismissive. He didn't want to be stuck with a faded Hollywood starlet.

"I want to see you again. I'm not used to begging. People have offered me a lot of money just to see my cock. You did a lot more than see it."

Walter felt a stirring of uneasiness. He glanced at Farley, assessing the shorter, slighter figure. He could handle him. "You aren't suggesting I should pay, are you? I've never paid for sex in my life."

"I shouldn't think you'd have to. Your body—it's absolutely fabulous. Most boys would envy that cock. I liked us together. How about making a date?"

Walter smiled more comfortably. He had been imagining things. "Well, sure. I liked it too. We'll see. I know it's not possible for the next week or two. I'm in town on business."

"No, you're not, Walter. Why tell me a thing like that?"

Walter's uneasiness became active alarm. He was a blasted idiot to think he could indulge in little adventures as if he were still an unknown kid. "Well, I've been away," he amended. "You know who I am, do you?"

"Of course. That's another reason I'd like to talk to you. I thought we could discuss your production plans."

"You mean for a job? If you know my work, you know I never use stars." It wasn't the first time he'd used the line. Actors were so flattered by it that they didn't notice they were being turned down. He had to handle Farley with kid gloves. Although he spoke quietly, something about his manner suggested danger, something corrupt, perhaps un-balanced. He hadn't forgotten the photograph. "Of course, if you want a reading like everybody else, I could arrange it when the time comes."

"No, I wouldn't like that. As you say, I'm a star. I don't take money, but everybody needs help at times. Considering what's happened, I sort of hoped we'd be friends. I can't wait to see that photograph."

The hint of a threat was unmistakable. This was turning into a nightmare. Only minutes ago he had felt something close to tender-ness for this man. He cursed himself for being a sentimental ass. Here was a face that was definitely going to get smashed, but he wanted to accomplish his purpose before permitting himself that pleasure. "I didn't say anything about not being friends." He would fire an actor who read a line with so little conviction. He had been about to put on his shirt but dropped it again. Perhaps a bit of nakedness would rekin-dle a sexual spark and give him an advantage. He moved closer to his adversary and tried to pump up his charm. "I'm counting on your let-ting me have that photograph, including the negative. You took it with-out asking. That's not the sort of things friends do."

"I didn't make you take your clothes off and get a hard-on. Lots of people have told me you're straight, having a wife and all, but I can spot a gay guy when I see one. I guess you're anxious for people not to know. I don't blame you. I thought it couldn't hurt me, but the studio cracked down when I got careless. If people knew who took that pho-tograph, it could be bad for you."

Walter's scalp crawled. His heart gave a leap of fear. His blood turned to ice. He glanced quickly at the bureau. He had the impression that Farley had left the camera there. He didn't see it. He remembered hearing drawers opening and closing while he was putting on his

**197**

socks. He made a dash for the bureau, prepared to demolish Farley if he tried to interfere. He pulled open the top drawer and ran his hands through the socks and handkerchiefs and underwear he found there. He shoved it closed and pulled open the second drawer and created disorder among some shirts.

"Here, Walter." Farley spoke from behind him.

He swung around almost with a swagger at having succeeded so easily and found himself facing a gun. Farley was standing near the bedside table pointing it at him. The nightmare had become an impossible real-life melodrama.

"I'm not a muscle boy, but I know how to take care of myself," Farley said. "Do you want me to call the house detective and tell him you made a pass at me and are trying to make trouble? I think you'd better go before something happens we wouldn't want. When I develop the picture, I'll get in touch, and we'll have a talk."

Walter stood without moving a muscle, trying to convince himself that somebody was actually pointing a gun at him. The only certainty was that he had to get the photograph. He didn't think Farley would want to kill him. If he got wounded, he wouldn't be in a worse mess than he was in already. He took a quick breath and sprang forward, expecting a bullet to rip into him at any moment and wondering what it would feel like. The shot made a sound like a cork being pulled. A shout of protest gathered in him as he prepared to feel the sting of pain, to be brought to a standstill, but his forward rush carried him on. He knocked the little gun aside with one fist and drove the other into Farley's face. Farley toppled back onto the bed. Walter was on him, pummeling him furiously. He felt his knuckles crack as they smashed into bone.

"Not my face," Farley cried.

"Where's the camera, you son of a bitch," Walter gasped. "Give me the fucking camera, or you won't have any face." His aching fists continued to pound flesh while his victim thrashed about under him and tried to cover his head with his arms.

"In the wastebasket," he cried. "Under the desk."

**198**

Walter landed a final blow and wrenched himself up and lurched to his prize, spent, shaking violently, his chest heaving. He found the camera and clawed at it with trembling fingers until he found the right knob and it sprang open. He tore at the film and ripped it out and sent it unrolling across the floor. He dropped the camera and returned to the chair where he had left his clothes.

Farley pulled himself upright and sat huddled on the edge of the bed. One shoulder of his dressing gown was ripped, his face was buried in his hands, he was weeping. "I wouldn't have done anything bad," he moaned. "Those bullets are just blanks. Oh, God, I've had a bad time. I thought you might help me."

He was pitiful, but Walter didn't pity him. His throat was still choked with rage and terror. It was a commonplace show-business story—up one day and down the next—but it shouldn't turn you into a blackmailer. Fuck him. He managed to knot his tie and got into his jacket and felt safer. He made a habit of carrying little cash, but he always kept a $50 bill folded away in his wallet. He pulled it out and dropped it on a table near the door.

"You're probably used to more, but that's all I have on me," he said, barely able to keep his voice even. "Don't threaten people."

A sob broke from the actor. "I'm still good, damn it!" he blurted through his hands. "You should've given me a chance."

Walter looked at the defeated figure on the bed and hated himself for being here. "You should try giving yourself a chance," he said. He pulled open the door and hurried down the corridor, breathing deeply in an effort to calm the tumult that was churning within him. He was out of it and safe, but he felt no satisfaction in his victory, only terror and shame at having got himself into the situation. He ran down several flights of the service stairs so that he wouldn't be seen getting into an elevator on Farley's floor. He mustn't let himself think about it now. He had to get through lunch with Aleck's influential friend. They were meeting at a nearby restaurant. Walter took time in the men's room to wash up and retie his tie and comb his hair. His hands hurt. He was grateful that he was no longer trembling. By not attempting the charm that he was in no condition to exert, he made himself sound like a tough-minded businessman, and lunch went better than he had any right to expect.

"I'll tell you something, Walter," his host said over coffee. "I don't want this to sound anti-Semitic, but if you were just another Broadway producer, I don't think you'd get the support you need. You know what I mean. I sometimes think we wouldn't have any theater without the Jews, but, after all, it's business with them. You're out to make a big cultural contribution to the country, and a few of us are happy to see one of us downtrodden Gentiles taking the lead. You've got a lot going for you—your family connections and so forth—but the main thing is you've served your country. You've got a fine record. I'm all for you. I don't mind saying that my faith in this country is strengthened by young fellows like you."

Walter blushed with shame. He was a fraud and a hypocrite. He felt obliged to stick his neck out to recover some shreds of his self-respect. "Of course, what I'm getting at is a theater for all the people," he said. "Jews, Negroes. For instance, most theaters make a policy of keeping Negroes out of the orchestra. I won't have that. I'm looking for plays by Negroes. We're not going to make concessions to anybody's prejudices. I want to make that clear because I'm going to want a lot of money from you guys."

"Well, you're getting into something that's bound to be controversial. So much the better, I say. We haven't fought this war to preserve all our old attitudes. We've got a scrappy president. Harry's a good friend of mine. I'm going to write him about this. You can count on me, Walter. I think it's truly inspiring."

He was a hero. He could do no wrong. Thinking of all that he had almost destroyed little more than an hour ago, he was appalled by his irresponsibility. If Farley had been tough, he would be done for. Cousin Myrtle's husband and the chauffeur. Cold sweat broke out on his body. He almost questioned his right to go on with the project. He was asking important people to commit an act of faith in him, right up to the president of the United States. Jesus Christ.

200

He was glad to find David at the office when he got there. He could not tell David, or anyone, about Frank Farley; but he could talk about what had led up to it and perhaps get some things straight in his mind. He counted on the strong currents of their mutual devotion to carry him through this awful day. He asked David to join him and told Alice not to disturb them.

"Is that all right with you, old pal? You're not expecting anything earth-shattering in the next hour or so?"

"Nothing that won't improve with age," David said. "You're looking pretty solemn this afternoon, honey."

"It's been one of those days." He shut them in. His office was furnished like a living room, with a handsome Directoire desk, where he sat when he had paperwork. He dropped onto a sofa, and David chose a comfortable chair. Walter told him about Clara and the scene they had had. David listened with growing concern.

"This is serious," he said. "We're going to have to do something."

"What? If she's going to run off and have an abortion when she feels like it, how can I stop her?"

"Arrange things so she won't have to."

"We're married, for God's sake, David. She has nothing to complain about. At least, she hasn't so far. What more can I arrange?"

"Did she say she wants me out?"

"I wasn't going to tell you, but that's what it amounted to. I'm sure she didn't mean it, but even if she did, she knows I wouldn't listen. It's pushing me in a way I can't be pushed. She's much more clever than that, more devious. If she really wanted you out, she wouldn't say so. She'd concoct some plot."

"Maybe she has, without our noticing. Anyway, this is a good time to think about it before we get going on something new. What else did she say?"

"The usual bit about your wicked ways. She says you're in love with me and everybody knows it. She was pretty overwrought."

David looked at him and threw his lighter into the air and caught it. "She's only partly right. Nobody knows."

"Don't be silly. We talked about all that long ago."

"No we didn't. We talked about falling in and out of love with each other like kids. That was way back at the beginning. Right? Right. I fell in love with you for real when we were doing *Forest*. So what? Clara must know you're somebody people fall in love with. *She* did. I don't think that has much to do with it, as far as she's concerned, except to embarrass you, which she knows it would. Let's talk about my getting out." He rose and moved around behind the chair. "Clara will find this hard to believe, but I want to give her a clear field."

Walter looked at him for a long moment, firmly holding his eyes while his embarrassment passed. "Come here," he said.

David came back around the chair. Walter reached for his hand as he approached and pulled him down beside him. He put his arm around him and stroked the side of his head and dropped his hand to his shoulder and gripped it.

"OK. You're the only guy I've ever known who's made me think it might be fun to be queer. Now let's talk sense. We'll fold the company. OK? There's no point keeping it on ice. We'll assign ourselves new identities. We'll think up a grand title for Clara. She'll like that. She can be executive director or something. You'll be business administrator. I'll be artistic god. Everything will go on the same as before. I'd like to make an announcement that Makin-Fiedler is being dissolved and get as much publicity as possible so when I talk to the money boys there won't be any confusion about our taking a profit. Is that all right?"

"Sure, as far as it goes. But let's talk about my quitting, honey. I mean it. Clara doesn't just want a title. She wants to run the show, and I completely understand her. I gave her a pretty free hand with the last one, and it wasn't her fault it flopped. I was watching for her to make mistakes, but she didn't. And she's right about this not being my kind of thing. You know me, honey. Showy. With plenty of dough to pay my bill at Cartier's."

It took Walter the time that David was speaking to realize that he meant it, and then everything in him rejected the suggestion. Was Clara right in saying that he would give up anything rather than lose

David? Probably. He was in a mood to question his qualifications as director of a semi-official institution. Kowtowing to political and financial powers wasn't his line. He had made that clear with Aleck and again at lunch. Why not go on as before, doing their successful but first-rate work? They had accomplished nearly as much as he would with the new project, and he could make another fortune. On a purely practical level, David was essential as a buffer. Working directly with Clara would be too nerve-wracking. He could battle fraternally with David over a production budget, but it wouldn't be the same with Clara. Nothing would be the same. He tightened his grip on David's shoulder.

"I'm not going to let you step aside, old pal," he said with finality. "I can't imagine doing anything without you. Maybe we should go on with Makin-Fiedler, and the hell with this other business."

"I thought we were supposed to talk some sense. Look at it from Clara's point of view. She's been in it from the beginning, and she's worked hard so she'd be able to take over from me. That's been more or less understood all along."

"Oh, no, it hasn't," Walter said. "I want her as a wife and the mother of my children, not as a business partner. If Clara were needed here in the office, she'd have all the more reason to go on having abortions indefinitely."

"I'm not so sure. If she felt firmly in control here, she'd probably find that having babies was an interesting sideline. She wants all of you. I understand that, God knows; but I can't have it, so it's probably time for me to make it on my own. To tell the truth, I've had a fantastic offer from Hollywood. I can have my own production unit—big money and no risk. I've been seriously considering it."

"I see." Walter felt a stab of resentment. How could be mention Hollywood compared to what they could do together? It was just talk, an effort to feel his way in a situation created by Clara. "This is insane," he burst out. "Clara has an abortion, and here we are talking about splitting up. Talk about devious. How does she do it? I'm not going to let her get away with it."

David put his hand on Walter's knee. "Let's forget about her for the moment. Let's look at it the way it is. I've watched you start out as my assistant and take over from me and move way out ahead of me. I've loved every minute of it. It's been bigger than anything I ever expected, and I've done all right. Now it's getting so we have to keep me in the background. Frankly, I don't want to hobnob with Harrimans and Rockefellers and Astors. I'll never be respectable, even when I'm married. I'll feel at home in Hollywood. There's always room for one more freak."

"But damn it, it wouldn't be any fun without you," Walter protested.

"Oh, honey, you're not going to have time for fun. It's going to be big, important, impressive work. Nobody but you would get into it. It's got to be your show, or it won't work. I know you. You'll be hand-engraving the tickets. All you need is a good production man, and you've got her. Aside from everything else, I'll never get married as long as I'm with you. I can't explain it, but I know I've let you get too big in my life."

For the first time Walter tried to face it and imagine what it would be like without him. No one to share the thousand private jokes that had grown up over the years. No flashing teeth and rolling eyes to remind him what it had been like in the beginning. No one to make fun of him. No one to turn to for unquestioning support and affection. Losing David and his child in the same day was too much. He leaned back and put his hands on top of his head and looked at the ceiling. His eyes filled. He closed them and let the tears spill over. "Oh, God, David," he groaned. "Why does everything get spoiled?"

David leaned over him and kissed his forehead. "Thanks, honey. I've had a few cries myself thinking about it. You'll never know what it was like being your best man. That's when I knew it couldn't last forever."

Walter pulled himself upright and brushed away at his tears and looked at him. "Because of Clara? You swear you wouldn't let her squeeze you out?"

"With Clara, I'm never quite sure of anything. If she were pregnant and couldn't do the job, I'd turn Hollywood down and wait and see. As it is, you don't need me. If I weren't sure of that, I wouldn't go."

"Does she know you've been thinking about it?"

"I don't see how she could. You mean, about the offer? I haven't discussed it with her."

Walter was alert for a beat of hesitation in his voice, a fleeting shadow in his eyes, but detected nothing. "And you really have a big offer? I guess I ought to be congratulating you instead of sulking over your walking out on me."

David laughed with the old exuberant toss of the head. "Oh, honey, I'm not walking out on you. You know that. There's no rush. I should stick around another month or two until Clara and I get the details ironed out. Things change. It's as simple as that. As far as I'm concerned, I can stop trying so hard and settle for what I was in the first place. I guess that's the way it should be at 30. We've had a good run, old pal."

Walter leaned forward and kissed him on the mouth. They looked at each other with laughter in their eyes. "Yeah," Walter said, drawing it out to encompass a wealth of years and shared accomplishment. If Clara gloated over this, a Washburn would finally get hit. He still couldn't believe it was happening. Was this the way the loving, working friendship of all his important years would end, with a quiet talk, an embrace? It would be easier if they had had a screaming row. He tried to think of things that would help him cut the bond. Perhaps he wouldn't have to read any more libelous innuendoes about himself in the columns. Perhaps this would satisfy Clara at last. So what? Nothing reconciled him to losing David. He preferred to think it would all blow over. David agreed that there was time. He squeezed David's hand and stood. "What're you doing later?" he asked.

"This evening? Nothing in particular. Meeting Paul for dinner."

"Can I join you?"

"Wonderful. Better yet, let's make it just us. I'll call Paul off."

"He won't mind?"

"I live with him, honey. I'm not married to him."

He would call Clara and, for the first time in their lives without a compelling excuse, tell her he wasn't going to spend the evening with

205

her. Let her have a bad day too. He looked down at David and chuck-led. "We ought to go out to New Brunswick and have a drink at that bar next to the theater."

"Oh, no. That would be too much like an ending. Nothing's ended, honey. I'll always be around when you need me." David rose, and they faced each other.

"You're sure of that?" Walter looked without embarrassment into his lively, loving eyes. "I'm going to take you at your word."

"You can, honey. You know that."

Over drinks at "21" they drifted easily into the intimacy of the old days. By the time they had finished a leisurely dinner, Walter was re-gretting that they hadn't had more evenings like this in recent years and promised himself that they would in the future. He was more than ever convinced that this afternoon's talk had been only exploratory; they had reached no decision. He said as much when they were both putting money on the table to cover the bill. Noting that the $50 bill was missing from his wallet, he flushed with shame and distaste and went on quickly to divert his thoughts. "You won't sign that contract without telling me, will you?" he demanded.

"You don't want me to?"

"Of course not. They'll wait, won't they?"

"Oh, sure, I can stall for time. Why?"

"I want Clara to ask you to stay. What would you say to that?"

"I'd say you're the Wizard of Oz."

Their eyes met, and the gleam in David's made it clear that they had both responded in the same way to the evening. Their partnership was too good to be dissolved. The battle with Clara had just begun.

It was almost midnight when they parted, and on the way home Walter had the taxi make a slight detour to pick up the first editions of the morning papers at the all-night newsstand in front of Grand Cen-tral. He glanced at the headlines by the light that bored intermittently into the back of the taxi like an erratic lighthouse as he was driven downtown. The front page of the *News* was splashed as usual with thick black ink. The light was tinged with red when the words leaped up at him: MOVIE STAR SLAIN! Then he was in the dark with an old movie still of the beautiful youth who had been Frank Farley imprinted on his mind. The lighthouse beam probed and lingered long enough for his eyes to scoop up the first few paragraphs of the story: "Discovered late yesterday afternoon... lavish East Side hotel... knife wounds... naked body mutilated..."

Darkness. Shock paralyzed his mind and body. A stab of light. "Police are following leads provided by a collection of photos of nude male models found..." Icy terror clutched his heart, and he began to tremble all over.

Knife wounds. Death hadn't been caused by a fluke blow to the solar plexus. The time of death had been fixed to within an hour or so of the body's discovery. He could account for every minute of the day from 1:30 on. Nobody had seen them speak to each other. He managed to light a cigarette with a trembling hand and sat with muscles tensed to control the shaking until he was deposited in front of his door. He let himself in to a silent apartment and made a tiptoed dash to the bedroom to make sure Clara was asleep. He returned to the living room and tore through the other papers. Only the *News* carried the story. Poor Frank probably wouldn't attract much more attention dead than alive. He poured himself a stiff drink and sat beside a lamp and forced himself to read the account word for word.

It was scrappy, obviously hustled into the paper at the last minute to provide a juicy headline. The sexual implications were cautiously stated but not clear. Aside from the reference to the nude photographs, no indication was given of what direction the police investigation was taking. Would they want to talk to everybody who had seen him during the day? His hand still shook as he took a hasty swallow of his drink. It was unlikely that the elevator boy had recognized him or noticed that he had got off at Frank's floor, but if necessary, he could deny it. He had got off at a lower floor. To see whom? No. That wouldn't work. He would have to say that Farley approached him as he was leaving the bar and asked to speak to him in private about a job. He had gone up to the room for a few minutes and that was that. Would he be expected to take the initiative in reporting the encounter to the police? Why should he? He talked to dozens of people about jobs every day. Unless he had some evidence to offer, it wasn't his business if they got murdered afterward. He drained his glass and rose to replenish it and roamed the room blindly. He became aware of the suit he was wearing, the suit he had worn all day. It was conspicuous. He would ask Clara to send it to the cleaner in the morning. There was nothing strange about that. She always sent this things out after he'd worn them a couple of times. Get it out of the house for a week. Why? He just didn't want to be seen in it for a while.

Did the police have some method of developing film even after it had been exposed? Certainly not. Was he sure he had exposed all of it? Yes, he had seen it snap back when it ran out to the spool. There were no grounds whatsoever for his being implicated.

He would have to tell Clara he had run into Farley in case anything came out. He had to have Clara on his side. He would tell her David wanted to go to Hollywood. It was probably just as well. He shouldn't stand in the way of David's big chance.

He found himself pouring another drink and saw that his hands were finally steady. Another drink, and he'd be able to sleep. He had himself under control except for a knot of dread somewhere around his heart and an occasional wave of weakness that seemed to affect his legs. It suddenly occurred to him that he might not have been seen leaving, that the murderer might have gone to Frank's room unobserved, and he stumbled to a chair and fell into it. Oh, Christ! His lunch date. Alice. David. He could answer any questions, but to be brought into it at all, even for a routine check, could wreck him. He gulped down his drink, trying to knock himself out, and dragged himself up unsteadily to slip into the haven of bed with Clara. He vowed to obscure gods that he would forget his grievance with her if he were spared any involvement with Frank's gruesome fate.

He woke up during the night with his heart pounding, fighting his way out of a dream. Frank Farley came crashing into his consciousness. He stifled a moan. In his numbed and agitated state, it seemed to him that he carried some fatal curse that threatened every male he touched. Lying in the dark was a torment, suspended by fitful sleep. He was up early, feeling ghastly, but thankful for the sanity of daylight. If the police wanted to question him, they would surely do so discreetly, without its getting to the press.

The story was in all the papers during the day, but only a couple of the more sensational ones gave it a big play. None of them carried any hint that the police were nearing a solution. The knot of dread continued to weigh on his chest. A random reminder of yesterday's events could make his legs feel as if they would buckle. He tried desperately to think of somebody who might be able to tell him what was going on behind the scenes, who wouldn't think it odd his asking. He didn't see how he could get through another day like this. He felt as if he were suffocating.

Clara noticed his strange mood but supposed he was upset about David's leaving. He suggested that she sound out the partner about his Hollywood plans. When she did so, David seemed puzzled at first, but when she told him it was Walter's understanding that he was accepting the offer, he agreed breezily that it was all settled. This long-awaited triumph so delighted her that she told Walter that evening that she thought they could start having children as soon as they had nursed Theatre Today through its first season. The announcement didn't pull him out of his strange withdrawal.

The Farley story dropped out of the news the day after that. Walter had to struggle with himself to keep from calling the police just to see if they were interested in what he was prepared to tell them. He even asked Clara if she thought he should, and she brushed aside the question as if it weren't worth a reply. He had read his Dostoyevsky. He knew he mustn't allow his sense of guilt to draw him into the crime.

When the papers announced the following day that a suspect had been arrested, he was so relived that he almost wept. He didn't even bother to read the story beyond seeing that it was a young waiter who had been fired by the hotel a week earlier. By this time he was resigned to David's departure. They had referred to it a few times as if it were a foregone conclusion. In retrospect, David's declaration of love seemed dangerous and unhealthy, a bar to their old, easy relationship. He and Clara would be Theatre Today. He would prove to Aleck and all the Washburns that he was a match for them.

She puts the telephone down and remains standing in front of it, but somehow withdrawing from it in a mime of displeased incredulity. Her back is turned, so he can't see what is going on in her face; but he will remember the moment always, a sort of watershed, marking Before and After.

"How very odd," Clara said.

"What's the matter?" Walter asked, looking over the paper, intrigued by her tone of voice.

"Three million dollars is the matter." She moved away from the fanciful Gothic console, which was the telephone's resting place, but cast a lingering puzzled glance back at it. "Guildenstern, Guildenstern, Rosencrantz, and Guildenstern say there's been a hitch. They say I should've received some sort of court order. There *was* a funny looking paper in the mail the other day. I don't understand. It's always been perfectly clear that the money was to be paid over to me on my 30th birthday."

"That's certainly the impression you gave me when I married you. I was counting on it for our old age."

"It's nice of you to joke about it, dearest, but I'm rather upset."

"Well, what's the problem? Your birthday isn't for another couple of months, thank God. I'm sure you're suddenly going to shrivel up into a ghastly old hag. Won't they give it to you then?"

"That's what I'm telling you, dearest. They've just told me they won't. On and on about writs and injunctions and things. I'll have to go see them. I couldn't make head or tail of it on the phone. They even said something that sounded as if Daddy had something to do with it."

Walter tossed the paper aside and stood, shoving his hands into the pockets of his dressing gown. "Aha. Aleck strikes back. He's taken his sweet time about it. Maybe this is what he's been waiting for all these years. How many years has it been since our last charming meeting? Four? Five? Good lord. Does he have any control over the money?"

"How could he? I'm not a minor."

"No, Clarry, you're not." Nor did she look it, although he couldn't see that she had changed much in the ten years or more since they had met. She had put on no weight, nor acquired any greater assurance, since that would have been impossible. There was a new slightly sharp brittleness in her manner, but this didn't suggest maturity so much as a habit of making decisions and issuing commands.

Or perhaps it was the visible face of sterility. He associated maturity with ripeness. Clara hadn't ripened; she was a splendid tree that had borne no fruit. He had come to think of her more as an extension of himself than as a lover. She had become too essential to the operation of Theatre Today for them to have thought much about children again. Their professional partnership was a complete success. He still missed David, but Walter knew now that he hadn't always been good for him. David had offered escape, an opportunity to indulge his sense of fun. Clara provided something more important for him, and he knew it; the steel of his ambition was welded to the steel of her ambition for him.

"I have a million things to do at the office," she said. They didn't approach each other or even consult each other with their eyes. Their sex life continued to be active, but their relations were unadorned with physical intimacies, except when they were actually in bed.

She went to the table where she had left a voluminous handbag and withdrew a leatherbound notebook and gold pencil and jotted some reminders for herself. "I'll have to try to work the lawyers in later this afternoon."

"We'd better not be careless about it. I don't intend to let Aleck swindle you out of $3,000,000, if that's what it's all about."

"It's probably just lawyers' fuss about nothing, but you're right. I've got to find out. I've been rather counting on it."

So had he. Would Aleck try to disinherit his daughter? Of course he would. Walter wasn't sure that telling Aleck what he thought of him had given him $3,000,000 worth of satisfaction. Knowing it was coming had been a comfort for the last few years, pinching pennies while he moved from triumph to triumph in one of the most spectacular careers of the day. He turned and checked the Empire clock on the mantelpiece. "You better get going anyway. Herbie and his naked boy will be here in half an hour. That shouldn't take too long. I'll get to the office by 1:00 at the latest. I can take over for you. Don't just try to squeeze the lawyers in. Make an appointment."

She went to a mirror and put on a velvet beret he had designed for her. She went about the room collecting her odds and ends, gloves, handbag, the slim lacquered stick with an ornate gold head he had found for her to complete her "executive" look. She posed briefly at the door, an original and striking figure, and waved her handbag at him. "OK, dearest. See you shortly."

Her departure drew a gust of warm air from Tenth Street in through the open window. It lifted the draperies, and they billowed and subsided as if to herald her advent into the outside world. He gathered up the morning's mail, most of which she had already opened, and settled down to look through it. The downstairs bell rang just when he was beginning to expect it. He rose and pushed the button to release the lock below. He didn't wait for Herbie to mount the stairs but opened the door and went back into the room. He heard him bumping about on the stairs, and then Herbie called out, "Can we come in?"

"Sure," Walter called back, and Herbie came shambling into the room carrying two large awkward cases of photographic equipment. He was a big untidy shapeless bear of a man and the best photographer Walter knew. He was followed by a trim, handsome young man. Herbie introduced him to Walter as Mark Something and shook off outer garments. Hat, raincoat, and jacket landed in a pile on a chair, and he crouched over his cases in rumpled shirtsleeves.

213

"Is there someplace I can hang my clothes?" the young man asked.

"Oh, sure." Walter appraised him with his casting director's eyes. He would do well enough for this job, he supposed; but he wasn't the spectacular beauty Herbie had promised when Walter had explained to him what he had in mind for the poster. There had been some sort of to-do about Mark's posing in the nude in the privacy of Herbie's studio, and Walter had suggested having the session here.

He took the model to the bedroom, continuing his discreet appraisal. His expression was grave, his features well-formed but slightly heavy, and he reminded him of someone. He was shorter than Walter and probably only a year or so younger. He was so impeccably groomed and his dark suit so sharply pressed that Walter went immediately to the overflowing closet to get him a hanger. He held it out, wondering why Herbie had made such a point of his beauty, and looked at the hand that reached for it. It was a beautiful hand, smooth and shapely, with elegantly tapered fingers, and what it suggested about the body's structure gave a clue to Herbie's enthusiasm.

He glanced again at the slightly swarthy face and placed the resemblance that had eluded him. Mark looked like the Olympian *Apollo*. Walter had always been intrigued by the statue because it conformed so little to the classic ideal of masculine beauty. It had a strong head, faintly archaic and forbidding and full of character. Mark's face was marked by a more contemporary, softer sensuality, but it had the *Apollo*'s brooding quality and the mysterious command. Walter went back to the closet and pulled out a floor-length black velvet cloak that he had salvaged from one of his productions and threw it on the end of the bed.

"You can wear that until Herbie is ready if you want." They acknowledged each other with slight nods, and Walter returned to the living room. Herbie was setting up his lights. Walter helped him push furniture around the crowded room while they chatted familiarly. They worked frequently together.

"Better get those curtains closed," Herbie muttered, peering into one of his cameras. He gave the impression of seeing nothing except through a camera's eye. A look of innocent benevolence somehow emerged from his face. "The kid's terrific-looking, isn't he?"

"I didn't see it at first, but he's perfect," Walter agreed. The model was working on his imagination. His Theatre Today posters had become a small feature of the city's life. The press usually gave space to each new one, and *The New Yorker* frequently ran a paragraph about them. They were usually designed by the young painters and designers who worked for the theater. Walter had planned a photographic layout as a novelty, inspired by a technique Herbie had evolved whereby the human body was given the look of marble yet remained hauntingly lifelike. Walter had been intrigued by the opportunity to become an instant sculptor and had found a loose allusion to the theme of an Italian play he was planning for the fall.

Walter went to the bookshelves and pulled out a rough sketch he had made of the composition, planning revisions if the young man's body lived up to the promise of his hands. Dismembered arms and legs were placed in surrealistic juxtaposition to a central torso. He would get the remarkable hands in somewhere. The young man reentered the room draped in the cloak, and Walter dropped the sketch on a table and circled disarranged furniture to join him.

"Herbie's about ready. If you don't mind taking that thing off, I'd like to see you under the lights."

"You wanted me to strip completely, didn't you?"

"Yes, we'll crop you where necessary, of course." Walter smiled and saw intelligence and response in the eyes that met his but none of the flirtatiousness that he so often encountered in the line of business. "That sounds rather drastic. The point is, I want to show as much of you as the law allows, so we have to start with all of you."

The grave expression lit with humor. "I see. I've never been asked to pose stark naked before. I didn't much like the idea until Mr. Uhlray— uh, Herbie—said it was for you. I hope I'm OK for the job."

"Herbie seems sure enough." Walter found it odd having this conversation with Apollo. "I have some ideas. If you'll just stand around for a minute without posing, I can see how they fit."

The young man turned from him and shrugged off the cloak and dropped it onto a chair as he passed and stepped out into the lit area that had turned part of the living room into a sort of stage. Walter followed slowly, his eyes registering a series of startlingly satisfying pictures—a broad back tapering to a long curve of buttocks that flowed into well-developed legs, proud shoulders with a dancer's rather than an athlete's smoothly muscled definition of chest and abdomen, firmly rounded thighs and calves without bulges that rested on big arched feet as beautifully articulated as the hands, the skin immaculate and unblemished and nearly hairless so that every line was picked up by light without blurring. Walter tried to exclude genitalia from his range of vision, since it wouldn't figure in the final results. His eyes traveled up to the solid column of neck, swelling at the Adam's apple, easily supporting the slightly heavy jaw. Isolated by light, the young man seemed to acquire height, yet the body retained a well-knit cohesive look, line flowing into line with no interruption, so perfectly proportioned that Walter felt an ounce more or less would mar its extraordinary symmetry. The most perfect body he had ever seen? Harry's had been a young athlete's body, and Walter knew that he might find it uninteresting if he saw it for the first time today. This one had the subtlety of sculpture, full of secret promises, waiting to be brought to life by the beholder.

"You're magnificent," he said, standing just out of the light a few feet away. "Really beautiful."

The young man's eyes found Walter's across the lights. He smiled faintly. "Thanks. Coming from Walter Makin, that means a lot."

"Thank *you*," Walter felt a small lift of pleasure at the realization that the brief exchange had put them in touch with each other. For an instant it struck him as wildly incongruous that there was a young man standing naked in his living room, and then he was recalled to the purpose of the occasion. Herbie wheezed and puffed at his side.

"Ready, Herb? Carry on. I don't see how you can go wrong. Oh, and Mark—is that right? Mark?" He crossed the barrier of light that separated them and was surprised to find himself looking down once more

216

from his superior height. "Now that I've seen you, I think I know what I want. Keep all your body open. I don't necessarily want to give you poses. Try anything that feels right. But open. Free." The intimacy he always felt when he was working with an actor was beginning to build between them. Mark watched him attentively. "Try reaching for the sky. Or embracing the world. Or flying, diving, anything. Think of all your body opening out." Walter accompanied his words with brief mimes of what he had in mind. They stood close together, their eyes seeking confirmation in each other; but the intimacy they were creating was the intimacy of shared creation, quite sexual. "I know. Try a big morning stretch."

Walter withdrew a step. Mark spread his feet and put a hand on his hip and shot his other arm into the air. He arched his back and flung back his head and thrust his hips off at an angle to his torso. His cock seemed to stretch too with this great easing of his body as if exposing himself so defenselessly around him.

"Christ, yes," Walter exclaimed. "You're fantastic. Get cracking, Herbie. I want him like that from every angle." He backed away from the lights, leaving Mark pinpointed alone in a lascivious moment of awakening. Only then was Walter aware of the sharp pang of desire that had awakened in him. It receded as all his professional attention was engaged in the job at hand.

He encouraged Mark to break the pose frequently and re-create it with variations so as not to let it get rigidly set. Walter was fascinated by the way he moved, without self-consciousness or cultivated grace but with natural, unemphatic masculinity. Walter's eyes were so satisfied by the line of his back, from shoulder to the elongated spheres of buttocks, that he was scarcely aware of the temptation it stirred in him. When he was sure he had all the shots he needed for his central figure, he had Herbie work on details of arms and legs, and his concentration on the job slackened, and his fascination began to engage him more personally. He focused on features that hitherto had registered only as part of the whole. His eyes lingered on the level brow that was somehow slightly forbidding, on the heavy eyelids that, when lowered,

217

gave the face a darkly seductive look, on the thick, dark straight hair that was shaggy around the edges and invited a hand to smooth it. The mouth wasn't fleshy, but the curve of the lips was stirringly sensual. Their eyes met frequently during his scrutiny, Mark's in turn questioning, as if he wondered what Walter found to interest him, or contemplative, as if it were natural for their eyes to rest on each other, with a spark of intensity in their depths.

At a word from Herbie, Mark lay on his back on the floor and lifted an arm, and the contact between them was broken. It left a void in Walter that was immediately filled with a rush of desire. His sex gave a leap, and his heart raced. He wanted to touch this superbly naked young man. Mark. He was Mark. He wanted to whisper his name to him and make him his own. Mark lay stretched out on the floor, naked, offering himself to any taker. He saw his chest and abdomen rising and falling with the infinitely thrilling breath of life. He wanted to lie with him and hold him and feel him breathing against him. He looked at the sex inert between his open legs and longed to see it spring up with desire. His mind raced back to explore every look they had exchanged. Had there been an invitation he had missed? Was Mark an adept who would take a sexual advance for granted, or would he dismiss him with contempt as a queer? Walter had no idea and didn't know how to find out. The boys who had flirted with him over the years hadn't taught him how to take the initiative.

Thinking of the complications of getting him alone and revealing his intentions cooled him. Just because a male with a beautiful body lay naked and tantalizingly available on his living room floor didn't mean that he would drop the restraints that had become a part of his nature. He turned away and immediately wondered if Mark would regard his withdrawal as a sign of indifference.

Ridiculous. The young man probably hadn't given him a thought except perhaps to wonder if Walter Makin might be useful to him. Herbie would be finished soon, and they would pack up and leave. And he would have the pleasure of constructing a striking poster out of the elements of Mark's extraordinary body.

"Good, kid. You're great," Herbie said behind him. "Just one more full-length, and that'll do it."

Walter turned back. Mark was once more on his feet, and his eyes were waiting to greet him. They were straightforward, uncomplicated, acquiescent in some odd way that might have nothing to do with sex.

"Feet apart. Arms up a bit, away from your sides. Let's see some of that old pelvic thrust."

Mark followed Herbie's instructions with his eyes fixed on Walter. At the last order, he smiled suddenly for the first time, and Walter's knees seemed to give way. It was a lovely smile, gentle, with more sweetness than humor, utterly disarming. Walter watched him as he found his balance on feet that seemed to grip the floor. His hips were thrust forward, his arms slightly lifted. It was a wrestler's pose and brought all the perfections of his body into taut balance. Looking at Walter, he moved his hands from the wrists so that he was no longer a wrestler but became an eager love reaching out for his loved one. Walter's eyes dropped involuntarily, and he saw the sex spring out, lengthen, acquire girth. He lifted his eyes hastily and saw the muscle of Mark's jaw flex and the intensity of his gaze deepen.

"Fine. That does it," Herbie announced.

Walter moved swiftly to the cloak and gathered it up and entered the pool of light. He dropped it over Mark's back and exerted a slight pressure on his shoulders. "Sit a minute. We've given you a real workout." He went about unplugging lamps, waiting for the excitement in him to subside. His sex was uncomfortably restricted by clothes. He went to the windows and pulled open the curtains. He could assume, he supposed, that Mark's brief partial erection had been for him. He wouldn't be dismissed with contempt. Then what? Did he really intend to give way to impulses he dreaded in himself? It was too complicated and threatened to become more trouble than it was worth. Forget it.

He joined Herbie and helped him dismantle the lamp stands. They discussed the shots Walter was most interested in. Mark sat near them. Walter couldn't bring himself to look at him yet. He felt the man's eyes on him while he crouched with Herbie, packing equipment.

"That pretty near does it," the photographer said. "You better get dressed, kid. Mr. Makin's a busy man."

Walter stood and turned to him, his heart beating rapidly again as the moment approached to let him go. Mark was sitting with a leg tucked under him, the cloak draped around him. Their eyes met. Mark started unfolding his leg to rise. The cloak was an encumbrance. Something caught. He teetered and flung out an arm to recover his balance. The cloak flew open. His cock was erect, not long but massive, an aggressive extension of his beautiful body. He tugged at the cloak and freed it and covered himself as he found his footing. Walter glanced down at Herbie; he was tucking in his last camera, oblivious. He lifted his eyes to Mark. He looked stricken. It had been an accident— not, as Walter had thought for a few flustered seconds, an outright provocation. He thought of the guileless smile. Mark hugged the cloak around him and started for the bedroom. Walter waited a beat. He wasn't conscious of making a decision. He found himself moving rapidly across the room so that he reached the door ahead of Mark and blocked it.

"Why don't you go ahead, Herb?" he said, looking into Mark's eyes. "I have some ideas I'd like to talk to Mark about, if that's OK with him."

"Yes, sure," Mark agreed, his gaze growing limpid and peaceful. He turned, and they stood side by side, facing Herbie.

He snapped his case shut and stood. "Some folks can talk the day away. I've got to get going." He looked around him and spotted his clothes. He clamped his hat on his head, with hair straggling out from under it. He heaved himself into his jacket. Walter knew he should go to him and perform his duties as host, but he couldn't force himself to move. He and Mark had imperceptibly eased themselves closer so that they were almost leaning against each other. His arms ached to hold the body that he felt now belonged to him. By moving only his fingers, he could lightly stroke the curve of buttocks. He was trembling slightly. Mark shifted his weight to encourage the caress.

Their proximity emphasized the difference in their height and filled Walter with a sense of domination and power. He was aware that his expression was frozen on his face as he blindly watched Herbie struggle into his raincoat and pull it around him, the collar catching under the collar of his jacket. He picked up the awkward cases.

"OK, Walter. I'll call you in a few days. You're great, kid. Be seeing you." He lurched toward the door, an absurdly disheveled figure. Walter was confident that he had noticed nothing. The door slammed behind him.

In one swift move Walter pulled away the cloak and took Mark in his arms. Their mouths met and opened to each other. Walter's senses sang as his hands discovered the feel of the back that had so entranced his eyes. His fingers strayed along the cleft between the buttocks, and muscles worked in welcome. Mark made a deep humming sound in his throat. His hands had worked through layers of cloth and found Walter's erection. They moved over it and lifted it against his belly and continued up over his chest under his shirt.

Walter broke away and pulled off his clothes with all his old elation, but his exhibitionism was curbed by the glory of his partner's body. He ran his hand thought the thick hair and took his mouth again. He dropped his hands to the graceful shoulders and down over his rib cage to the supple waist. Mark's hands covered his and moved them back to his buttocks. He thrust his body up against Walter's and arched his back and clung to him. Walter released his mouth. Mark's heavy breathing stretched the muscles over his chest. His thick lids were lowered in a face that had become a dark mask of passionate acquiescence.

"Christ," Walter muttered. "Come on." He put his arm around him and led him through the bedroom to the bathroom. He continued to hold him close while he fumbled about in the medicine cupboard and found the lubricant Clara sometimes used. They remained as close to each other as movement permitted, arms encircling each other, hands exploring, breathing each other's breath.

Mark kissed Walter's face and neck and took the lubricant and stroked it onto Walter's sex, his head averted over it. Walter took some and ran his hand between Mark's buttocks. His eyes avoided the gross virility of genitalia. He was ruled by his sense of touch. His hands reveled in the exquisite texture of muscle and skin. They moved rapturously over chest and abdomen and thighs. He lifted Mark's chin, and their tongues met again as they sank to their knees together. The bodies tangled and found the position they were seeking. Mark uttered little cries and groans as Walter entered him slowly. They thrashed about on the floor and quickly drove each other to orgasm. They lay together taking long, shuddering breaths. Their breathing slowly returned to normal.

"Are we gong to see each other again, or is this—" Mark began in a muted voice.

The unfinished question took Walter by surprise. He had assumed this would be written off as the passion of a moment. He answered with his body still singing with conquest. "That was too quick to count. I want you for hours. Where do you live?"

"That doesn't matter. I never stay in one place for long. Would you like me to move down here somewhere?"

"Could you?" It occurred to Walter that having this magnificent creature easily available might prove more of a distraction than his busy life would permit. An irresistible distraction. "That would be wonderful. Would you?"

"Sure, all I need is a furnished room. I can find one around here."

They were apparently laying the groundwork for a continuing affair. Words were being spoken at the prompting of their joined bodies; they would seem less binding when lust abated. "I won't always be able to see you when I want to," Walter said, forcing a note of moderation.

"I know. You're married. That's why I thought it would be easier if I'm nearby."

"Are you interested only in guys?"

"I'm interested only in you, Mr. Makin. At least for the time being. Don't worry about it."

"What's your name?"

"Mark Travere." He said it so that it sounded like "Travery." He spelled it out.

222

"That's good. I've never heard a name like it. I've never seen a guy like you. How old are you?"

"Twenty-seven. You?"

"Two years older."

"I thought you must be, but you don't look it. The Boy Wonder." He laughed softly. "You're the sexiest-looking kid I've ever seen. You look like a kid."

"You have a certain modicum of sex appeal yourself."

"Does this happen to you often? I mean, the boys? It's none of my business, but I can't help wondering."

Walter's first impulse was to resent the question—everybody knew that Walter Makin was straight—but he realized that he'd given him the right to ask. "No, only a few times in my life. I think this is the first time I'd have made a pass at a guy even at the risk of getting socked."

Mark laughed again. "That may be the nicest thing anybody's ever said to me."

Walter hugged him and kissed the corner of his mouth. "We better get going. I must be squashing you."

"You are. I like it. It's hard to believe I'm being squashed by Walter Makin."

"Maybe you'll learn to love me for myself."

"I may, but you're awfully damn glamorous, even on a bathroom floor."

"I'm sorry about that. It just happened."

"I'll say. There was a modicum of urgency about it."

They laughed together. Walter felt power accumulating in him again. In a few moments, he would be able to repeat the performance. The superb body beneath him communicated desire. Muscles moved insinuatingly. Walter remembered his promise to join Clara by 1 o'-clock and withdrew from him carefully, reluctantly. He sprang up and crossed quickly to the shower. As he turned on the tap, he waited to feel the distaste he remembered at having to wash away the traces of his pleasure. He felt only that he wanted a shower. He didn't expect to be overcome by guilt, but he was surprised that none of the brakes

223

seemed to be functioning. Until now the memory of Frank Farley had been sufficient to restrain him when he'd been tempted. That specter remained close to the surface of his consciousness, but he supposed enough time had passed for it to have lost its immediacy. Perhaps, like Aleck, he was taking a delayed revenge on Clara, revenge for the abortion, revenge for the loss of David. He knew that their sterile coupling had slowly changed his attitude toward his few adventures with boys. The body in his bed might just as well have been male for all practical purposes. The enormous danger remained, but he wasn't frightened of it in this case. He thought of Mark's smile and felt completely safe. What had just taken place had crackled with the excitement of rejuvenation. He hadn't been so deeply aroused in years.

As soon as he had soaped himself, he called to him. "Do you want a shower? Come on in." He was transfixed as Mark appeared around the curtain. He saw him for the first time with the eyes of a lover. He was above all astonished, astonished at having wanted the beautiful body, astonished at being allowed to have it. Now that he knew Mark physically, he was captivated by his head. He wanted to know what went on behind the gravity of the strong, well-balanced features. He put his hand on his neck and looked into the dark, reassuring eyes and pulled him closer and held their heads together. His cock stirred with unabated desire.

"God, Mark. You're something." He drew his head back and opened Mark's mouth with his tongue and ran it over his teeth. He spoke with their lips lightly touching. "I want it all over again. Please don't let me. I'm hideously late already." He glanced down and saw that they were similarly affected. He reached down and held heavy flesh. It filled his hand. He smiled. "It's good to know we still want each other."

"I don't think that's going to be a problem. You don't have to touch me there if you don't want to."

"I do want to. It's fantastic, like all of you. It takes a bit of getting used to, though."

"I don't know if you're interested, but that was the first time it's happened to me like that."

"The first time? You mean–"

"I've never been had like that before. I've thought about it, but I wasn't sure I wanted it. When I noticed the way you were looking at me, I thought, *If that's what he wants, I'm all for it.* Of course, I didn't know about this." He ran his fingers along Walter's sex and closed his hand on it. "I admit, I was scared when I saw it."

"Was it all right? I didn't hurt you?"

Mark's sweet smile spread across his face. "Agony. Don't be silly. It hurt at first, probably because I didn't know what to expect. Then it was sublime. You know that. When you came in me, I felt as if my life was just beginning. And a lot of other things I'd better not go into now."

"No. Please help me go. I've really got to." He turned on the cold tap, but they continued to hold each other, which counteracted any calming effect the water might have had. They were both erect when they emerged from the shower. Walter pulled a towel off the rack. "Do you mind if we share? Clara would notice if–"

"Sure. I wiped up the floor where I splashed."

"Thanks." They stood close together and used opposite ends of the towel to dry themselves. "Did you mean it about moving?"

"Of course. If you'd like me to."

"I want you to, but we're going to have to be careful until…well, until we figure a few things out."

"I understand. Even if you weren't married, I should think being Walter Makin would make for difficulties."

"Mostly it takes a lot of time. How soon do you think you can find something?"

"I'll look around today. I want to find something decent so you'll like dropping in. That's the idea, isn't it? You'll come to see me?"

"Yes. God knows how or when. At least my wife and I are independent during the day. Are you very busy?"

"I average about four jobs a day. That leaves plenty of spare time."

"You must make good money."

"Not bad."

"So how soon do you think we'll be neighbors?"

"Tomorrow, maybe. Or the next day."

"Oh, good." He didn't want too much time to think it over, or he'd talk himself out of it. "I was afraid you were going to say a week or two." The towel seemed to draw them together so that within moments they were in each other's arms.

"I promised to help you get out," Mark said. "This isn't a very good beginning."

"You can't help the way you look. You feel so wonderful too. I do have to go, damn it." He ran his hands slowly over the hard chest and abdomen and, with less reluctance now, down to the thick, rigid sex. "God, what a handful."

Mark reached for Walter's. "I'm afraid we're built so differently. Mutt and Jeff. It makes us go together somehow. It'll be interesting to see how we get these things into our pants."

"Jesus. It's too good to do it on the floor again, and we can't use the bed. Nothing in the world would stop me otherwise. Hurry and find that room."

"Don't worry, I will."

Walter put his arm around him and led him into the bedroom. He touched his hair. He ran the back of his hand over his cheeks. He put it flat on his chest, savoring the fathomless thrill of possession and intimacy. "I want time with you. It's a problem. Things seem to be happening that I'd like to find out more about."

"I'm glad you think so too. There won't be any difficulties as far as I'm concerned. It's been quite a modeling session. Did you know right away how much I wanted you?"

"No, I wouldn't have dared make a pass at you. There's nothing about you that...well, you know. Thank God you got tangled up in that cloak."

"I was horrified. What if Herbie had seen? You didn't guess I was queer?"

"No."

"I'm glad. I suppose everybody tells you you've got one of the most sensational bodies in town."

"Not many people have had the opportunity to."

"That's right. I keep forgetting I'm not just one in a long series. Why has it happened with me, Walter?"

"I thought you'd never call me by my name." Walter ran his hands lightly over his shoulders and down his arms to his hands and lifted them so that he could study them. He kissed one and then the other. "Beautiful. I think I fell for you when I saw your hands. Do you know the *Apollo* at Olympia?"

"Is that the one called the *Apollo Belvedere?*"

"No, that's the pretty one. The one at Olympia isn't pretty at all. Very handsome, very much a god, superb. You look like him."

Something happened in Mark's face. His mouth and jaw tightened. The intensity of his eyes sharpened. "I should've known Walter Makin would provide some dramatic surprises."

Walter unfolded their hands so that they stood palm to palm, sex lifted to sex, touching. "What about me? Am I one in a long series?"

"Well, sure, in a sense. I've been going to bed with guys for the last six or seven years, preferably a new one every night. There's no point in denying it."

"Does that mean I've got to fight off the competition?"

"There's no competition, Walter, not for the moment. I've made that clear. You don't want me to say any more, do you?"

"No." He spread their arms and stepped closer and released his hands. They wrapped their arms around each other and leaned their foreheads together, holding each other lightly so that their bodies were free to move against each other. "It's ridiculous to get dressed when we feel like this, but we've got to. If it can't go on all day, we might as well stop. Oh, God, Mark, you feel so divine."

"You…oh, please. This is beginning to drive me crazy. Let me get my damn clothes on and get the hell out of here."

They broke apart, and Mark strode quickly to the chair where he had left his shirt and shorts, the muscles of his magnificent back bunching and flowing rhythmically. In seconds he was covered. He sat to pull on his socks, and Walter stepped into the living room and snatched up the cloak and turned back with it around him. Mark pulled on his trousers and began to tie his necktie in front of the bureau mirror. Walter stood close to him and handed him a comb when he was finished. He found him even more desirable dressed than naked. He touched the full curve of his behind.

"You're so handsome," he said to him into the mirror. "It's funny. You're so unusually handsome, I didn't quite grasp it when you arrived. Now I'd expect people to swoon when they see you in the street."

The mirror reflected his faint smile. "Oh, they do." He returned to the hanger and slipped on his jacket. His sex was a prominent upright cylindrical form against his groin.

"That handful shows a lot," Walter said.

"It'll be all right when I go outside." He stepped up to Walter and gave the cloak a tug and let it fall to the floor. "My turn. This cloak is marvelous the way it comes off." He looked him over and shook his head. "*Sexy* isn't the word for it. You're enough to drive a poor faggot crazy."

Walter winced inwardly. He immediately labeled this small jolt of withdrawal as "coming to his senses," and it briefly crossed his mind to discourage his moving, but Mark had made it clear that it was no great moment. Let events take their course. He could have sex occasionally with a willing young man without altering life in any way. He let Mark kiss him lightly on the lips and drop down and kiss his cock without making a move to detain him. He picked up the cloak and trailed it after him as he followed him to the door.

"I'll be waiting to hear from you," Walter said.

"The way I feel, you won't wait long."

"Don't phone. I might not be able to talk. Leave a note in the box downstairs or ring and come up. If Clara's around, don't be surprised if I say I'm thinking of using you for more photographs."

"Right." He reached for Walter's hand and gave it a squeeze without looking at him again and went quickly to the door and let himself out. Walter turned back and gathered up his clothes from the living room floor while his erection subsided.

228

Feeling still the touch of Mark's body, it seemed that he had barely explored it. There was still so much more he wanted to know. All his lines of communication were open, waiting to be put to use. Clara could be thankful that he hadn't as yet fallen in love with a girl.

He re-created an image of Mark in his mind's eye and found it no wonder that he had been enthralled. He wandered to the bathroom while he put on his shirt and looked down at the bath mat that had served as Apollo's altar–appallingly inadequate. The thought of getting all of him in bed took his breath away. It also reminded him of what Mark had said about a new boy every night, and his lustful high spirits recoiled. Would there be a new one tonight? So what? Mark was queer, but he had said enough to indicate that he shared Walter's feeling that something special had happened to them. Life had acquired an intriguing new facet. He was bursting with curiosity to see what sparks it would strike from the dark corners of his spirit.

He was soaring when he reached the office. He hadn't felt like this for years. Something fabulous had happened to him. Minutes passed while he simply savored it without pinpointing its source, and then he allowed himself to conjure up a kaleidoscope of Mark in every moment they had shared: Mark stretching, Mark combing his hair, Mark racked by orgasm, Mark smiling, Mark writhing ecstatically in copulation. The images left him giddy with desire.

He sent word to Clara that he had arrived and shared his high spirits when she joined him. He was genuinely pleased to see her. Even his sexual response to her felt recharged and alive. She looked at him with interest.

"Everything went well this morning?" she asked.

"Very, I think. Herb found this gorgeous guy."

"Oh? Lovely. I wish I'd been allowed to look at him."

"You can keep the photographs under your pillow."

"Without a stitch?"

"Completely naked."

"Oh, goodie. We haven't been having nearly so much fun around here. Carl doesn't want to give us an option on his new play."

"The son of a bitch. The same old story?"

"I'm afraid so."

Walter's grand design was being wrecked by success. As soon as writers or actors were launched under his auspices, they were lured away by commercial managements or Hollywood. He had managed to keep his original concept intact for the first two years while everybody had still been fired by enthusiasm at participating in his daring experiment. Since then he had witnessed a steady erosion. When a new play had a big success, he was under tremendous pressure to give it an independent Broadway run, rather than keep it within the framework of his repertory program. He didn't mind losing his actors; it stimulated him to develop new ones. It wasn't so easy to develop new writers. He had found three good ones and half a dozen more who were capable of turning out a good play and who might do good work again but were undependable. Johnny Bainbridge had been one of the latter and had finally succumbed to Hollywood. The good ones, once established, showed little inclination for being used to subsidize their less-gifted confreres, although it was thanks to Walter's setup that they had got the hearing that the commercial theater might never have given them. He tried to be patient with their attitude, but since he, as the director of a nonprofit organization, was making only a small fraction of what he might have earned ordinarily, his patience was wearing thin. He had to admit that Clara's impending riches made it easier to toss fat offers from Hollywood into the wastebasket.

"Don't these idiot writers understand that they're successes because I give them better productions than they can get anywhere else in the country?" he demanded, more of the walls than of Clara, since they had gone over the problem many times in the past. "I can't let Carl go. Doesn't he know what a hack producer and hack director could do to his work?" He looked at the bowl of flowers on the table in front of him and thought of Mark and laughed. "Actually, I should let him find out, except the experience would probably kill him. Oh, damn. Tell him I'll give him 40 performances in the first four months of the season. If they all sell out–and I'm sure they will–I'll give him a run. This means tearing the company apart again. Blast him."

"You're in a very generous mood today, dearest."

"It's spring. I'm looking forward to Europe. Anyway, Carl is one of the ones that makes what we're doing worth bothering about. We'd better have him to dinner soon and subject him to a little of the Makin uplift. He's got to understand that a living theater isn't created by one playwright."

"How about next Wednesday?"

"Sure...no, wait a minute." He thought of Mark. He wanted to keep himself as free as possible for his initiation into the improbable mysteries of having a lover, if that was the way it turned out. He didn't know if it would last beyond another encounter, but he suspected it might take several weeks to wear out the excitement that continued to build in him. Their departure for Europe was a comfortable six weeks away. "Let's keep the social bit to a minimum for the next week or so. I want to tie up all the loose ends for the fall so we won't have to think about it while we're away."

"Suit yourself. I'm just off for lunch with Hannah. I'm going on to the lawyers after. I have to go by the theater. If I don't get back here, I'll see you at home."

He rose and went to her on a rare demonstrative impulse. He felt grateful to her for leaving him so free. It wouldn't be too difficult to find time for Mark. If he were already in his new place, Walter could have spent an hour or two with him later this afternoon. He gave her a little kiss and sent her on her way.

When he got home, he found her looking aggressive and very determined.

"It's Daddy, all right," she announced before he had had a chance to sit down.

"You mean, about the money?"

"Of course. It seems he's found some technicality in Aunt Maureen's will. He's ganged up with a stupid cousin of mine to get the money for her. I guess he didn't like my siding with you, dearest."

231

"Does it matter? Can he do anything?"

"It seems he can. Or has. Lawyers drive me mad. It takes them an hour to say yes or no. Then it turns out they mean maybe. I've decided to go to Cleveland myself."

"Whatever for?"

"That's where the court is with jurisdiction or something. Daddy's apparently already blocked everything, maybe for months. Rosencrantz and Guildenstern want to enter into negotiations with somebody out there, presumably by tortoise. I'm going out and find out what the hell it's all about."

Walter couldn't believe his ears. What had he done to deserve this reward? She was leaving the field clear for Mark. "When?" he asked, trying not to sound eager.

"Day after tomorrow, I thought. I could come back Sunday or stay over until Monday if it looks as if I can accomplish something."

"I don't see how I can go with you," he said tentatively, prepared to muster an army of reasons why he couldn't possibly go.

"Good heavens. Why should you, dearest? It'll just be business. I certainly don't intend to cross the ancestral threshold. I thought I might stay with Edith or somebody. I'll make some calls in the morning."

"I suppose it's important enough to make the effort," he said judiciously. A whole weekend with Mark! The money seemed insignificant compared to this.

"Important enough! Have you looked at our bank account recently? I wouldn't be surprised if I can settle the whole thing in a day. Lawyers like to play games with each other."

"If anybody can beat lawyers at their own game, I'm sure you can, Clarry. We better drink to your success." He would have the precious gift of time, time to get to know Mark, time to get his fill of him perhaps, time to think about it calmly so that he wouldn't unwittingly incur obligations because his judgment was clouded by snatched, unsatisfactory moments with him.

They had drinks together. She put together one of her slapdash meals that had improved with the growing availability of prepared and packaged and frozen foods. He was so stirred sexually that it spilled over to include Clara, and he was actually looking forward to getting her into bed instead of regarding it as an aspect of life to be taken as it came. They would never have children. Surely this freed him to make the most of a male lover if he chose. The thought of a male lover still brought terrors. Mark could conceivably ruin him, of course; but he had seen his smile.

He woke up the next morning riding a wave of happy anticipation. Yesterday he had discovered treasure. Today he could look forward to enjoying it. He asked Clara at the office if she were still planning to go to Cleveland the next day and was told that her plans were made. She was taking a plane the next morning. As the afternoon drew to a close, he worked himself into a fine pitch of excitement. Would there be a note when he got home? He felt there had been little time for Mark to look for a room, pack, and move into it, yet he had promised not to keep him waiting long. If the note were there, he should probably wait till tomorrow to see him, when Clara would be safely out of town. He mustn't push his luck.

He and Clara went home together. As soon as he stepped into the entrance, he saw that their mailbox was empty, but he opened it to make sure a slip of paper hadn't got caught on the side somewhere. "Nothing," he said.

"That was fairly obvious, dearest," Clara pointed out.

He made them drinks and changed into slacks and an old smoking jacket to make it clear that the day was over as far as he was concerned. He hurried so as not to be caught by the doorbell in the midst of changing. Once he had settled down in the living room with his drink, he relaxed. It probably would be better if Mark didn't show up until the next day. When Clara was gone, he would call the office and cancel all his appointments and stay at home and wait for him. Clara passed him on her way to the kitchen. She was barely out of sight when the bell rang.

He forced himself to sit quietly, while his heart leaped up in his chest. "Are you expecting anyone?" he called.

"No."

"I'll get it." He rose slowly, in case Clara came out, and sauntered over to the button to release the catch downstairs. He glanced behind him and darted out the door and closed it and ran to the head of the stairs. Mark was mounting them. He flung himself down them and they stopped, facing each other, between floors. Their eyes met and questioned each other. They were both breathing rapidly.

"God, I've been praying for you," Walter whispered.

"I guess it wasn't a dream," Mark said in an undertone.

"No."

Mark held out an envelope. "The address is in there."

Walter took and put it in his pocket. "Nearby?"

"Very."

"I'll be there as soon as I can. After dinner. I shouldn't be later than 10. You'll be there?"

"Of course."

Walter saw that he was wearing a light suit, which made his dark good looks even more striking than before. He put his hand on his shoulder and gripped it. His ears were alert for sounds. He glanced up and down the stairs and darted his head forward and quickly kissed Mark on the lips. "I've been thinking about you without stopping."

Mark lifted a beautiful hand and put it on Walter's. "You're my sexy kid," he murmured.

"Yeah. I can't wait." He squeezed Mark's hand and broke from him and leaped up the stairs two at a time. When he glanced down at the turning, the stairwell was empty. He patted the envelope in his pocket and took a deep breath and went to his door and rang. In a moment Clara let him in.

"Sorry. I locked myself out without thinking." He closed the door behind him and went to his drink. "It was an actor we know–I can't remember his name–he wanted to know if we're casting. It's incredible, people think they have the right to bother me at home."

"Somebody who's worked for us?"

"No, a friend of Sally's, I think. I'll remember his name in a minute."

Clara shrugged and returned to the kitchen. He waited till she was gone and then went to the silver box where they usually kept a spare pack of cigarettes. He found the pack, removed it, and went to the bookshelves and dropped it behind some books. He listened for sounds of activities in the kitchen and, reassured, drew out the envelope and pulled a single sheet of paper from it.

"I want you, M," he read, and an address that he knew must be right around the corner. He crumpled the envelope and threw it into the wastebasket and stuffed the paper back into his pocket. He was excited with the discovery that Mark was more openly appealing than the slightly forbidding image he had preserved in his mind's eye. He must call Herbie tomorrow and find out how the pictures had turned out.

His excitement remained, underlying his evening with Clara. They were never at a loss for conversation, and they launched into a discussion of the coming season that carried them through dinner and coffee and, to Walter's delight as he glanced at the clock and saw it was just after 9:30, through his last cigarette.

"Got any cigarettes, Clarry?" he asked as he stubbed it out.

"Of course, in that box where they always are," she said.

"Oh, good." He went on with the point he was making. "Thank God for an early evening occasionally," he said, rising from the table. "Two in a row is too good to be true. I feel like a nightcap. How about you?"

"I wouldn't mind a bit of whisky." She rose, and they drifted into the living room, still talking. He went to the silver box and opened it.

"There aren't any," he said, holding it out to her.

"Cigarettes? That's funny. I swear I put a pack in yesterday."

"I must've smoked them."

"You really ought to cut down, dearest. Let me think. Maybe…" She went to the desk and opened a black lacquer box. "No, I guess there aren't any."

"My fault. I'll run out and get some. Fix yourself a drink. I'll only be a second."

"What a nuisance. Are you going out like that? I hope nobody sees you. People will think Walter Makin has had the flop of the century."

235

"I think I'm rather fetching. The Bowery look." He kept all his movements easy and relaxed, making it look as if he were hesitating about going rather than flinging himself at the door as he wanted to do. Once out, he ran down the stairs but slowed to a stroll on the street in case she were watching him. As soon as he was sure he was out of sight, he sped up and turned the corner and within moments had found a dingy doorway with the number he was looking for. Mark was a genius. He couldn't have done better unless he had found a room in the Tenth Street building. Walter decided not to tell him about the weekend until he had had time to make sure he wanted further involvement. His being so close made it almost too easy for them to see each other. He pressed the bell of No. 3 as Mark's note instructed, and as soon as the door was buzzed, he crumpled up the slip of paper and dropped it. He took the stairs two at a time and found Mark standing in the second-floor hall. Their arms were around each other before the door closed behind them, and then their mouths were devouring each other. Mark was wearing only a shirt and trousers, which made his body gloriously accessible. Walter yanked the shirttails free and ran one hand up over his shoulder blades, the other down inside the trousers over his buttocks. Mark clung to him and made the odd humming sound in his throat. Their mouths relinquished each other.

"Hi, kid," Mark said.

"This is fabulous. You haven't lost your looks overnight."

"You haven't aged much."

"I haven't got much time. I shouldn't be here at all. I've got magnificent news. My wife's going away tomorrow for the weekend. Can we be together?"

"We can be together whenever you say. Right now, I want us together in bed."

"I swore to myself I wouldn't tonight." He was unbuttoning Mark's shirt. Mark interrupted him to remove his smoking jacket. They stood together and continued to undress each other. "Do you smoke?"

"Yes. Why? Do I smell of cigarettes?"

"You smell gorgeous. That's what I'm doing right now—getting cigarettes. If you have a spare pack, I won't have to waste time buying them later."

"Yeah, I have some."

They bent to remove shoes and socks and dropped trousers and shorts and were naked in each other's arms again. Walter experienced an eruption of sensuous delight unlike anything he had ever known. He warned himself not to attach any emotional importance to it. Repression had probably sharpened his special appetites. He was old enough to indulge them at last, sufficiently mature to take his pleasure where he found it, without worrying about its undermining his basic normalcy.

They somehow found themselves locked together in a wide bed. Walter had been determined to go slow, to learn every part of Mark with his eyes and hands and mouth, but urgency drove them again. A lubricant passed between them. Walter blindly grappled the beautiful body to him and took possession of it. They thrashed about together, laughing and shouting. Their orgasms were simultaneous and violent. Walter lay on him until stillness settled over them.

"You feel hard again already," Mark said.

"I am. You make it like that permanently."

"Do you have time to do it again?"

"I don't know about time. I'm going to."

"Please do. I can't get enough of you."

"Does my having you like this make you want to try it this way with other guys?"

"No."

"That's one of the things I've thought about—along with thinking how damn beautiful you are."

"Jealous?" Mark's body stirred briefly with laughter. "Me too. Knowing there haven't been many guys in your life is a big comfort. Oh, yes! Do that. That's an even bigger comfort. Oh, Walter! God, yes!"

Walter washed himself in the basin in the bathroom. In spite of his dismissive reference to time, his inner clock was working with precision. He hadn't been there for more than half an hour. He had run into—who should he say? He chose a newspaperman who worked in the theater department of the *Post* whom Clara scarcely knew. He wouldn't put a name to him unless she insisted. They had had a drink together.

He dried himself and returned to the room. He had given little attention to his surroundings but had registered that it was a pleasantly big room, rather bare, but clean and with nothing conspicuously ugly in it. He liked the bed's being a bed and not a contraption that turned into something else. A towel on the floor beside it was the only evidence remaining of what had just taken place.

Mark turned from a desk and approached him and dropped some keys into a palm. "Those are yours," he said. "There's a phone in the hall, but we can't be calling each other all the time. You can come in whenever you feel like it." His lips twitched with a small smile. "You'll also know I can't have anybody else here with me. This place is ours. I'm so glad you made it tonight. There've been moments when I've felt slightly nutty moving down here. It makes complete sense now. I know you want to get home. You better dress."

Walter moved his hands through his hair and down his neck and chest, beginning to feel familiar with him. He dropped his hands to his waist and pulled him closer, and they kissed. Their cocks stirred against each other. They drew their heads back.

"All right," Walter said. "Tomorrow—isn't it marvelous?—tomorrow I'm going to spend all day just drinking in your beauty. Do you have a lot to do?"

"I've got a few appointments. What time did you want to begin?"

"About 11? As soon as I know Clara's gone."

"Fine. I'll cancel everything after 11. Come when you can. If I'm not here, I won't be long." He put his arm around his waist and walked him to his clothes.

Walter bent to pick up his socks. As he did so, he paused experimentally to kiss his cock. Mark took a step back. "You don't have to do that. I know you don't like it."

Walter straightened and looked into the grave eyes under the strong level brows. "That's not true. It's not as simple as that. It's all still a bit strange for me. I mean, in theory I don't go in for that sort of thing. The faithful husband and so forth. That part of you makes it impossible for me to kid myself about it. You're a guy. You have a cock. I want to know it, along with the rest of you."

"All right, but don't push it. I don't expect you to turn into something you're not. You're fabulous in bed the way you are. You don't have to add any trimmings."

"I don't feel as if I've been to bed with you at all yet. Just a few wild convulsions of wanting you madly. I told you I want time with you—all tomorrow and tomorrow night and the next and all that night and the day after that."

Mark's face broke into his sweet guileless smile. "If we aren't sick of each other after that, maybe we'll really have something."

"I love having the keys," Walter said, staying close to him as he dressed. "If I wake up in the middle of the night, you may find me back in bed with you."

"I'll try to pretend you're here, whether it happens or not."

When he had pulled on his jacket, Walter stepped up behind him and held his naked body against his chest and lingeringly caressed his chest and abdomen and thighs with his fingertips. Mark kissed the side of his face, and Walter saw his cock swing out and lift in front of him. It was esthetically jarring because of the refined perfection of the rest of him. He couldn't deny he liked the feel of its hard thickness, if only because it told him Mark wanted him.

"I hate to leave you with this. I'll do something about it in the morning." He gave it a squeeze and kissed his ear and released him. He turned back at the door. Mark stood where he had left him. He surveyed him from head to foot. "I wish we'd had you photographed like that." He started to open the door.

"My God, the cigarettes," Mark exclaimed. He turned and strode to the desk. Walter watched the play of muscles as he reached into an open carton and returned with a pack.

"Thanks, beautiful. We make a good team." He allowed himself a final caress and touched his chin and let himself out while Mark moved around behind the door.

Clara left in a whirl of brisk efficiency in the morning. He waited until 15 minutes after her plane was due to leave and called the airline to make sure there had been no hitches. He called the office and told Alice to cancel his appointments. "And, Alice, you'll see me coming in and out during the day, won't you?"

"What? Oh. Oh, yes, of course. As a matter of fact, I just saw you go through a minute ago."

"You've got the idea. See you on Monday." He put on casual clothes and went out and around the corner and in less than three minutes was letting himself into Mark's room. He called out as he entered and was met with silence. He closed the door behind him and looked around. In the daylight the room was till pleasant, immaculate if spartan. The bed had been made but not covered. Walter smiled to himself and undressed and hung his clothes in the closet where there was an array of suits. He went to the bathroom and collected a towel and put it on the bedside stand.

As soon as he stretched out on the bed, thoughts of Mark's lying beside him gave him an immediate erection. He laughed and lay on his back with his arms and legs flung out and waited for his lover. His mind drifted. He hadn't taken a working day off since he could remember, perhaps never. He realized how much he longed for a rest. He would like to go off somewhere with Mark and just lie around and make love.

His eye was caught by a pile of books on the desk. There was another pile of books beside it. He couldn't see what any of them were, but they were real books. He would look through them later. Mark was a mystery that was about to unfold. He hadn't been able to place him in any way. He had an individual style, but most actors (or models) did. There was more to him than that. His commanding air suggested inner resources of cultivation and serious interests. He hoped that they would become friends.

240

It was a luxury not to have to think about time, but he knew only five or ten minutes had passed when he heard footsteps and a key rattling in the door. His sex gave a little leap on his belly, growing more rigid. He smiled and could almost feel his eyes slanting upward. Mark entered and saw him and remained motionless for a moment. He looked paralyzed with astonishment and delight. He pushed the door closed, moved forward slowly and stood looking down at him from the foot of the bed.

"My, oh, my. Imagine coming home to this. You look 18. I'm sure I'll be arrested for seducing a minor."

"Not if you stay there all dressed up, you won't."

He was as impeccably groomed as ever, freshly shaved, his hair meticulously combed except for the slight shagginess around the edges. His fingernails shone. Walter watched him strip quickly and arrange his clothes with sure, spare gestures. He crossed the room with the assured step Walter had admired from the start. When he reached the bed, Walter surged up and pulled him down to his knees on the bed with him and took a nipple in his mouth. Mark gasped as Walter darted his tongue over his chest and up into his armpit.

They sank down together and moved over and under and around each other in a balletic mime of passion. They were wrestlers and acrobats as well as lovers. They were brought up to their knees over each other and sank into each other's arms, moaning. Their mouths were everywhere on each other. They met from time to time for long enthralled minutes while their tongues drank from each other. Walter forced himself to learn the taste and texture of Mark's cock with his lips and tongue, and the last small resistance to his lover vanished.

He learned how to make Mark's body leap about with arms and legs flailing. He laughed with triumph when Mark cried out ecstatically. Their intent eyes told each other when they were close to orgasm, and they eased pressures to prolong the voluptuous interplay of their bodies. Mark came with a sudden shout when Walter's mouth was once more on his buttocks. He pulled the towel out from under him and made Walter lie back and gave him an orgasm with his mouth.

241

They lay together, their heads close on the pillows, and looked into each other's eyes.

"If that's what married men are like, I'm all for them," Mark said dreamily.

"You're fairly inspiring."

"Nobody's ever made love to me like that before."

"I'm glad. It's just a beginning. I seem to've been saving up all sorts of fancy tricks for you."

"Mmm. I'll say. It's the first time coming was almost an anticlimax. I had an idea I shouldn't go too far at first. I was afraid I might shock you. That lasted about two seconds. You don't mind my cock anymore, do you?"

"No. Why should I?"

Mark smiled. "It's a bit strange doing all these things with a guy who's straight."

"I don't think we need to worry about that." Walter sat up and dropped his legs over the side of the bed. He pulled Mark up with him and put an arm around him and ran his fingers over his tousled hair. "That's given me an appetite. Shall we go have some lunch before we get started again?"

Mark lifted both hands and gripped Walter's hair and looked deep into this eyes. "You puzzle me, to say the least." His grip tightened, and he pulled Walter's head roughly to him and thrust his tongue deep into his mouth. Walter felt a sudden male drive in him that threatened his domination. To retain the upper hand in the situation was essential to him. It was a guarantee that it wouldn't get out of control. Briefly there was a yielding in himself he had known to his sorrow with Harry. Mark pulled his head back but kept his fingers tangled in his hair. "I'm yours, but you're mine too, kid. I wonder how long that will last." He released Walter and rose and went to the bureau. Walter immediately wanted him back. They had been on the verge of some discovery about each other that he felt as a threat. Fair warning. He was prepared. Mark picked up his watch. "Good God. Do you have any idea what time it is?"

"About noon?"

"Almost 1. We've been at it for an hour and a half."

"Bliss takes time."

"What're you wearing?"

"Jacket and slacks."

"Fine. Same for me. I'll just be a second." He went on into the bathroom. Walter rose and began to dress, aware that he was getting in deeper and that he felt no need yet to pull back.

He knew a restaurant in a garden nearby, and they went to it. Walter didn't think there would be anybody he knew for lunch on a weekday, and he was right. He began to find out something about Mark. He was the youngest of five sons of a working widow and had been brought up in Queens. He had gone through high school and had been working ever since in all sorts of odd jobs, after a brief stint in the Army, which had ended with a prison term and a dishonorable discharge because of being caught in compromising circumstances with a fellow GI. He had read a great deal and given himself an education of sorts. The theater was a major interest.

"Jack and I really loved each other," he said, referring to the GI. "We weren't doing anybody any harm. If it hadn't been for that, I probably would've gone to college on the GI bill. Anyway, I decided I'd better go straight. I even almost got married at one point. Then it happened again, and I gave up. Why fight it when it's so much fun?"

"But never more than that? You never meet anybody you want to stay with?"

"No. I've never wanted to get involved. What's the point?"

"That's what I've always wondered about guys together. What about modeling? Do you plan to go on with that?"

"I wondered when you were going to ask that. It's a dumb sort of thing to do, isn't it?"

"Not necessarily, I just don't see that it leads to anything either."

"Exactly, a faggot model. It's about on a level with a whore," he said with no trace of self-pity. "A dishonorable discharge doesn't help when you're applying for a job. It's a problem, Walter. Modeling pays well. I

243

should be able to keep at it for another ten or 15 years. I could be a lot worse off."

"I'll think about it. We'll talk more about it. You know what I think of your looks. It went way beyond that the minute I touched you. Maybe we can figure something out."

Mark looked at him with a faint smile. "Do you honestly think we'll be seeing each other a week from now?"

"I know it," Walter said with conviction. Their eyes met and held until it became an agony for Walter to keep his hands quiet on the table in front of him. He wanted to reach out for him and hold him.

Mark was the first to speak. The habitual gravity of his expression was more pronounced. "I know I'm dreaming. I just hope nobody wakes me up. I think we'd better go home, don't you?" He insisted on paying. "It's the first time we've been out together. I know it doesn't mean much, but I'm sure you can understand my wanting to make a small gesture."

"You're sweet, Mark. Thank you."

They walked home staying close beside each other, both of them finding excuses to put their hands on each other, a corner to turn, a street to cross. As soon as the door was closed behind them they put their arms out to each other and kissed, less hungrily, more tenderly than before.

Mark drew back. "You can't even guess what this means to me." He offered Walter the sweetness of his smile. "Maybe after we've made love for another few hours I'll be able to talk to you."

They stood together and undressed. They used the bathroom together and put their arms around each other to walk to the bed. They stretched out side by side contentedly.

"We're getting to know each other, Mark."

"I know. At least that's what's happening in my dreams." Their mouths met playfully but didn't stay very playful for long. Mark's rejection of any big commitment made Walter feel safer than ever. They both knew that the limits of involvement needn't limit their pleasure. He stretched Mark out on his stomach and knelt over him and stroked his buttocks and watched them quiver under his caress and lift to him. He entered him and felt the rapture in the body he had joined to his. He drove into him and heard him cry out for more. He gripped him and felt him yielding to his will. He was making all of his beauty his.

When they had showered together and returned to bed, Mark lay out, his body cradled in Walter's arms, and arched his back and stretched and made a writhing, sinuous display of his body. He pulled up a leg, bent at the knee, and rolled his pelvis toward Walter and flung out an arm and offered himself with wanton surrender. Walter bent over to kiss his throat, and Mark dropped his hands lightly on his head and toyed with his hair.

"Oh, darling," he murmured. "I swore I wouldn't call you things like that, but how can I help it? I can't call you Walter after this. You've taken me. I've had guys. I've never been had. I've thought of having you, but I don't want to, after all, and I know you wouldn't let me any-way. You're not mine. I'm yours. Beloved darling. Does it sound silly?"

"It sounds wonderful. You can call me anything you like."

"Are you sure? You make it awfully easy for a faggot to make a fool of herself."

Walter's head shot up. "Don't say things like that."

"You hate it? So do I. Still, I *am* a faggot. And you're a married man. I don't think either of us better forget it."

Mark's thick lids were lowered. Walter saw a glitter of eyes in a face that had become smolderingly seductive. "Please, Mark," Walter protested, feeling something calculated in the look.

"What's the matter? Don't you want a whore? You're crazy about my body. You're not the first, but I've never let myself be had before. I'd do anything to make you go on wanting me. That's whoring. I want to be your whore."

"I don't understand. Haven't you wanted me to take you?"

"Yes, darling. I've never wanted anything so much. You inside me– it's the most thrilling thing I've ever known. Now that you have me, do you want me?"

For answer, Walter lowered his head to the body that lay out in his arms, indolent with pleasure. He felt a need to restore equality in desire. Mark kept his hands on Walter's head and guided his mouth over him, encouraging him to linger where he wanted his lips on him. Walter moved down over the deep hollows along the rib cage and pelvis. He encountered his upthrusting cock and ran his tongue around it.

"Don't try to–" Mark warned. "I want to feel your teeth on it. Yes, like that." He dropped his hands to his sides. Walter kept his lips and tongue on stout flesh. "Oh, darling. If you go on, I'll come in your mouth. Don't do it unless you like it."

Much later they sat side by side on the bed, the sheet covering them to their waists, hugging their knees in their arms. "I know what I want to do," Walter said. "I want to get dressed to the nines and go the grandest restaurant in town. How about it?"

"You mean, where everybody will see us?"

"Exactly." Walter laughed merrily. Mark was his. He wanted to parade him around in front of the whole world. "Are you very well-known around town?"

"I'm one of the top models in the business, but that's a small world. No, not really."

"I guess I was thinking mostly of your love life. I should think everybody would be after you. Have you had affairs with lots of famous and important people?"

"Only you. You mean, will people say, 'There goes Walter Makin with that notorious Mark Travere?' No, darling. Your reputation's safe. I've always liked 'em young. You're the only Boy Wonder."

"We won't make a scandal? Never mind. We can still have a good dinner. What do you say?"

"Getting dressed up might make an interesting change."

"Wonderful. I'll go around to Tenth Street and pick out something fancy. You come along as soon as you're ready. We'll stun each other." Walter kicked at the sheet; Mark helped him get rid of it, and they put their arms around each other and leaned their heads together. They shared a quiet moment.

"It's good, Mark."

"It's good, darling."

"You know something ridiculous? I don't want to leave you long enough to change. Get dressed and come with me. You can have a drink while I get dolled up."

Mark was silent. Walter moved his head and looked at him. His head was slightly bowed, his expression calm. Tears were streaming down his cheeks.

"Hey, darling, what is it?" He hugged him closer and kissed his tears. "Oh, my sweet baby. Don't. What's the matter, darling? Tell me."

"I've always been alone." He spoke easily, without choking or gasping. "It's the way I've always wanted it, but it can be damn lonely. Now all of a sudden you're here."

"Yes, darling. I'm here. You're not alone." His heart went out to him. He took a deep breath and put his hand under his chin and turned his face to him.

"I'm so afraid of making too much of it," Mark said. Tears continued to roll peaceably down his cheeks.

"Don't be afraid, sweet darling. You can trust me."

"How can you say that when you don't even know what it's about? I feel closer to you than I ever have to anybody."

"That's good, isn't it?"

"Yes, no matter what happens." Mark suddenly gave his big smile. "So what's there to cry about? Do you realize the things you've been saying?"

"How do you mean?"

"If you don't know, I'm not going to tell you."

"Now, come on, dar...oh!" The endearments had come so naturally to his lips that he realized only now that he had been saying them. He felt a small shock of self-consciousness and then threw his head back and laughed. "Well, why not? Sweet darling adorable baby. My own beautiful lover. You're right. It feels wonderful saying it, doesn't it?" He licked Mark's tears away.

"Darling," Mark said gravely.

"Beautiful, adorable darling," Walter said, laughing into his face. "I raise you."

"OK. You win." They fell back onto the bed, laughing. Walter rolled up onto him so that he was stretched out full-length on top of him. "I wonder if we'll ever manage to get inside each other's skin," Mark said with their noses and lips touching. "That's what we want, isn't it?"

"Yes, then I'll be as beautiful as you are. You're getting a hard-on again."

"So are you."

"Get dressed, my beautiful man. I want everybody in town to see how lucky I am."

Mark slid down him, then sprang up and headed for the bathroom. Walter wondered if he would ever be able to look at his back without wanting him.

Mark was very handsome in a dark suit. Walter kept his arm around Mark's shoulders in the dark when they went around the corner to Tenth Street.

Home seemed empty and alien to him. He felt that they were both interlopers as he poured them drinks. He called Le Pavillon and reserved a table. Clara would hear that he had dined with a handsome unknown. He had plenty of time to decide what he would tell her.

"This is a marvelous room," Mark said when Walter had put down the phone. "I was in no state to notice it the other day. It seems a hundred years ago."

"I blush. I'll never know how I dared to do it."

"What were you thinking—that you'd have me and then send me on my way?"

"I'm not sure I was thinking at all, except that you were the most magnificent creature I'd ever laid eyes on. Then I began to want you, and I've been wanting you more and more ever since."

"Still?"

They came together in the middle of the room and put their hands on each other. "That's probably the most idiotic question you've ever asked, and you know it."

"Can I come with you while you dress? I want to revisit the scene of the crime." They laughed and nuzzled each other.

"You have your clothes made for you, don't you?" Mark asked when Walter had changed. "It shows. I'm trying to love you for yourself, but you're still awfully glamorous. Walter Makin. The things I know now about Walter Makin."

Walter went to him and held his elbows. "I hope you know one of the important things. I like you, darling, as much as anybody I've ever known. We're going to be friends."

"I don't think we'd better start making declarations," Mark said, looking at him gravely. "You may get more than you bargained for. Just call me darling every now and then, and I'll be perfectly happy."

"Remind me not to do that in front of the waiters," Walter said. "Now let's go."

Walter knew people at four of the five tables they had to pass to get to his own, and he stopped at each and introduced Mark with a hand on his arm.

"Good lord," Mark said when they were seated. "Three movie stars, a famous writer, the greatest actor in the English theater, and a senator thrown in. These are the people you know, and you talk about liking me? *Glamorous* is hardly the word for you."

"You're the handsomest man here and nicer than any of them. I can't tell you how proud I am to be with you." He had noticed the eyes assessing Mark, the eyes turning speculatively to himself; and he wanted to burst out laughing with possessive pride. Mark could hold his own anywhere. His style was quiet and assured, his manners charming. He was going to keep him for himself for a while.

Despite his self-contained manner, Mark was a good talker, and everything they said was illuminated by the curiosity they felt about each other. Mark was familiar with all of Walter's work and admired it, with a few intelligent reservations. They liked the same books and films and music. During pauses, when waiters hovered over them, they exchanged looks of such passionate mutual approval that their breath kept catching, and they forgot to eat.

249

It was understood that this meal was on Walter, and he signed the bill with only a glance at it and distributed the substantial tips that were expected of him. Their departure was accompanied by the gratifying flurry of attention that his arrival had caused. In a taxi their hands moved to each other on the seat in the dark, and their fingers interlaced and teased and caressed during the silent ride downtown. They stopped at the Tenth Street place for Walter to pick up some things.

He threw a change of clothes and some toilet articles into a small bag, noting the risks involved if Clara should come back unexpectedly. He grabbed a bottle of whiskey from the bar as an afterthought. "OK. This is great. I feel as if I were really moving in with you."

"Careful, Walter," Mark said, his brow furrowing. "Don't give us any ideas."

Waking up with Mark in the late morning was a new turning point in this unfamiliar adventure, and Walter knew it without examining the implications. He hadn't spent a single night with another male–he didn't count Greg–since Harry, and he was filled with the camaraderie he remembered from long ago. The sheer fun of it struck him the moment he opened his eyes and saw Mark's dark tousled head lying a few inches from him. Mark's smile brimmed with sweetness in greeting. Memories of Harry brought warnings that he could too easily disregard. Walter gathered Mark into his arms with a muffled cry and kissed the side of his head. The strange rapture of holding a boy, a man! Suddenly it seemed to him that he had never known a moment with a girl to equal its complex satisfactions. An exclusive closed circle that somehow impossibly opened to contain an identical circle. Male to male. Mysterious magic. His fingers strayed among silken shaved strands in an unshaved armpit. His legs tangled with unshaved legs. The pubic growth felt sparse and patchy, checked by the bulky exterior equipment, a conspicuous manifestation of desire, gratifying to the touch. I want. I need. The poignance of an echo, a call from the hidden twin of self. Male to male, a riddle of infinite impossibilities.

250

"What a lovely sight to wake up to," Walter murmured.

"I didn't want to move for fear of waking you. Let me up for a minute, darling."

They took turns in the bathroom freshening up and fell back in bed, reaching for each other. They had spent 24 hours together, and Mark had become part of life. Walter laid his hands on him and felt his authority acknowledged.

"You're mine," he said into Mark's ear when they had recovered from the aftermath of orgasm.

"Yes, darling. Oh, God, yes. What's happening gets more and more tremendous."

Mark had an electric kettle, and he made instant coffee, and they discussed the day. It was sunny. They decided to go out and roam the streets with no fixed objective in mind.

"We can always hurry back here if we find we have to hold on to each other," Mark said.

They took a Fifth Avenue bus and rode on top with their arms thrown casually around each other's shoulders. They leaned their shoulders against each other while they watched the animals in the zoo. They had lunch and strolled to the Frick Museum and doubled back, stopping at several bookshops. Walter found an album of photographs of Greek statuary, including the Olympian *Apollo,* and bought it for his friend.

"My goodness," Mark commented. "I certainly wouldn't dare make a pass at him."

"You see what I mean? You're sexy-looking, and he isn't, but your features are a lot alike."

There was an exhibition of pictures by one of Walter's discoveries at a 57th Street gallery, and they stopped there. One of the pictures struck Walter's fancy, and he immediately wanted it.

"Damn. There's no point even asking how much it is, but I wish I could have it. Do you like it?"

"Yes, it's beautiful. But I'm not sure. I think you might get tired of it if you had it around all the time."

"You may be right. That's shrewd of you." Walter's eyes probed the composition for weaknesses. "Good. I won't buy any pictures without your OK. Not that I can afford to, anyway."

"Aren't you rich?"

"No, everybody assumes I must be," Walter said dryly. "It's a nuisance sometimes knowing that I could be if I wanted. I try not to think about it."

"But isn't your wife rich?"

"She thought she was about to be. There seems to be some difficulty with a will. That's why she's away."

"So I'm not a rich man's plaything? Tough luck. Let's go somewhere, and I'll buy you a drink."

They took another bus and rode down to the Brevoort and sat out on the sidewalk and had long iced gin drinks.

"I like being out with you almost as much as I like being at home with you," Mark said. "What a wonderful day."

"Yes, everything fits into one big perfect something or other." Their intimacy was so easy and so constantly expanding that Walter knew it was only a beginning. He kept pushing practical considerations into the back of his mind, but they were getting his attention nevertheless. The question of how he and Mark would be able to spend their days together in the future had an obvious solution, but he didn't want to examine it too closely until he had decided how he would present it to Clara. She was to call tonight to let him know when she was coming home. He would know then how much time he had. He looked at the handsome profile beside him and wanted to make the beautiful body his again. "It seems to me we've proved we're not just sex-mad. Don't you think it's time we get a reward?"

Mark turned with his lovely smile. "I'm all in favor of rewards, even if we haven't done anything to deserve them."

For the first time they closed a door behind them without rushing into each other's arms. They stood with their hands on each other, quietly relishing the return to privacy.

"I do love being with you, darling," Walter said.

"I'm beginning to believe you do. Maybe we won't get sick of each other, after all."

"It's possible."

They kissed while they took their clothes off, and they continued to kiss on the way to the bed. Walter stretched him out on his back and knelt between his thighs and moved in and took him in a way that permitted him to look into his eyes and watch the ecstasies of his body. Mark stretched out his arms to Walter and drummed his heels on his back and called to him. Walter handled his body and claimed it all, drove himself into it and held it where he wanted it, watched it being driven to thrilling contortions and held it again while Mark gave himself up to the power that possessed him as he shouted and sobbed with a wrenching orgasm. Walter prolonged his pleasure until Mark's body was once more heaving and panting and thrashing about in paroxysms of surrender and another ejaculation leaped from it.

They were spent and abashed when they showered together, scarcely daring to look at each other but touching and holding each other with tenderness and solicitude.

"I honestly didn't know it could be like this," Mark whispered.

"Neither did I."

"I'm not imagining things?"

"No."

They slowly recovered with strong shots of whisky, which they drank sitting close together on the hard little settee with their arms around each other and towels around their middles. Their voices and the sense of camaraderie returned.

"I better get fresh sheets," Mark said. "I came all over the place." They changed the bed together and dressed again for dinner.

"I'll get more clothes when we go to Tenth Street for Clara's call," Walter said. "I'm going to need a truck to move me out of here."

"Don't wake me up, even though it's almost time," Mark said.

They had a good cheap meal in a little restaurant Walter knew off Bleeker Street. Clara's call wasn't due until 11:30 or midnight, so they had time to kill.

"Have you ever been to a gay bar?" Mike asked.

"No. Why? Do you want a new boy for tonight?"

"Would you like to see one?"

"I don't know. Don't a lot of theater people go to them? I don't want to be seen."

"I can take you to one where nobody's ever heard of Walter Makin. Anyway, I don't have to say your name."

"If you want to," Walter agreed.

"I do, even though you probably won't like it. You wanted to show me off last night. That was part of the dream. I think I'm talking about something closer to reality. My reality. It has to do with my belonging to you." Mark's heavy lids lowered as he spoke; Walter felt a renewed pang of desire.

"If it has to do with that, let's go."

They took a taxi to the East 50s. Walter was nervous about the expedition. He felt that going to such a place was a commitment of some sort he hadn't bargained for and which Mark had no right to expect of him. His old dread of the brand was once more strong in him. He hated being deposited in front of the door by a taxi driver who probably knew what sort of place it was.

They entered a nondescript bar that was crowded, noisy, and populated exclusively by males. As soon as he could bring himself to look around, he was struck by the low esthetic level of assemblage. He had always thought of homosexuals as pretty youths, limp-wristed, shrill, perhaps even painted but more attractive in a strictly physical sense than the general run. A second glance revealed a scattering of presentable young men, but there was a generous share of paunches and bald heads and ill-formed features.

They found room at the bar and ordered drinks. He saw Mark nodding to several people. As he relaxed, Walter was aware of eyes crossing his in an effort at contact, but he was accustomed to this and paid no attention. After a few more drinks, they decided to leave.

"Did you hate it?" Mark asked when they were in the street headed for Lexington Avenue.

"No, not really, but I didn't like it. Can you see any connection between that sort of thing and us?"

"Not particularly. Except we're two men, and we're having an affair. We may belong there as much as anywhere. It depends on what you mean by 'us.'"

"Us? What do you think I mean?"

"I don't know. It's a subject you're not exactly eloquent about. All the things I've been trying not to say."

Walter hailed a passing cab and took Mark's arm and urged him toward it. "Let's wait till we're back near the telephone."

They drove downtown in neutral silence, the close connection between them suspended but untroubled by any sense of real alienation. It carried over while Walter was letting them in so that neither made a move toward the other after Walter closed the door. He went directly to the kitchen and got ice and made them drinks. He was amazed at how much he minded even this small coolness between them. He took a glass to Mark, where he remained standing tentatively in the middle of the living room. He touched his hand as he gave it to him.

"I can't stand being even slightly at odds with you, darling. This is the first time we haven't been completely right with each other. Don't try not to say things. Tell me why we went to that place."

"You hate everything to do with being queer. I wanted you to see the worst. It wasn't so horrible, was it?"

"No, of course not. I'm probably silly about it. I'm sorry."

"I've spent a lot of time in places like that, looking for sex, cruising. It was marvelous being there with the most attractive kid any of them had ever seen and not wanting to give anybody else so much as a glance."

"Oh, baby, darling," Walter enthused. He put his hand on his neck and pulled his head forward, and they kissed lovingly across their glasses. "That wasn't much of a quarrel, but I'm glad it's over. Come sit and say more things like that." He kept a hand on Mark's shoulder and went to the sofa and sat. Mark dropped to the floor on his knees and leaned against him.

"Can I stay down here for a while? I may not be able to look at you through what's coming. You said you liked me as much as you've ever liked anybody. I can't bear to say anything that might change that, but it's going to come out, so it might as well be now. We've been together for two days, and I'm bursting." He bowed his head and was silent. Walter touched his hair. "I'm...now that I'm going to say it, I'm scared. I don't have to. I could go on being your whore but...oh, hell. We're in love with each other, Walter. It doesn't make any more sense to me than it does to you. I didn't think it could happen to me. I don't want to make complications, but you can't be in love with somebody without wanting to keep him. I just hope it doesn't seem like more of the queer stuff you hate." He looked up with grave, intense eyes.

Walter met them without flinching. He took Mark's hand and moved it to the fabric stretched over his rigid sex. "That's what your saying those things does to me. It would be awfully easy to say the same thing to you. I just don't understand what it means when guys talk about being in love with each other." He had dodged the issue as long as he could. Surely he knew enough of his life to find an alternative to Mark's declaration. Mark was making the mistake of expressing what had happened between them in the vocabulary of normal passions. It distorted everything.

Walter stroked Mark's hand and looked him in the eye. "What do we do about it if we're in love with each other?" he demanded.

"Being in love is being in love," Mark insisted. "You'd know what to do about it if I were a girl."

"But, Christ, Mark, it's entirely different. If you were a girl, I'd already be thinking about divorcing Clara and marrying you and having a family and all the rest of it. Besides, I've never felt like this with any girl."

"Thanks." He dropped his eyes and took a swallow of his drink. "What are you thinking about? She's coming home tomorrow or the next day. What happens then?"

"I'm thinking about today and having hundreds more like it. You'll meet Clara. I'll tell her how much I like you. We'll do all the things friends do. We're going to be together. There's no question about that."

"Except that we won't spend nights together."

"Even that should be possible sometimes."

Mark lifted his eyes to him. "Don't you understand that today would've been entirely different if we hadn't waken up together and made love right off and known that our bed was waiting for us whenever we needed it? There's a difference between having an affair and living together."

"I haven't noticed our making love has much to do with whether it's night or day. Let's put it simply. Can you honestly imagine my divorcing Clara so that we can keep house together?"

"Stranger things have happened."

He touched Mark's cheek. He felt the proud shoulders against his arm, lightly balanced matador's shoulders. Their eyes searched each other out. "You're magnificent. Apollo. A divine body that makes male or female unimportant. All right. Let's say it could happen, but you must admit it's a peculiar thought for somebody who's never dreamed of having a serious affair with a guy."

Mark shot up, still on his knees, and pushed Walter's legs apart and thrust himself between them. He left one hand on Walter's cock and tangled the other in his hair. He pulled his head to him and kissed him hard, forcing his tongue into his mouth. Once again Walter felt his domination threatened. He reached out for him. Mark jerked his head back and looked at him with hard, demanding eyes. "Listen to me, damn it. You want me more than I've ever been wanted. You take me in a way that nobody's ever taken me. I've given myself to you more completely than I thought was possible. I've let myself be your whore. That might've been enough for me, but you won't let it be. I've tried to make it easy for you by not saying anything, but we've gone too far."

"I haven't asked you not to say anything," Walter said placatingly, thrilled by the strength he felt for him, feeling the unfamiliar yielding in himself but still unwilling to surrender his controlling authority. "You can say anything you like."

"Then listen. We're so in love with each other that I don't care about anything anymore. God, you really like me to say it, don't you? I'll remember that in case you ever have any trouble getting it up. You're queer for me. Why not admit it? God knows, I don't want you to be queer for anybody else."

"It's not a question of admitting anything. If you want to call it being in love with each other, all right. I haven't denied it. All I've—"

The telephone rang. They sprang up as if the police were battering down the door. Walter moved toward the phone, grateful for the release. He turned his back on Mark and answered. It was the expected call. He felt a brief numbing shock at being summoned back to Clara's world by the sound of her voice.

Mercifully, she had a lot to say. He listened with sufficient attention to make appropriate replies without attempting to take in all the business details. Elation soared through him so that he had to take a grip on himself to keep from roaring with laughter when she said she was staying till Monday, perhaps Tuesday.

"I'll call the office by noon and let you know, dearest," Clara said.

"Fine. I mean, I'm sorry you have to stay over. It's a damn bore. I'll be waiting to hear." He forced himself to continue to chat with her, leaving her the initiative to terminate the call. She finally did so, and he hung up and turned back to the room, beaming. Mark was leaning over a table leafing through an art book. He looked up, and they moved to each other and stood face-to-face with their hands on each other's waists.

"Did you follow that, sweetheart?"

"I tried not to listen."

"We're still in luck. She's not coming back till Monday, maybe even Tuesday. It looks as if we may end up having almost a whole week to ourselves." Walter pulled him closer so that they were touching all down the front. "So. Is it all settled? Have we decided we're in love with each other?"

"Thank God you can kid about it," Mark said, smiling. "You're right. It doesn't matter what we call it. All I care about is what we do about it."

"I have some ideas. I want to tell you what I've been thinking." Talking about being in love was thrilling in its way; he wanted to pin it down to practical considerations. Knowing that Clara wasn't about to land on him was a help. "Shall we have one more drink and talk about it before we go home?" They released each other, and Walter took his hand, and they went together to replenish their glasses. They went hand in hand to the sofa and sat, close enough to reach each other but not touching."

"First of all, how would you like to work for me?"

Mark sat back, his eyes fixed on his glass. "In what way?" he asked cautiously.

"As my assistant, private secretary, a little bit of everything. The money wouldn't be very good, maybe not as much as you're making now. You have no experience, but you're very intelligent; our tastes are the same, and, God knows, I'd be able to count on you."

Mark closed his eyes for a moment and opened them again. His smile was wide and ravishing. "The amazing Mr. Makin. You're still there, so I guess you're real, but I don't believe it."

"You think it's a good idea?" The thought of hiring Mark on a permanent basis had been maturing in the back of his mind almost without his knowing it. Mark had passed all the tests Walter may have subconsciously set for him. Clara was the only problem. "We can invent a bit of experience for you. We've got to be careful how we work you into the picture. Clara's got to like you. If we're smart, she will."

"Can we be lovers and work together and not have people suspect something?" Mark said with obvious reluctance, scrupulously giving Walter an out. Walter noted it as another high mark in his favor.

"Why should they? Maybe we'll invent an ex-wife for you. If you flirt a bit with the girls around the theater and not at all with the boys, there won't be any talk worth worrying about, so long as nothing dreadful emerges from your lurid past. I've always had a male assistant, anyway. We're going to Europe in five or six weeks. As soon as Clara gets this money business straightened out, we'll be filthy rich. If we get you launched properly, there's no reason why I shouldn't decide to take you with us to give you a look at what's going on over there. We're planning to move into a much bigger place too. I'll see that there's a room for you. When we get going in the fall, I'll work up some sort of crisis that makes it more convenient for me to have you available both day and night. Once you're in, it can turn into a permanent arrangement. It's high time I stopped sharing a bedroom with Clara. We're the only couple I know who still do after ten years of marriage. We'll be able to creep into bed with each other. How does that strike you?"

Mark was gazing at him. The smile had vanished. "My God," he said. "You really do want me to belong to you. As far as I'm concerned, I'm yours. I might even accept the creeping into bed part. I'm not sure. Let's go home. I've got to touch you, and I don't want anything to happen here. Let's get going. You'll have to say it all over again before I can take it in."

He was reacting just as Walter would have wanted him to, without gratitude but soberly with undemanding acceptance. It would be insane to consider tearing his life apart, but for them to have a life together in conjunction with the life he and Clara had created made exciting sense.

They rose and stood looking into each other's eyes, keeping their distance. "I'll tell you one thing," Walter said. "I wouldn't be talking about a job, no matter how much I love you, if I didn't think you'd be damned good at it. You don't know what I'm like when I'm working. I get awfully absorbed. You probably won't like it at first until you get used to it."

"I'll know how to handle you. I should think it would be good to have an assistant who adores you. Now please. Out. I feel a modicum of desire coming on. I don't want to end up on the bathroom floor."

Walter snapped out lights, and they left after exchanging a quick kiss at the door.

They stayed up all night and slept till noon. Eventually Mark pulled some clothes on and went out for the Sunday papers and brought them back along with some sandwiches and beer. Walter waited, wearing only a pair of Mark's blue jeans that were too short for him. Mark laughed when he saw him.

"God, you're cute and sexy. Seeing you in something of mine gives my heart the flips." He put the papers and the bag of provisions on the table. "I should've looked for a real apartment. I hate having to go out to restaurants all the time. I'd like to cook for you. I'm good at it."

"That's the longest time we've been apart for almost three days. I didn't like it."

"I know. It really hurts when we're not near each other."

Walter watched him as he slipped off his jacket and moved across the room to hang it up. He was his usual immaculate self, shaved and combed, shining with cleanliness. Walter felt as if they were mated, as animals mate, drawn together by some compulsion in the blood without the need of a conscious exercise of will, irrevocably bound by the fact of being together. Mark returned and moved in close to him and let his fingers stray over his bare torso.

Walter ran the back of his hand along his hard jaw. "I almost wish Clara were coming back today, after all. I can't wait for you to meet her and get you started at the office where I can look at you all day."

"I'm scared, naturally. Everything you say about the job sounds fascinating, and I think I can do it. It's the other part that worries me. You have to admit it sounds strange. What it amounts to is living as a threesome—a ménage à trois. Is that anywhere near the right way to pronounce it? I can't help feeling we're going to end up wanting to be on our own, but of course I'm prejudiced."

"Try not to be, darling. It seems strange to us because we know, but it shouldn't to her. It'll just be my finding a friend I want near me. Europe and being in hotels should be fun. She likes to go shop. We'll be able to do things together and rush off to bed constantly. Once we're back here in a big place, it'll be like being on our own a lot of the time. There'll be difficulties at first, I grant you. We're going to have to be awfully careful."

"I don't mind being careful if we have our private time. Like this."

"Like this, sweetheart. God knows, I'm tempted to tell her the works and sweat it out and see what happens. I even want to tell her, but I know she'd manage somehow to break us up."

"Would she? It's maybe none of my business, but I still don't have a very clear idea what you feel about her."

"Oh, lord." He gave Mark a hug and kissed his cheek and sat in a straight chair at the table. Mark began to take things from the bag. Each time his hand emerged from it Walter got a jolt of sensual pleasure. "She's the girl I've always wanted to be with. I love her. It wouldn't be fair to try to compare the way I feel about her and the things I feel with you. It's different with a girl. With you—it's a raging volcano that makes everything else seem pretty pale. I like you in a way that men probably never like women. Still, Clara and I are a pair. We've created a sort of legend together. That may sound silly, but I can't imagine doing anything to destroy it."

Mark moved around behind him and stroked his shoulders. "Yes. Well, I'll remember that. If that's the way it has to be, we'll try to make it work." Mark's hands grew possessive, and their caress moved down over his chest. "Let's get some food into us." He pulled the other chair close to Walter and sat. He unwrapped sandwiches and poured beer. Their talk returned to Clara. They had settled that he would come to Tenth Street for drinks one evening during the week when others would be there.

"She'll know you're the model for the poster, of course," Walter said. "The pictures should be ready tomorrow."

"You mean, she'll see all of me, before you do the cropping you talked about?"

"Of course. I don't think we should deny her that pleasure."

"That's enough to make a fella shy."

"I know she's going to like you. She likes people who look like somebody but who've done it on their own. Like me. I think we're definitely going to have to give you an ex-wife. You got married very young—when you were in the Army. You'd planned to go to college, but there you were with a wife and a baby so you had to go to work. You've had many jobs, but you were interested in the theater, and in your spare time—no. Hey, wait a minute. I know. Your wife was from New Brunswick, New Jersey, and you went there with her, and you had all

262

these jobs, but you managed to do a lot of work with the little theater group there. You knew people who had known me; and when your marriage broke up, somebody gave you a letter of introduction to me. When you came back to New York, you started doing more and more modeling and lost the letter and didn't do anything about it. Then when you met me the other day you naturally talked about it; we hit it off, and I immediately thought you might be the solution to the assistant problem. I took you to dinner at Le Pavillon to see if you'd make a good appearance in public. There. How about that? What could be simpler?"

"You're wasting your time in the theater. You should write a novel. That *is* why you took me to Le Pavillon, isn't it?" They looked at each other and laughed.

"I swear to God I didn't think about it until we were there, and then you were so superb that I couldn't help thinking how lucky I was to have found you. I don't mean personally. *Lucky* is hardly a word for that. I was already thinking about the job."

"When do you think it'll start?"

"I don't know when we can start paying you—that's Clara's department—maybe not till this fall. But in the next week or two, so's not to look as if we're rushing it, I'd like you to start coming into the office whenever you can and sit in on all the stuff I'm laying on for next season. By the time we take off for Europe, you'll probably be doing my job for me."

"Europe. God. I thought I was dreaming before."

They agreed that they must resume their normal working life the next day. They were up promptly, and Walter took his belongings back to Tenth Street and put them away. Longing for Mark began to gnaw at him before he was finished. He had been too grudging in the expression of his feelings. He should have told him he cared about him more than he had ever cared about anybody. Why not tell him that he was madly in love with him and get it over with? He was back at the old sticking point. He couldn't tell somebody he was madly in love unless he was prepared to rearrange his life accordingly. The way Mark

263

wanted him to. He still couldn't imagine doing it for a man. He could have Mark without disturbing the public facade of his life with Clara. Their physical passion could be kept a secret. He had found a devoted friend.

He couldn't get him out of his mind even at the office. He felt as if he'd been away a long time and ought to be busy catching up. He called Herb and arranged for the photographs to be sent around right away by messenger. Waiting, making calls, and taking others, he imagined Mark's being there with him and knew that if they could get through the next week, everything would be all right. He felt for the keys in his pocket. Mark was to call later. No matter when Clara got back, he would have to see him somehow, if only for half an hour.

When the photographs arrived, he tore open the heavy envelope impatiently and spread them out on the coffee table. His heart began to pound. Mark was magnificent. Mark was a god. Mark was male beauty, taut and erotic. The pose they had hit on together had resulted in a series of the most stunning photographs he had ever seen: front, three quarters, breathtaking back. He felt a hollowness in the pit of his stomach. Had he actually possessed this remarkable being?

Clara called at midday to say she was staying over one more day and would be back the following afternoon. She sounded cross and rushed, and he let her go as if she were an intrusion on his real life. Another night with Mark. It would cushion the shock of transition from the last few days' exclusive preoccupation with him to working him into a normal full life.

He spent an hour scissoring out bits of Mark's anatomy to compose the poster, with sensational results. Herbie hadn't yet applied his marbleizing technique to the negatives, which would make Mark unrecognizable.

When Mark called, he told him the good news about Clara. "You haven't found a new boy for tonight, have you?"

"That's getting to be a pretty bum joke," Mark said.

"I know. Does it hurt?"

"God. You?"

"Just about unbearable. At least I have the photographs to look at. Wait till you see them." They made arrangements to spend another night together.

The next morning Walter saw Mark off for an early job. They knew they probably wouldn't see each other till the next day, and their parting kiss was anguished. Walter went back to Tenth Street to change and turned up at the office on edge with fatigue and the prospect of facing Clara.

Late in the afternoon Clara called and said she was home. She still sounded cross. He told her he would be there in an hour. He finished his most pressing business by phone and took a taxi to Mark's room. He promised himself he wouldn't stay for more than half an hour. Clara might call again and find that he had left the office. He had to save his lies for the big occasions, whole evenings, or at least a couple of hours.

He let himself into an empty room. It was a blow. He had always assumed that he would find Mark when he wanted him. They would have to set up a system of regular communication.

He waited for what he judged to be ten minutes and then decided that too little time remained to make it worthwhile waiting longer. He left a note saying that he doubted he could get back that evening but would try. If not, Mark was to call the next day. He braced himself for Clara and went around the corner to Tenth Street. She was looking cross. They gave each other a peck on the cheek. Walter felt as if they had been away from each other for weeks and wondered if they would ever be really together again. He went to the bar and mixed himself a stiff drink.

"You've got a drink?" he said over his shoulder.

"Yes, I've had two enormous martinis," she said, "and I'll probably have two more."

He took a big gulp of his drink and turned to her. She had settled into the chair she favored. He sat on the sofa near her.

"All right. Tell me all about it," he said, trying to recapture the lightly affectionate tone he used with her.

"I won't tell you *all* about it. It would bore you to distraction. In a nutshell, my name was never actually in the will. It was the eldest daughter of the first son of the second brother of God knows who. It seems there was a family conclave, and everybody agreed it must be me. The only other person it could be was my disgusting cousin Marion, and she was already so rich that a lousy $3,000,000 would have made her nose crinkle with disdain. We were both about seven at the time. They all agreed I should have a nest egg to tide me over until my revered parents kick the bucket. Now Daddy and the beastly Marion have conspired to have it reviewed by the courts. It's one of those things that'll take forever. I tried to reason with Marion, but Daddy has hypnotized her. It's all for the good of the family or something." She made a sound of barely contained fury in her throat.

"What do you mean, forever?"

"At least a year. Maybe two. Maybe five. It depends on whether I have to appeal, and so forth."

He took another generous gulp of his drink and hastily put down the glass as the implication hit him. "But…you mean…we won't be able to go to Europe?"

"That's the first thing I thought. But we have to. It's a legitimate office expense. We may have to cut it short. We'll have to cancel the suites at the grand hotels. I won't be able to do any shopping. At least I've found good lawyers who'll take the case for a percentage. We won't have to cope with legal fees."

He waved his hand at her to cut her off. "But don't you realize? We don't have any money. We won't be able to move out of here."

"Not possibly. The lawyers think I have a perfectly good case, but if I win, they're sure she'll appeal. The problem is to line up–"

"Jesus Christ!" Walter shouted. He sprang up and turned his back on her. His eyes had suddenly filled with tears. All his plans and hopes were blasted. He couldn't take Mark to Europe. He couldn't have him move in with them. Everything had to be restudied and replanned. He rubbed his eyes and waited for his tears to subside. "Goddamn it," he cried when he was able to turn back to Clara and retrieve his drink.

"I'm sick to death of this. I'm the biggest figure in my field. I don't mean just here. In the world. People write articles about me in Russia, and I can't even afford to go there. I can't afford anything. I want to get out of this dump. You're the business genius. Arrange it."

She sat, straight and composed, not looking cross anymore. "We've never thought about money, dearest."

"No, because we thought you were going to have some. Your name not even in the will, for God's sake. Who does your father think he is?"

"I could kill Daddy. Doing a thing like this, then going off to Europe so I can't even discuss it with him. Don't worry. We'll win, dearest."

"When? Five years? I want out of here now. I'm sick of living like this. Oh, Christ." He went back to the bar and replenished his drink. He had a perfect excuse to say he wanted to go out and walk around and think. The words were on his lips, but he suppressed them. He didn't want to tell Mark yet. He didn't want to tell him until they had a whole night to make love and reassure each other. The thought of leaving him to go to Europe brought tears to his eyes again. He drank and kept his back to her. "Damn it, Clarry. Isn't there something you can do? Can't we get some money from the theater?"

"I don't see how, dearest. The contracts are very carefully drawn."

"I'm sure they are."

Clara joined Walter at the bar. "I'm not very happy about it myself, you know."

"Sure, darling." He touched her hand and snatched it hastily away. He had never called her darling in his life. He felt himself blushing hotly. He moved away from her into the room. "The hell with it. Let's forget it until I've had time to get used to it." *Until I've had time to talk to Mark,* he thought.

He got through the evening with her somehow. She made them something to eat, and then they switched to wine and drank a great deal of it. She wanted to know what he had been doing. He told her of a call from Mark Travere and of being interested in him and taking him to dinner, throwing in a few casual details from the story he had concocted.

"It would be nice to find you a dependable assistant. I wouldn't have thought a model would be the type." She made his work sound faintly disreputable.

"I gather the modeling was a stopgap, and then he was very successful and went on with it."

"Well, we can't put him on the payroll till fall. You haven't forgotten dinner with the Logans tomorrow?"

"It's tomorrow?"

"Yes, and we're having Tallulah and Evie and Clifton and some others for drinks on Thursday."

"I knew it was some time this week. Why don't I ask Mark Travere so you can meet him?"

"Would he fit with that crowd?"

"I think he'd fit with just about anybody. He's very much a gentleman. That's why I thought you'd probably like him in the office."

"What about his wife? Did you say he was married?"

"Divorced. Apparently the wife and child are still in New Brunswick."

"That's better. An extra man. And good-looking? Maybe he'll turn out to be a treasure. I want to see Herbie's photographs."

"They're marvelous, but they're not all that much like him. For one thing, they make him look much taller than he is."

"Is he a dwarf?"

They had both had enough to drink for this to strike them as very funny, and they laughed extravagantly. Walter was grateful for anything to lighten his mood. At least Mark had been brought into the picture, and very skillfully, he thought. He couldn't see why he shouldn't start coming into the office at the beginning of the week. There was no need to wait. Clara would be delighted with him. He would soon become a fixture at Tenth Street. He must remember to tell Mark that he'd been living around the corner for months.

They finished their third bottle of wine and fell into bed, neither of them in a mood for love. Walter woke up during the night and reached out for Mark. He heard Clara grunt and rolled away from her. He wanted to get up and steal out and run around the corner. He could say he'd been restless and needed a walk to put him to sleep. It was maddening knowing Mark was so near and not being with him. He let himself cautiously out of bed and found his dressing gown in the dark and went to the other room and switched on a light. Three o'clock. If he went to him, he would have to tell him what had happened, and this was hardly the time for the discussion they would have to have.

He sat and stared at his feet. He felt Mark's lips on them. He could see his body sprawled out asleep, his dark hair in disarray on the pillow. He ached to hold him. He was completely in Mark's power, and he knew he should fight it. Had it been like this with Clara at the beginning? He remembered the time he and David had packed her off to New York and he had spent two nights with Fay. He had missed her perhaps, but not in this crushing way. He had to get himself under control once more, learn how to direct it so that his joy was intensified when they were together but he could remain at peace when they were apart. He equated his vulnerability with weakness. Human experience was the poetry of the world. People individually were fascinating toys. He liked–*loved*–Mark, but he would soon get bored with him if he allowed him to take up too much of his life.

He dismissed all thought of going to him now. He might as well go back to bed. He didn't move. Let Clara get used to not finding him beside her. There might be nights when he would go out. She would have to accept the fact that he had turned into a night person, given to walking the streets in the early hours. He dozed, seeing Mark's body in every conceivable position, basking in the sweetness of his smile, hearing his charming voice declaring his love. He went back to bed eventually but was up early, bathed and dressed and ready to go. He told Clara that he'd had a restless night and wanted to walk at least part of the way to the office to clear his head.

He hurried around the corner and noiselessly inserted his key in Mark's door and opened it cautiously. Mark was standing a few feet from him, smiling at him. They burst out laughing as Walter closed the door behind him. Mark looked as if he had just stepped out of the

269

shower, combed and immaculate, naked except for shorts. They stepped to each other and kissed. Walter ran his hands over cool skin.

"Perfect timing, darling," Mark said. "I don't have to get dressed after all. It almost killed me to find your note last night. Is anything the matter?"

"Plenty, but not with us. Do you have some time, or shall I just tell you later?"

Mark looked him in the eye and nodded. "Bad, huh? I guess we better have it." He moved to the bed and picked up his dressing gown and put it on. They sat beside each other at the table. Walter told him about Clara's money problems.

"I'm not going to be able to take you to Europe after all," he ended painfully.

Mark's evenly balanced features were not constructed for the expression of petty emotions. They grew a trifle more grave, but he did not look downcast or reproachful. "No. To tell the truth, I couldn't quite believe in it. I expected Clara to make objections. We'll survive for a month, I guess. In a way it'll be easier knowing you're not here than hoping for you all the time. Missing you last night was bad. Besides, it was getting awfully close to my being a kept boy. You're the only person I've ever known I'd let keep me, but only in dire circumstances. I wouldn't like it. I suppose this means the big apartment is out."

"That's the worst part."

"Yeah," Mark murmured. He sketched designs on the table with a finger.

"I've made up my mind," Walter said quietly, coming to a decision as he spoke or believing that he had come to a decision. "I'm going to tell Clara. Not yet. Not till she knows you and you've started working for me in the fall. I won't leave her. I'll go on leading my public life with her. You and I have to have our private life together. Other men have mistresses. I'm going to have my friend. We'll find you a real apartment, like you said. I'll be able to give you at least $25 a week for my share. I want it to be ours. Our social lives will have to be a little apart, but the rest will be together. Clara will have to know where I am at night. I'll be sleeping with you. Maybe not every night, but as a natural part of life. Do you think it will work?"

Mark pressed his hands against his eyes and dropped them. "It damn well has to. I wasn't sold on the threesome idea. What about her? Will she accept it?"

"I'm counting on you two liking each other. I see it happening easily and gradually, without any great drama. If she can't accept it, well– I need you, darling. If it were only sex, I'd make sure I got over it. It's much more. I sat up thinking about you most of the night. I suppose it's being in love. I'm still fairly confused about it."

Their eyes met and called to each other. With one accord they rose and moved into each other's arms, and their mouths met. Their hips clamped together while their kiss deepened. They broke apart, but Walter kept his hands on the naked body under the dressing gown. "Can you think of any other solution?" he asked.

"I don't know Clara, so it's hard to say. If you want to know what I really think, I think we're going to live together. I'm so sure of it that I'm not going to push it. I'll try anything you say. If we both put up a hundred a month, we should be able to find something really good. When am I going to meet the lady?"

"That's all settled. You're coming for drinks tomorrow evening."

Mark took a deep breath. "God. We're really getting into it now."

"Yeah, the next couple of days are going to be hell. I've got a dinner tonight. Drinks tomorrow. After that, maybe everything will fall into some sort of pattern."

"I think we'd better go to a bed for a while, don't you? Thank God for sex. If I didn't know you're in love with me, I'd throw you out."

"I'm counting on your knowing all the things I don't know." Walter let go of him and shed his clothes.

The next day was dominated by Mark's impending meeting with Clara and went quickly. They were having only a dozen or so in for drinks, and most of them had arrived when Mark turned up. By then, Walter was in a fever of nerves but covered it with great calm. He greeted him carelessly without being able to really look at him and managed to keep his hands off him as he led him around for introductions. Clara took charge of him. When the tension of having him there had subsided, he was able to observe the others' reaction to him.

Mark was making an impression. The famous actor couldn't take his eyes off him. The even more famous actress looked tigerishly determined to take his pants off him. Clara, who had been entranced by the carefully selected photographs Walter had shown her, talked to him for some minutes before letting him go off on his own. Walter watched him doing so with the aplomb he had learned to expect of him. He was urbane but subtly discouraging with the famous actor. He was respectfully flirtatious with the famous actress. He ended by settling down with the distinguished writer and his wife and a lovely girl who was the best young actress in Walter's company.

He wanted to hug him for his unerring social sense. He could foresee his future. He had seen it happen before—people who were ignored until they were suddenly seen in the right frame and then were picked up and welcomed into the mainstream of the city's life. With his looks and as a member of the Walter Makin organization, Mark was about to make his mark. Walter felt a pang of jealousy but was aware that it was probably all for the best. When their passion cooled, Mark would be well-established in a new and rewarding life, and there would be no grounds for reproaches, as there might be if Mark weren't capable of fending for himself. Walter wouldn't want to be responsible for picking up a nonentity and eventually dropping him. Clara stopped beside him for a moment to sing Mark's praises.

"You're right, dearest. He is a find. Not as staggeringly beautiful as the photographs, thank heavens, but certainly one of the handsomest men I've ever laid eyes on. Did you notice him snub Clifton? It's rare that a young man knows how to make it politely clear that he doesn't like men making passes at him. Oh, dear, we need another bottle of champagne."

Walter circulated but managed to keep an approving eye on Mark. He saw Clara talking to him again. The Makins had another brief moment together.

"I thought Mark might be a loose end later, but Jack and his wife have already arranged to take him and Elaine off somewhere," Clara said. "You must fix it for him to come to the office and talk business."

Again, Walter could have hugged him. He was making just the right show of independence on his first evening, and he had linked up with a girl and the most unswervingly heterosexual couple in the room. He waited until a few people had left before he allowed himself to single him out for attention. "Everything all right?" he asked, standing over him. Mark immediately rose, and they moved a step away from the group he was with. "You're sensational," Walter mumbled half into his glass. He saw the muscles of Mark's jaw tighten.

"It's a great party. I'm enjoying myself."

"Clara likes you enormously. Can you come to the office tomorrow and talk about the job?" He didn't trust himself to look directly into Mark's eyes, but he saw that extraordinary things were happening in them. For an instant he was afraid they were filling with tears but realized that they were simply shining with happy excitement.

"Fine. What time?"

"Why don't you call? I'm always there by 10:00 or 10:30." His hand started to lift to touch him, but he clenched his fist and held it stiffly at his side.

Mark came to the office the following afternoon. Walter went to the door to welcome him when Alice announced him and closed it behind him and held it while they kissed. "Here we are, darling. It's really beginning now."

They moved apart, and Mark looked around at the handsome room. "This is your office? I wouldn't mind living here."

"You'll be spending a lot of time here. There's a cubicle for my assistant at the end of the hall, but most of the time I'll want you here with me."

"I hope so."

There was a moment of silence while they looked at each other, exploring each other in this new setting. Just by entering the office, Mark had acquired an executive look. Walter realized that there was nothing theatrical about his extraordinary good looks. He smiled impishly. "God. You're here at last. Work's going to be almost too exciting. I'll take you to see Clara in a minute so you can talk about money. Oh, I want to show you the poster." He went to him and put a hand on his shoulder and caressed it as he directed him to the desk.

"Don't, darling. Please," Mark murmured. "You know what it does to me. When can we be together?"

"We can go home as soon as we finish here," Walter assured him quietly.

"Thank God. Day before yesterday seems a long time ago."

Walter dropped his hand and moved a step away from him. "Here," he said, pulling a large sheet of paper around to face them. Herbie had processed his mock-up and had sent a proof.

"My God," Mark exclaimed. "It's terrific. You dreamed that up? You really are the Boy Wonder. Nobody'll know it's me, thank God."

"No. I'm rather pleased with myself. Did you have a good time last night after you left?"

"Yes, I missed you like mad, but Jack and his wife were very nice to me. I'm going to see them again next week. I like Elaine."

"Good. Cultivate her. She's going to be a star. I hear there're girls in the background. It might be good for both of you to be seen around together."

Mark lifted his eyes. For the first time, Walter saw resistance in them. "At moments I hate your being famous. I know. You have to think about things like that. It's all very new to me. I'll learn."

"I didn't mean–"

"I understand. If she's queer too and we like each other, what could be better? All of a sudden, thanks to you, I'm beginning to have a life. I've always admired Jack as a writer, and we had a nice evening together and ended up pals. It's amazing. As soon as I tell people I'm hoping to be working for you, they start paying attention to me. The next thing I know, they'll start wondering about my sex life. Right. I'll cultivate Elaine. If you're sure she likes girls, we should get along very well together."

"Now, listen. I told you people are bound to pay attention to you. They just need labels so they know what they're looking at. I see it all the time. You shouldn't resent it."

"I don't resent anything. Honest. That's not what I meant at all. I'm foolish enough to want to belong to you and not think about anything else. I know if I'm going to belong to you, I've got to think about lots of other things. I'm in love with Walter Makin, not just the guy next door. Who am I to make waves? I have to get used to it, that's all."

"I think what we both need is to get home as quickly as possible. Come see Clara."

Clara greeted him with brisk friendliness, and he left them together in her office. She returned with him to Walter's.

"It's all settled," she announced. "He's a willing slave. He says he doesn't mind coming in to learn the ropes without pay until we get back from Europe. You didn't tell me he lives so close to us."

"I didn't know myself until…" He looked at Mark for guidance. "When did you tell me?"

"Last night."

"Right. I knew you were somewhere in the neighborhood."

"He's been our nearest neighbor for months. It's all too cozy for words."

"Well, that's fine. Welcome." He approached Mark and shook hands with him. He immediately felt the electricity crackling between them and promptly withdrew. "I can show you some things here. Then I thought I might take him to the theater and introduce him to people. I have some other things to do over there. If I don't get back here, I'll see you at home." Clara left them. He could look at Mark. "Well? How is everything?"

"Wonderful," Mark said. "I think I'll get along with her. She's fairly awe-inspiring, but she thinks you're God Almighty, so we have something in common."

"Let's get that poster lettered so we can say we accomplished something, and then we can stop by the theater for a minute. After that, I'll show you who I think is God Almighty."

Before the weekend was over, it was established that Mark was welcome to drop in at Tenth Street when he was passing by. He even adopted a distinctive ring on the bell–two shorts and a long–to identify himself. He spent Sunday afternoon with them going over the plans for the coming season. It was settled that he would confine his modeling jobs to the morning and spend the afternoons with Walter.

"You like him, don't you?" Walter asked Clara when he had left.

"Yes. He's charming and wonderfully unspoiled, and he seems very intelligent. Still, he strikes me as something of an enigma."

Walter's heart skipped a beat. "How so?"

"I don't know. He's so self-contained. I have a feeling he must be hiding a deep, dark secret. I keep wanting to get to the bottom of him."

"Be careful, Clarry. You sound as if you were getting a crush on him."

"I shouldn't think that would do me much good. I'm almost sure he's in love with somebody. I wonder who it could be. Do you suppose Elaine could have been love at first sight?"

"Maybe," Walter agreed, breathing more easily now that a girl had been mentioned. "He's spoken of her several times."

"Did you warn him about her preferences?"

"Of course not. That's the sort of thing a man finds out for himself."

"He's so divinely handsome that she might change her mind."

The following week gave Walter and Mark the skeleton of a life together. They spent every afternoon working at the office or out seeing people. They generally managed to save an hour at the end of the day to make love before Walter went home to Clara. It was so much better than what they had had since their first weekend together that it took them both a week to begin to grow dissatisfied with it.

"What are we going to do?" Walter asked as he prepared to drag himself out of bed for the fourth afternoon in a row. He had lifted Mark so that he lay on top of him, belly to belly, chest to chest. Walter's hands were tangled in his hair. "Are we never going to get enough of each other?"

"I don't think so, darling. It's hopeless. We couldn't get enough of each other even if we lived together. People have told me about its being like this, but I never wanted it, any more than you did. We're still trying to get into each other's skin."

"It's insane. I want to take you around the corner right now and stand in front of Clara with our arms around each other and tell her we adore each other. Can you think of a more ridiculous scene?"

"Yes, but I won't tell you about it."

Walter rolled them over so that he was lying on top of Mark and held his head and fed on his mouth. "You see? It's starting all over again. If this sort of thing can happen, why does it have to be a secret? It's a natural phenomenon. Why can't we be proud of it?"

"I am."

"You. You're incorrigible. No, sweetheart, please go on being proud of it. I'm so proud of you. We work so well together, and I don't mean just in bed. Now I've got to get up and dress and go, which I want to do about as much as I want to shoot myself. Before I got to Europe, we're going to have another weekend together, all day and all night for at least three days. I've already started a plot."

"Thank God you've got an active imagination. Do you think you can manage Europe without me?"

"No."

"It's hard to imagine." Mark had begun to worry about it. It was hard to believe that Walter could be so dependent on him without seeming to realize it. Clara didn't count; Mark was almost sorry for her. "It's time to leave, darling."

"OK. Here goes." He gathered himself together and sprang up and made a dash for his clothes.

The week after that, Clara devoted some time to research and observation and came to a startling conclusion. She immediately prepared for action. One evening when the Makins were doing nothing, there was a phone call for her. Walter heard her voice become brisk and businesslike. She came away from the phone looking preoccupied. "It was Janice, dearest. Something terrible has happened with Bob. I told her I'd come right up."

"Do you want me?"

"No, it's girl business. She needs somebody to talk to. If I'm not back by midnight, I'll call you. What a shame Mark hasn't dropped in to keep you company."

"I've got plenty to keep me busy. Give her my love."

He waited for ten minutes after she had left and then leaped up, feeling as if he were being released from prison. He hurried out and around the corner and up to the room. It was empty. The smile with which he was prepared to greet Mark made him feel foolish. This was translated into a sense of being wronged. Why was Mark always out when he turned up unexpectedly? He wondered if he ever stayed out all night. His eye was caught by a volume of poetry he had never seen before. He knew Mark's books now, all first-rate, indicative of a cultivated taste. He flipped over pages and saw that the verse was erotic and frankly homosexual, lyrical and not remotely pornographic, but after reading a few pages he snapped the book shut with an obscure feeling of distaste. Wasn't what they were doing enough without Mark's wanting to read about it?

He wandered about the room thinking about getting undressed and waiting in bed. He resisted the temptation. Something was all wrong. Mark's absence. The poetry. He had let himself be drawn into a homosexual relationship, and it was turning out as he had always known it must. Furtive meetings. The constant nagging fear of discovery. Doubts about his lover's fidelity. Why should two men be faithful to each other?

*It needn't be like this,* an inner voice objected. Face the failure of his marriage. Face the fact that he was subject to desires that he could no longer repress. Accept Mark openly as the companion of his life, his lover and mate, around whom the day's activities would automatically turn. Everything he hated–the constant worry about where Mark was and what he was doing–were all the consequences of his failure to take this simple step. It didn't involve any extravagant gestures or even any great courage. He had only to divorce his childless wife and sign a lease on an apartment where he and Mark could live comfortably. If anybody wondered what they did in bed, what difference did it make? Nobody could know.

All very well–except that he couldn't divorce her now. He might have been able to consider it a few weeks ago when she was about to inherit a fortune, but he couldn't walk out and leave her penniless because of her loyalty to him. He couldn't afford to set her up on her own. Was it too late for the only alternative? He tried to think dispassionately of not seeing Mark again. His life had been going along smoothly a few weeks ago without his knowing Mark existed. It shouldn't be too difficult to make a small step backward and start again from there. He sprang up and strode around the room, striking out lightly at the furniture. He should go home and get his mind on other matters and have an early evening. He got as far as the door before he turned back. Mark might arrive at any moment. He could have almost two hours with him. It was a sickness in him. It was sick to allow his whole life to hinge on the hope of a moment with Mark.

He sat and tried to read. He judged he had been waiting more than an hour and a half when he hard Mark's footsteps and his key in the lock. He wanted to rush to him and throw his arms around him with relief but remained seated. Mark entered and stood, dumbfounded.

"My God. What are you doing here?"

"Not spending the evening with you, obviously."

Mark hurried to him and dropped to his knees in front of him. "How long have you been here, darling? This is awful."

His uncomplicated gaze was all the assurance Walter needed that his evening had been innocent. He took Mark's hand and turned it so he could see the watch. "Since about 9. An hour and three quarters."

"What happened? How did you get away?"

"Clara had to go out suddenly. I came right over."

Mark shook his head. "This is awful. What're we going to do? Should I sit here every evening on the off chance that you might come in unexpectedly? I will if you want me to."

"Of course not. You've got to have your own life."

"You're angry, and I don't blame you. There's nothing worse than waiting for somebody. I know all about it. But you're right. If you have your life, I'm going to have mine."

"You needn't sound so pleased about it."

Resistance came up in Mark's eyes, sharpened by anger. "Come on, now. This isn't the way I want it. I've told you. We're going to live together. It's the only way we'll make sense with our lives. You'll see it eventually. Until you do, I've got to try to keep from going nuts."

Walter was immediately conciliatory. "I know. I'm being ridiculous." He opened his legs and pulled him close and held him. "Oh, God. I've been wanting you so desperately, and now I've got to go."

Mark pulled back. "Oh, no. We're going to bed together. We've got to. It's important."

"I can't. I've got to get back by 11."

The protest went out of Mark's eyes, and his body lost its amorous tensions. "If you've got to, you've got to." He glanced at his watch. "You have only five minutes."

They rose together. Walter told himself that if he managed to leave now, he might find some small tough untouched area in himself on which to start rebuilding his independence. It would be risky to stay out longer, but he could explain it away somehow. Caution urged immediate departure. At least he knew Mark was here now.

Mark put a hand on his arm and headed him for the door. "It's all right. I know it's going to be difficult until after Europe. I just can't bear to think I've lost two hours with you."

"Oh, Christ." Walter stopped and turned to him and gathered him into his arms. "Shall I say the hell with it and stay all night? That's what I want to do."

"I know. That's why I can let you go. We've been so careful. We might as well be careful a little longer to see if it pays off the way you want it to."

They clung to each other and kissed until they both had trouble breathing, then whispered stricken little farewells and parted. Walter got home shortly before Clara arrived. He congratulated himself on his self-control.

Clara had completed her case. She waited until the end of the week, when Walter was to be out of the office most of the day for important meetings in which Mark wouldn't be included. She allowed Mark an hour after he had come in for his usual afternoon's work and then went to Walter's room and found him installed behind Walter's desk.

"Hello, darling," she greeted him breezily.

"Hi."

"You look frightfully busy, but I'm going to interrupt you," she said. "I'm going home. I want you to come with me. I have some things to discuss with you."

"Oh? Well, Walter wanted me to–"

"It's all right," she said. "I take full responsibility. He called just before you came in. He's running late. He told me to ask you to come by our place at 7. He made rather a point about my telling you that he wouldn't see you before then. I don't quite know what he meant, unless you were planning to meet him somewhere. He won't be back here for the rest of the day."

"He said something about meeting him at Berman's if he got through early. I guess that's out. You're leaving now?"

"Yes, darling. Come along. Let's go where we can be comfortable. We might even have an illicit drink before the afternoon's done."

She kept up a bright line of chatter in the taxi on the way downtown. She had planned it all carefully and wanted to take him by surprise.

"Oh," he said after she had made good her offer to pay for the taxi. "There's something I should do. I'll run home and be right back."

"Of course, darling. Don't be long." She went up and took off all her clothes and put on a voluminous dressing gown. It was a bit hot for the season, but she didn't want to look as if she were trying to seduce him. She hadn't decided yet about that part of it. She put her feet into loose slippers. When his familiar identifying buzz sounded, she was ready to let him in.

"I decided to get really comfortable," she said when he entered. "Why don't you do the same, darling? Take off your jacket and tie. It's much warmer today. Summer's coming."

She seated herself on the sofa and waited while he did as she suggested. He came around in front of her and sat in a chair near her. The

281

line of his body in shirtsleeves was superb. "Did you leave a note telling him where you are?" she asked.

"What?"

"You needn't have bothered. I told you, darling, he won't be free till 7. For once, that was for your information as well as mine."

"I don't seem to be following you, Clara." He couldn't believe his ears, but he knew that he was suddenly engaged in a fight for his life. All his instincts for survival were immediately alerted. His heart, after a brief flurry, was beating regularly. His fingers tensed and then spread out gracefully on the arms of his chair. "What are you talking about?"

"You know, but I'm perfectly willing to tell you if you think there's any room for confusion. I'm Walter's wife. You're his lover. We have things to talk about."

"I'm *what*?" he demanded with perfectly expressed incredulity.

"You're his lover, darling." His composure was so impressive that for an instant she almost doubted the ironclad case she had assembled. She shrugged the shadow of doubt away. "Or he's your lover, if I haven't put it properly. I didn't mean to get into technicalities. You're having an affair. That's all that need concern us."

"Really, Clara, I'm pretty new to the theater, but you people amaze me sometimes. Do you think everybody is off having sex with everybody else? Are you suggesting that Walter and I are a couple of queers?"

"I wouldn't put it that way. I've always known about Walter's little tendencies. I dare say you've brought them all rushing to the surface. I'm suggesting you're a queer."

"Damn it, Clara, I thought we were getting to be friends. You're making me very angry. What right have you to say a thing like that?"

"Oh, every right." She sat back, almost regretting the fate she had in store for him. He was splendid. His extraordinary good looks had grown dark and dangerous, his stern brow was almost frightening. She felt a masculine menace in him that she had never felt in any man. "The secretary of war is an old friend of the family. I have your service record. It's suggestive."

"All right." He sighed. There was no point in trying to fight that one. "Kids do things at 18 they're apparently supposed to go on regretting for the rest of their lives. So what?"

"The present governor of New Jersey is also an old friend of the family. Travere is a fairly unusual name. They're looking up all births registered in the name of Travere in the last—"

"Oh, come on, Clara. What if I tell you my wife and I weren't speaking by the time the baby was born and she had it registered in the name of the man she was living with? Never mind. What are you going to do with these startling revelations? Tell Walter? He knows. We thought a few little lies would make me more employable. He's been wonderful to me. We get along beautifully, but unless you have a photographer under my bed, I don't see why you think you know what goes on in it."

"You disappoint me, darling. You're being tiresome. I thought by now we could agree that I know and go on to something more interesting." She glanced at the clock. There was still plenty of time. "Do you want me to tell you all of it? Very well. You stayed here with Walter after Herbie had finished the modeling session. A rather private product I use was moved that day. I've always kept it in the same place for years. You moved into your room the next day, not months ago. I won't bother to mention all the hours you can't account for when you and Walter were supposed to be somewhere on business. The other night a convenient friend in distress called me. I waited outside in a taxi and saw Walter go around to your place. He stayed."

"Really? Well, as it happens, I wasn't there that night. I can prove that easily enough. I mean—" From her expression, he knew he had blundered seriously, but for the moment he couldn't see how.

She enlightened him. "Exactly," she said with a satisfied smile. "You weren't there to let him in. He has his own keys to your place. Is that usual with two men who are just good friends?"

There was nothing for him to do but brazen it out. He thought of the years of solitude. He wasn't going to be beaten easily. He was fighting for Walter as well as for himself. "You'd make a pretty good detective, Clara. I'm still waiting for proof."

283

"Do I need any? What would Walter do if I told him that I knew this much? Refuse to see you again. He hasn't the courage to face this sort of thing."

"You're assuming he has something to face. Tell him. He'll tell you exactly what I have–that we've become friends and have a good time together."

"I thought you knew him better than that. It's the suspicion he can't bear. He might've had affairs with dozens of boys if it weren't for that. He got rid of another friend of his simply because he was suspect."

"David. He told me." Walter had made it clear that it was she who had got rid of David, but that had had nothing to do with being in love. If worse came to worst, Mark thought he might be able to hold him; but he didn't want to put him to the test. He mustn't say anything that would give her an even greater hold on them. "What do you want, Clara?" he asked, surrendering ground.

"That's better. First of all, I want you to get undressed."

"What are you talking about?" He was briefly incredulous, and then he knew that this was going to be worse somehow than anything he could imagine.

"I want you to take all your clothes off. I want to see you naked."

"Now? Here?"

"Of course. You've been naked here before. You're a model. I've seen the photographs. Why shouldn't I see the real thing?"

"What is this? I'll show you mine if you show me yours? We're not children, damn it. What if Walter comes home unexpectedly?"

"I wouldn't want that to happen any more than you, would I? We're quite safe."

"I did leave a note. He'll know where I am."

"Not if he doesn't get it," she said. "I've told you that he's coming straight here at 7."

It occurred to him that Walter might not mind. He had shown Clara the photographs. If he ever found out, he would have to forgive because of all that was at stake. Clara must be placated, whatever her motives might be. "You're absolutely sure?" he asked, searching for the trap.

"Of course." She looked at him blandly. She could lie as well as he. "Can you imagine my being willing to run any risks?"

He couldn't. He detected no sign of desire in her. Perhaps she simply wanted to see what Walter found worthy of love. "Can I hang my things in the next room?"

"Certainly. You'll find a hanger in the closet." When he had gone, she glanced again at the clock. She had achieved her major goal. Whatever happened after he was naked would simply fill out and elaborate her basic plan. She had almost too much time.

He returned naked except for his wristwatch and a towel around his groin and stood expressionlessly in front of her.

"What's the towel for?"

"There's nothing very special about the rest of me." He choked back tears of humiliation. This was disgusting and degrading. She wanted to humiliate him.

"Let me be the judge," she said coolly.

He jerked off the towel and threw it aside. She looked at his body. She was struck by an impression of great power in spite of its not being heavily muscled. On the contrary, all its lines were light and fluid but seemed to stem from a core of compact virility.

"Walter's the only man I've seen naked. I think I've been missing something."

"All right. Can I get dressed now?"

"Good heavens, no. I want you to do the poster pose for me."

"I don't remember it."

"Of course you do. Walter must've worked it out with you. It's pure Makin if ever I saw it. Go on."

He looked at her for a moment, and then his body began to move. She stifled a gasp as she watched movement become poetry. A hip was flung at an angle, an hand placed on it. An arm shot up and bent at the elbow, and a hand dropped behind his head. He arched his back, thrusting his pelvis forward lasciviously. She had been fascinated by the photographs, but they hadn't prepared her for the prominence the pose gave to his sex or that she could be tempted by it. It jutted toward her at eye level, a heavy, dense mass of power. Her eyes were transfixed. She didn't think it was erect, but her limited experience left her in doubt. It's head looked a great deal bigger than Walter's.

"Don't move," she ordered. She rose and moved to him. She was almost as tall as he. She moved her fingers over a biceps and down into the hollow of his armpit and over his chest and along his groin and closed them around his sex. It felt firm but flexible. It filled her hand more than Walter's. She stroked it but felt no response in it. She looked up at him. She noticed that his eyelids were thick and that when they were lowered, his face became startlingly sensual. "Does it get bigger than Walter's?"

He broke his pose and stepped back from her. "Far from it."

"Is Walter's as special as he's always led me to believe?"

"Yes."

"Have you known many men?"

"Hundreds. Do you want to know about cocks? They usually come in three sizes: small, medium, and large. There are giants, but not very many. Walter isn't one of them."

"And you're medium? I'd like to see the difference between you. Can't you make it hard for a girl?"

"Of course, but not with you. You're Walter's wife."

"I shouldn't think that would make me unattractive. If anything, I should think you'd want to have me the way he has me. He still does, you know. I should think it would make you feel closer to him."

"I don't want to feel closer to him through other people."

"Are you in love with him?"

"Yes."

"Does he think he's in love with you?"

"I don't know. Maybe he'll tell you someday. Is it understood that you're not going to say anything to him about the things you know?"

"I don't see how I can now. I don't want you to tell him about this. It seems to me I've given you complete control."

It seemed to him too, and it frightened him. She wasn't the sort to relinquish control, but he could see no flaw in the position she had cre-

286

ated for him. "The only control I want is to go on seeing him. If you try to take that away from me, I'll fight for him."

"Who said anything about taking anything from you? I thought we ought to get to know each other better." She moved close to him again but didn't touch his sex. She moved a hand around to his buttocks and stroked them. Walter had made much of the beauty of his back. She ran her hand between them and felt a quiver beneath the skin. She had found the mainspring of his sexual response. The picture it conjured up was loathsome but suggested that Walter might be more enamored than she had bargained for. She glanced down and saw that his sex had filled out. She felt no vibration of desire directed toward her. She saw from the clock that she had almost another hour to keep him occupied. "Come along, darling," she said.

"Where?"

"We'll be more comfortable in bed. I want to try to make you hard just to see. You don't have to do anything."

He sensed danger everywhere, but he could think of no way of getting away from her without risking the truce he felt had been declared between them. He was sure she wanted to corner him into damning himself in Walter's eyes, but he didn't see how she could. He felt no desire in her hands when she touched him. He picked up the towel and glanced at his watch. Still more than two hours till 7. Danger was everywhere, but he couldn't identify it.

They went into the bedroom, and he stood beside her while she opened out the big bed. She turned and dropped onto the edge of it and put her hands on his hips and took his sex in her mouth.

He wanted to pull away but forced himself to submit. In spite of himself, he began to lift a partial erection. Maybe she did just want to see him with a hard-on. If she accomplished her purpose, this episode might end. Her mouth was soft and expert. She was doing everything right, including the ministrations of the hand that fondled his balls and strayed back between his legs into the most sensitive area of him. For a brief period of time he remained on the verge of a vigorous response.

Self-consciousness intervened. She was Walter's wife. He was permitting her intimacies that belonged to Walter. His groin began to ache with the strain of trying to respond. The moment passed. He couldn't get an erection with her.

She acknowledged the impasse by lifting her legs onto the bed and pulling him down and stretching him out on his back. She moved down over him and continued her efforts.

She remained bundled up in her robe. She supposed queers might find the sight of a female body repellent. She didn't want to add to her difficulties. There was no enjoyment in what she was doing, but it had become a challenge. If she could make him hard, arouse some semblance of desire in him, her triumph would be complete.

The persistence of her mouth on him locked him into a physiological need. His male pride was engaged too. He had to achieve an erection to show her that he could and to relieve the infuriating congestion in his groin. His hips rocked with the need for release. If he could believe that she wanted him, he might be able to take her. Perhaps Walter would want him to, to replace him and free him from her at last. A man whose wife had taken his lover would no longer feel bound to her. This thought achieved what her mouth had failed to do. He felt power gathering to fill and lengthen his cock. She redoubled her efforts and laughed as it escaped from her mouth. She lifted her head. Her mouth looked loose and wet.

"It's getting so big. I can't do it anymore."

He sat up and seized her head, pushing it down. "Go on. With your tongue. At the end. Like that." He dropped back and felt it tighten, harden, acquire independence. He no longer had to exert inner pressure to stiffen it. He let his whole body fall into a long slide of relief. He felt her lifting her head again. She held his sex upright and stroked it slowly.

"It's all hard now, isn't it? It's not nearly as long as Walter's, but I can hardly hold it. It's so different from his. It looks beautifully brutal."

He felt the shift toward orgasm tingling in him, and he lifted her hand away, finally master of himself. She moved up beside him and urged him up to his knees, straddling her.

"I want to look." She lifted her hands to his chest and let them run down over him to rest lightly on his sex. "Magnificent, darling," she said breathlessly.

He was proud to show himself to her as a man at last, but he didn't dare risk the return of self-consciousness. He dropped forward onto her. As he did so, she pulled her robe open so that without seeing her body he felt her nakedness against him. Lying with her like this, he was disarmed by the sweetness of human contact. He didn't want her, but he was capable of taking her if she wished. He could see no reason why she would want to create ugliness between them. Having gone this far, perhaps they could be affectionate rivals. Walter would like that. "I'm sorry it took so long," he said. "You do that awfully well."

"Walter likes me to suck his cock. I'm sure he likes you to as well."

"Can't you tell me what this is about? Do you want me to…to do it?"

She had caught a glimpse of his watch. She must be prepared to keep this going for at least another half hour. "That's one way we could get to know each other better. You don't feel any scruples about being unfaithful to him?"

He hesitated. She was able to speak plainly without any apparent anguish. He owed it to her to reply in kind. Perhaps they were achieving some sort of understanding. "He's unfaithful to me with you," he pointed out.

"That's true. I don't suppose I would've thought of it that way."

"Can't we all talk to each other? I know he wants to. He cares about you and your marriage and everything. If we all care about each other, I don't see why something good can't come of it." He felt his cock swelling against her at the thought of clearing the way to a life with Walter without causing him pain.

"Don't you think it's asking a great deal to expect me to care about you?" she asked.

Her voice cut into him, catching him in a vulnerable moment, and made him feel like a fool for relying on decent feeling. He reserved judgment for another moment. "We're here together. I wish you'd tell me why."

"Walter wants you. It's my business to know what he wants and decide whether he should have it. I decided about you a week ago."

"Did you?" Anger was growing in him. He started to move off her, but she held him. If she wanted him, she wasn't going to get him. "I suppose you're going to tell me what you've decided."

"You won't do. Walter's played with your body, and so have I. That's all you amount to. I made your cock hard, but I knew it wasn't worth the bother. What you really want is to be fucked up the ass."

"Goddamn you." He choked on the words. He seized her wrists and pinned her arms above her head. He stared down at her from under thunderous brows. He was breathing hard.

"Now what, he-man?" She laughed in his face, but her laughter stopped abruptly. She could feel his strength gathering in him. She was suddenly terrified. "No. Please, Mark. I'm sorry. I didn't mean it. Don't." She could feel the hard bulk of his sex pressing into her belly.

He released her wrists and with lightning speed got a grip on the top of her robe and yanked it down under her so that her arms were trapped in the sleeves. His body was moving on her with swift, implacable force. Her legs were wrenched apart. Her hips were seized in an iron grip. He entered her. "Oh, Christ, no! Oh, please. Don't. You mustn't. You're raping me. Oh, please, Mark. You're too big. You're tearing me apart. Oh, Christ. It hurts too much. Stop. Please stop." He continued to force himself into her. She tried to twist away from him, but his weight held her helpless under him. He seemed to grow huge within her, and she felt his belly come up hard against hers. She felt as if he had destroyed her, and then her body was pierced with bliss. She flung her legs around him and pulled him to her. "Oh, yes, darling. It's heaven. Do it, darling, do it." She was stunned that she wanted him. This was a vengeance she hadn't dreamed of. She was being unfaithful to Walter with his lover, and he filled her body with bliss.

He rolled over onto his back and swung her into the air over him, disengaging himself from her. His sex slapped down on his belly, and he lowered her onto himself so that she was sitting astride his thighs. She managed to disentangle herself from the robe. He looked at her naked breasts expressionlessly from his lowered lids. "Put my cock inside you," he ordered.

She raised herself and lifted it so that it could enter her and writhed on it to recapture the bliss it had offered her.

"Is it rape?" he demanded.

"No, darling. I want it," she crooned. "It's so different from Walter." He gathered himself together and surged up so that her head slammed back against the bed. He held her and remained within her, looming over her, while she clung to him with her legs. Her arms were free at last to hold him. "Take me, darling," she whispered.

"I know you now," he said with cold fury. "You're a killer and a bitch. You think you own him, but I'm going to take him away from you. Yes, he's in love with me. I'm going to tell him everything that's happened this afternoon. I'll tell him I fucked you, and I'll tell him why. He'll never be unfaithful to me again. Not with you, goddamn you."

She scarcely listened to him. His threats were harmless. Unless her timing went terribly awry, there were only a few moments left to enjoy him, and she craved more. She would be the victim of her own design. Walter had defined sex for her years ago, so that she was unprepared for discovery. He had always taken her in a way that made her a partner. Mark was doing something that made unfamiliar demands on her body. He was driving into her brutally, raping her, blissfully annihilating her. She stretched all of herself to receive his power and cried out as she began to feel the contours of his massive cock moving with miraculous freedom in her, opening her, still opening her so that she dissolved in a long, continuous orgasm. Muscles flowed against her under glowing skin. She placed her hands on him to imprint on them the feel of his rhythmically moving body. He was about to be ejected from her life, but she would still hold him. She heard indistinct sounds outside. The sounds she had been waiting for? She began to cry out to drown them.

"Come, darling. Come," she cried. "I want to feel you come in me." She continued to cry out disjointedly, praising his cock and the things it was doing to her.

The room exploded into violence.

Mark was torn from her. Walter towered over them. She felt momentarily bereft, and then she began to laugh. Mark tried to scramble up but was flung to the floor. She heard him cry out, "Let me tell you," but Walter was on him. His arms were flailing, and he was shouting obscenities. She saw his fists smashing into Mark's face and body. Mark staggered up under the blows and made a dash for the door. Walter was ahead of him. He seized the hanger on which his clothes were neatly hung and flung it into the other room. He found his shoes and socks and hurled them after it. He was back at the bed in a bound. He dropped down on it and began to beat her and curse her. She rolled onto her stomach and covered her head with her arms, laughing and sobbing.

He continued to beat her until his hands hurt. He spit on her and tore himself away from her and rushed to the living room. Mark's back was turned. He was shoving his shirt into his trousers. Walter leaped at him and struck him hard across the side of the head. Mark staggered and pulled himself up and faced him. Walter saw his fists lifting and braced himself to parry them and met eyes filled with love and torment. His guard faltered, and then he was on the floor with a chair on top of him. Mark stood over him, tears streaming down his face.

His voice was choked and breathless. "Even if you're not queer, I hope you get rid of her," he blurted. "I'll be waiting at home if you want me." He picked up his jacket and tie and walked to the door. His body slumped against it as he opened it, and then he was gone.

Walter pushed the chair from him and pulled himself up. The silence was numbing. He dragged himself to a chair and fell into it and put his head in his hands. He waited for his heart to stop pounding and for the total chaos within him to sort itself out. The slowing of his heart restored him to what he assumed was normal. He felt wonderfully dead. He had beaten his love into submission. He could feel his fists pounding into the worshiped body, releasing hatred to murder love. Now that it was done, it was clear that that was the way he had wanted it, the way it had to be. Mark had been right: They couldn't be lovers and work together without sooner or later giving people ideas. He thought of the speculative glances the night they had dined at Le Pavillon, and out of the depths of his deadened spirit crawled the horror he had always felt of having his secret laid bare.

He would never see him again. Would he be able to see Clara again? He hoped he had killed her but doubted that he had been so lucky. He felt nothing. His mind was dead.

He dropped his hands and sat back in the chair for a long time, staring at nothing while the numbing silence gave way to the everyday sounds of the street. He heard another sound and lifted dead eyes to see Clara enter, wearing a dressing gown. She was a stranger, perhaps an enemy. He noticed that the room was getting dark and rose heavily and went to the switch and snapped on the main lights. He looked at her, expecting her to be bruised and bloodied. Her mouth looked slightly puffy, but otherwise she was all right.

"What do you want?" he demanded.

"Nothing," she said coolly. "Are you mourning the end of an idyll?"

He made a conscious effort to concentrate on her. "I'm warning you, Clara. You better be very careful what you say—or I'll kill you. And I'm not speaking figuratively. I mean exactly what I say. I probably ought to kill you."

She crossed the room, her carriage regal, and stood in front of the fireplace. "Because I had a man you've had dozens of times?"

He lifted his hands in front of him and looked at them. The knuckles were swollen. He dropped them. "You wanted me to find you with him. Is that it?"

"Yes."

"How did you know I'd get here in time?"

"I found out when your meeting was ending. I knew you'd go to him as usual. You found his note."

He felt a dull admiration for her ingenuity and persistence. "I see. I suppose you tricked him into some sort of confession."

"I didn't have to. I told him what I knew. He denied it for as long as he reasonably could. He was very loyal."

"Then he went mad with desire and tore your clothes off. You're talking shit, but I'm not going to give you the satisfaction of trying to find out what really happened. I don't care. Amazingly enough, now that I've had time to calm down, I don't care that you dragged him into bed with you. That should worry you, Clara."

"Should it?"

"Yes, goddamn it!" he roared. "I cared about it being him. I don't care what you were doing. I don't care how you managed it. He should've told you to go fuck yourself instead of doing it for you."

"Charming."

"You haven't left much room for charm, Clara. Oh, Christ." He shoved his hands into his pockets and took a few paces back and forth in front of her. He stopped and looked at her and spoke quietly. "Mark and I were friends. What does it matter if we loved each other's bodies? It can happen and last a little while, and that's the end of it. When are you going to let up, Clara?"

"Never." She blazed with challenge, her shoulders back, chin up. "I'm your wife. I married a man. If you're a faggot, get out of here and go be one. I'll get a divorce. Daddy's always thought that's the way it'll end up."

"Daddy. One reason I'm still here is that I'd hate to prove him right. What's bloody Daddy got to do with it?"

"Thanks to you, I'm a pauper, that's what. What're you going to do about that?"

"Christ. I'm getting out of here." He headed for the door.

"Where're you going?"

"I haven't the slightest idea."

"If you go to him, I'll–"

He swung back to her with his devilish smile. "Well, well, well. For once you're not feeling so sure of yourself, are you, Clara? Perhaps it's not too late for you to learn a lesson. Let's make it stick." He made a rush at a draped table laden with a collection of porcelain figures and swept his arm across it. Sound was deadened by the carpet. He kicked the table over and heard a gratifying crunching sound as more porcelain was smashed. He sprang at another table and overturned it with his hands. A crystal lamp went and a few pieces of Etruscan pottery. He picked up silver and lacquer and porphyry boxes and flung them at pictures on the wall. Glass shattered, paper ripped, canvas dented. He continued around the room, gutting rare books, hurling carved marble candlesticks against the wall, splintering painted silk fans in his hands. He sprang to the tall windows and yanked at draperies and brought heavy rods and bits of the wall crashing down around him. He ripped delicate fabric to shreds. He charged the mantelpiece in front of which Clara was standing, toppling two more lamps as he went. She retreated hastily. He seized the Empire clock that had been measuring out his life to empty infinity. He lifted it over his head and sent it catapulting into the hearth. Time stopped with a magnificent crash. He would gladly have it stop forever. He paused, breathing heavily, and surveyed the shambles around him.

"I hope you're satisfied," Clara said imperturbably at his side.

He whirled to her. "Almost, you fucking slut. You're a pauper, aren't you? Naked went they into the night, or something." He sprang at her and seized her dressing gown and tore it from her. She went for his face with her nails. He grabbed her arms and dragged her across the room toward the door. She struggled and made herself a dead weight and shouted curses at him. He heard the word "faggot" and hit her hard across the face with the back of his hand. He caught her from falling and grappled with her naked body while he got the door open. He put his hands on her back and shoved. She careened across the hall and bounced against the banisters and fell to her hands and knees. He stepped back inside and slammed the door on her. He slumped against the wall, his chest heaving, waiting to recover his breath.

In a moment he heard her tapping at the door and softly calling to him. A memory came to him of one of the first evenings they had spent together. He remembered thinking how satisfying it would be to see her groveling now, but the sweetness was gone. Let her stay where she was. There wasn't much traffic in the hall. They had only a few neighbors above them. The chance of scandal was slight.

He laughed at the thought of Clara Washburn scratching naked at his door. Laughter swelled up in him. He howled and shook with laughter and rolled against the wall until laughter turned to tears and he was sobbing uncontrollably. He doubled over and tore at his hair. He dropped to his knees and pounded the floor with his fists until the paroxysm passed. He pulled himself to his feet unsteadily and leaped against the wall for support and wiped his face with a handkerchief. He had to get away. He smoothed his hair with his hands and straightened his clothes and pulled open the door.

She was curled up on the floor against the jamb in a fetal position to hide herself. A man's jacket had been dropped over her shoulders. There had been traffic after all. He stepped over her and ran to the head of the stairs and hurtled down them.

In the street he continued to move fast for fear his feet would betray him. He felt far less dead. He feared a return to the living. He dropped down a few blocks toward Washington Square and went into the first bar he came to where he could hope not to meet anybody he knew. Two quick double whiskies deadened him again. He started on a third and thought of the future and found an astonishing idea lodged in his mind. He wanted money. He couldn't see how money would have changed what he'd been through, but he felt sure that it would have. Money would have given him the freedom to act promptly as the occasion demanded. Money would have given him some choice. Money paid for trips to Europe and big apartments and privacy. He finished off the third drink and ordered a fourth. He wanted money. He had counted on Clara's. He would damn well make his own.

Having followed his thoughts that far, he found that others formed in lucid succession. He'd resign from Theatre Today. He'd call David and tell him to get him the best contract any Hollywood director ever had. The thought of getting out of New York lifted a great weight from him. He had no place to live now. He had taken care of that. He didn't see how he could ever go back to the office. Too many memories. Two weeks of enchantment and passion and joy. Never again. He ordered another drink.

Let Clara run the fucking theater. Let her have all the men she wanted to manipulate and destroy. How had she managed it? What had he done to make it happen? He didn't know how to handle love, if that was what it had been. He had no time for it. It was too confining and diverted all his creative energies away from the things he knew how to do. He didn't need it. He needed money to lead the kind of life he had always dreamed of. He would replace all the trinkets he had smashed with things of real value and surround himself with beauty. Let Clara follow him if that was to be his fate. She was all he had, all he was ever likely to have—best to make the most of her. There was no substance in relationships outside the recognized ones. They were too intense, too precarious, too dependent on the shifting sands of physical passion.

He drank some more until he was confident that there was no chance of a face, a body, a name materializing in his mind. He ate something somewhere. He went to another bar—or perhaps it was the same one—and had several more drinks. Long stretches of time slipped away from him, leaving him standing in the same place without knowing what he had been doing. The drinks began to play tricks on him. He was getting maudlin. He found himself weeping for no reason and impatiently dashed the tears away. There was a room nearby. Nothing important. He would like to see it maybe just once more, give him a chance to explain. He was sure there was an explanation. "Let me tell you," he had begged in an agonized voice before he had begun to beat him. With his erection just beginning to subside. Shit! Goddamn fucking shit!

He found himself outside, going somewhere. He couldn't remember where. He stopped in front of a door and had to focus carefully before he recognized it. He went into the drab little entry and fumbled with his keys. Was there someone here he wanted to see? No. Only a painful memory to be wiped away by time. Weaving slightly and with uncertain fingers, he removed two keys from the ring and stood with them in his hand. He couldn't see very well. Tears seemed to be rolling down his cheeks again. He lurched toward the letter boxes and put a finger painstakingly on a name and dropped the keys through the slot.

He hugged the wall as he stumbled slowly around a corner and headed toward home.

Hollywood was a new life, a one-dimensional life of work; and Walter found it fascinating until he decided that he had nothing more to learn. At the beginning he had everything to learn and a great deal to teach Hollywood.

David had outdone himself. He browbeat his studio into offering Walter complete independence, with final approval of script and cast and the right to cut and edit his own work. The pay was princely, and he discovered what it felt like to be rich. He liked it.

He didn't like the atmosphere of big business in which he was obliged to work. It took him the better part of his first year to teach the men who ran the studio that he intended to operate nearly as possible to the way he had operated as director of Theatre Today and as principal partner in Makin-Fiedler Productions before that. He had to invoke every clause in his contract that guaranteed independence before he could finish his first film to his satisfaction. It apparently hadn't occurred to the studio heads that anybody would take the document literally. David, assigned to Walter as producer, knew studio politics and had his own position to consider, but he backed Walter to the best of his ability.

Aside from David, Walter was on his own in a way he had never been before in his professional life. The studio isolated him from Clara. She was no longer there to spare him tiresome details, help him reach decisions, cow opposition with her commanding or forbidding style. He hadn't insisted on her coming with him. He had discussed the possibility of her staying in New York and producing on her own. Now she was restricted to the life of a housewife, and he wasn't greatly perturbed by her evident restlessness and frustration. They both had made sacrifices to stay together. Slowly the pain of his unacknowledged loss faded, and eventually he began to feel sorry for her.

Their house, a Spanish-Moorish-Gothic monstrosity that had once belonged to a silent star, was rented and provided no great stimulus to whatever homemaking instincts might be latent in her. They both found Hollywood's social life absurd or boring or both. It was an adjunct to work; people were always doing their acts, or films were being shown, or photographers were recording everybody for posterity. The fact that every gathering always included some of the most famous faces in the world quickly lost its novelty.

They found many old friends already there—David, of course, who had a nice young wife and two babies; Johnny Bainbridge, still alone; Greg Boland, on his fourth wife; and a number of others—but friendships seemed to get lost in the pecking order. As a vastly eminent newcomer, Walter was drawn into the industry's elite, and he found it took too much time and trouble to break out.

"If you're not making the greatest film that's ever been made, we're insane to be here," Clara commented from the sidelines.

Walter didn't think of his film as the greatest ever made; he intended it to be the only film to come out of Hollywood since the invention of sound. He put aside everything he had learned in the theater and set out to master the unexplored medium of pictures. His visual sense was highly developed. He rejected all the adaptations of plays or books that were offered him and picked out an intricately plotted thriller. He cut dialogue to a minimum and developed the action with numerous comic effects. When he finally allowed the studio heads to see the finished product, it was so completely unlike what had been expected of him that nobody knew what to make of it, but everybody had to agree that it was exciting and funny. When it was distributed eventually, it attracted a great deal of attention from serious critics and was acclaimed a refreshing landmark in filmmaking. The studio had been prepared to settle for prestige with Walter, so the fact that it did very well at the box office added to his status.

There was time for another trip to Europe between pictures, and he was gratified to be able to afford the luxurious travel that he had thought would be possible only when Clara's money came through. Passing through New York revived dormant memories. He was able to allow Mark to assume the substance of reality in his mind, at last, and he saw the episode as the final eruption of the unstable fires of youth, a childlike romantic passion that had been certain to burn itself out. He was finally 30 and old enough to know better.

Aided by his professional independence of Clara, they had entered a new phase and, he suspected, arrived at what marriage was intended to be: an unequal partnership in which he laid down the law and she followed. In the future he could indulge a fancy for any young body that caught his eye. It had been Clara's competing with him for supremacy that had inflated his response to Mark out of all proportion.

So they traveled in splendor, and nobody caught his eye, and he concentrated on buying paintings. He also acquired a marvelous French cook and her husband and shipped them off to Hollywood. He was going to adorn his life with the style he had always given to his productions.

Before going to Hollywood, he had been outraged by the growing harassment of the theatrical world, led by a congressional committee and concentrated on the film industry. He had signed protests and petitions and had dropped, professionally and personally, those who cooperated with the forces of repression. In view of the total irrelevance of Hollywood's product to the world, he was unprepared for the fear and insecurity that pervaded the industry, the raging paranoia that infected the whole studio system. Everybody was afraid of his own shadow. Johnny Bainbridge spoke gloomily of the "witch-hunt." Even David warned him not to talk too much about some of his New York productions, but Walter's associates over the years had been of such awesome distinction that he couldn't imagine any of these upstart movie moguls questioning anything he had done under their patronage.

301

Two days before he was to begin shooting his second film, he was summoned by the studio boss, one of the grand old men of the industry, Sidney Magnus. Walter had met him several times, but he was too old to take an active part in the community's social life. Walter supposed he wanted to wish him well on his new venture. He was a small mournful man who always wore dark business suits as if to disavow the lush tropical environment he had played a large part in creating. He didn't mention Walter's film but made a rambling speech about the greatness of America.

"There's a terrible threat to the industry, Walter," he concluded. "A handful of Bolsheviks and troublemakers are trying to take over. Perverts, Walter. To the public, we are getting a bad name. I am going myself, personally, to Washington, D.C., to tell the Congress of the United States that these people will be cleaned out. I will not have one of them left on my lot. We know who they are. I'm told you once produced a play by a Communist."

"I may have, Sidney. I've produced a lot of plays," Walter agreed cheerfully. Sidney reminded him of his father-in-law, and he responded with blithe defiance. "The only one I know by a Communist was the first I ever did. It was by a Frenchman."

"The name I have is John Bainbridge."

"He did the English adaptation. He doesn't work for you anyway."

"He does not. He never will. Those are the facts in a nutshell. You say John Bainbridge is a Communist. That's good, Walter. We know it, but I'm glad I can say you told me."

"I haven't told you anything of the sort. As a matter of fact, I don't think he is, but what difference does it make? There aren't many Communist films being made out here."

"Bolsheviks, Walter. Perverts. I don't understand such filth, but people tell me. A man likes another man. He wants to overthrow the system. I understand that much. Out. I want a clean studio, Walter."

"You sound like the department of sanitation, Sidney."

"You're a clever man. You laugh. I'm not laughing. I want you to tell me all such people you know. You're a great young American. Your beautiful wife is a great young American lady. Her family are great Americans. You're an example, Walter. I want you to tell me. I want the industry to know that you're with us."

"I'll tell you this, Sidney. If a man does his job well, I don't give a damn what he does when he goes home. I'd gladly give you a list of people who don't do their jobs well."

"You're young, Walter. You're the greatest man in the theater today. Fine. That's why I wanted you out here. But what's the theater? Peanuts compared to pictures. How much money have you made—a million, maybe? I'm worth $30 million as I'm sitting here. You're nothing if I say so, Walter. Don't you forget it."

Walter chortled. "You people really do have delusions of grandeur. OK, Sidney. Let me know when you decide I'm nothing, and I'll try to vanish into thin air."

Going back to the work Sidney had interrupted, Walter knew that he should be indignant, perhaps even to the point of invoking one of the escape clauses in his contract and walking out, but like so much in Hollywood, he found it aroused only contempt and a determination to go his own way. Getting rid of Johnny Bainbridge wouldn't be enough for them. They wanted to break Walter Makin, make him a good organization man. Their imaginations were too limited for them to grasp the fact that they had nothing he needed. He liked the work and the money, but he could go back to Broadway and make money this time, whenever they pushed him too far. It was almost unfair for him to be in such an impregnable position. It made him feel that he should assert his power on behalf of his less favored colleagues. He wished Johnny worked for the studio. He would insist on shooting any script Johnny had handy and let them try to do something about it. He was aware that he would be less capable of taking such a high-handed stand if his public record weren't spotless. A man likes another man. Out. He hoped David had buried his past.

David called the next day to tell him of a sudden change in the studio's plans. He wouldn't be the producer for Walter's new film but had been given a new assignment and was being replaced by a relative novice. Walter liked working with David and was annoyed, but his control didn't extend to the choice of studio personnel. He told David about his talk with Sidney as a warning to him.

David laughed. "Honey, I didn't marry Sidney's great-niece for nothing. You taught me that a well-connected wife can be useful."

It wasn't the only last-minute change. His assistant, who had worked with him on his first film, failed to appear on the first day of shooting. A stranger was there to replace him. Several errors had been made in the actor's calls so he had to reshuffle the schedule. He didn't waste time raising hell with the new assistant, but the better part of a half day's work was lost before he had begun. He was confident he could make it up, but for the first time he had committed the director's cardinal sin of running late.

He ran later still in the week that followed. There was a succession of accidents and errors that could happen to anybody but had never happened to him. Sets weren't ready on time, prints were spoiled so that scenes had to be reshot, actors kept going up in their lines. He regarded himself as being relatively free from paranoia, but he couldn't help having his suspicions. After a week he had no doubt that this was Sidney's revenge. He went home to Clara every night in a rage, which he was careful to control during the day. Temper tantrums were the greatest time-wasters of all. Clara listened thoughtfully to his reports of the day's woes, usually delivered over a drink by the pool, while she stared out at the space immediately in front of her, her mouth working as if to savor the taste of the situation.

"You know, of course," she said the first time he mentioned the possibility of dropping the film and getting out of Hollywood, "all you'd have to do is give him the names of half a dozen people that everybody knows anyway, like Johnny. It wouldn't do them any harm, and it would make him feel you're on his team."

"But I'm not. Blacklists. Prying into people's private lives. It's disgusting. Good men are losing their jobs. I knew it, but I didn't see that there was anything I could do about it. I'm beginning to wonder." He hadn't seriously considered dropping the film. He intended to stay and stay on his own terms. "I want to talk to Johnny about this. Do we have any spare time between now and Sunday?"

"No, dearest. We're having Betty and Bogey and that crowd for dinner tomorrow. Otherwise, it's one brilliant soiree after another at the Metros and the Goldwyns and the Mayers. Actually, it's the Selznicks tonight for a change."

Clara pondered the problem for two days while Walter reported mounting difficulties. She wanted to leave Hollywood—there was no question about that—but she wanted to leave in a way that wouldn't hurt his career. She had heard of Sidney's tricks being used on others. They would hound him until he quit and salvage their investment as best they could with a new director. Walter would be professionally discredited.

That would be bad enough, but if he allowed himself to be drawn politically, he might make trouble for himself that would follow him back to New York. She had a more realistic grasp of the situation than he. A wave of bigotry was sweeping the country that wouldn't stop with sinister politicians like McCarthy and California's own ghastly little Nixon, whom they'd had the misfortune of meeting. A quixotic embroilment with Johnny and others like him could dry up Walter's sources of production money.

She hadn't been happy with the way they had left New York. As soon as Walter had returned from Europe, he had rushed the play, for whose poster Mark had posed, into production while he was simultaneously liquidating Theatre Today. The play had been quite a success and was only now coming to the end of its run, but there had been something precipitate and undignified about their departure. Mark had been a close call. She had learned that her intervention in Walter's life could have dramatic consequences, so she weighed the risks carefully for two days before she called Sidney Magnus and arranged a meeting.

Sidney staggered to his feet when she entered his office. "Clara," he exclaimed as she approached. "A sight for sore eyes. Let me look at you. The embodiment of pure young American womanhood."

"Come off it," she said as she offered her hand. He took it and leaned over it to lift it up to his lips. She caught him as he was about to pitch forward onto his desk and put him back into his chair. She withdrew a single sheet of paper from her pocketbook. "There, Sidney. A list. You weren't very clever the way you handled Walter. You must know you can't bully a man of his stature."

The old man sat huddled in his chair and studied the list. "Good, Clara, good. What I would expect from the daughter of one of the most respected families of this country. The FBI might want to ask some questions about these people."

"Lay off, Sidney. You're got what you want. Naturally, Walter doesn't know anything about this. There's nothing in his contract that says he has to tell you about the people he knows. Tell the FBI to do their own homework."

"Clara, there's a terrible threat to the industry. A handful of Bolsheviks and—"

"I know, Sidney." Clara, who had perched briefly on the edge of Magnus's desk, stood. "You're going to clear them out. It's your responsibility. After all, you hired them. You wouldn't want the FBI wondering about that, would you? We won't talk anymore about it. Walter may be on your side, but he's a professional. He doesn't believe in doing anything that isn't stipulated in his contract. Now I must fly."

"It's an inspiration to talk to you, Clara. Your family—"

She hurried out before he could tell her about her family.

Walter came home the next evening in a much happier frame of mind, reporting that work had progressed almost without incident. In another few days, with everything going smoothly at last, he was so absorbed in his film that he literally had no time to devote to the witch-hunt, except as it affected his immediate concerns. When Clara heard that Johnny and a few others she knew had been dropped by their studios, she didn't bother to mention it to him. It would have happened sooner or later in any case. Walter would hear soon enough.

One of the things that bored Clara most at the parties they went to was the amount of time the ladies of Hollywood devoted to the discussion of their insides. They were fountains of gynecological lore about birth control and abortions and, under the subheading of pregnancy, about breast care and postnatal treatment for sagging abdomens and similar afflictions. In these edifying conversations, the name of Dr. Smallfield kept cropping up. The ladies of Hollywood couldn't do without him.

Clara had never accepted the possibility that her abortion had had anything to do with her subsequent barren state, but she had been to several specialists for what she told herself were routine examinations and had been assured that everything was in order.

Eventually the name of Dr. Smallfield had been so dinned into her ears that she decided she might as well see him. Not that there was anything wrong with her, but if he were such a wizard with birth control, he might know a trick or two about making things work the other way around. When she went back to him a second time to learn the results of the X rays, he spoke of tubes and scar tissue and suggested that she have a small operation. She agreed and was vague about it with Walter.

She stayed in a hospital for two days and went without intercourse for another week, and before Walter had finished his second picture, she was able to announce casually one evening that she was pregnant. He looked at her incredulously.

"You needn't look at me like that," she said, brushing aside six or seven years of waiting and wondering. "We knew it was bound to happen eventually."

"Is that what the operation was all about?" he asked, still not able to believe it.

"Don't be silly, dearest. I told you that was just a little female thing. Of course, I suppose anything that's done there could make some sort of difference." She watched his face light up with his impish smile and sat back in triumph. Her timing had always been right. After the lull of Hollywood, she would move back into the center of their lives. She had always known how to give him what he needed, when he needed it. Once he was a father, another Mark would be out of the question.

She gave birth to her first child after he had started work on his third film. Parenthood immediately set a limit to their time in Hollywood. Neither of them could imagine bringing up children there. Walter didn't expect that becoming a father (this time, of his wife's child) after all these years would affect him very deeply, but it did. Now that it had happened, he realized that it meant even more to him than he had thought. This was finally what life was about. The little flurries of passion, the small dissatisfactions and reproaches he had allowed to accumulate to Clara's discredit, were nothing compared to the wonder of their bringing children into the world together.

To his surprise he found his attitude to his work changing. He grew more relaxed, almost indifferent when he couldn't come up with an original solution to a problem. He was no longer driven to excel himself. He had been an innovator and a trailblazer; he began to look forward to a future of interesting but undemanding work that wouldn't impinge on the comfortable framework of money and family life. Tenderness of a sort that had never existed between them entered into his relationship with Clara.

She was pregnant again in less than a year's time after the birth of the first boy. He made a fourth film, started a fifth, and began to read play scripts that were still being mailed to him from New York. He found several that he liked and, shortly after the birth of the second son, notified the studio that he was leaving on completion of his current picture.

He had saved a lot of money, and he put most of it into the purchase and remodeling of two houses on East 75th Street. Alice had kept the office going during the four-and-a-half years he had been away. He was soon back in business as Walter Makin Productions, with the very big difference that Clara didn't pitch in with him.

She had examined the role of mother and found that it suited her for the present. She was aware that his imagination was no longer wholly gripped by his work. He liked spending time with the babies. A lot of his energy was going into the creation of a grand setting for them. He was more interested in discussing with her the acquisition of a picture or a piece of furniture than his production plans. He was looking forward to the elegant dinner parties she would be able to give in the dining room he was planning. She knew her new value to him as a wife and hostess and mother; to become his business partner again would be a retrogression.

The independence he had enjoyed at the studio was consolidated as he became once more his own boss, and he made the most of it. In reaction to Hollywood's repressive atmosphere, he went out of his way to find staff that would be shunned by the movie moguls. He found a business manager and old friend of David's who had been one of the first victims of the Hollywood witch-hunt. He heard of a newspaperman who had refused to testify before some congressional committee and hired him as his press representative. A bright, personable–probably homosexual–young man came to him with high academic qualifications and a strong recommendation from an experimental theater in Texas and became his assistant. As the father of two, Walter didn't see why he shouldn't hire gay youths if they were good at their jobs. He let it be known that he would give receptive attention to plays by Hollywood writers who figured on blacklists. He told Alice to try to find out where Johnny Bainbridge was. He had dropped out of sight several years earlier.

It was one of those coincidences that were constantly occurring in the city. On the day he told Alice to look up Johnny, he ran into him in the street. He saw him approaching, as light and worn and self-contained as ever, and had a moment to remind himself not to expose Johnny to the full flamboyance of his manner before they were in front of each other. Johnny looked at him without a flicker of expression or break in his pace. Walter swung around and grabbed his arm.

"Hey, Johnny. What's up? Have you gone blind?"

Johnny stopped without looking at him. "Let go. I don't want to speak to you. Isn't that clear?"

"What is this? You must be mad. Only this morning I asked the office to look you up. I was hoping you might have a play."

"If I had, I wouldn't give it to you. Now, can I go?"

"No, damn it. What's it all about? You've got to tell me?"

"You know."

"Do I? I'm Walter Makin. You're Johnny Bainbridge. We went to school together. I've produced a couple of your plays. I can't see any reason there for our not speaking to each other."

"Oh, for God's sakes. You've never heard of the House Un-American Activities Committee? You've never heard of Sidney Magnus? You've never heard of a list denouncing your friends and working associates?"

"I've heard of some of it. I've never heard of a list. Do you think I would... This is insanity, Johnny. What in hell are you talking about? Tell me, please."

"I'm talking about the list you gave Magnus. Everybody knows about it."

"A list? *I* gave Magnus? Come on, Johnny. This is serious." Walter assumed that his indignation was convincing because Johnny allowed himself to be hustled into the first bar they came to on Rockefeller Plaza. Walter had been on his way to the office. He ordered drinks for them and turned to Johnny. "All right. Let's have it again. Everybody knows *I* gave a list of my subversive friends to Magnus?"

"So Magnus says. That's the rumor."

"It would've been quite a list. When am I supposed to've compiled this major work?"

"I don't know. Three years ago? I know you'd finished your first film. About the time I got dropped, not that you had anything to do with that. I'd have been out much sooner if I'd been more important."

"You were on my list? Yes, that figures. I remember Sidney asked me about you. Come to think of it, he did want a list. In essence, I told him where he could shove it. They put the screws on me for a while at the studio, and then they let up. I guess Sidney told somebody I'd cooperated so he could save face."

"No. I remember Gilbert Lukas was mentioned. That could only have come from you."

"Gilbert Lukas? That musician friend of Clara's? I hardly knew him."

"You. Clara. Six of one, half a dozen of–"

"Oh, no, Johnny," Walter cut in harshly. He peered into his glass. He didn't want to believe what he was thinking. He continued his interrogation. When they parted, the tenderness he had been cultivating in his relationship with Clara had turned to cold condemnation. Johnny had presented conclusive evidence of her having acted on his behalf. Again. His arrogant assumption that he could make Hollywood dance to his tune was criminal nonsense. Thanks to Clara, his success there had been an abject defeat. He could forgive a personal injury. He could never forgive being put in the position of betraying everything he believed in. Even thinking of her as the mother of his children didn't soften his heart toward her. It was finished. He would never turn to her again as the partner of his inner life. There was no point in confronting her with it on the off chance that there had been a misunderstanding. Confrontations with Clara never led to anything. He had already isolated himself from her in his work. He would isolate himself from her in every area of life that was important to him. They would act out a charade of compatibility and glamorous living. If he ever wanted to leave her, there would be no further need for justifying himself.

His return to the city soon created a stir. He started lucky with two successes, and his old reputation as the Boy Wonder was revived. There was a big project brewing regarding a cultural complex to be called Lincoln Center, and he was asked to revive Theatre Today for it as a showcase of the nation's theater. He was tempted—he would have a chance finally to be in on the planning of a theater from the ground up according to his specifications—but finally refused. He could no longer afford to be an innovator and a leader. He had put himself in a position where he had to make lots of money. The alteration and decoration of the house, or houses, on East 75th Street was costing a fortune, and he was determined to fill it with treasures. He needed money to live in a way to which he had yet to become accustomed. He needed money for instant mobility. He needed money to retain some control of the children, whatever happened. If this required lowering his professional standards for a while, he was at least aware why he was doing it.

When his third show flopped, he had to scramble for cash for several months. He raised a loan to pay the office staff and was grateful when the French couple suggested that they could wait for their wages. His fourth production was a trivial bit of nonsense and a smash success. He paid off his debts and bought some pictures and realized that this was the way life was going to be–ups and downs, the sense of adventure and the vaulting ambition gone, the routine of a craft mastered, which had earned him an eminent place in the city's life. Honors and awards became commonplace. At 35 he had become as much of an institution as anybody could in the unpredictable world of the theater. Just when it couldn't matter less, Clara's case went to a final court decision, and she was awarded possession of her money. It had grown considerably. As far as he was concerned, it was entirely hers. It simply enforced his need for money of his own to match it.

Groping blindly for something that seemed to have eluded him, he had brief affairs with several young actresses, but this too quickly turned into routine. It taught him that he couldn't expect a body, his own or any other, to offer any more revelations.

He dropped in at gay bars with his assistant from time to time when they had been kept late at the theater. Alone, he went back to the first one he had been taken to, with the half-formed hope that he might hear some news of Mark or even run into him. It had been too long, as time was measured in the constantly changing city, for this to be likely, but he was in the neighborhood and went in. One of the bartenders remembered Mark and said he had left town long ago.

There were others that weren't frequented by a theatrical crowd, and Walter found them a cheerful convenience when he felt like shedding the demands of being Walter Makin. He liked the anonymity and the air of expectancy, eyes sliding to the door to check each new arrival, the sense of impending encounter. He always attracted suitors, so he was assured of companions who didn't know who he was.

One night a particularly uninhibited group of youths swarmed around him immediately upon his arrival at one of the places he sometimes visited. The exclaimed over him shrilly.

"A divine man."

"Take your hands off him, Gladys. He's not yours."

"Look at his smile. What a wicked dish."

"We've got to take him with us."

"Calm down, girls. Let him take his pick."

Walter laughed as he disentangled himself from them to order a drink. There were five or six of them, all appearing to be in their early 20s except for one who was even younger, probably not out of his teens. They continued to carry on behind him. The young one pressed up beside him while he waited for his drink.

"I'm Kenny," he said. "You're the most gorgeous man I've ever seen."

The boy was tall, almost as tall as Walter, and very slight. He had a dissolute and expensive look. His pale skin and chestnut hair looked as if a lot of money had been spent on them. His features were agreeable but without marked character and reminded Walter of someone.

"I'm Walter." He took his drink from the bar and eased himself around to face the boy.

"I do anything. I have a big cock, if you're interested. You will come with us, won't you?"

"I don't know where you're going."

"To Roger's. For an utterly depraved orgy. There's a prize for the biggest cock. Something tells me you might win. You're such a gorgeously big hunk of man."

His voice and manner were also reminiscent of something. Walter began to puzzle over it. "Aren't you awfully young for this sort of thing?"

"I'm 18." The boy put a hand on Walter's crotch and coolly evaluated what he found there. "I thought so. That feels like the answer to a maiden's prayer. I can't wait to see it."

Walter laughed. "I doubt if you ever do."

"Why not?"

"Lots of reasons. For one thing, I'm old enough to be your father."

"You'd have had to be awfully young when you had me. I'll bet there's less than ten years' difference between us."

"I ought to take you up on that. I'm 38."

"I don't believe it. You can't be. I've never fallen for an older man."

Walter touched his arm kindly and felt his slightness under his jacket. He was a dreadful boy, yet there was something appealing about him. Walter hadn't the slightest twinge of sexual interest in him, but he felt a parental urge to protect him from his dubious playmates. "If you've fallen for me, why do you want me to go to any orgy with you? I should think you'd want us to go somewhere alone."

"You haven't asked me."

"That's true. What's your name, Kenny?"

The boy smiled slyly. "I don't usually give it in these bars. It's not Kenny. My real name's Jerry, for Geraldine."

Walter knew him instantly. He was looking at Fay as a young girl. "And Kenny is for Kennicutt?" he asked with a fluttering around his heart.

The boy looked startled. "You're a mind reader or a seer or whatever they're called. How did you know?"

"I knew you when you were a little boy. You look very like your mother. Your parents are friends of mine."

"Uh-oh." Alarm replaced amazement in his eyes; then the sly smile returned. "Well, I guess neither of us is apt to tell anybody where we met. Why don't my parents have more friends like you? Their baby daughter might stay home more often."

"What are you doing here? Why aren't you at school, or something?"

"Geraldine was a tiny bit naughty at school. She got caught being fucked by one of the gardeners. Twenty-five, built, and dreamy, with a cock like this." He measured off a generous length of bar. "Even so, he wasn't half as gorgeous as you. Are you going to take me away from all this? I'm your slave for life."

"I have to go." Every word the boy said made Walter wince. His son was appalling. Anger, directed at the Kennicutts, stirred him. Why had Fay let this happen? He still felt the boy's appeal in spite of so much that repelled him. Somebody should tell him that he could be queer without making a spectacle of himself. He put his money on the bar beside

his empty glass and ran an arm across the boy's back, feeling its fragili-
ty, a vulnerability that pierced him with tenderness. "I want to talk to
you, Jerry. You're living at home? I'll call you in the next day or so. I'm
Walter Makin."

"Walter Makin! But you're... What are *you* doing here? You've just
been nominated Father of the Year. My mother was talking about it the
other day."

"Yeah, well, there're all kinds of fathers. I'd like us to get to know
each other."

"We can't help that if you take me where I want to go."

A hand moved over Walter's crotch again. Walter looked at the boy
expressionlessly. "I think I'll have a word or two to say to you about
groping people in public."

"What do you expect? A girl can't keep her hands off you. I think it's
getting a little bit hard. Why don't you take me home with you now?"

"Because I'm Father of the Year. Fathers don't generally go to bed
with their children. If I find I can make any sense with you, I may make
an exception. We'll see."

"You're the most glamorous father I've ever seen. It gives me goose
bumps. You really will call?"

"I'll call."

"I'll be glued to the telephone. You're the most utterly thrilling man
in the world."

"Have a nice orgy." Walter gave the boy's back a pat and made his
way through clutching hands and voices shrill with protest at his departure.

He walked home feeling strangely disturbed. The boy, Kenny, had
interested him only mildly. The minute he had known he was Jerry,
all sorts of unfamiliar emotions had begun to clamor for attention.
Blood responding to blood? A sense of responsibility for having
brought this misguided kid into the world? Neither would explain the
sexual element that had intruded undeniably on his consciousness.
Jerry perversely excited him. He wanted to talk to him and try to
straighten him out, but he also wanted to hold him. If Jerry persisted

315

in making passes at him, he knew he would probably go to bed with his son. The hell with incest.

That he had a son old enough to offer himself as a bed partner made him acutely aware of the passage of years. He wasn't yet 40, and as far as he could see, the big adventures of life were all behind him. At Jerry's age, he had been so desperately eager to get started. He wondered if he hadn't perhaps rushed it a bit.

W alter swept across the lobby of the Gladwyn, carrying his jacket over his arm, and went directly to the elevators without bothering to have himself announced. Tom knew he was coming. The room number was seared into his brain. Tom. Tom Jennings. Tommy. The love of his life? Unlikely, but he intended to give it a whirl.

Going up in the elevator, he tried to gauge what he was feeling in comparison to the way it had been with Mark. It was hard to bridge the gap of so many years, but he remembered that he had tried to think of Mark as a sensual rather than emotional experience. Tom had none of Mark's physical splendor to blind him to what was taking place in himself, although he found him very sexy. If he understood Tom correctly, he had refused to go to bed with him because he felt there might be something much more important at stake. Clever Tom. It had seemed to grow more important with every hour they had been apart.

He knew that his sense of lost time was making him impatient. The age difference between them wasn't enormous, but if he were thinking in terms of a lifetime, 50 was a bit late to start. So much had happened to him so early that he felt awfully old to be given a second chance. Perhaps it had already slipped past him in any case. In the last couple of hours, Tom might have fought free of the spell they had instantly cast on each other. Walter too might see Tom with different eyes. Their second meeting might prove to be an anticlimax, an embarrassment to both of them. He was prepared for anything.

317

The elevator door opened, and he strode down a corridor, barely able to take in the numbers on the doors. His heart was beating rapidly. His excitement was making his senses unreliable. The number he was seeking leaped out at him. He stopped and pressed the bell. He heard it within as if it were at a great distance. He wondered if he would be able to speak at all. He had been struck deaf, dumb, and blind. The door opened, and Tom was a shape in front of him. His eyes were shining.

As Walter looked into them, their expression deepened and filled with welcome. There was something naked and exposed in them that affected Walter's joints so that he didn't trust himself to move.

"Aren't you going to come in?" Tom asked in his deep, gentle voice.

"Thanks." Walter knew he could have him now without meeting any resistance, but it was impossible to reach out for him while the door was open. When it was closed, they were somehow separated by the room. He was vaguely aware of suitcases standing about the floor.

"They said it was urgent," Tom said.

Walter was beginning to be able to see him whole. He was wearing jeans and a tight, thin knitted jersey that revealed the supple angularity of his body. He had good shoulders and slim hips without any heavy muscular accents. It was a keen, swift body. "Urgent? Yes, it was. It is— to me," he said.

"Yes. I can see. You've changed. You're more stunning than ever."

"Don't talk to me about that. My driver, my secretary—they're all nuts about you."

Tom grinned. "It must be some sort of peculiar disease that's going around."

"Thinking about you has turned me into a blithering idiot. I haven't the slightest idea what I've said to anybody for the last two hours."

"My thoughts haven't been exactly lucid."

Walter took a few steps toward him and felt a great glow of triumph when he didn't retreat. "I can't let you go. I know we have an awful lot to talk about. If we're going to make sense, I suppose we should try to keep sex out of it. At least, I'll try. Hadn't we better sit down?"

318

Tom stepped back and dropped onto the bed. Walter disposed of his jacket over the back of a chair and sat facing him. Their eyes met and delved into each other. Walter felt light flooding him. It was going to be good. He felt complete just being with him.

A little grin, shy, almost apologetic, played around Tom's mouth. "You've got it bad, Mr. Makin," he said, each word carrying a teasing lilt of joy. He found it incredible that Walter Makin should be in a blaze of passion for him. The highly theatrical manner that had given an air of make-believe to everything Walter had said in the car had been burned away. The passion remained. With luck he could make Walter Makin his. "When I left you, I knew what I was doing, but God—when I got your message, I was over the moon. I didn't know why you wanted to see me. I still don't. It doesn't matter so long as you're here."

"That's all I wanted—just to be here." His eyes were drawn to the smooth hollow where his collarbones met. He wanted to rest his mouth there forever. He raised his eyes to Tom's again. "Where to begin? I think I'm going to want to be part of your life. For that to make sense, I'd have to tell you a lot about Clara, and we haven't got time. Let's say she's a phenomenon that has nothing to do with the rest of my life. That sounds like nonsense, but it's true. It's been a good marriage in lots of ways, but…that's all. But I'm talking about something big, not picking up guys in bars. You say you're gay and I'm straight—with fringes. Do you still believe that?"

"From what I've heard, maybe that's what you want to believe. That's good enough for me. I talked about being in love with you, but…oh, hell, Walter, your life has no room for a man, and mine—mine's a great void waiting to be filled by someone I can love. I thought I'd never find anybody, but now I know different. That's what I want to hang on to."

"I want you to hang on to me." His eyes dropped to lightly muscled arms, and he wanted to be held by them. He felt Tom's frank, searching gray-green gaze on him, and he met it with all the longing that was in him. "What can I do to convince you? Believe me, Tommy, in my business I could have had an attractive guy every day of the week for the last 20 years if that's what I wanted. You're something else. Everything about you delights me—just being near you, everything." His eyes fixed on long-fingered hands spread out on thighs, thumbs pointing in toward the substantial bulge of crotch. Tom's grip on his imagination, emotions, thoughts, desires seemed to broaden and strengthen. He lifted his eyes and caught a slight frown crossing Tom's brow. "Why shouldn't we be in bed together, Tommy?" Walter asked, not insistently but for information.

The frown became perplexed, but the deep-set eyes remained direct and affectionate. "I told you in the car, if I go to bed with you, it'll just make it harder to leave you, but that's not all of it. I'm shy with you about sex. I'm bound to be a lousy lover. I've had no real experience. I was faithful to one guy for 15 years, and sex was never our trump card. I know you're sensational in bed. I've heard all about it. If we were going to live together, I'd learn fast enough, but not like this, not here, not a quick roll in the hay and see you next week."

"No, not that at all. I want to make love to you, Tommy. It's as simple as that. I don't want a demon lover. I want you. We don't need bed to prove anything. We already know—"

The telephone rang. The shattering of the intense communion between them was like some vital organ being severed. Walter took a deep breath and watched the movements of the rangy body as Tom stood and went to the head of the bed. He looked more powerful from behind. There was a spring of power in the well-rounded buttocks. He listened to the deep voice dealing courteously with whoever was at the other end of the line.

"Yes, I'm sorry. Something came up… Of course… I understand. I'll pay for another night… I'm not sure. I'll let you know later."

A crucial moment was behind them. Tom was no longer in a hurry. He hung up and turned and lifted his arms from his sides, his hands open, his tight clothes molding his body, poised as if inviting an embrace. Walter gathered himself together to spring to meet him. but the arms extended into a stretch, the hands closed into fists, he grimaced and uttered a little grunt and dropped his hands back to his sides. The milestones of Walter's life were apparently to be marked by young men stretching. He thought of the dramatic poetry in Mark's body. Tom stretched in a straightforward easing of tension. He wasn't being seduced by tricks of physique.

"God, how I long to cling to you," Tom said with a hint of playfulness. "Or do I mean cleave? Yes. That has a nice ecclesiastical sound. How I long to cleave unto thee, O my husband, wife, master, mate. Do you grasp the dimensions of the problem?" A low roll of laughter broke from him; and he returned to the place on the bed where he had been sitting before, which was the closest place in the room to Walter's chair. Walter was aware of it and knew that he couldn't have borne it if he had sat anywhere else. Their feet almost touched.

Walter leaned back and looked for a suspenseful moment at Tom. He was beyond caring whether any of this was real. He was prepared to pretend that it was, say words that might be true, follow it wherever it led. He was discovering endless unexpected attractions in the face that confronted him attentively. It was a face of extraordinary character and appeal.

Tom watched the imp take possession of Walter's face, the lips curl, the eyes slant upward. He shivered with delight and desire. Walter had the fascination of originality. Tom never knew what he was going to say or do. He wanted them to be naked together so he could see if the things he had been told about Walter were true. He wanted to feel the magnificent body wanting him. He wanted to be seized and used and stripped to the soul. That he could fall in love with him threatened disaster, but he was past his initial panic. He was playing for high stakes, with little chance of winning; but he felt it essential for his own survival to play it out to the end. He grinned in response to rich laughter. "What're you thinking?"

"Oh, Tommy, Tommy, dearest Tommy," Walter exclaimed. "I'm wondering how to say it right. I think I could spend the rest of my life with you. It may sound silly, but I mean it. I told you, I'm no prize. I'm spoiled. I don't have much money. I'm used to having people do everything for me. I'm vain and famous and expect attention. I'm getting old. There you are. If you want me, you can have me."

Tom straightened, and his shoulders seemed to grow broader. His long fingers clutched convulsively at his trousers. His lips parted, and he moistened them with his tongue. "If I thought you knew what you're talking about, I'd scream the place down with ecstasy," he said in a muted voice. "You just can't get it through your head. I have to live with the guy I love. I mean really live. It's not the same as being married, but that's the rough idea. I'm demanding too. I've been in a bad way. A transcontinental affair is one thing I don't need. But that's aside from the point. I can live anywhere. I'd live here if you wanted me to, but together, as a pair, so that everybody would know and treat us accordingly. I think we're both out of our minds."

The imp in Walter grew more pronounced. "Am I to take it that you're proposing? I accept. I don't care where we live. We have time to decide about that. First, I want a California honeymoon."

Tom didn't laugh. Walter was approaching the dissolution of his life with gaiety and insouciance, as if he didn't expect to be taken seriously. He mustn't let himself believe in it yet. "What about all that weight, Walter?" he reminded him.

"Weight? I suppose if I step out from under it, it'll fall with a hideous crash. The boys are grown-up. They'd be the only serious reason for second thoughts. The younger one is just the age I was when I had my first experience with a boy. Harry was his romantic name, and I've always been inclined to hate him everlastingly, but there have been times when I've been grateful to him—now more than ever."

"I think I *will* scream the place down." Tom flung himself back onto the bed and bounced up again. Walter's heart raced at what had taken place in his face. It had all come alive. His eyes danced. His grin had spread into a dazzling smile of barely contained delight. His throat swelled with laughter. Light radiated from him and warmed him like the sun. It made him almost believe that he could escape Clara.

"When do you want to go to California?" Tom asked through ripples of laughter.

"Soon. The next day or two? You're not still planning to leave today, are you?"

"You said you were tied up for a week."

"I was. I'm either tied up for a week, or I'm going to drive to California with you. You leave me no choice."

"Jesus. That's not right. I'm sorry. I'll stay. I keep forgetting we hardly know each other. You must have a thousand things to think about, with the big event tonight and everything. You'd be mad to decide anything until that's out of the way."

"What if I skip the big event tonight?" Walter's laughter was wickedly gleeful. "That would simplify matters. The only trouble is that I'd miss seeing Clara's face if I don't show up."

"Cut that out." Tom was winning so triumphantly that it scared him. He was a gambler and superstitious. Never push your luck, he warned himself. He kept feeling as if he were dropping in an express elevator when he thought of their bodies touching. "We'll have all day tomorrow to decide what we want to do. Tonight you're going to collect your award."

"I'm not so sure. The award has nothing to do with you, so it's really a nonevent. If you'll let us go to bed, maybe I'll do what you tell me. I'll be yours, and you'll be mine, and nothing else in the world will matter."

*Nothing,* Tom thought. "Now listen, Walter. This is getting serious," he said. "I'm not a wrecker. Your career. Your marriage. I'm just beginning to realize how big it is. I've been thinking too much about myself. Maybe we'll be sexually incompatible." A sparkle of humor returned to his eyes, and he mocked them both. "I know what you like. It's never happened to me. What if I don't like it?"

Walter smiled into the humor of his eyes. "Sex. It's love, Tommy. You can't know what I like, because I've never been to bed with you, and I don't know myself. There's so much more of you than there is of me. I think you can bring me back to life. Forget all that weight. Marriage? Career? One is an aberration, the other a fake. The words are interchangeable. I want you."

"No, darling. Please." Tom sprang up, and Walter was immediately standing in front of him, holding his arms but not touching him elsewhere. Tom lay his sinewy hands on Walter's forearms. They both took deep breaths at the sudden longed-for contact. They remained still, breathing in unison, steadying themselves in preparation for the act of love they both knew couldn't be postponed.

"Oh, God, Tommy," Walter murmured. "I've got to hold on to you. Please let me. You've got to stay with me every second until we're safe. Please get me away from here. You don't know how important it is."

"I'm beginning to." Their eyes searched and probed, so close that they seemed to reach into the most secret depths of each other. "Yes. Now," Tom breathed. "We can talk about everything later."

"Are you sure I'm not trying to get you out of my system?"

"That was long ago. I'm sure now."

Walter moved his hands up to his shoulders and down his back. Tom's body became a reality, and he found it thrilling–hard, lithe, agile. "I'm feeling a bit shy myself. It's fairly tremendous when you know it could be for life. I've got to get it right this time. I can't afford mistakes, Tommy."

"You know, I almost come every time you call me that. Nobody has before."

"That's nice. I used to be known as an innovator." Walter laid a hand on his cheek. He touched his lips with the tips of his fingers and ran his hand through his hair. "How did you know exactly how I wanted you to look? I think I'm going to faint when I kiss you. We'd better take it a bit at a time. Where shall we start?"

Tom grasped the bottom of his jersey and peeled it off over his head, exposing a broad tanned chest, lightly shadowed with hair, the pectoral muscles flat and barely defined, the nipples large and brown and smooth. There was a faint ripple of abdominal muscle above the concavity of his belly.

"How beautiful of you not to have a lot of hair." Walter's fingers brushed against smooth skin and strayed into his armpits and encountered a few soft curls. "Not even here."

"What about you? Are you a great hairy ape?" Tom chuckled and slowly began to unbutton Walter's shirt.

Walter's eyes misted at the quiet intimacy of it. He awaited the revelation of some ultimate secret, the secret of love that he might have
learned with Mark but had resisted. He slipped his shirt off. Their eyes
signaled to each other, and they moved their heads to each other. Their
lips touched. Their mouths opened, and they moved into each other,
their arms around each other, their bodies pressed to each other and
straining for total contact. They broke apart and tore off their remaining clothes.

They caught only a brief glimpse of each other before they were in
each other's arms again. They both uttered incoherent sounds at the
feel of their nakedness against each other. Their mouths were joined
as Walter moved him toward the bed. Urgent little cries came from
Tom's throat. They fell on the bed. Tom tore his mouth away.

"Oh, God," he cried. "Walter. No!" His body pitched about with his
orgasm.

Walter laughed and moved his hips against him and came quickly
after him. Schoolboy sex, but no less thrilling for that.

They lay still for a minute for two, and then Tom pulled away and
made a dash for the bathroom. He returned with a towel, trying not to
act as self-conscious as he felt. Walter was even more magnificent
physically then he had imagined, and he had done nothing for him. He
was the man he had dreamed of ever since he had first heard of him.
He wanted to lie at his feet and worship him dumbly. He wanted to
howl in adoration. Years of repression and inhibition hadn't tamed the
fierce cravings in him. Walter wiped himself off and pulled him down
close again.

They lay together finding worlds of bright, infinite promise in each
other's eyes. Tom shuddered slightly and smiled. "I told you I was lousy
in bed."

"That was lousy? We both came in two seconds. What's wrong with
that? It just proved how much we needed it. God, Tommy, just being
with you like this, touching you and smelling you and looking at you,
is the most exciting sex I've ever known. You couldn't be lousy in bed
if you tried."

"You're a nice man, Uncle Walt." He put a hand on Walter's hair and inched a little closer to him. "I wonder why Mark didn't make you sound nice."

"Oh, lord, poor Mark. I wasn't very nice with him. I couldn't imagine living with a guy the way he wanted it. It's taken me 50 years to find out. Actually, it took me 38 years, about your age, and I've been waiting around ever since."

"I suppose I'll find out what that means eventually. At least we have Mark in common. It makes me feel as if I've known you a long time."

Walter lifted himself on an elbow and eased Tom onto his back and looked at last at the long, angular, loose-limbed body that he had only begun to know. His narrow midriff bore the pale imprint of very short shorts. His cock was modest in repose, but it had made a fine, lusty display of itself when incited by desire. A few small freckles or moles were scattered over him and pinpointed the places Walter wanted to explore. He was a man, and Walter found him totally desirable. "Tommy the cowboy," he said, bending to kiss a nipple. "You're a country boy. That's one thing that's wonderful about you. You smell of the country. Thank God you're not beautiful. You must be the most attractive guy I've every seen, but you're not a goddamned statue. That's what went wrong with Mark. I've always pretended that caring about male beauty had nothing to do with the big homosexual scene."

"He was beautiful, wasn't he? He wanted me to do what you did with him… *No,* damn it! You've got to help me talk straight about sex. That's the first thing. He wanted me to *fuck* him—that's better—and I couldn't. He really turned me on, but I couldn't give him what he wanted. I suppose at 18 that counts as a trauma. At least, you don't want that."

"Don't count on it, Tommy. I want you in every way known to man until we don't know which of us is which."

"Beautiful. Upset the old male-female balance? That's what I need. I've never really been one thing or the other. You'll help put it together for me."

"Yeah." Walter lowered his head until their lips touched. Tom opened his mouth, passive but responsive. Walter moved his tongue

326

slowly over his lips and teeth into his mouth. Tom put his hands on his shoulders and gripped them as Walter drew back.

"I love your teaching me how to make love, Uncle Walt."

"Is that what you're going to call me?"

"It's what I'm going to call you in public. You'll know what I'm thinking. Shouldn't we be deciding what we're going to do?"

"Haven't we?" The reminder that another life existed outside of Tom dazed him, making his thoughts collide and tumble over each other. The award. It would soon be time to dress for the evening. A distinguished gathering was due for drinks. The spotlight was about to be turned on him as he moved to center stage. Without Tom? Impossible. He slid an arm under Tom's shoulders and put the other hand on his waist and threw a leg across him, seeing that he was still wearing one sock, and gathered him close. They were beginning to get hard against each other.

Tom grinned. "As far as I know, all we decided was that we had to be like this. Oh, God, it feels good. Jesus, Walter. Listen. I'd like to sort of work out a timetable. You've got to go soon. It doesn't matter if you're busy for the next week. Then what?"

"California and... How can you expect me to make sense when you're getting a hard-on? All I want is to get out of town."

"What shall I tell the hotel? Shall I keep the room another week?"

"God, no. Tell them they can have the damn room as soon as we're able to let go of each other." He slid off him and made love to all his body with his mouth until Tom was shouting and laughing and leaping about under him. Within moments he felt Tom's orgasm gathering, and he moved quickly the receive the ejaculation in his mouth. He lay back in his turn when Tom moved down over him, but Tom had made such a point of being a sexual novice that he was prepared to pull away at the first sign of awkwardness or reluctance. The ease with which Tom's mouth took charge of him suggested that this was his particular predilection, and he let himself be carried to a peaceful orgasm. Their bodies were no longer thrilling strangers to each other but were attuned to what felt already like a familiar harmony.

"Now, let's try again," Walter said. "Do you have enough cash lying around to get us both to the Coast?"

"I guess so, if we take it easy on champagne and caviar. Why?"

"Because I can't get any money without going home, and I don't want to."

"Don't be silly. You ought to be getting dressed right now. We've got to talk sense."

"We are. We're going to California together. Let's go."

All of Tom's face was alive. His eyes sparkled. Their arms and hands tightened on each other. "I keep forgetting. It's too incredible. You're going to drive out with me."

"Can you imagine my letting you go without me?"

"OK. OK," Tom said excitedly. "Will you come back tonight and spend the night with me?"

Walter laid a hand on the side of his face and looked at him thoughtfully. "Just a minute. Let's see." Talking about not going to the ceremony had left a residue of genuine resistance to the whole idea of the award. All the people he admired most in the profession had banded together to honor him. He didn't want to let them down, but it was time to put first things first. He didn't need the award; he needed to work things out with Tom. If he were committing a folly, he might as well do it with style and leave himself no lines of retreat. He wanted to mark his liberation from himself, his liberation from the past, his liberation from Clara. Having got to the point of making a decision for which Clara would never forgive him, he was far from sure that he could go through with it. This made him sure that he had to.

He moved his hand over Tom's face, across his brow, across his straight nose to his strong chin. He tapped it with a loosely closed fist. "There. That's settled. Let's get out of here." He sprang out of bed and reached down and pulled Tom up with him. They stood face to face, their eyes level with each other, their midsections and thighs touching. Walter swept his hand over Tom's shoulders and down his back to the trim, firm buttocks. They didn't react to his touch. He lifted his hands to Tom's waist and gave his mouth a quick kiss. "For heaven's sake, put some clothes on. If you don't, I'm going to want you again in a minute, and we'll never get out of here."

Tom laughed. "Maybe you know what you're doing. I don't."

They jostled each other as they went to the chair where they had thrown their clothes. They quickly pulled on shorts and socks and trousers. Walter started to slip on his shirt. Tom remained bare-chested, his hands on his hips, watching him. Walter looked at him questioningly.

"Go on," Tom ordered. "Finish dressing. I want to talk to you, but not till you're ready to leave."

Walter buttoned his shirt and tucked it in and pulled on his shoes. "I'm going to carry my tie and jacket. I'm ready."

Tom smiled and shook his head. "You should see yourself. You're adorable, but people might wonder." He went to him and took his hand and led him to a mirror.

Walter chortled. His hair was in wild disarray. "I look as if I'd had a high old time in bed. Well, I have." Tom handed him a comb, and he used it. "How's that?"

"Fine. Now beat it. You may have other ideas, but you're going to collect your award. A lot of people have gone to a lot of trouble for you. I'd never forgive myself if you didn't show up. You can come back here afterward, and we'll take off, or we can spend the night together and leave in the morning, or we can wait for a few days while you get yourself organized. Take your pick, but you've got to show up tonight." He didn't know how long he could remain firm, but he had to make the attempts. His eyes were spellbound by the famous impish face. He took a quick breath, and his voice came out in a taut undertone. "Walter. Walter. Let's be careful, baby. Don't let's go too far until we're sure."

Walter stood in front of him with his hands on his naked shoulders. "When you say 'we,' everything you suggest is what I want to do, but you still haven't got the picture. I can't be away from you even for an hour. I found that out at lunch. I'm not going to risk it. We could go get the award together, but the minute Clara saw us, she'd know, and I'm not going to risk that either. God knows what she could do about it, but

I'm sure she'd think of something." A premonitory shiver ran down his spine. He looked at Tom intently as if the bond between them might become visible. His face was so firmly modeled and yet so expressive that it seemed to possess a number of personae, one superimposed on the other. As one replaced another, like slides, it became the definitive Tom, with no hidden areas in it, no suggestion that this was just one face of a complex personality. The country boy was gone, replaced by a friendly counselor, a doctor, or a lawyer. Walter gave his shoulders a little shake. "Come on, Tommy. I must be in love with you. It's the first time I haven't thought for an instant of running away from it. I can't let anything go wrong. Don't make me go to the award. Take pity on an old man."

Tom smiled. "You won't get very far with that line." He swung them around to face the mirror. "Look at us. If anything, I look older. I know 50 isn't Methuselah, but I don't see how you've done it. It makes me want to go out and stock up on creams and lotions." He made a face at the mirror and ran a finger from the side of his nose to the corner of his mouth. "Look at that. Lines. You don't have any." He leaned to Walter and kissed his neck. "A sexy mole on an alabaster throat. It's pure Dorian Gray." He left Walter's side to put on his jersey. He knew that he risked being carried away helplessly in the sweep of Walter's personality. He was bewitched. He had touched only the surface of the depths of passion he sensed in this extraordinary man and was afraid to plumb them until he had regained some possession of himself.

He pulled the jersey on over his head and ran his fingers through his hair. Being dressed armed him. He had lived for 15 years as the willing servant to a friend on whom he had made no demands, and when death had ended it, he had found that he had been stripped of all his resources. He had painfully survived with the discovery that love must be demanding. Without demands, one became a cipher. He had resolved that if he ever fell in love again, he would start by staking out his own claims in the partnership—the way he wanted to live, for instance. The importance of his work. His sexual appetites, whatever they proved to be. He mustn't let himself become Walter's willing servant.

Walter stood beside him with a hand on his shoulder. "What are we waiting for?"

Tom resisted an impulse to put his arms around him. A slight tremor passed through him at his proximity. "I'm terrified of letting you do something you'll regret."

"Please, Tommy. You've got to get me out of here. You say you need somebody to build a life with. Don't you think I know what that means?"

"I'm not sure. You don't have any idea what you're letting yourself in for. You haven't a glimmer what it's like leading a homosexual life."

"You lead one, so I guess there must be something good about it," Walter persisted. "After what's happened with us, don't you think it's about time I found out?"

"Oh, darling, yes. I just want you to take time to think what you're doing. I'll want you all to myself. I'll want you to care about my work, and you haven't read a word I've written. You have a wife and children and a big, established career and all the other things we've talked about. Maybe even girls, for all I know. All you will have is me, with a touch of scandal thrown in. Have you ever thought about that? I'm not saying we can't make it work. You make me feel that maybe we can. But...Christ, Walter. Are you sure we're not crazy? How long has it been? Five hours? Already I want to live with you and love you and make you happy. I'll feel the same way tomorrow. It doesn't matter about tonight."

"You're wonderful, Tommy." Walter's smile was gentle and only faintly impish. "You've said all the right things, except that I don't want to let anything come between us for the time being. I don't trust myself. I'll just disappear. When we've had time to settle down, I'll start picking up the pieces from out there. I presume you have someplace I can live."

"I won't let you starve on the streets."

"I hope it doesn't come to that. As long as I hang on to you, I don't think Clara can spook me. I have about $10,000 in my own account. The shows will be adding to that every week. Everything else is tied up one way or another, and it'll be some time before I can straighten it all out, but I don't think I'll be a burden for you."

"You definitely know what you're doing about tonight?"

"Yes. I have to go to California in a few minutes."

Tom threw his head back with a quick intake of breath and sat on the arm of a chair with his eyes closed. Was there anything else he should say?

Walter marveled at the ambiguous grace of his body as he perched on the chair, one arm extended to prop himself on its back, the long legs bent at the knee, one foot touching the floor for balance. He was almost girlish. He was very much a man. Walter could see his heart beating rapidly under the tight jersey.

Tom opened his eyes and gathered himself together and stood. They met and opened their arms to each other and held each other close and exchanged a kiss. For the first time in his life, Tom felt in charge of a love affair and responsible for making it work for both of them.

"The only major problem I can see," Walter said, "is managing to stay out of bed with you. I keep wanting to take your clothes off."

"Good. You'll turn me into a sex fiend. I think that's what I've always wanted to be." He thrust his hips up against Walter's. "I swear to God, I could wait for you for weeks if necessary."

"I couldn't. Stop worrying about tonight, baby. Believe me, it's unimportant. I'll tell you what's going to happen. David will guess immediately. He'll call here and find out I've left with you. He'll make up some story for Clara and convince her that she has to announce that I'm sick all of a sudden. One of them will read my speech for me. Clara will thrive on covering for me—again—and David will be laughing his head off. He's been waiting for this to happen since I was 18. A jolly good time will be had by all—especially us."

"Isn't *Time* about to do a cover on you?"

"In a couple of days."

"Then the press is apt to be a nuisance. You'd better really disappear. Let's be brothers. Tom and Walter Jennings. It'll be better when we ask for double beds anyway. OK?"

332

"Perfect. It sounds like being married. I'm a bigamist."

Deep ringing laughter burst from Tom. "God, what a day. And the night is still to come. I love you, Uncle Walt."

"I love you, Tommy."

Their mouths met in another long, lingering, kiss, quickly becoming passionate so that they were both breathing rapidly when they drew apart.

"You're right," Tom said with slight unsteadiness in his voice. "It's going to be no mean feat to stay out of bed. I'm gay, baby. Don't forget it. Things are going on in me that you probably know nothing about. Those fringes. I'm going to make you gay too." He broke away and went to the telephone and called down to ask for help with his bags.

They got out into the worst of the evening traffic. As they began to inch their way across town, Walter was immediately assailed by second thoughts. He was behaving like a naughty kid. Tom had said himself that a day or two didn't matter. He held himself in his seat and longed to jump out and run home. A glance from Tom riveted him to his side and sent him soaring on clouds of joy. He was with a man he could love. Faced with something so momentous, he couldn't behave as if it were a day like any other. He had to celebrate it with some definitive act. He was discarding the past and making a commitment to the future. But couldn't he have done it just as effectively tomorrow? He dropped from the clouds and touched the handle of the door. Still only a few minutes' walk from home. He couldn't expect anybody to make him indifferent to the consequences of what he was doing.

The highs and lows followed each other in rapid succession. His sense of time deserted him. He kept trying to catch a glimpse of the watch on Tom's lean wrist. He longed for it to be too late so that there would be nothing more to think about. By the time the Holland Tunnel disgorged them onto the Jersey shore, he knew it *was* too late. Only a wild dash back could have got him, dressed as he was, to the beginning of the ceremony. He began to relax and open himself to the powerful appeal of the presence beside him. The wanted each other; he could feel it almost palpably even though they weren't touching and were further separated by Tom's preoccupation with driving. He had craved the big experience of love all these years; this must be it. It had to work, or there would be nothing more to hope for. He had discovered a fine edge of desperation in Tom that added to the excitement of it. They couldn't have got through the evening without each other.

They remained silent while Tom maneuvered the car expertly thought traffic. As night fell, another glance at the watch told Walter that the ceremony had begun. He had done it. He had run away from Clara. He might go crawling back to her in a week, but meanwhile he would have risked everything for a purely personal satisfaction. Weight after weight dropped from him. He was free to submit himself to a whole new unfamiliar set of demands and obligations. Even at his advanced age, life could be an adventure.

After stopping for something to eat, they drove across part of Pennsylvania in the dark. Then they began to talk, without pause, insatiable for each other's pasts, both of them keenly aware of the pleasure they were finding in each other's company. Tom was a native Californian; his parents and an older brother and sister were scattered about the state. His father had been a successful accountant and was now retired near Monterey. Tom had been brought up in affluence. His was a straightforward California story, except for the anomaly of his talent and his sexual makeup. They talked about sex. Tom had been committed to men as early as Harry but had been less active about it. There had been Mark, and after Mark there had been no thought in his mind that his tastes might change as he grew to manhood.

"What's it like to be gay?" Walter asked. "If that's what I'm going to be, I should be prepared."

"It's excellent training for secret agents. You know, working up a cover and sticking to it so you're never caught being who you really are. I don't know. Plenty of guys don't bother with a cover and take on a lot of silly mannerisms. I've never seen why I should go around saying 'Get you, Mary' just because I like to suck cock. With us, well, we'll see. You're famous, and I'm getting near the top of my field. We're going to attract attention. It scares me because you may not be able to take it, but I'm sure I'm going to have to blow my cover with you. Naturally, my attitude's been affected by living with John."

"John's the one who died?"

"He was killed in a car crash last year. I was 22 when we met. He was 30. He was a wonderful guy–handsome, bright, funny. He was also a very successful businessman. He lived in two entirely separate airtight compartments. I was in one of them, the rest of his life in the other. We lived in the same house, but when he entertained, I split. He went on living exactly the same as before. We were in love with each other–it was wonderful when he joined me in my compartment–and he made a very convincing case for why that was the way it should be. I accepted it because I adored him. I wouldn't accept it again. I'd rather be alone than try to live such a big lie. I've tried to warn you all day, but it's no use. You have to find out for yourself. When his family turned up to…to do the things you have to do when somebody's dead, they were amazed that I knew so much about him. They were even more amazed when they read his will. I wanted to drop dead–for his sake. And it hurt. God, it hurt. Fifteen years, and I couldn't break down and decently mourn the guy they loved too; not the way I did, but what did that make me? A dirty little cocksucker. I couldn't let them guess that he was a cocksucker too. The sex part of being gay is a mystery to me. Why do I want to suck a cock and not put my nose between a girl's legs? I haven't the faintest idea. You'll have to forgive me for being crude, darling. It's good for my soul. I'm a cocksucker, but that's pleasure, not love. I've never been convinced it's the surest way to a man's heart. I'm not even sure two men can express their love with their bodies. Maybe I'll find out with you. I can understand it must be different with a man and a woman who love each other and have all the procreative pizzazz to work with. The physical part must seem almost divine at times. Does it?"

"I don't know, Tommy. Doesn't it have an awful lot to do with being in love? I may've mentioned the fact that I never have been. I've always loved sex with boys. Girls too. I think it's going to be better with you than it's ever been."

335

Tom dropped a hand from the wheel and gave his knee a squeeze. "Just keep saying things like that, and I may yet turn into a demon lover. Frankly, I'm hooked on the phallic. It's a deep, dark secret–I've always felt so silly dreaming of big cocks–but in your case it has a certain relevance. *Fantastic* is the only word for it, darling. I'm terrified of becoming a slave to it. No, not really. I'm not going to be a slave to anything anymore, but I'm going to let myself fall in love with you more thoroughly than anybody's ever been in love before. I want to make you fall in love with me in the same way, no holds barred. Do you think you're ready for that?"

"Yes, Tommy. If it isn't going to be like that, I shouldn't be here. There've been times today when I've been happier than I thought anybody could be–right now more than ever." He sat with an arm running along Tom's shoulders. He gave him a little hug. "Do we believe in love at first sight?"

"Of course, that's the only way the big things get started. It means we're not apt to fall out of love, but we may have a long way to go before we're sure we can make it work."

"Yes, because I'm me. It'll take time before I can trust myself. I don't think I ever have really. I have my little genius that's made it awfully easy to sidestep the big issues. I've coasted on it right from the start. I don't mean I haven't worked hard, but that's another matter. You're going to have to slap me down if you catch me playing my tricks with you. I maybe shouldn't say it, but your life with John sounds like a nightmare. I'm much too egotistical to play it like that, although I admit I talked to Mark along the same lines. My public life with Clara and him in the attic somewhere. I haven't got any ideas like that about you, but I had to prove it to myself. That was the point of cutting the award. I don't want any cover. I want to live with you openly. I don't want to know anybody you don't know. I want everything about our life to be ours."

"You know, this may be a miracle. Maybe we're made for each other. I'm going to tell you something fairly weird. I've hinted around about Mark, but the fact is that ever since he told me about you, I've had a feeling that we belonged with each other. I guess he made you sound like someone I wanted, and it just grew from there. It was very strange, knowing all these years that there was somebody out there that I'd eventually be with—strange and wonderful. When I met David and he started talking about you, I knew it was going to happen. I was with John, but I began to be unfaithful to him with you. My being in New York the last few weeks wasn't exactly a coincidence. David had promised to introduce us. When it happened today, I had to get away from you to make sure it wasn't all happening in my head. Twenty years of wanting you, Mr. Makin. Maybe that's why we know what we want without having to talk about it."

They didn't stop talking about it. Tom drove fast and very well, so Walter could relax into the growing comfort of being with him. He felt that they were utterly complete together. It was the best way he could express it to himself. Tom's fanciful tale of wanting him for 20 years was part of it. It might explain why he had been able to respond so unguardedly almost from the start and why he felt so confident with him. He didn't know what resistance in himself might be aroused once they tried to settle down to daily life together, but he was sure they were going to have a wonderful trip to the Coast.

It was almost midnight when they pulled into a brightly lit luxurious-looking motel. The VACANCY sign was on. Tom stopped the car near some others.

"I don't suppose you know how to take a room in a motel," he said. "Have you ever been in one?"

"I've heard of them."

Tom chuckled. "OK. Wait here."

"Be sure to keep account of all this."

"Why?"

"So I can pay you back, dummy."

"Really, darling." He turned and put a hand on Walter's and looked at him in the half-light from the motel. His eyes were only a glitter in the shadow of the deep sockets. "I thought we knew things we didn't have to say. What's mine is yours, and vice versa, with the under-

337

standing that neither of us spends any big money without discussing it first. John kept accounts. That's not us. I'm assuming, naturally, that this is just the beginning of a long life together."

"Is that the way it's going to be?" Walter asked, stroking the long fingers interlaced with his.

"That's the way it's going to be."

"It sounds like us. Now get in there and get us a room, or I'm going to make love to you out here."

Tom climbed out of the car, and Walter watched his graceful figure moving toward a neon sign saying OFFICE. He thought of the award. The ceremony would be over by now. He hadn't felt any regrets all evening nor even any curiosity about what had taken place. He was too absorbed in the wonder of finding Tom to feel any loss for Clara and family and home. This might come later, but he hoped that by then his spirit would have revived and expanded and become so intertwined with Tom's that the past would have melted away into a harmless memory. He and Clara had created a brightly bedizened life, but he had known for a long time that beneath the splendid panoply the machinery ran in a small rut of self-deception. He took a deep breath of real air, and his heart swelled with happiness as he saw the figure returning.

Tom waved a key and pulled a suitcase out of the car, and they moved into a pleasantly antiseptic room. They took turns freshening up in the bathroom.

"Somerset Maugham says you know you're in love if you can use the other person's toothbrush," Walter said as Tom emerged looking dewy and country-boy–fresh from the shower. "Can I use yours?"

"Who else's?"

They fell into bed and gathered each other close with moans of relief and need. They were both emotionally drained and physically exhausted. Their sex play was brief and schoolboyish and happy.

"When I wake up and find you beside me, I may start yelling with joy," Tom said, his eyes soft with love and sleep. "I just wanted to warn you beforehand."

"Wake me first, and we'll yell together. Our first night. We're going to sleep together tonight and tomorrow night and every night, I hope, forever. Do you sleep on your back or how?"

"Wrapped around you."

Tom loved again. After the months of frozen anguish and heartbreak, everything was thawing and colliding within him. It was almost too agonizing to be borne. For the moment, all his mind could encompass was the depth of his body's bliss.

"Oh, Tommy. You feel so wonderful. I could stay like this for a week."

They turned out the lights and nibbled each other's lips and laughed softly until they were breathing deeply, and they slept. They woke early in each other's arms.

"What are you going to wear for the next few days?" Tom asked as they were putting on their shorts.

"Your things, I suppose."

"Can you? You're such a strapping lad."

"I can wear your pants." Walter demonstrated by fishing a pair of jeans out of the suitcase and putting them on.

"God Almighty. Sexier and sexier. If you show that basket in Sausalito, you'll be mobbed."

"I'm counting on you to keep the crowds under control." He found a shirt and put it on. "A bit tight across the chest, but it'll do. How's that?"

"Wonderful. We won't be able to tell which of us is which before we've even begun to do it all in bed. I don't know what we can do about certain glaring differences."

Walter went to him as he was about to put on his shirt and ran his hands lovingly over his bare chest. "I've had about enough out of you. Now it's your turn. I adore your body. Your cock is the way I'd design a cock for worldwide distribution. Your face is so beautiful with intelligence and sweetness and humor and love that it makes me want to weep half the time. I connect with everything about you and everything you are, including your beautiful voice. Good morning, beloved Tommy."

"Good morning, darling Uncle Walt."

They were well into Ohio when Tom said, "Darling, do you mind if we drive like hell for the next few days? I thought we might take it easy and enjoy it, but there's something unreal about it that bothers me. Traveling isn't like ordinary life."

"I know what you mean. Let's get it over with quickly. I'd forgotten how it is. I won't let you do this alone again."

"That's good. Everything's good. That's why I'm in a hurry to start living with you. It was so beautiful waking up with you this morning and fooling around getting dressed. I wanted it to go on through a normal day, everything growing and shifting and getting more exciting until we'd be back in bed again whenever we felt like it. I guess I feel sort of the way you did about the award. Contact isn't broken when we're driving, but we have to keep it in its place. You'll tell me if you start getting tired?"

"Don't worry about me. You haven't worked in the theater. I can go for days with only a couple of hours' sleep. Didn't you say you had to be back in five or six days anyway?"

"That was yesterday. I promised to be back for a friend's birthday. He's in love with me, and I'm very fond of him. We've toyed with the idea of getting together. That's a fairly dead issue now."

They drove through or near many places where Walter had been with shows, and he told stories that made them both laugh. They took turns driving and stayed on the road well into the night. The weather remained warm and mostly sunny. Nothing occurred to test their tempers or high spirits. Their sexual activity remained brief, tentative, almost casual. Walter found it restful and sweet and completely satisfying. He felt in Tom a holding back, a reluctance probably to go too far in circumstances where it would be impossible to explore and evaluate new experience. They weren't, as Tom had put it, expressing their love with their bodies, and Walter was content to wait. Being with him, looking at him all day and holding him at night, was all the expression of love he needed.

"Do we know each other well enough now for you to tell me what happened when you were 38?" Tom asked in Iowa.

"We're beginning to read each other's minds. I was just getting around to that. Actually, it was important. It involves a little family history." Walter told him about Fay and their baby. "Jerry must have spread that story you heard about my being in a gay bar when I was Father of the Year. Nobody else knew. He was a monster, a real screaming little queen, making wild passes at me. It's very peculiar being faced with a son you don't know and yet feeling responsible for him. He was only 18. I decided to take him in hand. I did, in many more ways than one."

"How fascinating. You mean you..."

"Yeah, I took him to bed. It was only sort of half incest. I didn't recognize him when I met him. I hadn't seen him since he was a child. Of course, he didn't know I was his father and still doesn't. There was nothing remotely attractive about him, skinny, no more than pleasant-looking with all the worst faggot mannerisms–calling himself Geraldine, that sort of thing–and yet when I knew who he was, he drew me like a magnet. I wanted to straighten him out–if he'd been older I wouldn't have bothered to try–and the only way I could reach him was through sex. He was mad for me and wouldn't listen to anything I said until I took him. I still don't understand it, but there was something wildly sexy about fucking my own son. He inherited his cock from his Daddy, which should've finally put me off–a gruesome, great thing on a scrawny kid–but it didn't. I suppose you might say we had an affair for several months, but to me it was more like a seminar in the good life. In spite of sex, I loved him like a son. And it worked. I got him over all the faggot stuff. I made him see that there was more to life than a big cock. I got him going to a gym. God knows what went on there, but it certainly improved his looks. I talked to him about love, which he'd apparently never heard of. I also raised hell with his mother. By fucking him, I think I made myself a better father to him than I've been to my real sons. When I last saw him, he was living with a nice guy he was in love with. Come to think of it, it seems to me I heard he'd moved out to San Francisco. Have you ever heard of him? Gerald Kennicutt?"

"No."

"In any case, I made such a strong case for homosexuality and a decent life that I finally began to understand what I'd missed with Mark. After giving the word to Jerry, I swore that if it ever happened to me again, I'd grab it. It's mostly thanks to him that I had the sense to cleave to you. Are you shocked?"

"I'd like a moment of silent gratitude to Jerry. I'm stunned, darling. You're incredible. You give the impression of being totally in charge of life in a slightly inhuman way, as if you'd never had any doubt or been thrown off course. It's not that at all. You have a fantastic confidence, it's really self-confidence, in humanity, as if people could supply all the answers. I have a feeling that I could turn myself over to you and you'd know exactly which strings to pull to make me work. It's a temptation to resist. I'm beginning to realize that you're a great man, Walter. I intend to make myself good enough for you."

"Do you suppose we could be prejudiced about each other? I have the distinct impression that you are already."

In Colorado they began to find Walter looking at them everywhere from the cover of *Time*.

"He looks so glamorous," Tom said. "I never get to meet people like that. Where did I pick up this tramp? Shouldn't we buy a copy?"

"God, no. Everything in its good time. When we get there, I'll call David and find out what's been going on. Drive on." He stretched and looked at Tom and immediately had an erection. He slid his arm along his shoulders and gave him a little hug. "Oh, Tommy. Do you have any idea what you do to me? I'm so happy that I feel as if the top of my head is going to blow off. I can't begin to say it. You might be able to write it, and I want to try to put it on the stage someday, but at times my body almost goes mad wanting to tell you what it's like."

"Have you got a hard-on?"

"Sure. More or less as usual."

"Me too. You're usually way ahead of me, so I suppose you know I'm dying to get into some heavy sex with you. That's the main reason I'm in such a hurry to get home. I want to be completely alone with you and in our own surroundings and with plenty of food in the house so

342

it can go on for days if we want. That's the most truthful speech about sex I've ever made in my life. Do you mind very much waiting?"

"I'm not waiting, in the sense of not being satisfied with what we've had. I love light sex with you, if that's what it is. I love the buildup, getting to know how your body feels. Every inch of us must've touched each other by now and told us how right we are together. There's a place behind your knees I'm particularly mad about. I haven't waited to find that."

Deep laughter rolled from Tom. "You're such an idiot. If you make sex funny just when I'm getting turned on by the whole idea, I'll never forgive you."

"Sex was never spoiled by a good laugh. Anyway, I know where you're ticklish, so you haven't a prayer."

At the first place they stopped in Nevada, they found a row of slot machines, and Tom lost a handful of quarters before he could be led back to the car. "I might as well confess before you find out," he said when they were driving again. "I have a secret vice. I like to gamble. Shall we knock off early this evening? We haven't much farther to go now. We can make it by tomorrow night or the next morning. How about it? There's a town coming up that has a couple of gambling joints. Shall we stop?"

"I hoped I was your only secret vice, but if you have others, I suppose they too must be indulged. Sure, baby."

They found a motel near the town and then drove back to the garishly lit main thoroughfare. They had dinner, and Tom gave Walter $50. "If you're not a gambler," Tom said, "just remember one thing—the idea is to win."

"I play a dignified game of roulette. I've never won or lost anything in my life."

"I've found you, so I shouldn't expect to be lucky at cards too, but I'm the blackjack king. Let's give it a try."

They walked a little way down the street, and Tom led them into a large, not very crowded room with a haphazard attempt at Wild West decor filled with noise and tables. Tom made his way directly to a blackjack game and put some bills in front of him and signaled the dealer for a card. He had become noticeably keyed-up and intent.

Walter smiled at the signs of an addict and left him to wander around the room. There was a bar at one side, and he had a couple of drinks. He found a roulette table and lost $10 and won them back again. He knew that if he continued to play he would end up with exactly what he had started with, so he wandered back to Tommy and saw that he had an impressive pile of bills in front of him.

He knew that gamblers didn't like to be distracted and had all sorts of superstitions about their luck so he tried to stay out of sight, but Tom felt his presence and turned and winked at him. He looked adorably pleased with himself. Walter gave him an encouraging nod and returned to the bar. A few more drinks and the realization that the end of their trip was in sight relaxed him, and he was suddenly aware that, in spite of his blithe remark about going for days without sleep, he was very tired–abnormally tired–more tired than he could remember ever being. *That'll teach you to run off with a younger man,* he taunted himself. He waited long enough to have another drink that he didn't particularly want and then went back to Tom, who was intent on his cards.

"Will you be ready to go soon?" he asked in a quiet, unaccented voice so as not to intrude on his concentration. "I've about had it."

Tom fumbled in the pocket of his denim jacket and held out the car keys at the end of long fingers without looking at Walter. "You go ahead. I'll get a taxi back." He hoped Walter wouldn't notice that his hand was trembling slightly.

"I can wait a little while," Walter said without taking the keys. "I'm not sure I can find the motel."

"It's right out at the end of the main street and then to the right. You can't miss it."

The keys changed hands. Tom felt a scream of pain building in him, about to be torn from him. He clenched his jaws and held it in. He mustn't let it all start again. He had to learn not to jump at Walter's bidding. He mustn't swamp him with slavish devotion. Walter wanted to

344

go. He felt like staying. There was no reason why they shouldn't both do as they wished. He had spent a year reassembling the elements of his individuality. If he allowed himself to become a cipher again, he would be no use to either of them. They had to retain some degree of independence so that all they had to offer each other could flourish freely and acquire independent strength. He settled down resolutely to study the cards.

Walter drove back to the motel feeling bereft and offended. He knew he was being unreasonable. Gambling wasn't something two people shared. He and Tom had been together continuously in a way he had never been with anybody else before. It was natural for Tom to want to indulge his vice on his own for an hour. Walter was too tired to be reasonable.

The starkly lit modern and characterless motel room didn't improve his mood. He thought of his splendid house, of his staff waiting to do his bidding, of his decorative family completing the picture of worldly felicity, and he wondered what he was doing in this bleak outpost of American civilization—alone. Had he taken leave of his senses? He dragged himself to bed before attempting to examine the question. His body luxuriated in the instant easing of fatigue, and his spirits lifted. Tommy would come in soon and get undressed and lie down beside him. What could a fine house offer compared to that? They had been together long enough for there to be no doubts. They were perfect for each other. He could truly believe now in their going on through life together. It was all that he had hoped it might be. He didn't care if he never worked again; making Tommy happy would be enough. If it made Tommy happy for him to work, he would do the best damn work of his life. He thought of the unclouded hours they had spent together across the vast breadth of the nation, of Tom's lean, graceful body against him, of the loving light in his eyes. He was smiling to himself when Tom came bursting into the room. He looked shamefaced and defensive. Walter sat up in bed.

"Well, it's old Gaylord himself, the scourge of the Mississippi river-boats. Did you win?"

Tom looked at him defiantly. "Are you all right?" he demanded as if it were an accusation.

"Of course. All of a sudden I felt absolutely dead. I had to lie down. I'm fine now. Come on. Show me your loot. Did you break the bank?"

Tom appeared briefly bewildered and then sat on a chair in front of the empty television screen. He had stayed away only long enough to convince himself that he could do it. After 15 minutes, he had been so assailed by worries that he couldn't concentrate on the game. Would he find a taxi easily? Had Walter got lost? Would he be angry? To find him cheerfully naked in bed was rather an anticlimax. "I was way ahead for a while. Your leaving threw me off. I ended up about $40 to the good."

"That's not bad. I'm sorry about leaving."

"Why should you be?" Tom said. "We can't expect to do everything hand in hand."

Tom's manner was defensive. His loose-limbed body was tied up in knots. Walter wasn't sure he understood what it was all about. "Of course not, darling, except that I sort of like to whenever possible. I wouldn't have left if I hadn't been feeling so rotten. Come to bed, sweetheart."

"Sure, in a minute. First, you might as well say it."

Walter had never seen him like this. He had taken on a wild, fanatical look, his face drawn, his eyes tormented. Walter wanted to hold him and comfort him, but he also wanted to let him get it out, whatever it was. "Say what?" he asked mildly.

"Tell me what a shit I was not to leave with you."

"Oh, Tommy. Don't be absurd." He tried not to find this tiresome. "You had every right to stay. I admit I was cross for a minute, but that's because I'm spoiled and I was tired. If I want to be with you every minute—and do—I should've stayed too."

Tom studied him with anguished eyes. "I don't understand you. Don't you want to pull the strings?"

"No, I've pulled enough strings all my life. If anything, I want you to. I don't see why we can't pull them together."

Tom slumped in the chair and dropped his head back and looked at the ceiling. "I fall in love so badly. It's got to be all or nothing. I almost died when you left. I'm so afraid of turning all gooey and faggoty and boring the hell out of you."

"Whatever you do, you'll never bore me. As it turned out, it was good for me to be alone for a while. It gave me a chance to think of all I've left behind and realize more than ever how glad I am."

Tom's expression cleared. He lowered his head and looked at Walter with the light of love once more in his eyes, reverting to the country boy, with no trace of the complexities and tensions that were in him. "It's hard for me to believe that I can let it all out, that you don't mind my loving you to distraction and wanting all of you."

"You'll find out."

He stood and shed his clothes and disappeared briefly into the bathroom. When he dropped into bed, Walter grunted, as if he'd been hit in the stomach, with the impact of his nakedness against him. They gathered each other into their arms and opened their mouths to each other and drew apart and looked at each other with wonder.

"Do you feel it too?" Tom murmured. "When we're like this, everything I want in life is here. Have you ever felt like this with anybody?"

"No."

"We create a whole universe with each other. It means that nothing that's happened in the past is any help. I've got to learn everything all over again. Oh, God, Walter. Dear Lord Jesus. How can bodies get so close to the sublime?" His grip suddenly tightened. "Oh, God, darling. Oh, please. Christ. I'm going to…" His mouth stretched open, and he uttered a strangled cry as his body was lifted and tossed about by an intense orgasm.

They drove hard the next day and crossed into California at nightfall. By early afternoon the following day, the Golden Gate Bridge was behind them, and they were driving through Sausalito and around the bay. Everything had been much built up since Walter had been there, and he had trouble placing himself. They passed through some nondescript country and more development and suddenly entered a lush garden area of great trees and flowing shrubbery. Handsome houses could be perceived behind tropical foliage. Walter caught glimpses of water.

"We've been here before," he exclaimed.

"Have we?"

"Sorry. I meant Clara and me. There was a party at a big house on a hill overlooking the city. We drove along this road. I guess I wasn't paying attention to where I was. This is Belvedere? What is it?"

"It's a posh real estate development. I think it's rather beautiful."

"It is. It's like a botanical garden with houses. My goodness, Tommy. Fancy you bringing me here. Aren't we grand?"

Tom laughed. "I told you Belvedere."

"I know. I didn't make the connection. I don't mean I thought you lived in a hovel, but I wasn't expecting anything like this."

"Stick with me, man."

"I will, man."

They drove for another few minutes, and then Tom slowed and made a sharp right turn into a drive that descended steeply through several lavishly planted terraces to a long, low house nearly concealed by spectacular greenery. The bay stretched out just below it. They came to a sliding stop in a crunch of gravel.

"Here we are," Tom said.

"It looks as if we'd need machetes to hack our way in. Sleeping Beauty."

"I want to tell you about it before we start hacking. It's up for sale. Whether we leave it on the market depends entirely on you, so you don't have to say you like it if you don't. Johnnie and I lived here, but I never felt it was mine. It's full of ghosts, but not in the way you might suppose. They're all my ghosts, my happiness, my stupidity, my despair. Now that you're here, they'll all fly screaming into the night, so that's all right. Johnnie wasn't the sort to leave ghosts. He just picked up and left. It was his house. Now it's mine, as if I'd bought it. It will be ours if we want it, or we can find some place you like better."

"Well, let's go see."

"My heart is doing some peculiar cartwheels. Come on."

They stopped in front of a hermetic-looking door while Tom coped with several locks and keys. When the door finally opened, the effect was a shock. They stepped into light and air, enclosed by glass. Outside the glass was a flowering terrace with garden furniture, and beyond, the seascape of the bay. Tom crossed a big room and pushed back sliding doors, and the house was filled with the warm afternoon sun. He returned to the paved entrance and collected a pile of mail from a table while Walter looked around him.

He could see that it wasn't a big house, but the space and proportions were admirable. The layout was open planning of the sort he didn't much like–the kitchen was too visible and the "dining area" lacked the intimacy he felt a dining room should have–but his mind was immediately active with plans for screening and masking to achieve better separations. The furniture was modern and, to Walter's mind, rather dull, but there was a big stone fireplace at one end that could stand being featured. He could see that the carpeting and fittings were of the best quality, with the overall effect being solidly luxurious. Within moments he had rearranged and replaced some of the furniture in his mind's eye and created a handsome set. The Oriental touches would have to go.

Walter turned and found Tom looking at him expectantly. He went to him, and they held each other lightly and kissed. "It'll be easy to make it look like us," he said.

"That's nice. It doesn't matter if you change your mind, but I'm glad you like it. Come outside."

The wide terrace was paved, and wooden steps led down from it to the water's edge and a short jetty. A small sailing boat was moored at the end of it.

"Is that yours?" Walter asked.

"That's my baby. She's *Eaglet*. She's too small to be an eagle, but I soar when I'm on her."

"I'd like to go soaring with you." All the small property was beautifully planted to give the effect of vistas. Trees had been astutely placed to provide some shade for the terrace and break the undistinguished line of the house. "The garden is superb. Has it always been here?"

"No, I did most of it."

"I thought so. And John was more or less responsible for the inside of the house?"

"Yes."

"There's something about it that almost breaks my heart, but that'll pass. You at 22 tackling this garden. You must've been a joy to behold. And being here all alone for the last year. I very nearly can't bear it." Inexplicable tears filled his eyes.

Tom looked at him wonderingly. "What a very nice man you are, darling. I'll show you the rest; then we'd better have a big drink, or I'll burst into tears myself—of sheer happiness, utter impossible happiness." He leaned forward and kissed the side of Walter's face. Walter instinctively drew back. Tom smiled. "It's all right. Nobody can see us. I planned it very carefully."

They went back inside, and Tom led the way to a small den at the end of the big room. It was lined with books, and a cluttered desk turned its back on the view. "This is where I work." He went to the desk and picked up a framed photograph. "I might as well show you this, and then I'll put it away." He handed the photograph to Walter.

Tom was standing looking only a little younger and slightly heavier, with a pale smile on his lips. A shorter, slightly heavier youngish-looking man stood beside him. His smile was so bright, there was an air of such eager vigor about him that Walter despaired of ever knowing what John had been like. He handed the photograph back.

"Don't put it away on my account."

"No, on his. It's not fair to him to be reminded all the time of how much he let us miss."

They put their arms around each other's waists as Tom led them back to the entrance. Short corridors ran off it to left and right. Tom turned to the left, and they entered a pleasant bedroom whose most attractive feature was a view of a tiny, densely planted courtyard. Tom went to the door and opened it and returned to Walter's side.

"This was my room. There's a bathroom in there. Believe it or not, this is where I slept most of the time. I thought if we put a desk in here and another phone, you could use it as an office. What do you think? As far as I'm concerned, the bed will be pure camouflage."

"Fine. I won't have to muss it, will I?"

"I'd rather you didn't. It'll save wear and tear. Come on." They crossed the entrance and followed the other short corridor to another larger, more elaborately furnished bedroom, with a similar, larger courtyard off it. "Now, darling. This was Johnnie's room. I've been living here for the last year, for company. As far as I'm concerned, it's mine now; but if you don't like the idea, we can change everything around or get the hell out."

Walter looked around the room. He knew this wasn't easy for Tom despite his breezy manner. "The bed looks like us," he said. It was an outsize double. "Wouldn't it be better over here? I love the courtyards. Were they your idea?"

"Yeah. Thanks. The bed here? That's where I always wanted it." Sinewy muscles swelled, fabric stretched over the lithe body as he grappled with the bed and shoved it into its new position. He stood back beside Walter and surveyed the effect. "Obviously, that's where it belongs."

"OK, Tommy. I think we'd better have that big drink."

Tom's hand touched Walter's. "The bad part's over, darling. Thanks to you. Yeah, a drink to celebrate. But I mean, celebrate. I don't know where to begin."

They fixed themselves drinks in the kitchen area and carried them to a big sofa in the living room and sat side by side while Tom looked at his mail. He sorted it into two piles and handed one of the piles to Walter.

"Will you look at those, darling? These are all bills."

"You mean, open them?"

"Of course, they're for us. You'll let me read yours, won't you? I said all of you."

"I mean all of me."

351

They drank and opened envelopes. "Anything interesting?" Tom asked when he had glanced at his pile.

"A couple of fan letters. Very nice. An invitation to appear at some sort of symposium that sounds fairly heavy. Something to do with the end of civilization. This seems to be a love letter."

"That must be Steve, the birthday boy. He never got me, poor guy; and now he never will. We'll have to have him out and be nice to him. You'll like him." He swung his feet up onto the arm of the sofa and stretched out and lay his head in Walter's lap. "God, here we are at last. You and I. Us. We're together. The two of us." He rubbed his cheek against the hard bulge of Walter's crotch and lifted a hand to stroke Walter's cheek. "Thanks, darling. That's the way I want you to be. For us. Not me anymore. Us."

He doubled up and rolled in against Walter and buried his head against his abdomen and clung to him. His body was shaken by sobs. They quickly passed, and he stretched out again and dropped his head back onto Walter's lap. Walter's arms held him. His cheeks were streaked with tears. He looked up and smiled. "Another attack of hysteria. Only it wasn't. It's love. It's getting so big that there's no more room for it inside me. It's going to spill out all over the place." He pulled himself up so that his arms rested against Walter's chest, his head against his shoulder, and he kissed his neck. "I better unload the car; then I'll run out and do some shopping." He sat up straighter and propped himself on an arm and looked into Walter's eyes. "Listen. What should I get for us? You know. I've heard a thousand jokes about K-Y. Is that what we should have?"

"Sure, it's fine."

"I won't get arrested if I ask for it?"

Walter chuckled. He held him at the sides of his ribs and pulled him closer and gave his mouth a quick kiss. "You're safe. You can say it's for your wife."

"Really? How very peculiar." He laughed and shook his hair back and sprang up. He gave a hitch to his jeans as he swung off toward the front door. He snapped his fingers and veered back toward a telephone on a table. Walter heard him address somebody named Marjorie and then stopped listening and simply gazed at him, more profoundly moved than he had ever been by a human being. He was capable of love. He knew it at last. All of his being seemed to have risen to the surface of his skin and yearned for Tom's caress. He was wholly exposed. He felt as if he could be as easily crushed as any creature that had just shed its carapace, but for the first time in his life he didn't fear his vulnerability. His only fear was that he might still fail Tom in some way, prove unworthy of him. He thought of how carefully he had contrived only a week ago to make it difficult for himself to run back to the stale protection of life with Clara. It wouldn't be necessary now; nothing could tear him away. Tom's challenge was that he made no challenge but accepted him in an act of faith. He stood when Tom hung up.

"That was Marjorie," Tom explained. "She'll clean for us. She's one of the last local ladies who lives around here. She's been a good friend. Why don't you fix yourself another drink?"

"Can't I come with you?"

Tom smiled. Light seemed to flow from him. "You don't have to. I'm used to doing the chores. Aren't you tired?"

"Probably, but I don't feel it when I'm with you."

"Then come here, damn it."

Walter went to him and put his hands on his waist. Tom's lips were soft and tasted of whisky. Walter relinquished them with an effort. "I'll help you with the bags," he said.

Tom showed him around the Tiburon Shopping Center, and they were soon home again. They emptied the luggage onto the bed in Tom's old room. "I'll sort it all out later," Tom said. "Do you want a shower as much as I do?"

They undressed in the room that immediately became theirs. Tom had an erection before he was out of his jeans. He stood in front of Walter and began to masturbate slowly and without self-consciousness. "Goodness. This is a lovely tease when I know you're going to take over. I amaze myself. Nobody's ever affected me this way. You make my body feel so wonderful that I'm falling in love with myself. That's good. That's enough. I'm just making myself want you."

The soaped each other under the shower, and Tom gave Walter an erection. "I'm so glad we waited," he said when they were drying themselves. "We belong to each other now. Anything we do is right. I'd have had a nervous breakdown a few days ago. Your cock in me. Jesus." He handed Walter the tube of lubricant they had bought. "Come to bed and show me, darling. It looks impossible, but I'm sure nothing's impossible for you."

Walter led him into the bedroom, and they lay in each other's arms while he applied the lubricant, stroking it between Tom's buttocks and gently inserting a finger into him. Tom gasped. His eyes were wide and brimming with tears.

"My darling," Tom whispered hoarsely. "You're going to take every-thing I am. I'm going to give all of myself to your cock. Your cock, dar-ling. I worship your cock. You. Do you know what it means? You won't leave me after this, will you? You can't."

"I'll never leave you, Tommy." He knew what it meant. They had passed beyond desire. The act had become a consecration of all they could offer each other. He felt a great tender concern for the friend who moved against him and offered his body to be joined to his. He shifted him around and held him in his arms and entered him carefully. Tom cried out. Walter held him and waited. After a moment he exerted an additional small pressure.

"Oh, Christ," Tom cried. "Is it supposed to hurt so much?"

"I don't think it will, darling," Walter soothed him, "but I told you it wasn't necessary. Do you want me to stop?"

"No, please. I want it. Just slowly, darling. Please."

Walter lay still. Their breathing carried them closer to each other. Walter felt himself slipping almost imperceptibly into him. He stroked him gently and felt the strain in him easing. He remained motionless and became aware of a small movement of Tom's hips. He responded with a pressure no greater than a deep breath. Tom laughed. Walter gripped his hips and felt resistance passing, and all of himself seemed to gather in the act of possession as he made a long thrust into him. Tom shouted. They were caught up in an ecstasy of union. Their bodies moved in rhythmic unity. Consciousness was suspended. They were gripped and bound by an impossible need to be one; then they flew apart. They lay together gasping, as drained and spent and bewildered as if they had been dashed up on some unknown shore. After another few minutes, Walter withdrew slowly and rolled out of bed and went to the bathroom and washed. He knew something had eluded them in the final moment. Some resistance remained in Tom, something withheld. When he returned, Tom was lying facedown where he had left him.

He dropped down on his stomach beside him and flung an arm across him and kissed his hair. "Tell me, baby," he commanded.

"I'm ashamed, and I'm trying so hard not to be."

"Good God, darling. Why?" He pushed in closer to him and tried to unbury his face from the pillow.

"I don't know. For wanting it? For worshiping your cock? It's terrible to want anybody so much."

"Did you feel that? I love wanting you so much, but it doesn't have to be that particular way. It's probably just not your thing, that's all. Why should it be?"

Tom turned onto his side to face him and put an arm around him. "Because it's yours. I felt as if doors were opening down endless corridors. Revelation after revelation. And then there was a door that wouldn't open. I didn't want it to. I was ashamed. It's an awful way of putting it, but I can think of lots of guys whose cock I'd suck, in theory, but I wouldn't let anybody except you do that. Do you know what I mean? I felt as if I were making a sacrifice."

"So you didn't like it. It doesn't matter." Walter meant it. He knew they would find satisfaction in one form or another. He was already looking forward to the next step.

"It does," Tom protested. "Maybe I liked it more than I want to admit. You've got to go on. You've got to open that final door for me."

"I know what to do about that."

355

"Do you?"

"Of course. That's why we waited, darling. So we could go on and on and find out everything. Let's have another drink and put your things away and have an early dinner. Then we can come back to bed."

"I go on amazing myself. Once has always been enough for me. Now I want it and want it and want it. Right now. More."

"We don't have to wait till after dinner. Let's see who gets a hard-on first."

They climbed out of bed and put on dressing gowns in the other room, and Tom began to organize clothes. Walter left him to call David from the big room. David laughed until he choked when he heard his voice.

"You're something, honey," he finally managed. He reported that the big evening had gone much as Walter had predicted. Clara had carried it off in her characteristically regal fashion. She had worn a dress that conspicuously displayed the brooch and had left the cocktail party several times pretending to go up and see how Walter was feeling. The presentation dinner had gone well, and Walter's acceptance speech had been read by Richard.

"Have you heard from her yet?" David asked. "Well, brace yourself, honey. I didn't tell her anything, but she knew Tom had been there. She didn't come right out and ask for his address, and I didn't let on that there was any reason for her to have it. But it was obvious what she was thinking. She'll find you easily enough. I don't want to be nosy, but how is everything?"

"Heavenly."

"It's like that, is it?" David laughed some more. "Well, you've certainly kept me guessing for the last 30 years. I've got to hand it to you. When you finally make up your mind, you don't fool around. You couldn't have found a greater guy to run away with. What are you going to do now?"

"Think." Tom appeared with a handful of ties, and Walter beckoned to him. "Just a minute." He put an arm around Tom's shoulders and handed him the instrument.

"Hi there," Tom said. He listened, fingering the cloth over Walter's chest. He spoke in broken phrases interrupted by bursts of deep laughter. David was doubtless being outrageous.

"Tell him to call us if he hears anything."

Tom relayed the message and hung up with another burst of laughter. "We seem to've made him happy, anyway. How about that drink you mentioned?" He dropped the ties in a chair, and they fixed themselves drinks and went out onto the terrace. The sun was dropping behind the high hills that barred the sea. There was a slight chill in the air. It wasn't a real sunset, but it marked the end of their first day in their new home, and Walter was moved and reassured as he stood beside his love, looking out. The long drive had effectively cut him off from his habitual interests and preoccupations. He felt nicely isolated and secure. The small sexual hitch seemed unimportant. There were probably things about Tommy he still didn't understand, aspects of his homosexuality that set him apart and made some of his reactions difficult to grasp. He would learn. They should probably get their minds off sex for a while.

"How rich are we, Tommy?" he asked. "Or poor, as the case may be."

"I want to go over it all with you. I have about $25,000 a year, not counting my earnings, but they're unpredictable. You're probably used to spending that much in a month."

"Not quite, but the money has flowed, especially since Clara got hers. I liked being able to buy pictures, but the rest hasn't meant all that much to me. I'll have a lot coming in for the next year, more than double what you have, unless Clara manages to tie it up somehow. That should adequately feather our love nest for the time being. I want to read your play. I don't see why I shouldn't produce plays out here. I'll look into it when we've settled down. Do you expect to go back to work soon?"

"Yes, on the new novel. I'm anxious to get back to it."

"How do you work? Do you have a fixed schedule?"

"Yes, every morning for at least four hours and another hour or so in the late afternoon to go over what I've done."

357

"That sounds good." He moved closer to his side. "Everything sounds good. Do we have a busy social life?"

"It's all there if we want it. I'd like to give a party for you when you're ready to come out of hiding. What're you going to do about Clara?"

Walter laughed. "I was wondering the same thing. I'm trying to figure out what she's thinking. She'll probably decide it's a momentary madness and wait for me to come to my senses."

"What're the chances that you will?"

"Tommy, if I'm not in my right senses now, I hope I never will be."

"I won't put you off, being so queer? It's all going to come out now. I didn't mean to tell you that I worship your cock; but it's going to be increasingly obvious, so I might as well say it."

"I love hearing it. I worship all of you. You don't mind my not picking out one particular part, do you?"

"I'd rather you didn't. I want you to think of me as an irresistible ensemble. I haven't begun to make you queer yet, so I don't even mind if you think you're attracted to my intellect."

"I am. You don't think my falling in love with you is queer? I have, you know. I don't mean at first sight. I mean the works. I don't know when it happened, but I've been very aware of it this afternoon. The trip's over. We're home. I'm wonderfully in love with you."

"Oh, darling," Tom growled. It came out like a groan. They moved closer to each other. It was getting chillier. Walter put his hand under Tom's arm, and they went back inside.

Tom pulled the sliding glass door behind them. "I'll make a fire in a little while. I'm going to cook for you at last. I'm good. Thank God we're back in wine country. I'll never forget the look on your face when I ordered a coke with my hamburger. Yes, darling, this is the beginning." They stood close together, facing each other, and drained off their drinks and looked at each other questioningly. "Is it happening?" Tom asked.

"Yeah, am I going to be the first?"

"No, I think it's going to be more or less neck and neck. I'm beginning to tremble, idiotically enough, like a virgin bride."

"Let's go."

They put their arms around each other and headed toward the bedroom. They threw off their dressing gowns when they reached it and were both immediately ready for action. Walter went to the bathroom for the lubricant and made a quick application and returned with it to the bedroom. Tom lay on his back in bed. His erection rode up his belly, nearly touching his navel, a daunting display. Walter wondered if he could cope with it. He knelt over him and began to stroke the lubricant onto it.

"What are you doing?" Tom asked with a note of alarm.

"That should be fairly obvious."

"But I told you, I've never been able to."

"You've never tried it with me."

"But honestly—are you serious?"

"Of course, it's a cure for being ashamed. It also might help me become gay."

"Oh, God, darling. I feel as if I'm falling apart in a thousand pieces."

"We'll put you together again."

"I'll either wilt or come in two seconds."

"You can come as quickly as you like once you're inside me." He dropped down on his side with his back turned to Tom. "I've never done this. You better take it slowly too. There's a lot of you." He held Tom's cock and directed it into him.

Tom uttered a cry of alarm and disbelief and flung an arm over him and held his sex. Walter was stunned by the pain. How could anybody want this? He gritted his teeth, determined to go through with it, and urged him on with a hand on his hip. He felt Tom slipping deeper into him, and the pain grew more intense. For a moment he almost hated him, but he reminded himself that it was Tommy. He had to make their bodies work right together. Tommy had the right to take him as he had never been taken before.

Tom's chest was heaving against him. In another moment he realized that the penetration was complete. He had survived. He had a moment of soul-shattering joy as he felt the hard, lean body master and possess him, and Tom's shouts and the frenzied contortions of his body told him that it was over. He rolled onto his stomach and brought Tom up onto his back and held him there. He wanted to fight free of him, but he still felt hard and demanding and painful in him. He thought of the demands he'd made in the past. He lay still and waited for Tom to release him.

"Oh, Christ," Tom gasped after a long silence.

"Was it good, baby?"

"Good? You belong to me. I've taken you. You're mine. Was it good for you, darling?"

"If it was like that for you, that's good enough for me."

"You didn't come."

"We can't have everything right at the start."

"I can't believe it. I'm still hard. I want it again."

Walter took a difficult breath and steeled himself. "I belong to you, baby. Take what you want. Fuck me again, Tommy."

"Yes, darling. I've fucked you. Tom has fucked Walter. I can't believe it. *My* Walter. You're mine. Nobody's ever belonged to me like this. You. Oh, Christ, you. I'm going to make you come." He pulled Walter's hips back to him as he worked himself onto his knees. He got a grip on his shoulders and began to drive slowly into him. "Oh, Jesus. I've never felt anything like it. Does my cock feel good in you, darling? Tell me."

"You cock feels perfect, Tommy. Take me with it. Do anything you want with me, so it's perfect for you." It was still agony, but the pain was dimmed by the triumph Walter could feel in the body he loved. The long, strong fingers that moved over him and gripped him were electric with desire. Strong thighs were clamped to him. All of Tom's body was charged with desire. It revived his erection. He wanted to give himself until he was past pain—or caring. He felt an orgasm building in him, an orgasm of giving. He could even offer Tom the illusion of pleasure.

They put on their dressing gowns again and had a couple of drinks while Tom cooked dinner. A fire blazed at the end of the living room. Walter learned where the silverware and linen were kept and set the

table. When they were near each other, Walter loved the new possessive way Tom touched him. He put his hands on him at any excuse as
if he were afraid he might escape. They had spoken very little since
they had left the bed as if the experience had made speech inadequate
or superfluous.

"God, what you do for me," Tom blurted, finding his tongue while
they finished their drinks in front of the fire and waited for dinner to
cook. "It's like a huge singing in me or maybe like organ music crashing through me. It makes my head swim. It's funny I was so worried
about bringing you here. You obliterate everything that's ever happened to me. I feel as if we were moving into the house for the first
time. We're in love with each other. Isn't it amazing?"

Walter looked into his face leaning eagerly to him, keenly intelligent
and ablaze with young passion. He marveled at his luck. He could
never do enough to deserve the passionate devotion he saw in it. "It is,"
he agreed with quiet conviction.

"The old male-female balance is still screwed up, but in a lovely
way. You're doing everything I've always needed. I'll soon be able to do
things for you. It changes everything knowing you belong to me. It's
obvious I belong to you."

"I've counted on that. It'll be one of the major mistakes of my life if
you don't."

Tom uttered a few rich notes of laughter. "You don't make mistakes.
That's one of the marvelous things about you. I'm going to know myself as well as you know you. God, darling." He stretched and placed a
hand firmly, possessively on Walter's shoulder. "You're giving me myself. I always thought it had to be the other way–giving myself
to somebody. Let's eat and drink a few bottles of wine and tell each
other things in front of the fire. And then bed and all the divine things
you know how to do with our bodies."

Walter read Tom's play the next morning, sitting out on the terrace
in the sun with nothing on but Tom's brief swimming trunks. He was
gripped by it and so genuinely impressed that he counted it as one
more gift of luck. He had expected intelligence, but the taut poetic nat-

uralism of the dialogue put it above anything he'd read for years. One aspect of it bothered him, however. He was just finishing when Tom came out with Marjorie to introduce them. She was a sensible-looking middle-aged woman and immediately addressed Walter by his Christian name.

"I'm glad you're here," she told him. "This guy's been moping around here by himself for too long. You're a fine-looking fella. I hope you stay awhile."

"I expect to."

"That's just dandy. I'm sorry I'm late, Tom. I didn't expect you so soon. I'll be back on my regular hours tomorrow. I'll just be an hour, and then you guys can go on about your business."

Tom waited until she had returned to the house and then turned to Walter. "How's it going?" he asked cautiously. He was wearing a scruffy dressing gown he called his "work dress" and had spent the morning "building up steam" to get back to his novel.

"Fine. I'm not quite finished. I'd rather wait till she's gone to talk about it."

"OK. I'll go back to my hole. I'm getting my desk straightened out."

Walter spent the hour flipping back through the play. When Tom joined him, he had shed his work dress and was also wearing brief trunks and looked his most beguiling–loose and lanky and boyish. He stood with arms crossed on his chest, looking down in the direction of his little boat.

"OK. Let's have the verdict," he said.

"It's damn good, Tommy. That's putting it mildly, but I don't want to sound as if my critical sense can't function where you're concerned. Really good. If it had come to me a couple of weeks ago, I don't think I'd have worried about whether it would be a moneymaker, for once. I would've wanted to do it. I love you, but now I'm going to turn into a fan. I want to get started on the books right away."

Tom looked at him with a shy smile. "Wow. That's a relief."

"There's only one thing I wondered about. When you wrote the girl, were you ever thinking of a boy?"

Tom pulled a chair near him and sat as if settling down for a serious discussion. "That was my original idea, of course. I hoped it wouldn't show."

"It doesn't really, except maybe to me. Once the thought occurred to me, I read the rest of the play as if she were a he. It's tremendous. It makes the reticence about sex ring much more true. Would you consider changing it?"

"I don't know, darling. Wouldn't that kill any chances of its getting produced?"

"I'll produce it if you do."

"Not otherwise?"

"I didn't mean it like that. I'm thinking about the play. Should you be thinking about getting produced?"

"That's telling him. Of course, you're right, darling. Except I think the play is valid the way it is."

"The girl isn't absolutely convincing all the time. That's something I could cover in a performance, but when a play's as good as this, why cover? It should work on its own."

"Well, since I believe in the way it is, it's hard for me not to think about production. Wouldn't there be legal problems if I change it?"

"I'd fight for it. Besides, the world isn't what it used to be. Look at the stuff that's being done now. When I think of all the taboos when I was starting out, it's incredible. This might be more daring than anything that's been done so far, but what the hell. I'd like to blaze a few more trails before I'm through. You aren't thinking of your reputation or family or anything, are you?"

"No, I'm ready to stand up and be counted. You'll see. I went pretty far in my last novel."

"Then at least read the play through again with that in mind. I think you'll see that you have to change it."

"Do you suppose we're going to be good for each other's work, on top of everything else?"

"I doubt if you need anybody to be good for your work, aside from the odd editorial suggestion. There's no doubt what you're doing for me. I've told you. It's going to be a whole new career. I'm going back to the way I did things at the beginning, cutting costs way back and taking risks on things I believe in. I can count on backing if I don't lose too much money. If you can give me another play or two, I'll get all the kids back who've given me up as hopeless. I think I can do it here. I'm thinking of tying in with somebody in New York to move things East after I've tuned them up here so we won't have the curse of being a regional operation. I'll start with your play. We'll stir things up, Tommy."

"I guess maybe we were born for each other." They looked into each other's eyes. Their gaze intensified, and then they both burst into laughter. "It's happening, but then it does all the time. Is it immoral to go to bed before lunch?"

"I'm willing to risk it."

They had several days of total peace and isolation while Tom got to work on the play's sex change. Walter wondered what it would be like when they let the world in. So far, it was still a bit like a dream, but he was tired and was content to drift. He supposed he was getting old enough to need time to recover from the trip. It wasn't unpleasant, simply a lethargy that made reading and admiring Tom's three novels and making love to the author a sufficient expenditure of energy. He was going to have to call Clara in the next few days if he didn't hear from her first, and he wanted to be able to offer her more than lethargy. If he talked to her in his present condition, he would sound bored by anything they had to say to each other, which wouldn't be polite.

There hadn't been time for him to feel really separated from her. He tried not to think about her but had constant impulses to turn to speak to her about something—a habit he had to break. He even wanted to discuss Tom's work with her. He thanked God for the steel in her nature. She would be in a rage with him, not weepy or hurt. He laughed wryly to himself at times when he thought of her. Dear old friend. That's what she could be if she ever let up on him. He didn't think she would want anything as simple as a divorce. There were money matters to be straightened out, but she was rich, so that shouldn't be a problem. The test would come when he and Tom began to be seen together and word spread of a clearly homosexual liaison. Clara would no longer be able to pretend that the Makins were still the ideal couple of popular myth. He was willing to postpone that day as long as possible.

He was lying out in the sun one morning on a big beach mattress, not even reading, having finished Tom's novels and gone through them a second time. Marjorie had gone, so he had been able to strip. A towel covered his loins. He was getting a good tan. Tom was in his study, near enough to make his presence felt. All was right with the world. He was surprised when Tom appeared in the door well ahead of schedule wearing his scruffy work dress. He saw his erection thrusting out from between its folds as he approached the mattress. Walter sat up with a chuckle. "What's up?" he asked.

"Don't be rude. I couldn't concentrate. That is, I was concentrating all too well on you, as you see." He slipped off the robe and dropped down between Walter's legs, pushing the towel aside, and curled up against him with his hands flat on his chest. Walter put his arms around him. "I'm feeling ridiculously kittenish. I'm not really built right to be kittenish, am I?"

"A kittenish cowboy? Why not?"

He stroked Walter's hardening sex and watched it lengthen and fill out. He put two fingers under it and lifted it so that it stood upright between them. "Is it over a foot long? I wonder."

"Don't be silly. I've seen one a foot long. Unbelievable."

"Well, I know mine's well over seven inches, maybe eight, depending on how you measure it. That's the sort of thing a serious writer knows about. Look at the difference between us."

"An inch or two maybe."

"Listen to him. An inch or two. As if that didn't count. Never mind. It's two feet long if that suits my poetic fancy. I know at last where I want it."

"Do you, baby?" Walter had been waiting for this. Tom was still tinkering with his precious "male-female balance." Walter had continued to give himself to him, hoping that repetition would reduce the pain, wondering if he might even learn to like it. He didn't share Tom's phallic preoccupations, but he liked the feel of a man's body, the play of a man's mind, the poetry of a man's love. He had learned that much over the years, although he wanted to substitute Tom's name for the collective noun. Honesty obliged him to make some acknowledgment of being gay. If Tom hadn't turned up, it could have been somebody else, although he found it difficult to imagine.

Tom lay his head on his shoulder and kissed his neck in the area of his mole. He was fascinated by the mole. He worked himself down and ran his tongue around his cock, and for a moment, while he stroked his hair, Walter thought that this might be where his experiments would end. Tom straightened and looked searchingly into Walter's eyes as if pondering a decision, and then he swiveled and lay back with his arms flung out above his head, his legs thrown over Walter's thighs. "Do it, darling. The stuff's in the pocket of my work rag."

"Out here?"

"Yes. God, yes. I want to be fucked right now. I never dreamed I'd ever know anybody well enough to say it. I want you to fuck me in broad daylight so there's no mystery about it. Your cock inside me where I want it."

Walter disentangled himself from Tom's legs and lifted himself to his knees and found the tube in the heap of his robe. Tom pulled his knees up and hugged him with them as he moved in between them.

"Let me watch you getting ready. Yes, like that. More. God, it glistens in the sun. You're magnificent, you and your two-foot cock."

"You've gone mad."

"Maybe. I'm demented about that—your huge gleaming cock. Let me have it, darling. Drive it into me. It's going to open all the doors."

Walter slipped a hand under his balls. Tom lifted his hips and groaned with pleasure. "Christ, I can let you touch me there without being ashamed. You can take all my body. I'm so proud your cock wants it. God, does it ever. Look how it wants me. I want it. I want a man to take me and use and come in me. I want it to be you, darling." He started to twist around onto his stomach, but Walter restrained him.

"Stay there."

Tom looked puzzled, and then his face lit with rapture as Walter lifted his legs over his shoulders and entered him. He slipped slowly but easily into him. "Yes!" Tom cried. "God, yes, darling! That's it. What heaven to be able to look at you." He stretched his arms out and toyed with his face with his fingers. "You're beautiful when you're fucking me. I make you look like that. Oh, yes, darling! This is it!" He shouted as his body plunged about under Walter and his ejaculation sprang from it. He laughed with an exultant note. "Now, yes. Oh, God, I can give you what you want. It's immense—your cock is immense, darling. Oh, Jesus. You're doing what you want with it. You know. Yes, I want it. I want it. Wow! Beautiful. Yes! Now! Oh, darling…" They shouted into each other's eyes with naked recognition, and Walter collapsed onto his chest. Tom kept his legs jackknifed over him and held him close until Walter slipped from him and sprang up. Tom followed him into the shower, and they exchanged slyly ambiguous and exploratory looks as if they were testing each other's reactions but didn't speak until they turned off the water. Tom giggled, and they both burst into a gale of uncomplicated laughter.

"You think I'm crazy," Tom said while they dried themselves.

"A bit, in a fascinating way."

"Oh, darling, we're going to have such fun. We're going to live together for the rest of our lives. I know that. I'm ready to show you who you're living with. You've got to be gay to understand."

"I'm not sure I know what you mean by that. You don't just mean about sex?"

"No, everything. It leads in and out of sex. All the doors are open for me now. No more shame. I know you didn't like my, you know, fucking you, but you're gay enough to understand what it meant to me. It's made a man of me. I can let myself be yours now without being swallowed up by you. That's what you want, isn't it?"

"Of course."

"Well, that's not like being married, is it? That's being two men together. You'll let me be myself and still belong to you in the way I must. You know what I mean. It's the way I'm made." They pulled on brief

367

trunks and went to the kitchen, where Tom began to prepare their usual picnic lunch. "I'm stunned at how much I want to be fucked," Tom said. "This morning I literally couldn't think about anything else. To make sure, I thought of guys I wish had fucked me. There were quite a few. I had a hard-on for an hour before I let myself go out to you. If you didn't have that divine cock, I shudder to think what might have become of me."

"I don't like the sound of that."

"No, I don't either, but you can't let me become myself without looking at the dangers. I don't mean I want to go out and get laid by the whole town, but I might if you couldn't do what you just did for me. It's a side of me I didn't know about. You found it. Before, I was just a simple cocksucker. Now look at me."

"I'm looking. I like it." They kissed playfully across the mayonnaise. "Just drop any idea about getting laid by the whole town—or even a small part of it."

Tom laughed. "We're going to make each other jealous. That's obvious. I know I'll have to behave myself—that's never been a problem—but I want you to look at the boys. I want you to want them. It'll make you want me more. You're much more masculine than I am, as we both very well know. I'd cleave, no matter what you did. The only thing that bothers me is that I don't seem to change you. I turn into 12 different people before your stunned eyes, and you go on being the same—enchanting and adorable and fiendishly sexy. I suppose it's maturity, but it's a bit frightening. It makes me feel you haven't any faults. Hurry up and turn gay, darling. I know I'll be able to hold on to you if you do."

"Without the slightest difficulty."

"Do you realize we haven't been together two full weeks yet? I feel as if we'd packed a whole lifetime into a few days. If it goes on like this, I'll be able to write a ten-volume novel about it before year's end."

They took sandwiches and fruit and a bottle of wine and went down the wooden steps to the water. Walter's eye was caught by the little boat. "When are you going to take me for a sail? There should be a nautical bit in our novel."

"Soon, darling. I don't want to take the time yet." They sat on the jetty and ate. "I know we can't go on like this indefinitely. Real life is going to come in the door one day soon, and we'll have to start rushing around doing all the necessary everyday things. First, I want to have an orgy of belonging to you. I want you to take me as often as you possibly can, beginning in about five minutes. I want to learn to be the best lay you've ever had. I keep thinking of things. Let's spend the rest of the day more or less in bed."

"No argument, Tommy. It's a sport I'm very partial to. I told you it would be more divine with you than anybody. You're wrong about my not changing. I'm not remotely the same as I was two weeks ago. To begin with, I'm happy for the first time in God knows how long. Maybe truly happy for the first time ever. It started the first moment I really looked at you, so you'd have no way of knowing what I was like before."

Tom looked at him, and his heart accelerated. The chestnut wave fell across his forehead. The eyes slanted. The corners of his mouth curled up impishly. There was a change. He was no longer the worldly Walter Makin he had first met. He was a thrilling, naked, ageless faun. Tom swallowed with difficulty. He had surrendered all of himself to him and felt wonderfully whole. He leaned his naked body against him and brushed the side of his face with his lips. "Darling Walter. Beloved Uncle Walt. I'm going to make you happy all our lives. We can express our love with our bodies. Your cock in me. It doesn't sound like much, but it joins us completely. Did you know I'd find out I needed it?"

"I knew we'd find what we wanted in each other. We had to. We always will."

"You must be gay to believe that, darling. I do. You see what I mean? Only a gay would talk about love and forever in the same breath these days. It's the cockeyed vision of total lucidity."

Another dreamlike day passed and another. For no particular reason, except for the feeling that if he didn't do it now he never would, Walter decided he could no longer postpone calling Clara. He waited till mid afternoon, when by her time she would almost surely be home getting ready for the evening. He carried the phone to the sofa and made Tom sit beside him. They had been making love and were in their dressing gowns. Tom opened Walter's all the way down the front. He tucked his legs under him and put his arms around Walter and lay his head on his chest.

"I'm listening to your heart beating. I won't move a muscle. I can suck your cock from here if you should happen to want a little light diversion."

They chuckled, and Walter moved an arm around his shoulders. He wedged the phone into the sofa and dialed with one hand and took a deep breath and waited. A male voice answered, probably the pretty new young thing. He asked for Clara.

"Is this Mr. Makin?" The voice sounded flustered.

"It is."

After a good deal of clicking and popping, Clara was on the line. "There you are, dearest," she said briskly. "I thought perhaps I was never going to hear from you again."

He was grateful for her instinct to attack. It was just what he needed to save him from any possibility of getting maudlin. "David gave me the impression that you had a pretty good idea where I was. I knew you'd find me if you wanted me."

"He knew?" she snapped.

"I told him when I got here."

"Well, what have you called about?"

"I thought it was about time we were in touch. I didn't want to make it any more awkward than necessary."

"How very considerate of you. I've had to tell this ridiculous story about your being sick. I've considered letting it be known that you'd gone out of your mind and had to be put away. I suppose everybody on the Coast knows you're thriving."

"No, I haven't seen a soul."

"The boys will be home in a week. What am I supposed to tell them? Fortunately, they'll be leaving almost immediately for Hopie's ranch, but they'll doubtless notice your absence."

"I don't see why we don't tell everybody as much of the truth as you like. I'm here with a well-known writer. I'm interested in his work, and I'm planning to put on his first play. I'll be working out here for the foreseeable future."

"And what's the rest of the truth?"

"I'm very much in love, Clarry." He refrained from adding "for the first time in my life." Tom hugged him closer. Clara made a sound of contempt in her throat that came winging across the nation.

"I suppose you've forgotten that Claudette is expecting us at Cap Ferrat at the end of the month and that we're due at Majorca for two weeks at Hal's."

"I hadn't exactly forgotten. I just haven't given it much thought. I'd better wire them polite little notes explaining that I'm involved in the most exciting project of my life. Shall I say you're coming anyway?"

"I'll decide that for myself. What are we supposed to call this? Desertion?"

"That should sound all right in divorce court, I suppose, if that's what you want."

"I'll talk to the lawyers. You must be aware that I can probably block your money."

"I can't blame you if you decide to be unpleasant. It won't make any difference. I've hit it lucky. Tom can afford to keep me."

"He has a name, has he?"

"Sorry. Didn't I say? Tom Jennings. Alice was supposed to order his books for me. If they're there, you should read them. They're marvelous."

"I'm really not interested in the life and works of your catamite."

His arm tightened on Tom's shoulders. "Maybe we'd better not talk anymore now, Clara. You have every reason to be angry, but you must know why I did it like this. You haven't forgotten Mark."

Her sudden laughter lashed at him. "You're really pathetic. A middle-aged man with a wife and grown sons running off to find romance with an almost middle-aged faggot. Yes, I know all about him. When it's over, I suppose you think I'll be dying to welcome you back."

He was awaiting her familiar threat to find another man but realized that it was a bit late for that. A woman past 50 was more or less out of the running unless she was ready to settle for hustlers. He was touched by compassion for her and by a sadness that all the years added up to so little. "I think we'd better leave it for now. We'll write. I'm ready to accept anything you decide."

"Then I take it I needn't expect you home for the summer at least."

"I am home, Clara. That's the point." Tom lifted his head, and their eyes met. Walter spread his legs to make room for what was happening down there. "As a matter of fact, since the boys will be so near here, I think I'll arrange for them to come see us at the end of the summer. I'd like Tom to meet them."

"And seduce them?"

"Don't go too far, Clara."

"How can I? You don't have any respect for yourself. You never have had. Whatever I do, I'll see to it that you don't ruin yourself utterly."

"That's fair warning. I know what to expect when you're looking after my best interests. Let it go, for God's sake. There's absolutely nothing you can do about this. You're dealing with two very determined men." His sex lifted as he said it.

"We'll see about that. Good-bye, dearest."

He heard the click of the broken connection. He dropped the instrument into its cradle and reached for Tom's head and held his ears and met his parted lips. Tom withdrew from the long kiss and dropped his head to Walter's upright sex. Walter lay back with a contented sigh and caressed the back of his neck. "There, Tommy. For our purposes, I guess I'm divorced. We can get married whenever you like."

Tom paused in his play, and his lips moved against Walter's flesh when he spoke. "I'm glad it's settled, darling; but don't let's get married. We'll go on breaking the law." His mouth opened and moved voluptuously over the object of his worship.

The call seemed to bring them back into the world, as if they had been waiting for it to define reality. They began to integrate themselves into their surroundings in practical ways. Tom took Walter to his bank, and they arranged to have a joint account and have Walter's money transferred to it. Tom had a telephone installed in his old room. They drove into the city and found a desk and went shopping for some essentials for Walter.

"I suppose I'm going to have to think about having a few suits made," Walter said.

"Made? Do you have your clothes made for you?"

"Of course."

"It's awfully expensive, darling. There're plenty of shops where you can get good things for a third the price."

"Really? Things that would look all right?"

"That would look beautiful on you, darling. You're not exactly deformed."

"Well, we'll see. Maybe I can arrange to have some of my things sent out from New York."

He was displeased to be told where he could buy his clothes, and it took him most of the drive home to shake off a sense of oppression. When he realized he was sulking about clothes rather than Tom's sensible concern about needless expenditures, he burst out laughing. "Really, I'm such an ass. Clothes, for God's sake. I can wear yours. Ours. They're ours, aren't they?"

"Of course."

"I've lost some weight. All that exercise in bed. I can even wear our shirts now."

They came to a final decision about taking the house off the market. Tom began to call people and to receive calls in return, and he talked again about giving a party. He took Walter to his barber.

"My ex-barber," he amended. "I'm going to let my hair grow. Would you like it long?"

"Sure. I'd love to see a cascade of blond hair on the pillow beside me. It's picking up lovely coppery tones in the sun."

Tom finished the revisions of the play with Walter's enthusiastic approval. "It was your idea, and you were right, darling," Tom said in response to praise. "The fact that the changes practically made themselves proves that this is the way it should've been. You don't think it's too shocking?"

"It's not shocking at all. It's tremendously moving. That doesn't mean it won't shock the pants off a lot of people."

Tom returned to his novel. Walter bought screening material and paint and lumber and a few tools Tom didn't have and amused himself by transforming the kitchen and dining area. Tom expressed delight, but Walter had a feeling that he wasn't much interested. He sensed an increasing withdrawal in him. Love flowed from him unstintingly, but it was confined to their more intimate hours. During the day Walter began to notice that he was frequently vague and unresponsive. It filled him with dread. Perhaps he couldn't expect them to maintain indefinitely the high pitch of the first days, but should it pass so soon? He had gambled everything on Tom and had happily abandoned himself to love. It was even more wonderful than he had imagined. What would become of him if he lost it? He was only beginning to realize how totally dependent he had become on his lover.

"Is anything wrong, Tommy?" he asked one day at lunch.

"Wrong?" he replied. "How could there be?"

"I don't know. You're different. You act as if I weren't here most of the time."

"Oh, no, darling." He looked stricken. "How awful for you to feel that way. What do you mean?"

"Just that. You don't talk to me anymore."

"Don't I? Oh, darling, I'm sorry. I was thinking about the work."

"Do you always think about the work?"

"I guess I do. I don't know. It feels so wonderful knowing you're here that I'm working better than ever."

"Are you, baby? That's marvelous." He laughed suddenly, realizing that work affected him the same way. It had never occurred to him that anything could be so absorbing as putting on a play. "Love must be making me stupid. I was afraid you were getting bored with me."

"Don't say that. Please, darling. I'd never work again if I thought it was spoiling anything for us."

"It's not. I should've recognized the symptoms. How strange to be jealous. It's something I've never wanted to be."

"Please be jealous, darling. I love it. It's something new about you. I feel as if there were a great wall of happiness around me, and for the first time in my life there's nothing to interfere with my writing what I want to write. I suppose we'll have our bad times like everybody else, but so far I can't imagine it." He couldn't. He had worried about Walter's being bored. When they had set off on their wild dash across the country, he had been prepared, if all went well and they found they wanted to stay together, to shut up the house and turn around and go back. San Francisco. New York. It didn't matter. For Walter to want to do his play, and do it here, was an unexpected bonus and gave them a chance to settle down; but they could have worked things out without that. The one thing he couldn't do was let anybody interfere with his work, but until Walter got started he could cut his work time to a minimum. He took Walter's hand and looked searchingly into his face. "The way you look at me—as if I were the most fascinating person in the world. If you ever stop, I'll shoot myself. Work's been turning me into a dull dog. Help me pace myself, darling. If I get carried away, I have to do it all over again anyway. Let's give that party."

"Fine, but there's something else I'd like even better. I'd like to go for a sail with you."

Tom looked away. "Sure, one of these days. It takes a lot of time to get the boat ready, and she's such a dinky little thing. You'll probably think it's a lot of fuss about nothing."

A rebuff. There was no mistaking it. His reserve about the boat had nothing to do with his work. Something to do with this life with John? Walter found it almost unbearable for there to be anything about him he didn't know and understand, but if his evasiveness about the boat was the greatest wound love was going to inflict on him, he hadn't much to complain about. "Any day," he said casually. "Who're we going to invite to the party?"

Tom gave his party, and Walter met a dozen of his best friends and their mates, all male. They were newspapermen and decorators and painters and actors and an airline pilot. It was Walter's first public appearance as a homosexual, and his pleasure in finding social recognition for his relationship with Tom almost counterbalanced his discomfort.

Invitations followed, a handful that soon swelled to a torrent, and the oddness for Walter of living in a world without women slowly wore off, although he couldn't get used to being kissed as a matter of course by his hosts. He supposed that this was the sort of thing Tom had in mind when he complained that Walter wouldn't let himself feel really gay.

With summer upon them and the likelihood that his production plans would soon be taking him into the city frequently, they decided Walter would have to have a car of his own. Tom was responsible for their choosing a practical little compact rather than the Jaguar Walter had his eye on. He also insisted on paying for it. "Let me handle the money, darling. You're not used to thinking about it."

Walter came close to losing his temper. "Unless I'm mistaken, I've just had something like $20,000 paid into our account. Is there any reason why I can't spend my money the way I want?"

"Our money, darling."

"Sorry. Our money," Walter corrected himself impatiently. He hadn't adjusted yet to a communal approach to money. His financial affairs had always been managed for him by Clara or the office, but he had known that the money was his. "I can't go around in a mini whatsis— or whatever you've picked out for me. People will think I've gone broke."

"No, they won't, darling. They'll think you're keeping me and that Clara's bleeding you white. Or maybe they'll think you're too smart to get stuck in traffic in a flashy car."

Walter looked at him and prepared to attack. He was standing in front of the fireplace in tight shirt and jeans, lean, tan, rangy. His cowboy, impervious to citified tantrums. Walter's anger collapsed. "All right. Have it your way. But don't blame me if somebody runs into me and I get carted away in a tangle of tin."

"If I thought you'd let somebody run into you, I wouldn't let you have any car."

"You wouldn't, would you?"

"No, I wouldn't. Frankly, I hate the idea. I'll probably go gray worrying about you. You're used to being driven."

"What a sweetheart you are."

"Your money yet," Tom growled.

"Oh, shit, Tommy. I said I was sorry. Come here. Please." Tom moved slowly to the sofa and sat on the edge of it beside him. "I meant *our* money. You know that. Of course it's ours."

"Yes, ours. Everything is ours. It goes without saying. That's why I haven't even bothered to tell you I'm having the house put into both our names. You'll have to sign some papers."

It took Walter a moment to be able to speak. "Tommy. Tommy, darling. You shouldn't do that."

"Why? Because you don't want to be bothered with it in case you decide to clear out? Don't worry. You can…" His voice broke, and he toppled over into Walter's lap and flung his arms around him and buried his face against his stomach. His shoulders shook, and then he was quiet. They hugged each other. Tears welled up in Walter's eyes. "Mad as a hatter," Tom said thickly against his stomach. "He was dragged away screaming 'I love you.' My love. My life. You. Us. Ours. Not our fucking money. Our heavenly life. We'll never have enough of it. You're not going to clear out, are you?"

"No, Tommy. Never."

"Never." He edged himself around until he was lying out flat on his back with his head on Walter's lap. He lifted his arms and let his hands toy lightly with Walter's face. He looked up with shining tear-streaked eyes. "You've been crying too. What a sissy. Why are we so damned pleased with each other? I know you're just a guy in a body like everybody else—well, almost. Aside from the fact that nobody's ever had a face like yours or such a beautiful body or has been so sweet and bright and funny, there's nothing very special about you. I guess it's just because you adore me. I like that. Adore me, darling.

377

Worship me as much as I worship you. And please drive that silly little car carefully."

Adjustments. Walter was only beginning to discover the many adjustments that love required. He wasn't used to thinking about somebody constantly to the exclusion of all other thoughts, of wondering what he was doing, what he was thinking every minute of the day. So far, Tom had shown no sign of being attracted to anyone else; but that didn't make Walter less jealous. He was obviously attractive to others, and Walter was always slightly on edge at the gay gatherings when a young man attached himself to them. He had lost his social touch. He was too intent on hearing what Tom was saying, gauging his reactions, intervening if he seemed to be enjoying himself too much, to be able to make easy contact with others. When Tom's eyes strayed below a belt, which they frequently did, Walter was always quick with a question to divert his attention. He felt an ache of deprivation when a chore took him out on his own and was always in a hurry to get home. He was completely content and relaxed only when they were alone together, preferably touching each other. He wasn't aware that he was suffering some of the agonies of love that experience had taught him to avoid.

He wondered what people were saying. His cherished heterosexual image was smashed beyond repair, of course, and he minded less than he had expected. Everybody would be buzzing from coast to coast by now. Have you heard? Walter Makin has gone completely gay. He wished the truth were known, if only for the kids' sake. Even if they were both as gay as toads, which would raise hell with the law of averages, it wouldn't be pleasant for them to hear that sort of gossip about their father. He hadn't gone gay. He was in love with a fascinating friend. There was a difference. He wished all the gays here could make the distinction. He hated the eyes welcoming him as if to some charmed inner circle.

"Don't you know any women?" Walter asked with a sharp edge he couldn't suppress after they had been going about in public for more than a month. They were having an after-dinner bottle of wine in front of the fire.

378

"Sure. I have some good friends in the sort of literary university crowd. They're mostly away by now. I'm a big literary gun out here, the biggest there is. We won't have to get into that till fall, thank heavens. They're not going to be happy about you. They might admit that their hero is a bit odd and he's taking a long time to find the right girl, but an out-and-out faggot is going to upset them. John never mingled." Tom chuckled. His hair was almost down to his shoulders. In the flickering firelight, he looked like a romantic frontier figure. "You getting tired of gay guys, darling?"

"Yes and no. Your real friends—Steve and Bill and Sidney and that bunch—I like them a lot." Tom knew how to disarm him. It had never occurred to him that he might be a liability. The edge was gone from his voice. "I still find the big parties a bit peculiar."

"I don't usually go to them. It's been fun showing you off, letting everybody know we're together. I admit I've never been so popular. You're a star, darling. Everybody wants to say they know Walter Makin. Why don't you take over our social life? You must know lots of grand people around here."

"No particular friends. People I've known with Clara. It's not worth the bother to get in touch with them."

"An out-and-out faggot might be awkward?"

"Two out-and-out faggots might be awkward. Do you think anybody can look at us without knowing we're mad for each other?"

"It's a problem. You'll have to get used to being an outcast."

"I don't feel like an outcast except at the big fancy parties. I take it Mark doesn't travel in your circles."

"No, I haven't seen him for a while. Do you want to try to find him?"

"No, I've been hoping we wouldn't run into him. I don't think I'd like to see him aging."

"He has. The last time I saw him he'd gone completely gray. He looked a good ten years older than you. How about Jerry?"

"I've asked about him. People seem to know him. He works for Talbot, the decorator. He's in Europe. They say he'll be back in a few weeks. I'd like to see him."

"I'm dying to meet him, naturally. Your son. Fantastic. Now that you've more or less settled in, what do you think, darling? I know it's all different for you. Not very glamorous. No stars of stage or screen. Do you think you're going to like it?"

Walter hesitated. They had been to some outrageous gay bars. They had seen some shows Walter found well-meaning, sometimes exuberant, but rarely professional. They had been to parties. He found the city—despite its vaunted cosmopolitanism, its exotic touches, the flamboyant drag prevalent in some of its streets, its sumptuously decorated houses and apartments—as pleasantly provincial as he remembered it. The atmosphere was casual and diffuse. He doubted if he could take it by storm, even with Tom's play. He felt an enormous complacency that could easily be defeating to an innovator. It was a challenge. It was a relief to be challenged by a place rather than a person.

"To be perfectly frank, I'd be quite content on the moon as long as you were there. Well, maybe not the moon—all those funny suits and things. We couldn't have much fun in those. But you get the general idea. I talked to David this afternoon. He says he and Flossy might come up for a weekend soon. George Cukor may be coming too. I'd like to see all of them. Maybe we could give a little dinner party if it wouldn't be a bore for you to cook." He had not yet adjusted to asking Tom for services he was accustomed to having performed by servants.

"You know I love cooking for you. You'd like some ladies to fill up the corners? I can dig up a couple. Millie. You'll like her. We haven't really started living a normal life yet. Your going to work will make a big difference. We'll slowly get things sorted out."

Walter was gradually getting to work, although he still felt a curious lack of energy. It was perhaps a lethargy of love, of wanting to let himself drift at Tom's side. He had discovered that Artie Solvering, who had worked for him several years earlier, was the director of one of the city's theater groups; and he began to have regular meetings with him to feel out the ground. He looked at properties that might be suitable for what he had in mind. He didn't necessarily want a theater; but a large space that he could turn into a sort of theater he was formulating in his mind. He found a girl in Tiburon who would come in for a couple of hours in the morning for secretarial work. He had some stationery printed and bought a typewriter and a tape recorder, and business began to fill more and more of his day. He had been in touch with Alice almost since his arrival—about the shows running in New York, about money; about sending some clothes; later about Clara, who was in Europe; and about the kids, who were at the ranch. Now he began to have almost daily telephone conversations with her about his San Francisco plans.

One afternoon, when an appointment in the city ended sooner than he had expected, he drove all the way home for a few needed minutes with Tom before he would have to drive back again for a meeting with Artie. He called Tom as he entered the house and received no answer. He went through the terrace and looked around. He was about to go back inside when he was suddenly rooted to the spot. He stared down at the jetty, stunned. The boat was gone.

As he recovered from his initial astonishment, he began to concoct a melodramatic scenario in which Tom was the courier of a Bay Area dope gang, dashing about in his little boat to pick up and deliver the contraband. When this nonsense failed to amuse him, his thoughts turned more serious. Did Tom have waterborne assignations with a boyfriend? Or did he simply like to go sailing alone? The more Walter thought about it, the less he liked it. Tom had said being gay was like being a secret agent. Was the total, open, loving relationship Walter thought they were achieving based on some sort of deception? He had been determined not to be demanding. For once, he had been prepared to dedicate himself wholly to another person's happiness. Did Tom have needs and interests he knew nothing about? It was all so new to him. He had never understood permanent homosexual matings or how they could possibly work. Had Tom deceived him in allowing him to believe that their passionate devotion would be enough? How did his going off alone in his boat, *if* he were alone, fit in with everything being theirs? If he went for secret sails, what other secrets might he have?

He told himself that he was getting overwrought—as usual, where Tom was concerned. Tom had had a sudden impulse to go for a sail. He would hear all about it this evening.

This thought helped him through the meeting with Artie and kept him from breaking all the speed limits on the way home. As he neared the house, he was suddenly appalled by the magnitude of the crisis that might be facing him. If Tom lied, could anything be salvaged? He believed in him to the roots of his being. He had to believe that he was as straight and true and dependable as he knew him to be, or everything he had done was idiocy.

Tom welcomed him with his usual loving warmth, but within minutes Walter knew, with a numbing dread close to horror, that he wasn't going to say anything about the boat. Walter tried a few cautiously leading questions ("How was your afternoon? All as usual?"), but Tom slid around them with admirable dexterity. He didn't actually lie. Walter wanted to believe that it was a vast misunderstanding. Perhaps he'd been out only briefly and didn't think it worth mentioning. Perhaps he'd forgotten. By the time they had fixed themselves drinks, he wanted to come right out with it but realized that it was too late. It would look as if he'd been testing him, trying to catch him in a lie.

Walter took him to bed before dinner and made love to him with a passion verging on violence. Tom had to be his. This being, this mind, this adoring body was all that he cared about in life. He didn't know how it had happened; but he knew now more than ever that it was true. Tom hadn't lied. There was some simple explanation. He would let it go for a while, and when an opportune moment came, he would ask him point-blank if he ever went out in the boat. Reason warned that, meanwhile, he should be more watchful, more cautious, more guarded in the unthinking confidence he felt in being with him, but he knew that reason wouldn't prevail. He couldn't be cautious when he melted with love at the sight of him. He couldn't be guarded with the storm of passion that shook him when he held him. He took him violently and listened to his shouts of adoration. Tom was his as surely as he was Tom's.

Work went on apace. He wrote to his list of backers outlining his plans and received quick replies with enough promises of support so that he could proceed. He decided to give Tom's play a straight, professional production and go with his other plans when he found the material he was looking for. He gave the play to Artie, who was stunned by it and was eager to help cast it locally. He entered into negotiations with one of the city's commercial theaters for a month's booking in late October. He would start rehearsals in mid September and keep the production on the Coast until the end of the year and send it to New York in January. All this suited Tom, who expected to finish the first draft of his novel by the end of the summer.

They cut down their social activities to people they both really liked. Walter kept Jerry in mind and called him at home one Saturday morning when he thought he would be back. He recognized his voice immediately. "Hello, sonny. I hoped you'd be back."

"I don't believe it. It can't be. Is it really you, sweetie? You sound so clear. Where are you?"

Walter told him, including the circumstances of his being there. Jerry exclaimed appropriately. There was something old-fashioned about his light, mannered voice, like a '20s debutante–or like Fay. "My word. You've finally fallen. How heavenly. You were such a divine lover. I never believed Clara was the whole story. I'm going to be madly jealous. I've always heard he's an utter dish. You must be the talk of the town."

"I wouldn't be surprised. When do you want to come see us? How about lunch in a little while?" It was one of the things he was getting used to–that you could invite people on the spur of the moment instead of a month in advance.

"Oh, damn, sweetie. I have a lunch. Later?"

"Sure. We'll be here. Come for a swim and stay for dinner. Are you unattached?"

"Yes. Too sad. You met that adorable boy I was with, didn't you? That broke up a couple of years ago. Shattering. Still, it lasted for five years. I never dreamed I could be faithful for so long. Well, in my fashion. It

383

was every bit as good as you said it would be. I'm still hoping for the right man to come along. What a shame it can't be you. Is 3:30 too soon? We have so much to talk about."

"That's fine. I'm looking forward to seeing you, sonny."

The prospect of seeing his son again, of introducing him to his lover, of meeting on the equal footing of shared and acknowledged sexual inclinations excited him and loosed a nice warm flow of love in him. He told Tom as soon as he came out of his study for lunch.

Tom's face lightened up. "How wonderful. I'm going to meet your son. I feel already as if he were a little bit mine. He's 30 now?"

"Yeah. A bit old to be yours, but still. His manner's rather silly, but I think he's a good kid."

The last few days had been unusually hot. Both Walter and Tom had been having plunges in the icy water of the bay just to stay cool. They decided to stay up on the terrace so that they would hear Jerry when he arrived. Walter carried out their usual light picnic lunch, and they ate in the shade.

"There's something very sexy about meeting your son," Tom said. "I must be jealous. Once you've been to bed with your son, I guess you'd go on wanting to. It's not like a passing affair."

"I don't think we need to worry about that." Walter looked at Tom's lanky body and fine, intelligent face. His pale hair was getting long all over and lay on his shoulders in back. At times in bed, with a long lock falling over an eye, he looked startlingly feminine, but generally, as now, it gave him an adorably shaggy, boyish look. "He'll undoubtedly fall for you. Watch out."

"You always think that about everybody, darling. It's very sweet of you, but a letdown when they all fall for you instead."

They went to bed for half an hour. When they got up, they put on their trunks. "I'll go on down so you can have a minute alone with him," Tom said. They kissed, and Tom left him. Walter straightened up here and there around the house, looking forward to the impending visit, amused at the thought that Jerry was largely responsible for his being here.

He heard a car in the drive and opened the door to the house just as Jerry reached it. He closed it behind him and kissed him lightly on the mouth, immediately drawn to him again with that odd mix of feelings both erotic and paternal. For the brief moment that he held him, he could feel Jerry's trying to turn it into a close embrace, offering himself. He held him at arm's length and laughed, shaking his head. "None of that, youngster."

"You can't blame a guy for trying. You're still the best. It's true even after 12 hectic years. And now you've finally found out what it's all about. How can I resist?"

He had changed little in the five years since they had last seen each other, except that Jerry's hair was even longer than Tom's. It fell in rich chestnut waves around his shoulders. He was tanned and healthy-looking, dressed in expensive casual clothes, with several chains around his neck. There were bracelets on his wrists, and he carried a shoulder bag. A few years ago Walter would have assumed that he was wearing some sort of fancy dress. Now he simply looked with-it. He had become an attractive young man, characterless but agreeable. He communicated a will to please that was disarming. "You brought your trunks? Good. Put them on in there." He indicated the office bedroom. "Let's go on down. Tom's waiting for us."

Walter went on into the living room, examining the potent pull his son still exerted on him. It wasn't, never had been unmanageable, but it was there. It probably always would be. As Tom said, it wasn't like a passing affair. Jerry joined him in a few moments in the brief trunks. Walter saw at a glance that he had arranged his cock to make it as conspicuous as possible, upright against his belly, inviting instant surmise about its potentialities for expansion. His body, which Walter hadn't seen since he was 18, remained almost completely hairless, lightly developed and long-limbed, a smoother, less masculine, more urban version of Tom's. The tanned skin had a satiny texture. The head, with its extraordinary burnished hair, was a pretty girl's head. The prominent sex added a troubling hermaphroditic note. He was much more tempting now than he had been 12 years ago.

He stood close to Walter, looking at him with flirtatious eyes. "This is thrilling, sweetie. I can't stop thinking about it. You here with a boyfriend. I should never have let you get away. You're as gorgeous as ever. Why don't you get older? That body. I'd forgotten how sexy it is. My word." He dropped his eyes and looked up with a naughty smile. "I haven't forgotten *that*. It's been my goal in life to make mine its equal. Tell me about lucky Tom. I know he's a divine writer. Is this his house?"

"Yeah, we've been here a couple of months. Getting on to three, I guess. We met, and we've been together just about every minute since."

"What heaven for you. I'm going to hate him for getting you."

"Come on and meet him. He's looking forward to it."

"He knows I was one of your weak moments?"

"Sure. I heard you were out here and told him all about you. Now that we've got together, I hope we'll be seeing something of you."

Walter was careful not to touch him as he ushered him out and across the terrace. He dropped behind as they started down the wooden stairs and observed that Jerry's bottom was rounder and friskier than Tom's. He used it as bait. Tom was lying on a towel on the jetty and rose to greet them. The little boat bobbed innocently in its mooring. They stood together exchanging pleasantries. Walter noticed that they were all almost exactly the same height. He saw Tom glance from Jerry's hair to his own. Something else Jerry had inherited from his father. He waited for Tom to take in the well-filled trunks. He did so very discreetly as he was spreading towels. Walter wasn't surprised to see his eyes lingering after the first quick reconnaissance.

"Have you been in yet?" Walter asked hastily.

Tom looked at him dutifully. "Yes, for a minute." He looked at Jerry, his eyes darting all over the place as he tried not to fix them on one area. "If you get hot enough, it feels wonderful," he told him.

They sprawled about on the jetty together. Jerry made much of their love affair, teasing them and congratulating Tom for "bringing Walter out," flirting with both of them. It was all light and frivolous, but Walter could feel it reinforcing his sense of being joined, mated, paired.

Tom sought his eyes with amusement and complicity and love. Walter was pleased with Jerry for making a point of their union, but he knew it wouldn't stop him from making a pass at Tom if he struck his fancy. Walter watched for an arm or leg to make an artful contact. When a move was made, Tom made it so overtly that it might not have been intended as sexual. Tom sat up and lay his long strong fingers on Jerry's back.

"You've got a good tan. You should put some suntan stuff on it."

Walter's stomach turned over. He wanted to tear the hand away. Jerry was lying on his stomach. "Be a doll and put some on me, will you?" he suggested.

Tom lifted himself to his knees over Jerry and began to apply it. The association of tubes and ointment and Tom's caressing had unsettled Walter's nerves. His heart raced. A vivid picture of them making love together flashed through his mind and gave him a perverse thrill. They were a study in contrasts–light and dark, strong and weak, genuine and artificial. Their long hair gave them a heraldic beauty. Walter amused himself by imagining them in various period costumes and stage roles. He saw Jerry look up over his shoulder, his hair falling over the side of his face, and slowly, lingeringly assess the body that was bending over him. Walter checked Tom's trunks. They were tight and confined him snugly so that he could be aroused without it showing.

Tom sat back on his heels and asked Jerry about some people they apparently both knew. Walter breathed more easily. Under the guise of gossip, Tom was asking writer's questions, drawing Jerry out. He was evidently interested in him, but it was natural that he should be. Tom and Jerry. He almost laughed as he made the connection. Cat and mouse? Lovers and sons. Fay would be fascinated.

Jerry sat up and swung around so that he was sitting with his legs spread out flat in front of him, his hands on his upper thighs, his back slightly turned to Walter. Walter craned his neck and saw that lying on himself hadn't diminished Jerry's display. On the contrary, it had probably been stirred up by Tom's hand on him.

387

He dropped his head and stopped listening to their words and concentrated on their speech pattern. Their voices overlapped, building to laughter, coming to sudden stops, wandering in soft murmured bypasses before getting on the track again. It was a vocal flirtation, the melody carried by Jerry in a voice filled with flutes and strings, complete with obbligatos, the bass accompaniment provided by Tom. Walter picked up every shift and nuance. There was a passage in Tom's play that might lend itself to this treatment. He made a mental note to check the script tomorrow and see what he could do with it.

There was a silence, and Walter lifted his head. Tom began to speak animatedly, and Walter saw why he felt a need to. His son's cock had developed a strong outward curve and slanted along the top of his trunks, stretching the fabric and barely covered by it, obviously aroused. Jerry was running his thumbs along the inside of the elastic near his hips in a blatant tease, as if he were about to expose it. Walter felt himself stirring as Jerry flaunted himself.

He turned away and missed something. The other two suddenly sprang up, laughing, and took a running step to the edge of the jetty, their backs turned to him, and dived in. The splashed around together, laughing and shouting. Walter rose and dived in after them and shouted with the cold and climbed right out again. The other two soon followed him, spluttering and gasping. Jerry paused at the top of the wooden ladder and reached into the front of his trunks and lifted his strikingly shrunken cock upright once more. He caught Walter's eye on him and smiled mischievously. They all moved toward each other and stood together rubbing themselves down and exclaiming about the icy water. Jerry's hair hung in long glossy strands. Tom was toweling his vigorously. He tossed his head about and threw his arms around father and son and drew them closer.

"I'm fascinated by this guy," Tom said to Walter. "I'm glad you found him again."

"You two are a heavenly pair," Jerry said. "Walter knows I've always been mad for him. Now there's you. I don't know which of you to try to seduce first."

Their eyes roved from one to the other, conveying private messages, taking each other in. Walter felt a strange collusion developing among them. For an exquisite moment they seemed to achieve a perfect physical and emotional balance. Then he saw Tom's and Jerry's eyes meet and hold a beat too long, their bodies sway almost imperceptibly toward each other, and he broke away. It was natural. In the complexities of connection, they were the two who were strangers to each other. Again he felt a perverse thrill at the thought of their bodies' meeting.

"We'd better go up and put some clothes on. It's going to start getting chilly soon," he said.

They gathered up towels and started up the stairs.

"It'll take me an hour to get my hair under control," Jerry said. "Can anybody lend me a brush?"

"Sure," Tom said. "Your hair's beautiful. Mine's getting there."

"I adore streaky blonds. What do you do when it's wet?"

"I just sort of shake it and hope it'll fall into place."

"I have a whole routine. It's a bore, but the result's rather gorgeous. Would you like me to show you?"

"Sure."

Walter listened to them and wondered where they thought their flirtation was leading. He knew, as certainly as Tom knew that everything was theirs, that they had to be true to each other. He saw Tom put his hand on Jerry's shoulder as they entered the house. A hospitable gesture. They parted in the corridor, and Tom and Walter went along to their room.

"Don't forget the brush," Jerry called.

"I'll bring it in a second," Tom replied.

Walter closed the door on them. Could he allow Tom to be alone with Jerry? He didn't see how he could prevent it. Tom would be justifiably indignant at his making a fuss if all he wanted was to have his hair arranged. They peeled off their trunks. Not to his surprise, he saw Tom's cock spring out stiffly. His own was conspicuously elongated. Tom eyed it and laughed as they dried themselves more thoroughly.

"Your son is quite a number. We need hardly comment on the obvious. Is it as big as yours?"

"Practically."

"Not quite, I'll bet. I have an eye for such matters." He turned to the mirror and ran a comb with difficulty through his hair. He tossed his head and picked up a brush and started for the door.

"Where're you going?" Walter demanded.

"Taking him the brush."

"Put something on, for God's sake. You've practically got a hard-on."

Tom chuckled. "That's been going on all afternoon. We might as well look. That's better than getting mysterious and uptight about it. If it weren't so public down there, I'd have suggested we all take everything off. I'm not going to let him do a big production with my hair. I'll be back in a minute."

"Wait, damn it," Walter said as he watched the naked body stride swiftly out the door.

The process Walter had seen beginning was quickly concluded in the corridor while Tom hurried to the other room. His erection was satisfyingly complete when he pushed the slightly open door wider and called Jerry's name. He appeared around the bathroom door holding a towel in front of him. He looked at Tom and dropped it and uttered silvery laughter.

"That's the way I like a gentleman to come calling." He advanced into the room with a slight sway of his hips. The visible evidence of his pleasure grew spectacularly as he approached.

"Let's get a really good look," Tom said briskly. He tossed the brush on the bed and went to meet him. They reached out and held each other and moved their bodies tantalizingly against each other. "You're such a tease. I've been dying to get my hands on this all afternoon." He was holding, being held by Walter's son. He felt an intense sexual curiosity about him and an extraordinary instant affection for him.

"I've been dying to have them there, Thomas," Jerry said with a little thrust of his hips to show himself off to advantage. "At least, I show what I've got. Those trunks of yours are so chaste. I can't make head or

390

tail of cocks and balls when they're covered up. Who could guess you had all this tucked away in there?"

"All what? Tell me about it. You and Walter are apt to give a guy an inferiority complex. It's not much more than average, is it?"

"Average! We'd all be so lucky if it were. You're one of nature's noblemen, Thomas. Hasn't anybody told you? Aside from Walter and half a dozen others encountered in a long and busy sex life, you're about as big as they come. An eight-incher if I ever saw one. I never allow myself to dream such extravagant dreams. Life is full enough of disappointments."

Tom laughed, ridiculously pleased with himself. "It's about time I knew how I stack up against the other boys. You're a pal, Jerry."

"I want to be much more. Hadn't we better lock the door?"

"Of course not. I'd never do anything I didn't want Walter to see."

"Really? In that case, we'd better concentrate on your hair. Come over here."

Tom saw that he had placed a chair in front of the long mirror on the closet door. He could give himself a couple of minutes more. He slumped into the chair with his legs sprawled out indolently in front of him and watched Jerry come up behind him in the mirror holding a comb. His big cock came sliding over his shoulder and up along the side of his face. Tom swung around and took it in his mouth. He drew back and measured it with his eyes. "You and Walter," he murmured. "If you only knew. What a pair."

"You do that divinely. Don't stop. It'll only take a minute."

Tom stood. "No. You're too tempting. I better do my own hair. I told you I won't do anything behind Walter's back."

"I'd adore for you and Walter to do things behind my back."

Tom chuckled and put his arms around him and pulled his hips in against his. "I'm excited about your being here. Let's see how it goes. Maybe you should consider staying all night."

"I always consider staying all night when I'm with beautiful men."

Tom pulled him closer, and their open mouths met. Walter's flesh and blood. A delectable mouth that Walter had made and that he was

391

making his. All sorts of fragmentary thoughts tumbled around in his mind. He broke away. "OK. Make yourself pretty and come join us for drinks. There's no rush, but I'll be waiting for you." He gave Jerry's frisky behind a caress and briskly left the room.

Walter sat on the end of the bed, where he had collapsed. He felt as if all his senses had been knocked out of him. His stomach was in a turmoil. What was Tom doing? *Nothing's wrong*, he insisted to himself. Tom wouldn't have gone charging out intent on sex under Walter's very nose. It was all perfectly innocent–as innocent as it could be, given Jerry's nature and Tom's nakedness. Kids these days didn't think anything about being naked together. That was all very well for Jerry's generation, but Walter didn't want to feel a generation gap with his lover.

He stood up and sat down again. Jesus. His son, the stripteaser. Enough to unsettle Tom's mind. Damn Jerry. Why didn't he go watch them doing their hair? There was nothing private about it. And if they weren't just doing their hair? Tom wouldn't let anything happen. He wouldn't even if they were off alone somewhere. Tommy was his, and they both knew it. If he took the trouble to go into the hall, he'd probably hear them talking cheerfully together.

He was trying to gather his forces to get up when Tom came bursting into the room, his erection waving jauntily in front of him. At least it was erect. Nothing had happened to make it subside. He was torn between anger and desire. Tom's color was high, his eyes were shining, he looked triumphant and utterly irresistible.

"Where've you been?" he demanded, giving precedence to anger.

"With Jerry, of course."

"You let him see you like that?"

"I could hardly help it, darling. We were both as naked as jaybirds and as hard as rocks. He says I've got a big one. How about that?"

"I've told you that," Walter snapped.

"Oh, you. What do we know about it? We haven't been around enough to make comparisons. He's an expert. I'm pleased as punch. It's going to stay like this forever."

"Goddamn it, Tommy. I won't have you running around showing your cock to everybody and letting people play with it." He watched Tom's high spirits dying and hated himself, but life wasn't all high spirits. There were things they had to get straight between them.

"Don't say things like that to me, darling." Tom spoke quietly, with gentle reproach. "You won't have it? Don't try to scare me. I've been scared of my own shadow all my life. We're together. Nothing can scare me now."

"You don't think you might do things that'll make us stop wanting to be together?"

"No." His voice immediately rose with conviction. "I can do anything I want because I know I'll never do anything that's wrong for us. Jerry and I give each other erections. We were both dying to see. We feel close to each other because of you. I put his cock in my mouth. Oh, I kissed him. That was it."

Walter stared at him, incredulous. "You dare tell me you sucked his cock, and you say—"

"No, I'm not telling you that," Tom cried. "I put it in my mouth. For a few seconds. Your son's cock. Part of you. It was the most natural thing in the world. I knew you might come in. I didn't do anything I can't tell you. Your lover put your son's cock in his mouth. It's something your lover is inclined to do. It's not a jawbreaker like yours. It happens that I find jawbreakers more exciting. Do you want to leave me for that?"

"I don't want to leave you, Tommy." He reached for his towel and hitched it around him. He went to where Tom had left his and picked it up and handed it to him. "Go on. Cover up for a while. I don't want to feel like a member of the general public." He ran a hand over his forehead and dropped back on the end of the bed. "All right, Tommy. Tell me about it. Try to make me understand. What's it all about? What does Jerry mean to you?"

"What does Jerry mean? He's yours. You made him. It's like anything you make, a play you produce, the way you made the dining room out there. I love everything you've touched. His big cock makes him even more yours. That's all. Oh, God, I sometimes wish you were a cocksucker. Maybe you'd understand. I don't mean you don't suck my cock very sweetly when you think of it, but that doesn't mean you're a cocksucker. Will you ever be gay?"

"Does being gay mean running after anybody who comes along?"

"Certainly not. It means understanding what men are like. Men without women to goad us. We're animals. We're curious but lazy. We'd rather make love than war. Holding a guy's cock isn't a love affair. It's a simple instinct."

"Just a minute. Let me tell you something. When I was sitting here wondering what in hell was going on, you running around stark ass and so forth, I thought some of the things you're saying. I thought you might want to get him out of those damn see-through drawers. He was begging you to. I knew you wouldn't do anything. I believe in you, Tommy. I know we're animals, but we don't have to behave like them. How would you like it if I started holding guys' cocks?"

"I don't know." A small smile twitched at the corners of Tom's mouth as he sat on the bed near him. "It's so hard to imagine, I'd have to wait till you do it to find out. No, darling, of course I'd hate it. That's not us. We're talking about a special case. Jerry's your son. The whole idea has me all steamed up. I know you have two other sons, but they're a bit young, and as far as I know, you haven't thought of going to bed with them. You have with Jerry. You still want to. That's perfectly obvious. I saw the way you looked at him. I wasn't jealous, because he's yours and has nothing to do with your being attracted to a pretty boy. In case there's any doubt in your mind, I intend us to be faithful, and I'll fight like a wildcat if you get other ideas. Listen…" He paused. He felt that they might be headed for the sort of ultimate confrontation that he suspected they needed. Everything had been almost too perfect, too smooth, too easy. Walter had invented life without grit, without the abrasive quality that Tom knew couldn't be avoided. Now that they'd had their honeymoon, he felt they should be locked in sweaty combat over some issue that hadn't arisen. He wanted to provoke a holocaust of passionate commitment that would bind, weld, cement them together, prepare them for anything life might bring. Clara. Walter had slid out of his marriage; but he was glad to avoid any real showdown. His boat. He had kept it to himself and gone for secret sails to prove to himself that he could keep something of himself apart as Walter kept Clara, even though he'd left her. He wished Walter had insisted on going out on the boat or taken it out himself and risked his anger. Silly, trivial, but significant. He teased him about not being gay, and that was part of it. If he couldn't accept himself, how could he accept his lover? They hadn't got down into the muck and mire of life, and until they did he couldn't be sure that they'd survive it. That was as close as he could come to expressing it to himself. His random thoughts about Jerry were coming into focus. Excitement stirred him. "All right," he said urgently. "I'll say all of it. You want Jerry. You admit that?"

"In a way. It's sort of a fantasy. Nothing that I'd let touch us." Walter hoped he was being honest. Jerry had an apartment in the city. The thought might have crossed his mind that they could meet easily without Tom's knowing, but the notion was so fleeting that he had hardly been aware of it.

"But he's your son," Tom exclaimed. "God. To make love to somebody you've created. It must be one of the summits of human experience. I should think all parents would want to make love to their children, but they usually have to watch them grow up, and that must take the icing off the cake. How wonderful for you to have a son who's a sexy stranger."

"Fine. That's one fantasy. I'll tell you another. This afternoon I caught myself thinking about you and Jerry making love together. It was exciting." The gaiety that had swept Tom into the room was being rekindled. He sat up straighter. There was a light in his eyes. He was slightly mad, but beautifully so. Walter was sorry he'd made him wrap the towel around himself. He wanted to look at all of him. He added firmly, "That doesn't mean I'd want it to actually happen. Or allow it."

"But, darling, it's marvelous," Tom burst out with a roll of laughter in his voice. "Maybe you're gay after all. What a marvelous thing for you to think about. I want him. I want him because he's part of you. I

395

want everything that's you, but nothing could happen when you weren't there. We both want him. We could make it part of us."

"Are you suggesting a threesome?" Walter tried to convince himself that he was shocked. "As far as I'm concerned, love and sex have to do with two people. It's not a spectator sport."

"Why not? You want to see me with your son's cock in my mouth. You do, darling. You've practically said so. I understand. I'll give him a nice blow job for you. I know what you want. Our bodies are sort of alike. Your lover and your son. I'm wild to watch you take him." He laid his forearm across his lap and leaned on it. "There it goes again. I have a big one. How about that? I told you it was going to stay like this forever."

It was happening to Walter too, in spite of himself. Everything Tom said filled his mind with images of perverse delight. Could they play with this fire without getting badly burned by it? It drew him and terrified him. The fact that Tom was eager to accompany him, lead him along these strange twists of his psyche, opened up vistas of relationship that stunned and moved him. There was no limit to what they could give each other. "Are you sure we wouldn't get into something that might change the way we feel about each other, Tommy? I'm not sure fantasies should be allowed out. Isn't it dangerous to share some things?"

"Sure, but I'll tell you. I'm not scared of anything anymore. I'm ready for danger if it gets us closer to each other."

"And you think seeing each other make love to Jerry will make us closer?"

"Of course it will. I'll bet you've already thought of meeting him in town when I'm not around. That might seem safe enough, but it would be the beginning of the end. We're gay, darling. We've got to learn our own rules." He had convinced himself that Jerry offered them the opportunity for a great flight of imagination that would bridge the distance that remained between them and bring them to a final meeting of spirits. He wanted to expose himself in ways he never had, hoping that Walter would do the same so that everything in them would be known and accepted. "You've made me all free and open. You've got to be the same. I don't mind your still wanting Jerry if we can want him together."

"You're fairly breathtaking, Tommy."

"Hold me, darling." Tom stood and threw aside his towel. Walter followed suit, and they took a step to each other and put their arms around each other. "Talk about hard as rocks. You're the rock of my life. You and everything about you and all of you. Let's have a demonstration of how much we want each other."

"Just remember, baby, whatever we do with him, if we seem to be getting into something that might hurt, I'm counting on you to call a halt to things."

"Don't worry. I could never hurt you."

They had a very satisfactory demonstration and then went through the routine of preparing for the evening. Tom spent more time than usual on his hair. When he was done, he was looking very dashing. It was a vigorous tawny blond mane with a recalcitrant lock that threatened to fall over one eyebrow.

"I swear to God, Tommy, you get more and more handsome every day," Walter told him.

Tom grinned and squeezed his hand. "I've got to keep up with the competition."

They made a fire, and Tom started making preparations in the kitchen and got out things for drinks. They had fixed one for themselves when Jerry appeared. He had got his hair very much under control. It was glossy, with soft waves falling to his shoulders. He was dressed in white, a sheer cashmere turtleneck sweater and tight pants. His chains and bracelets gave him a festive party look. Walter saw immediately that he was wearing eye makeup, very subtly applied to give his eyes depth and mystery.

"My God. A vision has appeared before us," Tom exclaimed. He went to him and kissed him lightly but familiarly on the mouth. He placed a hand with equal familiarity on the bulge of his pants. "Is all this really you?"

"You should know. I told you I like to show what I've got." He glanced hastily at Walter. "Oops, have I spoken out of turn?"

"Of course not," Tom said. "I told him all about our passionate love scene." He put an arm around Jerry's waist and swung around to face Walter. "He's not new to you, but I find him a very decorative addition to our rough bachelor quarters."

"He is, isn't he?" Walter knew already that Tom had been right about getting everything out into the open. The tensions of the afternoon were gone.

Tom dropped his arm from Jerry's waist. "Go kiss Daddy," he ordered firmly.

Jerry laughed with a touch of astonishment. "That's the first thing he ever said to me–that he was old enough to be my father. I remember, because it's hardly what you expect when you're trying to make out with a gorgeous man in a gay bar. Look at him. Can you imagine having that for a father? I'd have fallen for him the minute I emerged from the womb." He went to Walter where he was standing in front of the fire and looked at him expectantly.

"You're looking very special, sonny. I never would've dreamed you'd turn out so attractive."

"There must've been something about me. You were the most fabulous lover I've ever had."

"Thanks." He put a hand on Jerry's arm and urged him closer, and they kissed. The excitement of holding this new, glamorous son was more potent than anything he had felt with the 18-year-old boy. Jerry's soft mouth was open to his, and for a moment he gave way to its seduction. Let Tom have some of his own medicine. Love for the foolish young man briefly raged in him. He squeezed his arm, and they broke apart. He looked at Tom. "Well?"

"Yeah," Tom said with a tight little smile.

They settled on what Jerry wanted to drink, and Tom brought it to him. They toasted each other.

"I love being with you two," Jerry said simply. "I think it's going to be the nicest Saturday night I've had since I can remember. You know,

398

you're both much too attractive to've found each other. It's one of those things that should happen but doesn't. It's in that new novel–it's a big best-seller–called *The Lord Won't Mind.* It's about two beautiful boys who find undying love. Utter fantasy, but I love it."

"Do you still think love is utter fantasy?" Walter asked as they settled down in front of the fire.

"No, of course not. It's just almost impossible to make it work. What happens when you're being pursued by one of the local gods, one of the great blond beauties they seem to manufacture here? I find that my feet turn to lead. It causes trouble in the home. I'm sure you two are pursued constantly. I hope you don't develop 'blond god' problems."

"Tommy says he won't let us," Walter said.

Tom leaned against the back of his chair and touched his hair. "I think we'll know what to do about them, darling." He sat beside Jerry on the sofa.

Conversation flowed. They finished their drinks, and Tom rose to replenish them. When he returned, he resumed his seat beside Jerry. They both suddenly reached out blindly to set down their glasses as they exchanged a look that had become electric, as if they were seeing each other for the first time. Tom moved a hand around Jerry's waist and leaned to him and covered his mouth with his. Walter was immediately relegated to the sidelines. He watched their bodies strain to each other, and then Tom pulled back. He was wrenched by a sudden violent stab of desire for both of them. They were so touching together: Tom, manly and aggressive; Jerry, artfully yielding.

Tom gazed into Jerry's eyes. "I guess we really do want each other, don't we? I guess we can safely say we all want each other. As long as you remember that Walter and I are madly in love with each other, I don't see how it can do anybody any harm."

"I adore both of you," Jerry said, his eyes held by Tom's. "There's no secret about that."

Tom laughed. "Our messages are getting through loud and clear." He stood and hitched up his pants and looked at Walter with a smile. "OK, darling?"

Walter chortled. "You're a monster."

"I better go concentrate on dinner."

Walter watched him go. He felt a bit shaken but not disagreeably so. Tom apparently intended to pursue his plan and could probably make it make sense. He rose and replaced him beside Jerry.

"He's a wonderful guy," Jerry said with more unmannered sincerity than he had yet managed.

"I think so. I suppose this is a bit peculiar."

"What is, sweetie?"

"Oh, nothing." Jerry was probably accustomed to threesomes and foursomes or any multiple thereof. "You and Tom look sweet together. I'm glad you don't use much makeup on your eyes."

"I should've known you'd notice. Do you think he did?"

"Probably not. You do it very well."

Jerry put a hand between Walter's legs and exerted pressure. "I'm still trying, sweetie."

"You may yet succeed. But don't try when he's not here. You can do anything you like when he is."

"Really? He said something of the same sort. It's an interesting switch. Quite amazing." He withdrew his hand.

"We're amazing people." Walter talked to him about Tom's play, and Jerry listened and asked questions as if he found him spellbinding. It was his particular charm. Tom returned and announced that dinner was ready. Jerry rose and went to him and held his hand. "We were talking about you. We missed you. I made a pass at your lover, but I'm beginning to feel lost with one of you without the other. I guess it's because you're so right together." He turned to Walter. "You don't mind if I think he's as sexy as you are? It's as if you were the same person."

Walter stood and went to them and kissed Tom. "Is that it? Are we the same person?"

"Of course."

"That's good." He moved between them and put his arms around them, and they went in to dinner. It was excellent, featuring braised sweetbreads expertly prepared. They drank wine copiously and grew quite merry. Walter was proud to note that Jerry didn't once refer to himself or any other male in the feminine gender. They carried wine back to the fireplace and built a larger fire. Tom turned out most of the lights, and they sat in a row on the sofa, Jerry in the middle by mutual unspoken agreement. Walter's arm lay along Tom's, behind Jerry's head, and they gripped each other from time to time. Jerry took off all his ornaments.

"They do make such a clatter," he said. "I wonder why I even bother with them."

"They suit you," Tom said.

"I suppose they do, but I'm not sure they should. You two look so divine with nothing." Jerry held heir knees and let his fingers stray teasingly over them.

They talked through their second bottle of after-dinner wine and got a good start on their third. They were beginning to get repetitious without being aware of it. Jerry wanted to know more about how Walter and Tom had got together in spite of Walter's resistance to homosexuality.

"I pretty much worked it all out with you, sonny," Walter said, "so I was ready for him when he turned up. I still wasn't completely convinced I could fall in love with a man. I guess I had some sort of block that you two haven't had. At least I have my sons. They mean more to me than you can imagine."

"Are they as dishy as you?"

"Tommy's met one of them. Ask him."

Tom was seized with a fit of laughter. "You bastard," he gasped.

"Writers are often incoherent," Walter pointed out. "We must make allowances."

Jerry's laughter tinkled. "You two. What a divine evening. I think I'm a wee bit tipsy." Once more he slipped a hand up the inside of Walter's thighs; this time Walter made a sound of assent.

Reticence was forgotten. They all had their arms around each other in a close triangular embrace. "Do you think we should ask this pretty baby to spend the night?" Tom inquired.

"I don't suppose he should drive in this condition." They all looked at each other and leaned their heads together and burst out laughing.

Walter tipped Jerry out flat on his back across his lap and got a grip on the bottom of his pullover and peeled it over his head, baring his son's hairless torso. Tom's hands moved up over it, and Jerry dropped his on them and pressed them to his breast.

"Oh, Thomas. Your hands are fabulous. They're strong and yet so gentle." He moved them down over him and folded them on the swelling mound of his crotch.

There was no doubt about where Tom's attention would be directed for the moment. This was the part Walter expected to be hard to take. He lifted Jerry's shoulders and gathered him to him and took his eager mouth. All his paternal-erotic tenderness flowed to this man who willfully remained a child. He felt his hips lift and heard the light sound of his trousers being pulled off. Their kiss deepened, and Jerry's arms tightened around him, and he moaned and shuddered against him. Walter steeled himself to look at what was taking place and drew back and surveyed the shapely body of his naked son.

Tom had worked his way down and held Jerry's sex upright. His open mouth moved over it. Jerry's pubic hair looked as if it had been trimmed into a small neat triangle from which the astonishing masculinity of his sex lifted to Tom's face. Walter gazed transfixed at the lips and tongue paying obeisance to his son. He supposed being slightly drunk made the sight bearable. Jerry lay in his arms, his head back, his lips parted, moaning ecstatically, little shudders of delight passing through him. Tom's pleasure was so open and unabashed that Walter couldn't help being proud of having a son that Tom wanted. He ran a hand over Jerry's chest and belly, feeling keenly aware of being father to the flesh he was caressing. Tom reached for his hand and folded it around Jerry's cock. Walter was on the verge of orgasm. He hadn't dreamed it was possible to achieve such depths of intimacy with another being. Through Jerry, he and Tom were growing together, growing into each other. Tom lifted his head, and they stared at each other intently.

402

"It's almost you," he murmured. "Get undressed, darling. I've got to see you naked together." Somehow Tom was making it all seem natural and right.

Walter extricated himself from Jerry and laid him back on the sofa and rose with a slight lurch, and his clothes seemed to drop from him. When he turned back, Tom was still dressed, but Jerry had got his clothes open down the front and they were locked together, writhing in a kiss. Walter leaned over and lifted Jerry's nearest arm. They immediately released each other, and Jerry let himself be pulled up into Walter's embrace. His hair was beautiful in lustrous disarray. Walter ran his hands through it and turned him in his arms and held his slight back against his chest. Jerry swayed his buttocks against him.

Tom pulled himself onto his knees and leaned against the back of the sofa, surveying them. His face looked bruised with desire, and his hair tumbled over his brows. He was coming out of his clothes as if he had been raped. "God, yes," he muttered. "Come here."

Walter held Jerry at his side and moved closer to the sofa. Tom shrugged off his shirt as he edged forward on his knees. His eyes were riveted on taut skin, swelling veins, sinew, muscle, whatever it was. The staff of life. Two. They loomed enormously toward him in the unsteady light of the leaping flames. Swelling with power. The focus of all his desire. One was father to the other, the father clearly master.

He slowly reached for them and brushed them with his fingertips and watched them lift and sway to each other and touch, the great thrust of Walter's power conferring power on his son. He clung to Walter's hips and lowered himself and stretched his mouth for him. Walter gripped his hair and thrust himself into him. Tom groaned in an ecstasy of submission. It was what he had been longing for. He felt the power newly unleashed in Walter, no longer confined by his sweet restraint, fierce and intoxicating. He somehow tore off his shoes while Walter's power swelled in him and strained his jaws. Walter pulled him up, and he kicked his feet free of his trousers while Walter held him close, rough with passion.

"Now, darling. Take me. Take us both. We're both yours. Take us."

"You're incredible, baby." Walter's arms gripped him, and he kissed him hard on the mouth. "Come on."

They moved together to the bedroom, jostling each other, all of them careening when one of them underwent some vagary of balance. They fell into bed together. Walter drew the two slim bodies to him, and they rolled about together, laughing wildly.

Walter seemed to enter a dark tunnel of sensual rapture from which he emerged in the shower. He wasn't quite sure how he'd got there. The wine had really caught up with him. He knew he had taken Tom and had encouraged him to suck Jerry's cock while he was doing it. He had held Tom in his moment of climax so that Jerry could take him into his mouth. The world of exclusive male sexuality that he had avoided all his life held back no more secrets from him now. He had enjoyed it all and felt more at ease with his body than he ever had. Tom had pulled off some sort of miracle. He hadn't attempted to disguise his attraction to Jerry but neither had he ever made him feel that his primary attention had been diverted; the current between them had dominated everything they had done and had run strong and hot between them. The shower was reviving him. He wanted to get back to them. God knows what they'd be up to while he was gone.

When he reentered the bedroom, Tom and Jerry were tangled together in a complicated knot, whispering and giggling together, their slim, long-limbed bodies interlaced. He stopped and studied them and felt an opening up of love for them both. He knew how they felt in each other's arms. His imagination summoned up his small gallery of partners—cheerful Harry, angelic Philip, grave Mark—and his heart contracted with little spasms of love as he saw them in moments of physical perfection. One by one, he had blocked them out as exceptions to his ordinary needs, but he knew at last that the mystery of male union had always dominated his life.

As soon as they saw him, the rearranged themselves on the bed to welcome him. Tom stretched out on his back with total abandon, his head on Jerry's stomach, Jerry's revived erection nestled against his cheek.

"We've decided we're both slightly lesbian but madly in love with the same man. The role-switching has worn me out." Tom lifted Jerry's cock and moved it over his face. They burst into laughter. "Come on, Gerald, let's show him a willing harem."

They lifted themselves and reached for him and pulled him down to them and made love to all of his body with their mouths. Walter stroked arms and legs and backs and chests and bellies and tumbled them over and kissed leaping cocks.

They slept, Tom wrapped around Walter as usual, Jerry stretched out beside them. Walter woke up in broad daylight in an empty bed. He reached out for Tom in the first moments of awakening, and it took him another minute to piece together the events of the previous evening. Had any of it really happened? Hot sweat broke out all over him, and his heart began to beat heavily. Taking stock, he couldn't find the residue of ugliness he assumed it must have left. Memory told him that it had contained an excitement of discovery that transcended sexual excitement. He knew he would be speechless with embarrassment when he saw them. Where were they? Had Jerry already fled in shame? No, not Jerry. He would have accepted it as normal. But surely Tom must be suffering some remorse. Why? They had done shocking things together and had loved it.

He chortled and grabbed a dressing gown and tossed it aside. He wanted to show himself to Tom the way he was. Tom wouldn't mind if he gave Jerry another look.

He went out the door that had been left open. He had reached the entry area before he heard them. He stopped abruptly and listened. He changed direction and forced himself forward on legs that suddenly felt numb.

The door to the office bedroom was open. He moved to it with difficulty and put a hand on the frame for support and looked in. They were tangled together on the bed. Tom was taking his son. The cries were ecstatic. Tom's body was an arc of power, riding Jerry hard. A great shout of outrage gathered in Walter's throat. He turned and stumbled and almost fell and rushed blindly back to their room.

He closed the door and fell into bed and pulled the covers around him. All his body trembled with rage. He would wait till they were through and throw the little whore out of the house. He would tell Tom what he thought of him and clear out himself. Even better, he could leave with Jerry. Thoughts of revenge raged through his mind and gave him the illusion that righteous wrath was carrying him beyond the possibility of being hurt. He was sick of the whole thing. They would end up living in a male brothel. Home. They had been drunk last night. Tom wasn't drunk this morning. He would smash his god-damned face in and leave before he wrecked his whole life. He despised him. He was in love with him. He was lost. He had made his bid for life and freedom and had nowhere left to turn. He was a victim of the flaw he had always suspected must be there, the flaw of a love unsanctioned and undefined by any law. How could two people make their own rules and expect them to mean anything? The rules were there to be broken. Tom had practically said as much, but he hadn't listened. He had wanted to believe that Tom offered something real and true. Fidelity between men was a farce. Tom had driven him and broken him. Now he was alone. Misery engulfed him.

He hypnotized himself into a sort of drugged semiconscious torpor that didn't exclude his misery but made it almost bearable. He heard the door burst open, and he was immediately awake and trembling violently with some emotion he didn't attempt to identify. Tom was with him. He would beat the shit out of him.

"Hey, darling," Tom greeted him exuberantly. "Wake up. We've been waiting for you. Are you going to sleep all day? Jerry and I have—"

He threw back the covers and sat up. It was surely rage that was shaking his body. "Get the fuck out of here!" he shouted. "Both of you. Get out!" They were standing close together, naked, looking young and vibrant and perfectly matched. He saw the happy expectation in their faces replaced with dismay.

"But, darling—"

"Don't call me darling," Walter roared. "Get out of here! Christ. I'm sick of men. Get your fucking cocks out of my sight." He fell back, exhausted, and gathered the covers around him and buried his face in a pillow. He heard murmuring, then the sounds of movement and the door closing. He tried to work himself back into a torpor, but his heart was pounding, and a great ache of loss was in the pit of his stomach. If Tom went anywhere with that little shit, he would kill him. The possibility began to gnaw at his nerves. He tossed around in the bed trying to find ease. Grown men didn't tear up pillows and smash watches. Grown men killed. He couldn't kill Tommy. Kill himself? He was back where he had started. His god with a gold head at his side. He was suddenly racked by great tearing sobs. Why did he do this to himself? He was in total command of life when he stuck to things he was good at. Why get into emotions that were beyond his depth? As soon as the sobs were under control, he crawled out of bed and went to the bathroom, fumbling through his morning ritual. As soon as he was finished, he'd go pack, except that he felt so lousy, he didn't see how he could. Strong black coffee might help, but he couldn't go out and face them again.

He was standing irresolutely in the bedroom when he heard a car start up outside and the crunch of gravel as it took the steep drive. He wouldn't go looking for him. He headed back to bed, wearing his dressing gown. He had just got the covers over him when the door opened. A great wave of comfort and relief swept though him. He glanced at Tom and looked away. He was wearing the shirt and pants he had had on the night before. It was all over, but he needed a few final nasty moments with him to help him out of the house.

"Is anything the matter?" Tom asked calmly.

A long silence followed. Perhaps the greatest punishment would be to refuse to speak to him, but he found the silence unbearable. "Good heavens, no," he said finally with heavy irony. "Nothing could possibly be the matter, could it?"

"I'm sorry, darling, but Jesus—you were dreadful. Jerry's terribly upset. You've got to call him later and tell him it's all right. You've ruined everything."

"I've ruined everything." He sprang out of bed and stood in front of him and unleashed his rage. "It was all for us, wasn't it? We had to have

**407**

everything together. Sure. That's why you had to get him off by your-self and fuck him in peace. Jesus Christ. To think I believed in you. Shit. All of it. Utter and total shit."

"You're wrong, darling," Tom said, facing him resolutely. "You were asleep. We didn't want to disturb you. I hoped you'd wake up and come join us. I left all the doors open. There was nothing sneaky about that. If you saw us, why didn't you come in?"

"Because I don't think your little games are very pretty," Walter roared. "They're disgusting. I suppose you let him fuck you while you were at it."

"No, I wanted it, of course—God, that cock and his being yours—but not without your being there. He didn't think he could, like I used to be. He said your being there might make it work. He knows you're his father—maybe not consciously, but he knows something. I'm exciting to him because I'm your lover. My taking him—you must've known that had to happen. You did it. I did it. It was part of it. I don't understand what's bugging you. When I was fucking him—"

"Shut up, goddamn you. Don't you ever think about anything else? I understand one thing. You have a problem. A big problem. I'm clear-ing out. You can figure things out on your own."

Tom lifted his chin, and his eyes hardened. "Back to Clara? I sup-pose I've been sort of half prepared for that all along."

"No, not Clara. I'll go somewhere and try to get my life straightened out. I can't with you. That's finished. I believed in you, you shit." He gathered together all his strength and swung away from him and went to the storage closet and pulled out one of the bags Alice had sent him. "I think this is mine, unless it belongs to you too now," he said icily.

"Oh, please, darling. Don't do this." His eyes were pleading. "Don't say anything's finished. Certainly not because of this morning. If that was wrong, you've got to tell me why."

"If you don't know, there's nothing I can tell you," Walter said. "There's nothing I want to say to you about anything." He threw the bag onto the bed and turned from it and tried to concentrate on what he was going to put in it.

"You've got to talk to me, darling. I'll help you pack if that's what you want, but I know you don't. At least, I'll do everything I can to see that you don't. Later, darling. Shall I bring you some coffee? You haven't had any breakfast."

"Why is that? I can't move in what I was told was at least partly my own house without finding you fucking somebody or getting fucked."

Tom controlled his laughter so that only a slight chuckle broke from him. "Now, darling. Last night was tremendous, and you know it. Things happened that I've often thought about but never dreamed I'd actually know for myself. All you. So many things. Everything's you."

"Listen, I don't want to hear about your dirty little urges. I was there last night. It's not a memory I want to cherish for the rest of my life."

"I do. It was one of the most amazing things that'll ever happen to us. We're going to be faithful to each other because we've discovered so much to be faithful to. Who else could give us what we give each other? We're more together than any two people have ever been. Won't you let me put this suitcase away, darling?"

They stood near each other, Tom at the end of the bed, Walter at one side of it. Walter assured himself that he never wanted to get any closer. He had seen the light of reason. Tom was trying to turn sordid debauchery into some sort of poetic vision. "It seems silly to put it away, since I'll just get it out again," he said uncompromisingly.

A slight frown crossed Tom's brow. "All right, darling. I better get you some coffee."

"If you've said everything you have to say," Walter said, giving an inch in spite of himself.

Tom dropped onto the end of the bed and brushed back the beguiling new lock of hair that fell across one eye. "I always have something more to say. You know that. Don't you understand the things I've been trying to tell you? People talk about gays as if we're just like everybody else except that we happen to like our own sex. We're supposed to want what everybody else wants—acceptance in the community, marriage after our fashion, and all of the rest of it. People talk about our minority rights, as if we were blacks with a legitimate grievance.

409

That's not it at all. We're unique. I'll never be your wife, no matter how much you fuck me. We're two men. We're rebels. I don't need anybody to protect my rights, except you. I don't want to be integrated into a gay community or a straight community or any other kind. I belong to you. I don't want a model homosexual marriage so that everybody can say we're 'really nice–considering.' I'll break any law if it means getting closer to you. I'm dangerous because I'm bursting with the kind of love that only men can feel for each other. You're dangerous too, darling. I know it. I feel it. We're dangerous because we won't let anybody stand in the way of our loving each other. Look what you've done for me already. The only people who can stop us now are ourselves. We've both tried to control it because we're frightened that it'll destroy us. That's what's finished. I'd rather be destroyed by it than lose it. I talk a lot, and I think I understand certain things, but if I've hurt you, I don't see how I can ever forgive myself. You're the–" He stopped abruptly and seemed to be having trouble getting a breath "–the only hope of happiness I have." He ground the last words out in a choked voice and bowed his head and covered his eyes with his fists. His shoulders shook silently.

Walter wanted to drop down beside him and hold him and end his own agony, but he steeled himself to resist him. Tom could put such conviction into his beautiful voice that anything he said became the truth. He waited until the shoulders were motionless. "Very nicely played, Tom," he said, making his voice as cutting as a knife. "I hope you make notes so you can use these gems in your books."

Tom lifted his head slowly. He tossed his hair back and wiped his eyes with the palms of his hands and looked at Walter incredulously. "I don't believe it. You're not Uncle Walt. Who are you?"

The words wounded Walter in a way that felt fatal. It was all ending. Let it go. "Somebody who cares about decency," he said recklessly. "You probably think we shouldn't."

"Decency?" Tom was on his feet in a blaze of passion. "I'm probably the most decent guy you've ever known. Guilt is indecent. I suppose you feel guilty about last night. How sad and wrong. Hurting people is

indecent. I may've hurt you, but God knows I didn't mean to. You're trying to hurt me. You want to."

"If that's what you think, why don't you clear out?" He had the advantage, so long as Tom didn't act on his suggestion. It felt good to be
independent again, his own master. Tom's presence permitted him to
savor it. "If you want to help with the packing, you could sort out the
shirts."

"What is this, darling?" He touched his forehead with bewilderment, a plea once more in his voice. "Because you were asleep I got out
of bed to do something I could have done right there. I thought you'd
be pleased to know what a man you've made of me."

"Very gratifying, I'm sure. Anything else?"

Tom wanted to lie at his feet and howl. Again. He had to stand up to
him. He knew the barriers people erected around themselves when
they were hurt. If he couldn't get to him any other way, he must dare
to attack. "All right. If you really want to leave, go ahead. Go."

Walter had seen his expression harden and close, and it frightened
him. A chill passed through him. He had decided to leave. Tom wanted to keep him. That was what it was all about. They mustn't lose sight
of that. "If you'd clear out so I can pack—"

"You'd better go back to Clara," Tom cut in. "If you don't, I know
what you'll turn in to. You're going to want boys. You always have, but
you've kept yourself under control all your life. I've corrupted you.
You'll start chasing them. You'll be just one more pathetic queen. You'll
get all you want for a while, but eventually you'll be an aging queen,
and there's nothing more pathetic than that. You'd better go back to
Clara. At least she'll keep you out of trouble."

"You're really asking for it. I'm warning you—"

"I'm warning you. I've started something you won't be able to stop.
You're used to people falling for you and having everything your own
way; but when you start chasing, things change. Lots of pretty boys are
tough cookies. The great Walter Makin will start paying for cock. That's
all it'll be—cocks and asses, cocks and asses. You're as hung up on cock
as I am. Your own mostly, but—"

"Goddamn you!" Walter shouted. He made a fist and took a quick step forward and hit Tom hard in the face.

Tom reeled back against the bureau and remained there, leaning against it. He looked at him with dead eyes. "I loathe people who hit people. Maybe I should've told you. Now I have. I probably should throw you out."

"I'd like to see you try." He wanted to hit him again. That was the surest way of ending it. Make them both hate each other. Then what? His mind reeled through the possibilities—staying with David, going ahead with Tom's play, joining the kids at the ranch, doing the bars to find a boy—and rejected all of them. Killing himself? He doubted if he could. Life on the whole had been marvelous. It had made him an optimist. He didn't want to stop living. He kept his eyes averted from Tom's face. He didn't know what he would do if there was a mark on it. "I don't see why you don't go and let me do what I want to do," he said, wording it to leave room for a reply.

"This is going to come as a big surprise to you, but that's exactly what I'm going to do." Tom remained leaning against the bureau for another moment and then slowly pulled himself upright and started casually, almost indifferently toward the door.

Walter's heart skipped a beat and began to pound violently. The idiot hadn't understood anything. Walter had simply been trying to make him understand that he'd behaved outrageously. The room suddenly felt empty. "What're you…Tom…Tom…" His voice failed. Tears started to fill his eyes, and his chest heaved with a sob he managed to choke back. He wasn't going to give in to it. He was tired. His control was a little unsteady. He heard an infant wail and realized that the strange sound was being forced out of him. He heard the strange wail again. He swayed slightly on his feet. There was a flurry of movement behind him, and Tom's arms were around him. He gave himself to them, and the torrent burst. Great cries were torn from him. They sank down to the edge of the bed and clung to each other. He felt Tom sobbing against him. They beat on each other's backs and shoulders with their fists. They slid off the bed and fell to the floor on their knees, still clinging to each other. They slowly found peace in each other's bodies.

"Darling. My beloved. Sweet darling," Tom prayed against his ear. "Let it all go. I hurt so. I hurt you. We'll never leave each other. We'll be together always. There could never be anybody else for either of us. We're going on now. Together. Always."

They loosened their hold on each other and drew slightly apart. Their faces were streaked with tears. Tom laughed unsteadily. "I'm not trying to get out of making you coffee, darling. I just got sidetracked." His smile faded, and his eyes searched Walter's. "I've hurt you, darling. I can't stand it. I've hurt you."

"Oh, God, Tommy. Yes. If all this means I've got to watch you making love to somebody else, I don't think I can take it. Last night was all right. I understood what we were doing. This morning almost killed me. I'm maybe being stupid, but I can't help it."

"We were taking risks, darling. I know that. We have to take risks if we're going to know all of each other, but I should've waited till you waked up. I swore I'd never hurt you. Something went wrong. It's not easy for me to face myself." His hands tightened on Walter's arms. "We're getting at something, aren't we? We've had to get at it together."

"We're getting at things. I certainly know I can't go back to what I tried to be before. When I was trying to convince myself I had to leave, I honest to God wasn't thinking of Clara."

"I'm glad, darling. I want us to know that we've gotten into something so dangerous that we can't stop thinking of each other and watching out for each other for a second. There's nothing to fall back on. If we think there is, we're done for."

"Can we make it, Tommy? Are we strong enough or good enough or whatever it takes? Will we cleave?"

"Yes," Tom said. "I've hurt you, or you wouldn't have to ask. I know you'll forgive me, because you love me; but that isn't good enough for me. I've got to prove to you that you can trust me."

Walter looked into the depths of love in the deep-set eyes. Straight, true, dedicated. How could he have doubted him? He moved his hands

**413**

over Tom's arms and shoulders and touched the long hair on the back of his neck. "I trust you, Tommy. Still. Again. No. Still–and always. I haven't quite got over being frightened of loving you so much. Are you really going to make that coffee?"

"Poor darling. Can I put the bag away?"

"I wish you would. I don't want to see it again."

They kissed gently and gave each other a little hug, and Tom rose and moved around the room. "I'll change the bed later. We've got to start all over again in virginal sheets. OK, darling. One coffee coming up, with a beer chaser. That'll fix our hangovers."

They went out to the newly enclosed kitchen, and Tom put on the espresso pot. Walter sat at the little table they sometimes used for breakfast. "You think I should call Jerry?" he asked.

"You've got to, darling. He said he was going right home."

He went out to the living room and did so and apologized for his fit of morning bad temper. They promised to see each other soon.

Tom brought the coffee to him. "I'm obviously not going to get any work done today," he said. "You know what I want to do? I want to take you for a sail."

Walter looked up, startled. "You mean in that thing out there that's painted on the water? I don't believe it's real."

Tom laughed. "I'll explain about it so you know how silly I can be. Being with Johnnie made me feel that I should keep some things for mine. I've been out in it a couple of times when you were in the city. I've hurt myself by being alone so I'd know how wonderful it is being with you. All that sort of thing is over since last night."

"Last night seems to have had its effect."

"It has. I think we'll be feeling it for the rest of our lives. Do you know about sailing?"

"Sure. I've done a lot of it in the south of France."

"Aren't we stylish! As a matter of fact, so have I. Let's have some beer, and I'll fix some sandwiches. There's enough breeze."

Walter sat back and looked at him and felt depths of surrender in himself that even Tom hadn't hitherto revealed to him. It imposed a

414

suspension of reason. Tom summoned him to an adventure that would test all of his capacity for daring and survival. He proclaimed the impossibility while urging them on. He had let Walter witness his physical passions as a demonstration of what they could find in themselves for each other. He had carried them beyond any possibility of withdrawal. One didn't withdraw from life.

Tom was smiling happily as he turned and headed back to the kitchen. Walter was immediately on his feet to follow him, feeling better than he had for months. They drank beer and made sandwiches and went back to the bedroom to dress in shorts and sneakers and T-shirts. Tom put on a windbreaker and handed Walter a sweater. "You'll need that. It gets chilly out there."

They collected their provisions, including a bottle of wine, and went down to the jetty and jumped onto the little boat. Less than 20 feet long, with an open cockpit, it rocked wildly in the water. Tom pulled sails out of a locker, and they put them on together. When everything was in order, Tom cast off. It was a simple rig, and Walter knew enough so that he could have been helpful, but Tom was so evidently and delightedly in charge that he sat out of the way on the narrow deck and let his adoring eyes revel in the beauty of Tom in action. He got the sails up, main and jib, and Walter watched the spring of his long legs as he ran back to the tiller. He watched the assured reach of his arms as his long fingers gathered in lines and secured them expertly for immediate release. The sails took the wind, and the little boat tilted and nosed down into the water, and he saw an exultant look light up Tom's face. The cords of his neck swelled as he tilted his head back to adjust his course to the dictates of the sails.

In a few minutes, the city appeared before them, rising startlingly out of the water. Great rolls of fog crowded in under the vast span of the Golden Gate Bridge. Many sails were dotted about the wide bay; some in packs suggested that races were in progress. They began to gather speed as they moved away from land and picked up a fresher breeze. The little boat heeled and kicked up some spray. Walter moved back along the deck and sat close to Tom.

The latter put his free arm around Walter's shoulders and hugged him. "Isn't this marvelous? We're together, darling, completely and forever. I feel it even more out here. I may never take you back to shore."

"I'm with you, skipper." They were both exhilarated by the rush of water and the dazzle of sun and the clean air that filled their lungs and whipped their hair around their heads. Sky and water seemed immense once they lost the shelter of land. It added a special poignance to their dependence on each other, so that for a moment tears gathered behind Walter's eyes. Tom put the boat through its paces, beating into the wind, easing the sheets to take it on the beam while they ate their sandwiches and drank wine from the bottle. In time, he jibed and headed in almost dead before the wind. He dropped down into the cockpit and settled himself comfortably, with the tiller against his neck.

"Is it all right for me to come down there with you?" Walter asked.

"Of course, darling. I'm going in closer to home. I don't like to go too far in case the wind drops."

Walter sat beside him and smoothed his hair with a possessive hand. "It feels marvelous long. I can't wait for it to get even longer. Can anybody see us?"

"If anybody has their glasses on us, they'll see the idiot bliss of my face. It's not the way a potentially distinguished man of letters is supposed to look, but I don't care. Isn't the *Eaglet* a honey?"

"Like her captain—swift and lean and alert. Her captain has something I want to look at in the clear light of day." He unzipped Tom's shorts and drew out his cock. It grew only partially rigid as he did so.

Tom chuckled. "You're diverting my attention from my pure, sexless love for the *Eaglet*. I think you'll succeed if you want to."

"In that case…" Walter slipped his hand under Tom's balls and lifted them out, then worked his way down in the cockpit and lowered his head and played with them with his tongue. Tom giggled, and his cock gave a sudden leap. Walter drew it into his mouth and felt it growing and hardening. Tom made contented sounds in his throat. Tom's cock suddenly surged up and escaped Walter's mouth. Walter lifted himself on an elbow to look at it.

416

"That's what's known as a cock," Tom said. "You may not have noticed, but it's been there all along."

"I've noticed it more than you realize. I've loved it right from the start. It's such a fine, manly thing."

"It's big enough to sustain my ego, but just barely. Now that it's received Jerry's seal of approval, I may start being cautiously proud of it. Not everybody can be built like you. Let me for a minute, darling." He curled his fingers around it, taking over from Walter's hand, and began to stroke it slowly. "Yeah. I remember. That's why I wanted to jerk off for you. There was a bunch of us one summer that used to do this together. Mine was the biggest. The others must've been dwarfs. I guess I wanted to feel like that again, sort of showing off for you." He removed his hand. "It's all yours, darling. I'm glad you like it."

"I love it. I'm going to be as good a cocksucker as you are."

"You have quite a lot of practice to make up for. Hey, do you suppose that's why this is called a cockpit? It never occurred to me."

They shook with laughter. Little spurts of laughter continued to erupt from Walter while he applied himself to perfecting his technique until they were both seized with the excitement of Tom's approaching climax, and they cried out together as he exploded into Walter's mouth.

They returned to the house in an almost ungovernable flood of love and physical well-being.

"How marvelous," Tom said when they had changed their clothes and fixed themselves drinks. "That's everything, darling. We've been sailing together. Now you know all of me and have all of me. Isn't it fabulous to know that everything from now on will be happening to both of us? There won't be any old private secrets that we have to go back to and dig up."

They got the fire going and sat in front of it with their arms thrown loosely around each other.

"Tommy," Walter said incredulously. "I've just realized there isn't a corner of me that isn't full of love for you. I wonder where I've kept it all these years. I feel it in my heels and elbows. I'm ready to believe that nobody except you could do that to me, but you'd suppose some of it would've spilled out sooner. I guess maybe it did a bit for Mark. What a waste. I'm absolutely saturated with love and never knew it. I'm jealous of Mark for having found you 20 years ago and jealous of Johnnie for having had you for 15, but mostly I can't help feeling a bit sorry for myself for never having felt like this. When I asked you to save me that first day, I didn't really know what I was talking about. I do now. Thank you, Tommy."

"Jesus." Tom's eyes searched Walter's. When he spoke, his voice was husky. "Walter. Darling. Darling gay Walter." He closed his eyes and suddenly gathered himself together and sat up, bursting with vitality. "We're going to have so much damn fun," he exclaimed. "I need only about five more days for the novel. Then we'll be together all day and all night, like it was in the beginning, only better. I can't wait to see you at work. I don't care if we fight a lot. It's so marvelous making up. You're going to have to start casting soon, aren't you?"

They were immediately engrossed in details of the production. Walter accompanied Tom to the kitchen; they continued talking while Tom cooked dinner. The realization that they were about to become creative partners took hold and created an electric excitement between them. Their imaginations opened and fed on each other. They were joined, mind, heart, body, in a union as real to them as existence itself.

The hot spell broke the next day. Walter completed his financial arrangements for the production. Tom put away the finished first draft of the novel. Walter ordered actor's sides of the play prepared, and they began auditioning actors at Artie Solvering's theater.

Walter's methods were his own. He had candidates walk around the stage. He had them improvise some simple incident like entering a crowded room or phoning a lover to cancel a date. He rarely had them read a line from Tom's script. In almost every case, he chose an actor that Tom didn't like. Tom was ready to accept his judgment, but it puzzled him.

"I've always known what I can do with actors," Walter explained. "It's the thing I trust most in myself. If a movement or the intonation of a voice scores with me, I know I've got the right person. We've got some

418

good ones, Tommy. I'm going to make this the best production I've done since before I went to Hollywood."

"I trust you, darling. God, just the fact that you're doing it is enough. I fall in love with you all over again every day just watching you work. The more you're you, the more I worship you."

"That's the funny thing about us."

They were so enthralled by each other that they didn't bother to wait to have such conversations in private. They spoke to each other when they had to, and Artie or their friends or casual passersby were welcome to listen. Walter decided reluctantly—he had grown accustomed to working at home—that he had to have an office in the city, so he leased a couple of rooms that reminded him of David's uncle's office way back at the beginning and hired a full-time secretary. He sent an announcement of the production to the local papers, and the world rediscovered him. San Francisco's acquisition of Walter Makin was big news in artistic circles. The fact that he was doing a first play of a controversial nature by the novelist Thomas Jennings was also news. Magazines and the features editors of newspapers besieged Walter for interviews, with interest also shown in Tom.

They agreed that they preferred to respond to these requests together. They were friendly and relaxed with the press and said things to and about each other that left journalists gaping. They lunched daily in the city's smarter restaurants and frequently dined out too. The cooler weather permitted Walter to deck himself out in the finery that had been sent from New York. They were conspicuous wherever they went, always intent on what they were saying to each other, touching when the need arose, two men openly and triumphantly in love with each other. They made the transition from being private people to public personages with no effort. They did nothing for effect. It never occurred to them that they shouldn't behave exactly as they felt.

They were scheduled to go into rehearsal in less than a week when Walter nicked the mole on his neck with his razor. It bled a lot, and he noticed that it felt a bit odd while he was trying to staunch the flow, slightly lumpy and sensitive. The next day he carelessly nicked it again, and again it took some time to stop the bleeding. He examined it more closely and saw that it looked angry, possibly infected, like a small boil. He put some tape on it and hid it with a colorful scarf.

"That damn mole is getting to be a bore," he told Tom. "I probably should get something to clear it up. Do you know a doctor who might work me in today?"

"I wish you'd stop hacking at it. I like that mole."

"I have to shave. You wouldn't like it if I have a great tuft of whiskers growing out of my neck."

"I think you just want an excuse to wear that scarf. It's very becoming, darling." Tom had a doctor friend and called him and managed to fit an appointment into their busy day. The appointment was for right after lunch, and he and Tom had had a bottle of wine, so he cheerfully obliged when the doctor, a youngish earnest man, told him to take off his shirt. He paid little attention while the doctor fiddled with equipment and palpated his neck and shoulders and listened to his heart and did something painful to his sore with some sort of instrument. It seemed an overly conscientious approach to a shaving cut, but Walter had never been seriously sick and rarely went to doctors, so he accepted it as part of the usual routine.

"Can't you just give me something to dry it up?" he asked finally.

"I should think so. However, we might as well be thorough since you're here. When you come tomorrow, I'll recommend something."

"Tomorrow? I can't possibly come tomorrow. I'm about to start rehearsing a show. I'm swamped."

"Oh, yes. I've read about it. Tom's a remarkable writer. You're starting soon, are you? Splendid. Well, I guess you can manage to get away for half an hour."

"It's not convenient. If I call you, couldn't you tell me what I should do for it? Naturally, I'd consider it a regular consultation."

"That's not the problem." The doctor was putting a bandage on his neck. "I think I'll have to insist on seeing you. There's some infection there. I'm going to have a few tests run. You come in tomorrow, and we'll get you fixed up."

"What time?"

"Well, let's see. We better make it 11:30."

"That couldn't be worse. Can't it be earlier, before the day starts rolling?"

"Unfortunately, it doesn't depend on me. I'm afraid I can't count on the results any earlier. No, you be here at 11:30, and I'll let you go just as fast as I can."

"What're the tests *for?*"

"Who knows? We'll have to wait and see what the detectives at the lab find out. You may have anemia, for all I know."

"What's anemia got to do with a cut neck?"

The doctor laughed briefly. "Absolutely nothing. I was just mentioning one of any number of possibilities. You're a remarkable physical specimen. I'm sure we'll pull you through, whatever it is."

Walter recognized the medical witticism and laughed on cue and left. Tom waited outside in his car.

"That seemed to take forever," Walter said as he climbed in beside him. "I'm sorry, Tommy."

"Newton's not a laugh a minute, but he's good. Did he give you something?"

"He's going to. He says it's infected. He's doing some tests, and tomorrow he'll prescribe something. He wants me back at 11:30."

"Oh, well. We have to take care of Mole. We've got to get a move on." They went through their crowded schedule and stayed in the city for dinner. Before they were finished, their eyes were lingering urgently on each other, making food a distraction. As soon as they were home, they made a hilarious rush for bed.

"How had we better handle this?" Walter wondered out loud while they were driving into the city in the morning. "Maybe I should've brought my car. No. We'll go about our business, and when the time comes I'll grab a cab. Your doctor friend said something about half an hour. I'll catch up to you about noon. That's when we're due at Harold's. It'll be the first time we've been apart for half an hour for weeks. Do you think we'll manage?"

"No. Can't I come with you?"

"I'd like you to, but we'd better act like tough businessmen. We've got to get all these odds and ends settled before rehearsals start. We won't be able to leave each other's side for a minute then."

"That's the way I'll write lots of plays, and we'll stay in rehearsal forever." He dropped a hand from the wheel and held Walter's. "It's fun being Siamese twins, darling."

"Bliss, Tommy."

The young doctor seemed a trifle absentminded when Walter showed up for his appointment. He expected him to remove the bandage and look at the sore, but he waved him to a chair and sat behind his desk. He drummed his fingers on its surface for a moment and then swiveled around and checked a desk calendar scrawled with notes.

"We've got a problem here," he said without looking at Walter. "Frankly, I was almost sure of it yesterday. There's no point beating about the bush. We've got a big problem."

Walter felt his feet go cold. Pins and needles started to climb his legs. "You mean, there's something wrong with me?" he asked lightly.

"I'm afraid there is," the doctor said. "I'm not very good at this. Let's start by telling you what it's called. People like to put names on things. What you have there is called a malignant melanoma. Does that mean anything to you?"

A barrier went up in Walter's mind. It couldn't happen to him. He obviously hadn't understood what the doctor was saying. He smiled slightly. "One word sounds familiar. You aren't by any chance trying to tell me that I have cancer, are you?"

The doctor swung around to face him. "I'm always pleased when the patient can say the word. These days there's no need to cloak it in mystery."

There was a beat of silence while Walter grasped the fact that the denial he had been expecting was not to be forthcoming. Visions of Tom filled his mind. The floor tilted. His hand shot out to steady himself on the edge of the desk. His mind blacked out for an instant. He found himself sitting back in the chair, looking at nothing. The barrier

422

was still fairly intact. This was happening to somebody else. He was responsible for the victim. He had to make him function.

"Now what?" he asked in his own voice, competent and decisive.

"Time is of the essence. I've arranged for you to go into the hospital this afternoon. I'm turning you over to specialists. We have some very fine men out here. I think you'll find San Francisco is right up in front in every field. They're taking a special interest in your case, naturally. You're very much in the public eye, what you might call a celebrity."

"You mean, my obituary will get a big play in the papers?"

The doctor smiled thinly. "That's the spirit, but we mustn't get morbid about this. There's every reason to hope that an operation will fix you up. You'll have it this evening or early tomorrow morning. The sooner the better."

His heart stopped. His blood was ice in his veins. Tommy hovered over him, holding his hand, pleading with his eyes. Walter passed a hand over his forehead. Now was the time to come to the aid of the victim. He had to function for him. "What kind of operation?" he asked coolly.

"I'm in no particular position to go into details. I don't know how far it's spread. The usual procedure is to cut into the area and remove all the diseased cells." He moved his hand from his neck to the end of his shoulder. "If they're able to get all of it, you're sitting pretty."

*Sitting pretty*, a voice screamed within him. I'm dying. I'm being taken away from Tommy. Sitting pretty. But that was the victim misbehaving, understandably upset. Walter struggled with him and overcame him. "I'm sorry we don't know each other better, doctor. I don't know how far I can trust you, and I suppose you have professional ethics to consider—the psychological effect on the vic...on the patient, and all that sort of thing. Can you believe that I'm much less concerned for myself than I am for others who are going to be profoundly affected by this? I have to make decisions that may literally destroy at least one other person. You can help me avoid that. Can I trust you to answer my questions truthfully?" He studied the doctor intently so that no flicker of his expression would escape him.

The doctor met his eyes directly. "You seem to me a man who can take the truth. I'll do my best."

"Thank you. OK. How good are the chances that the operation will be successful?"

"Excellent. With the reservation that we're dealing with something that we don't know a great deal about."

"Fine. Is it possible to know, when it's over, whether it has been successful?"

"It's possible to make a good guess on a short-term basis. We don't speak of cures in these cases. *Remission* is the word. We'll know pretty well if all the diseased cells have been removed. That would be considered a success. If there's no recurrence of the cancer for five years, we could hope that the remission would be of a more or less permanent nature."

"Five years?"

"The specialists can give you the statistics. I'm speaking generally."

"And if it's not a success, is it over with quickly?"

"In a matter of months—one, three—maybe as much as a year, there would be symptoms of recurrence. In your case the spread would probably be to the eyes or the chest, but there're other possibilities. It could take several years."

"My eyes? You mean I could lose my sight?"

"You must understand, very radical surgery is involved. A man can't let himself die. It's too painful. Everything must be done to save his life, or we go into the very tricky area of murder. I don't presume to give you advice, but I can tell you what every medical man would say—in your case, the only certainty is that there are no certainties. Now I think we should make the final arrangements for your entering the hospital. I can't emphasize enough the importance of time."

"Just a minute, doctor. This may sound mad, but what if I don't do anything at all? What if I just ignore it?"

The doctor shrugged. "In a matter of days you'd be in such pain that you wouldn't be able to go on. You'd be dead before you could get your show on."

Talking about it quietly made it seem more ordinary to Walter and also less real. He was definitely discussing the victim's case, not his. His mind had even been able to leap forward and consider some practical problems. "What time is it?" he asked.

The doctor looked at his watch. "Ten to 12."

"Will you make a call for me? I'm not sure I can speak to anybody at the moment." He drew out a notebook and gave the doctor the number. "Tom should still be at the lawyers'. Don't ask for him. I don't want him to know the message comes from you. Just tell them I've been held up and I'll meet Tom at our office at 2."

The doctor made the call, and Walter could tell from his end of the conversation that Tom was there. The doctor hung up and looked at the instrument for a moment. "I don't generally ask personal questions, but I think we'll agree that this is serious enough for me to waive conventions. Are you and Tom in love with each other?"

"Yes." Years of shame were dispelled with a proud monosyllable.

"And you don't want him to know?"

"He mustn't." His breath caught. His chest heaved. Tears rushed to his eyes. In an instant he and the victim were one. He bowed his head and kneaded his forehead and tried to force his breathing back to normal through the heaving of his chest. He couldn't break down now. He had too much to do. The doctor stood in front of him and put a glass on the edge of the desk near him. Walter was able to lift it to his lips and smelled whisky and drained half of it. He sat back with a shudder.

"Sorry," he said.

The doctor returned to his chair. "I don't know your motives, but I always respect my patients' wishes in these cases. What you're suggesting is impossible, Walter. I'm willing to lie, but you're going to be in a hospital, where everybody will know. You're going to have a very serious operation. You may lose an arm. I don't think that's likely, but it's a possibility. Tom will have to know. I want you to be prepared because you won't be in any state for emotional strain for some time."

"Then I better get the hell out of town." As soon as he said it, he knew what he had to do. He didn't know how he could do it, but he had to.

425

"What do you have in mind?" the doctor asked.

"I'll think of an excuse and go to New York. Can I trust you not to tell him? He may put two and two together and try to get it out of you."

"Doctors have plenty of experience of talking without saying anything. You can trust me. You'll be losing valuable hours. Professionally speaking, I strongly advise against it."

"Advice noted."

"But you're going anyway. You have people there who'll arrange for your arrival? I'm sure they'll put you into the hands of the best men. I suggest you have them call me. I can give them a reading of our findings. It might save a little time. Are you all right now? Finish that whisky. I want you to get moving. You should be on a plane in no more than a couple of hours."

"That may be pushing it a bit, but I should be there—let's see. Yes, I should be able to get there about midnight their time."

"They'll undoubtedly want you to go straight to a hospital." The doctor handed Walter his card. "I'll be expecting a call. I'll cancel my arrangements here." He rose and came out from behind the desk. Walter pulled himself up—a bit shaky, but he could manage. The doctor shook his hand. "Good luck. There's every reason to hope that you have many good years ahead of you."

Walter moved automatically. He walked down a street and found a cab and asked to be taken to the St. Francis. He hadn't got the hotels here straight. It was the first name that occurred to him. He had to be somewhere he could think and be alone and make phone calls. Take things one at a time.

Tom. He couldn't see Tom. The thought of it made his chest begin to heave. *You're not going to see him*, he told himself hastily. He couldn't look at him without breaking down. Could he leave word that he'd been suddenly called back to New York and would let him know later when he would be back? Keep him dangling, waiting, hoping, wondering, his life at a standstill? Better for Tom's sake to make the break clean and final. He wasn't going to let him watch him die. That was the one thing he had known from the moment the fatal word had been

426

spoken. They had been together barely four months. Months or years of agonized suspense was too great a price to pay for such brief happiness. His body repelled him; it was rotten with mortality. He couldn't demand Tom's devotion while it was being hacked and maimed. At best they would always be shadowed by the knowledge that their time might be cut off at any moment.

Tom's deep caressing voice spoke to him: *You can't leave me. We're the same person. I have the right to share this with you.*

His sight dimmed, and he closed his mind to the voice. He had the right to spare him. If their positions were reversed, he would want every moment with Tom that fate allowed, but he was older, his life had been free of tragedy, he would know that he had nothing more to hope for after Tom. Tom had barely recovered from tragedy. He was young enough to still find everything he wanted in life: success, new love, fulfillment. Let him think that he had betrayed him. It would break Tom's heart, but time healed such wounds. Let him think he was a shit. Anger and outrage would help him over the first shock. Whatever he did, he mustn't leave any ambiguous loose ends that might bring him running after him.

When the taxi stopped, he got out and paid and was able to deal efficiently with the people at the hotel desk. He was recognized, and they were eager to be helpful. He asked to be put on a New York plane any time after 3:00. He asked for a room and a bottle of whisky. He had little cash, but luckily he had credit cards with him. He was ushered into a room and was finally alone to cope with his crisis in any way he wished. He hoped he could keep tears at bay. He went immediately to the phone and called David.

"Listen, old pal," he said, cutting through his exuberant greeting. "This is important. I'm about to leave for New York. There's something wrong with me. I want you here as fast as you can get here."

"Now wait a minute, honey–"

"I haven't many minutes to wait. We're about to start rehearsing Tom's play. I don't want anything to go wrong. You can come up for a few days and take charge and then carry on from down there. The production is all set up. I'm going to ask Alice to have a power of attorney drawn up or whatever we need so you can take over for me. I want Herbie Sklar here. If you can't get him, get Sid Linden. Either of them can direct the show beautifully. I want this play to have the best production you can possibly give it. This may be the last thing I ever ask you to do for me."

"When do you want me there?"

"Right now," Walter said. "Take the first plane you can get. I want you here with Tom."

"Listen, are you telling me you're sick?"

"Yeah. Bad. You know nothing, you understand. I don't know what I'm going to tell Tom, but I'm not going to tell him that. All you know is that I called and told you I had to go to New York and asked you to come up and handle the production. I sounded perfectly normal and natural. Right? Stay with him, for God's sake, David. Keep his mind on the play. Don't let him go off the deep end. Find him a boy if you think it'll help. He likes big cocks. Do anything, goddamn it. Just keep him on the play and keep him going. I'm counting on you sweetheart."

"The studio may come to a grinding halt, but I'll get there. You know that, honey."

"I'll get Alice going on Herbie and Sid. Don't waste time on that till you're here. You usually stay at the Mark Hopkins, don't you? I'll leave word with Tom that you'll be there. I don't think he'll really take it all in till he's talked to you. Stay with him, for God's sake, David. Stay with him."

"Sure, honey. Needless to say, you've knocked me for a loop. I mean, about you."

"Yeah. Don't say any more. That's the way the cookie crumbles. You don't know anything about it, remember. Good-bye, old pal."

"Good-bye, honey."

Walter hung up and, not allowing himself time for self-pity, put in a call to Clara. If she had gone out for lunch, she should be home by now. Alice answered and told him Clara was there. He gave her instructions about Tom's production before asking to be passed on to her.

She was suddenly speaking to him. "Have you found out already?"

"What about?"

"About the money."

"What money?"

"Let's not go on sounding like Abbott and Costello. I obtained a court order stopping any further payment of money to you until we get a few things settled. I thought that's what you were calling about."

"Oh. No, I haven't heard anything." That was a question he hadn't even thought about. Who was going to pay to have him chopped up? Certainly not Tom. "I'm not much interested in money. I'm just about to take off for New York."

"Really? Is this the end of the romance? I told you you'd probably expect me to welcome you home with open arms. I don't think it's going to be quite as simple as that."

"Let's make it as simple as possible. The doctors here think I've had it, Clara. I've got cancer."

There was a silence. When she spoke again, her voice had altered. Hostility had been replaced by tough defiance. "What can you expect of those quacks out there? You'd better get here as quickly as possible."

"That's what I'm talking about. I'm getting on a plane in an hour or two. I'll have the airline let you know when I'm arriving. It seems I should go into a hospital right away."

"Of course. Cousin Clarence is one of the biggest cancer men in the country. I'll let him handle everything. Don't worry, dearest. We'll have you fixed up in no time."

The tremor of alarm in her voice touched him more than he wanted to be touched. He gave her the local doctor's name and telephone number. "He's expecting somebody in New York to call him. He can tell them what they've found out here."

"Good. We'd better hang up, dearest. I want to get everything organized immediately."

"Thanks, Clarry. See you in a few hours." He hung up and rose and went to the bureau, where whisky and ice had been left. He poured himself a stiff drink and took long swallows of it while he wandered around the room. He wondered why he had felt so rushed. There was nothing more to do except the thing he couldn't imagine doing. What could he say to Tom that he would believe? There hadn't been a discordant moment between them since the night with Jerry. Last night they had made love as exultantly as they had every night for months. The perfect harmony they had achieved had transfigured his life, but it didn't make it easy for him now. He longed to find some flaw he could seize on as a convincing justification for what he had to do.

*Think of Tommy, and you can do anything,* he told himself.

He replenished his drink and swallowed some of it and sat at the desk. He placed several sheets of hotel stationery in front of him and drew out his pen. "My very dear Tommy," he wrote. His hands began to shake. The pen slipped from his fingers. He flung himself forward on the desk, and racking sobs were torn from him. He let himself go, knowing that he was beyond control, that his only hope was for his agony to wear itself out. His sobbing slowly subsided, and he was able to see himself, a sick, aging man slumped over a hotel desk wailing like a child. It wouldn't do. Would it help to think of it as some sort of judgment? Just as he was learning to handle forbidden love, it was forbidden him? Neat but not comforting. Death was too arbitrary and meaningless; it offered no lessons. Should he have recognized love (Mark's?) when it was first offered him? The spirit's evolution couldn't be forced. Magic failed. Death followed. There was no point trying to rationalize it. He pulled himself to his feet and went into the bathroom and dampened a towel and bathed his eyes. He returned to the desk and sat down with determination and finished his drink.

He picked up his pen and put a fresh sheet of stationery in front of himself and tried to think of the right words. He could face dying if only it would happen quickly. Tom's long, lithe body would still be moving about in the world. His cock would get hard for somebody else. He wished him joy. He couldn't bear to hurt him, but the very fact of Walter's being alive here, there, under any circumstances, was bound to hurt Tom now. All he could offer him was to make it as easy for him as he knew how. He wrote in his bold decorative script:

My very dear Tommy,

This is an impossible letter to write. You said once that you've always been half prepared for me to go back to Clara. You were right to be. This has been building up in me for a long time. I've discovered that 30 years is too strong to break in the way I tried to do it. You know how hard I've tried to accept being gay. I can't. If you find this hard to believe, considering all the happiness we've shared, remember that I'm a theater man. The theater is good training for secret agents too.

You'll probably be as shocked by my quitting on the play as by everything else. I told you that if I didn't feel up to doing a good job on it, I'd rather see it done by somebody else. That's the way it is. I find that the conflict that's been growing in me is making me more and more unsure of myself. Everything is being taken care of. David will be at the Mark Hopkins later this afternoon and will be expecting to hear from you. You've written a beautiful play. You owe it to yourself to be tough and see it through. That's the one thing I think I have the right to ask of you.

If in the next few months I discover that I've made another hideous mistake, I won't be too proud to come crawling back to you. If I do, I hope for your sake that by then you'll be able to tell me to go to hell. I won't ask you to forget me, but I beg you to believe in yourself and in all the good in you you've offered me. I can't even ask you to forgive me. I'd rather anger made you feel that I'm unforgivable and help you kill regret. Maybe someday we'll be able to meet with the love that will always be in my friendship for you. I'm sure you'll agree that we mustn't see each other or try to get in touch with one another soon. I'm sorry.

W.

He folded the two sheets hastily, unable to force himself to reread what he had written, and sealed them in an envelope. He couldn't imagine Tommy's believing a word of it, anymore than he would believe it if Tommy wrote such a letter to him. He hoped that he would be so lost and confused that his first instinct would be to get in touch with David as quickly as possible to find out if he could shed any light on Walter's inexplicable behavior. He could count on David to handle him as well as anybody could.

He went to the phone and asked the switchboard if the plane reservation had been made. He asked the time. He was surprised that it was so early. Only a little after 1. He had left word for Tom to be at the office at 2. His theatrical sense of timing hadn't failed him. He considered asking the hotel to have the letter delivered, but he knew he'd be tormented by the possibility of a slipup. He had to know the letter was there.

Only two dangers remained. He might run into Tom on the street. If he got held up at the airport, Tom might trace him and intercept him. He would use his VIP privileges to forestall him. He looked around the room and picked up the letter and the whisky.

Downstairs, he signed for the room and the whisky. He filled out a blank check on his New York bank and cashed a small amount. He wondered if what Clara had told him meant that it would bounce. No matter. He couldn't draw another check on his account with Tommy. He was told that his ticket was waiting for him at the airport. He asked for something to carry the whisky in and was given a plastic bag. The solicitude with which he was surrounded irked him. You might suppose they thought he was about to die. He asked for a taxi and went out and got into it and gave the address of the office on Market Street. He looked around cautiously when they pulled up in front of it and told the driver to wait and made a dash for the decrepit elevator inside. The dim woman he had hired as a secretary was there. He handed her the envelope. "Tom will be here in a little while. Make sure he gets that. It's very important. I've got to rush."

He was out and back in the taxi, and they were off for the airport. He breathed a sigh of relief. It was unlikely that Tom could get at him now.

432

He could make his mind a blank and forget everything. From here on, Clara would be taking charge. He took a long swig from the bottle.

He was met with more solicitude at the airport. Officials took him under their wing. He told them that if anybody tried to reach him before takeoff, they were to say that he was already gone. He suggested that he was being pursued by the press and wished to travel incognito. It turned out that there was an earlier plane he could board in about 20 minutes. He asked that Clara be notified of his arrival and was escorted to a deserted lounge, where he took several more swigs from his bottle. By this time he had almost forgotten what he was doing. When he boarded the plane he felt as though he were walking though a dream.

The dream continued. For a while he actually slept and dreamed of Tommy and sailing the boat over land and laughing gleefully with him about something he couldn't quite place. He awoke in a state of agitation, staring around him, looking for him. He fell back in his seat and almost broke down again. He fought back the tears and, as soon as he could, ordered a drink. He seemed to have lost his bottle.

A stewardess came to him when they were approaching New York and told him that his wife would be waiting at Kennedy with a car. He would be the first off the plane and would be escorted to her. The transition had been made. He was now Clara's property.

He saw her flanked by officials standing at a doorway. The officials at his side made him feel for an instant that they were both being marched off to prison. Then he held her briefly and kissed her. The Makins were together again. She was looking majestic and glamorous, a member of the elite of a world he had fled. She made him feel like an urchin who had been called to order after wallowing naughtily in the mud. They thanked the attendant officials and went down a ramp, and he saw Mike waiting at another door. They shook hands.

"It's good to see you back, Walter," Mike said. "We gotta have a talk sometime."

"Sure, Mike. It seems I have to let the doctors have some fun with me first."

"Aw, that won't amount to nothing. You look like a million bucks."

He and Clara settled into the back of the limousine. Mike took his place in front. "OK, Mike. Shut us in." The panel of glass rose between them. Memory stirred. *You were alone the last time you were in this car,* he reminded himself, *so don't get sentimental.* He was enclosed once more in the sterile, hermetic world he had created for himself. Some part of him seemed to go slack, as with a struggle ended. Perhaps that was the only meaning he would find in death: that he was no longer young or adaptable enough to follow the thrillingly perilous road Tommy had opened to him.

"You're looking marvelous, dearest," Clara said.

"You're looking superb yourself, Clarry. With better reason, it seems." This brief exchange told him instantly that whatever had remained of sexuality between them was finally dead. She no longer challenged him. Her manner had softened, but not too much. She wouldn't smother him with solicitude. She was bright and matter-of-fact and affectionate. He felt himself relaxing into the habits of years of sharing. She had the right to officiate at his death, if she chose to do so.

"We're going straight to the hospital," she was saying. "I thought we might have a little welcome-home supper together, but I don't think we'll be allowed to. You've eaten, I suppose."

"Something rather inadequately disguised as food was put before me," he said.

"Poor dearest. Perhaps I'll be able to sneak you some caviar before you're taken away. They want to do some exploratory surgery as soon as you get there. Nothing important, apparently. The big show is for tomorrow morning. There's a surgical team waiting for you. Fortunately, you're here earlier than I expected."

"Have you told anybody about this, Clarry?" he asked. "I don't want anybody to know."

"I thought you might feel that way. I quite agree. People are so morbid. We don't want the vultures to start hovering over us. I've arranged with the hospital not to put your name on the list of patients. They're not to give out to anybody that you're there. You'll have a phone so you can call out, but no calls are to be put through to you. It can all be changed, of course, if you want."

"No, that's perfect, Clarry."

"I've told Alice to tell the staff at home the same thing. You're in the city, but very busy. You'll call back when you can. They're all getting used to your being the Invisible Man." She uttered abrupt laughter, less harsh than Walter remembered. "I don't know what we'd have done without Clarence. He's organized everything. Well, after all, the family practically built the hospital, so he's in a position to give a few orders. He says that in well over 50% of these cases, there's nothing to worry about. It's unpleasant, naturally, but not serious. We'll have you up and about in no time."

"It's good of you to take all this trouble, Clarry. I've thought of you quite often."

"I don't believe that for a minute. I'm sure you were having a glorious time. I've managed. We both needed a vacation from each other. I'm sorry about the money. The lawyers were after me about not leaving everything up in the air indefinitely. It was just a legal ploy."

"I think you've shown admirable restraint."

Long before Mike had brought the car to a gliding halt in front of the hospital entrance, Walter was convinced that he had made the only possible decision. They wouldn't cause each other pain. This was something that two people who had lived together for 30 years could take in their stride. No pain. No torment. Bleak and sad, perhaps, but they wouldn't be presented daily with each other's agony. If he died, he would have died in her care. She would find some satisfaction in being Walter Makin's widow, until Walter Makin was forgotten. She would have the boys. She would have money. If he lived—well, if he lived, he would have to learn to live all over again without joy, without passion, without the radiant light of love. He had managed before.

Their arrival was a confused bustle of orderlies and nurses and interns. He was installed in a luxurious suite full of flowers. There was a bath and a room beyond. When he saw that Clara had moved into it, he realized that this was a bit more serious than she was letting on. He saw immediately that she had brought his most prized possession from the house, a small Cézanne still life. He was delighted to see it again. She had hung it so that he could look at it from the bed. Again, he was more touched than he could allow himself to be.

Young men and women in white kept coming and going, asking him questions about every aberration of his body in the past, filling out forms, demanding specimens of this and that, taking his temperature, his blood pressure, his heartbeat. He was told to get into a peculiar-looking hospital robe. He was told to get into bed. Clara moved about serenely, a still center of order in a fever of medical efficiency. Somebody came and shaved the side of his head, which puzzled and annoyed him. Somebody gave him something to drink.

Clara stood beside the bed and looked down at him with calm, dry-eyed commiseration. "I think you're supposed to go to sleep, dearest. This must've been a frightful shock for you. Don't worry about anything. We'll manage."

"Sure, Clarry." He reached for her hand and gave it a squeeze. She bent and kissed his forehead. He felt the inevitability of their being together for this. He looked up at the vulnerable place under her chin that he had always found so touching. It was looking a bit stringy and haggard, but he smiled as he remembered fondly, vividly, all the times she had stood before him, defying him, challenging him, spurring him on with her fierce loyalty. "I can't let anybody see me with my hair like this. You'll have to find me a turban. Or one of the *Lawrence of Arabia* things. I'd look cute in one of those. The Shuberts probably have some lying around from an old *Desert Song* company."

"He always was a vain man." They laughed, looking at each other with understanding appreciation. He closed his eyes, feeling sleepy all of a sudden. He felt her still standing beside the bed when he took a deep plunge into unconsciousness.

He was aware of a long struggle that ended with the realization that he was waking up. The sensation that seemed divorced from him and yet made him want to cry out in protest became recognizable pain. His neck hurt like hell.

"Christ, it hurts," he muttered, opening his eyes. Clara was sitting under a single light reading, wearing a dressing gown and the glasses that had been increasingly in evidence in the last few years. She looked up, immediately removed them, rose, and came to him. Her carriage was as superb as always and showed no sign of fatigue. "What's going on?" he asked, barely moving his lips. He had found that it hurt to talk. The bandage on his neck felt considerably bigger, but otherwise he seemed intact.

"It's the middle of the night," she said to him quietly. "They've been looking at that place. When you wake up next, the whole thing will be finished."

"When will that be?"

"About noon tomorrow, I think. Well, today to be precise. You're full of sedatives. I'll see if the nurse should give you another shot." She went through the bathroom into the other room. Walter was almost asleep when he heard whispers and felt a needle prick in his arm.

Something was very wrong with Tommy. He was trapped some-how, caught in something. Walter gave a heave to whatever was in the way and awoke with a cry.

"Everything's all right, dearest." Clara's face swam above him. He was aware of a white form at the end of the bed. The whole side of his body was torn with pain. He couldn't move. His left shoulder seemed to be crowded up against the side of his face as if he were wearing foot-ball padding.

"What have they done now?" he whispered. He remembered that it hurt to talk.

"You're all taken care of, dearest. It's finished. You're going to sleep a lot, and the pain will go away. They say you can be out of here in about a week."

"The pain… Can't they…"

Clara turned away, and the white form moved around from the end of the bed. He felt a needle prick his arm again.

Clara watched over his feverish sleep. He looked very beautiful with the chestnut waves falling damply across his brow. She and the nurses had been combing his hair over to one side so that it almost hid what had been done to it. The modeling of his face looked purified, and his flush made him look younger than ever. Her adored and adorable, eternally youthful, eternally foolish boy. She was glad they had been apart for a while. She didn't think she could have borne this if it had fallen on them out of the blue in the midst of the peaceful but lively routine of their life. His incoherent, drugged ramblings about Tommy suggested that their time together had been stormy. She supposed that it had been on the verge of ending when he discovered the disease. He wouldn't have been so eager to return to her if he had still imagined himself to be "very much in love." He wasn't suited to his homosexual caprices, which arose from a twist of his nature that she supposed was bound to burst out from time to time. He was too romantic about them for them to last. He was too masculine to submit to masculine demands, no matter how effeminate his boys had been. She didn't care about them anymore so long as they didn't damage his career. She had been ready to start divorce proceedings to bring him to his senses, but the Makins had been a celebrated couple for too long for an actual divorce to be conceivable. They had more important things to think about now.

She had a conference with her cousin Clarence and the other doctors working on the case.

"I'm afraid we're far from satisfied, Clara," her cousin told her. "The malignancy was very widespread. The biopsies we're coming up with show that we didn't get at all of it. There's a limit beyond which you can't go on sawing away at a man unless you know it's absolutely necessary. We've got a lot to go over before we settle on a treatment. The best thing we can do now is to get him on his feet and get him out of here so he can lead a normal life. The next few months should tell the story."

"You mean, he might have only a few more months to live?" She looked from one to the other of them, challenging them.

"Not at all. There're various operations we can attempt, depending on how it develops. If we don't get it right the first time, we might try the second. I'd say if we get him through the next year, we'll have every right to hope for five more, and after that, maybe indefinitely."

She looked around at them. They nodded. Her cousin detained her as the others were leaving. He handed her a small pillbox. "I want you to have these with you always, Clara. In a case like this, pain can suddenly strike when we least expect it. I'm talking about the kind of pain that nobody can bear. We'll be standing by, but things can't always be arranged at a moment's notice. I don't hand these out indiscriminately, but I can trust you. You're a Washburn. Don't leave them lying around. They're killers. Never give him more than one at a time, and space them out as far as possible."

She dropped them into her bag. "Thanks. You know me. I'm tough. Is there anything you can tell me that you didn't want to say in front of the others? I'd like to be prepared."

"We gave it to you pretty straight. There's only one thing I didn't want to say in front of my colleagues. We may have to turn into butchers. I'm worried about his eyes. He may lose the left one."

"Only one? Do what you have to do, Clarence. I want him to live."

On the morning of the second day, Walter woke up feeling better. The pain was still bad, but lessening. He was aware of feeling drugged instead of just accepting it as a normal condition of existence, which he supposed was a sign of improvement. His thoughts were dull and disordered, but he found he could speak more easily and was ready to talk after the long blanked-out period of almost no communication.

"What's the verdict?" he asked when Clara had finished reading him bits from the morning papers. "The man in San Francisco said I should have a pretty good idea of what to expect after the operation."

"It's not quite as simple as that, dearest. There's apparently a very fine line between success and failure in these cases. They think the operation was reasonably successful, but they don't rule out the possibility of another."

"Come on, Clarry," he said. "Tell me all. This is a perfect time to. I'm still pretty woozy. I don't much care whether I live or die. Which is it going to be?"

"Live, of course. If the operation wasn't a complete success, there'll be a recurrence in a few months and another operation. That should really do the trick. Five years is apparently the magic number. If there's no recurrence for five years after that, all the statistics are in your favor."

"What about my eyes? Did they say anything about my eyes?"

"Nothing in particular. In cases like yours, it seems the eyes can be affected. You might lose one. So what? You'd look very dashing with a patch. You could get a job modeling shirts."

"Oh, Clarry. Is this what we really want? Have me reduced to a few functioning organs so that I can be rolled out for state occasions for the next five years? I'm pretty hideously disfigured already, aren't I?"

"Nonsense. Your neck will be scarred, but you can wear scarves for that. Your shoulder will be a bit peculiar, sort of caved in and bumpy, but your tailor can fix that with some padding. It's all so unimportant."

"I'm going to be such a frightful sham. How will anybody love me for myself if most of me is hanging in the closet?" He could never have had this conversation with Tom. They would be sobbing in each other's arms by now. She offered him the catharsis of indifference.

She made the impatient sound in her throat. "I don't quite see what alternative you can suggest."

"Wouldn't it be simpler if I slit my wrists? It's going to be such a bore for us, especially you."

"I'm not bored," she asserted indignantly. She drew herself up, her eyes alight with conviction. "I'm with you. I've never been bored for an instant since I first saw you. We'll make life even more exciting, knowing that we want to make the most of every minute. After you're 55, we can relax and lead a nice boring old age."

She could touch him. He wished he could make such an impassioned affirmation regarding their life together. It had been good, in the beginning. Something had gone wrong, probably in himself. His mind wandered, trying to follow the thread of a thought that had already eluded him. So much talk was making him sleepy. "Have the boys started college?"

440

"Last week. Think what the next five years are going to mean for them. We'll be watching them get started in life."

"Yeah. Does my mother know about this?"

"No. I told you, dearest, nobody knows."

"I suppose I ought to see her when I get out of here. When did I see her last?"

"Quite recently. Sometime last winter."

"I don't suppose I've been much of a son to them."

"How do you mean? You've given them a lovely house and scads of money."

"Really? So I have. How frightfully decent of me. Still, Dad's retired. It's the least I could do."

"Your father's dead, dearest."

"Dead? Of course he is. I went to his funeral, didn't I?"

"Naturally. You're getting tired. Why don't you have a little nap?"

"No, I'm thinking profound thoughts about parents and children. We're really quite a nuisance to each other, aren't we? I hope I haven't been as redundant to my sons as my parents were to me. I've been meaning to tell you something. You know it already, but just to make it official in case there's any reason to: Jerry Kennicutt's mine."

"I know that, dearest."

"I've seen him recently. He's gay, but he's turned out pretty well. I haven't been redundant to him. I'm very fond of him." Thoughts of Jerry made him restless, and he grew more wakeful. "Have there been any messages for me in the last few days?"

"Not that I know of. Alice knows how to reach me here. She'll let me know if there's anything important."

"If I begin to sit up and take notice in the next day or two, I'd like you to fix it so David can get through too. He's doing business for me."

"The Tom Jennings play?"

"Yeah. It's good. They're probably just starting rehearsals."

"Now that you mention it, Alice did say she had a paper for you to sign when you were able to."

"Fine. Anytime."

441

"It'll be rather marvelous having a new Walter Makin production coming to town. You'll be able to give it the final touches."

"No, I'll leave it to David. I don't want to get into it again." There was some of the old vigor in his voice when he said it.

She allowed a moment's silence to pass. "Do you want to tell me about the last few months?" she asked.

"No, it wouldn't be pleasant for either of us. Have you had any nice men, Clarry? I wouldn't blame you if you did."

"Good heavens, no. Never. I've never been much interested in sex except with you, and I've certainly never fallen for anyone else. I remember I used to say that women are the same as men, but they aren't. I think I'm like most women. If things are right with one man, that's enough. Men stay such children in lots of ways. They think there's a wonderful new adventure around every corner."

"What if there is, Clarry?"

"It's all in the mind. Women's minds are more practical. We want to keep what we have, not go jumping about from adventure to adventure. You've been all the adventure I've wanted. It's not done yet."

"I'm glad you feel that." His energy was beginning to ebb again, leaving a pleasant impression that they were arriving at a new companionship, without the complications of sex. He felt as if he never wanted sex again. Perhaps they would end by being able to talk about anything.

He continued to feel better. His strength began to return. After another few days, he felt up to using the telephone and put in a call for David. He found him in Hollywood. He had been back only a day. He wanted to know about Walter's health and settled for an assurance that he was surviving. He reported that all was well with the play. Rehearsals had been delayed only 24 hours. Herbie had taken over and was enthusiastic about it. Tom was quiet and withdrawn but seemed more thoughtful than emotionally overcome.

"I just don't think he believes it," David said, referring to Walter's departure. "He seems to be waiting, like he's expecting something to happen. We've talked a lot about you, of course. I've made a big thing about the hold Clara has always had on you. That seemed to be the right line to take."

"He's not angry with me?"

"Not remotely. More worried, if anything. He's a remarkable guy. You're his life. He seems to be trying to fit everything together in terms of what you mean to each other. God knows what he'll do when he thinks he has all the pieces in place."

"Oh, Christ, David. You better start telling him what a shit I am. Help him to get me off his mind."

"I think that would probably require brain surgery, but we'll see. I'll be going up there every weekend. I'm introducing him to every stud I know, and I know quite a few, but he just looks right through them. I hope you know what you're doing, honey. I'm not sure."

"For God's sake, David, what else can I do? I don't want him eating his heart out for the rest of his life. You should see me—and I suspect this is just the beginning. There's nothing left of me for anybody to build a life on."

"Jesus, honey, I want to see you. How do you think I feel watching it all go on? This is the worst thing I've ever got into."

"I'm sorry, old pal. I always thought I'd make a more graceful exit."

When he hung up, he wished he weren't feeling so much better physically. He wondered whether he could face the ordeal of recovery. The torment of uncertainty that he had thought was ended when he had sealed his letter to Tom was beginning again. His mind began to turn in circles. If it looked as if he might be more or less well for a while, if Tom were trying to come to terms somehow with what he'd done, shouldn't he see him, tell him the truth, face with him the necessity of being parted? And keep Tom tied to him always, cut off from life and new experience? Pain and drugs had insulated him from emotion. Now that they were wearing off, the familiar fierce craving for Tom was getting a grip on him again. If Tom found out somehow or suspected, Walter would be relieved of responsibility for the decision, and they would learn together what they had to do. *Oh, Tommy, please find out*, he prayed.

Clara kept his mail, on the grounds that he wasn't well enough to be bothered with it, but she screened it carefully with special attention to letters with California postmarks. Letters began to arrive forwarded from the Belvedere address, all redirected by the same hand. She studied it carefully so that she would recognize it. She was puzzled about Tom Jennings. It was hard to believe that he knew nothing of Walter's illness if they'd been living together, equally hard to believe that he would make no effort to inquire about him if they still had the slightest feeling for each other. Walter's reticence about him could mean anything, perhaps simply that he wished to close that chapter of his life, but instinct told her to beware. Tom Jennings might represent more of a threat than she had at first supposed.

Messages were piling up at home, just as they had a few months ago when he had failed to appear for the award. Then, she had been wild with humiliation and frustration, not knowing how to handle the situation. Now, at least, she was in control. She was eager to get him home, where her control would be even more effective. Anybody could wander into the hospital and, with ingenuity, might even arrive at Walter's door. In a week or two they could begin to give small dinner parties, and everybody would see that the Makin household was functioning normally again.

Walter had several more talks with David when Clara was out of the room. Rehearsals were going well. Tom seemed unchanged. He had taken care of a few revisions very effectively.

"There's beginning to be a lot of talk about you around here," David told him, speaking from Hollywood. "People are connecting your flit last spring with your quitting the production and are coming up with all sorts of way-out theories. I've heard you have a serious drinking problem. Some stories are closer to the truth. I don't know where they're coming from. Maybe there's a leak in the hospital. You've got to be prepared for Tom's hearing something."

"Oh, God. I'm getting out of here tomorrow. People will be seeing me around soon. That should end the talk. Anyway, he knows more about the flit than anybody else. He won't pay any attention to stories that try to make something of that. He knows you're in touch with me, doesn't he? It's up to you to convince him that I'm all right." If Tom was going to find out anyway, shouldn't he let David tell him now and end any doubts that he might have about Walter's fidelity to the pledges they had exchanged? Knowing that Tom must doubt him was beginning to drive him mad. But that had been the point. He wanted Tom to doubt him. He wanted to make it easy for Tom to cut him out of his life. He couldn't trust his judgment in his weakened condition. He had known what he was doing when he had written his letter. Stick to it.

He hung up in a torment of indecision. *Please find out, Tommy,* he begged.

The next day he was made ready for the return to the house. His bandages had been reduced to manageable dimensions. He had trouble getting his arm into sleeves, but with help he was able to get more or less dressed, with a jacket thrown over his shoulders. Putting on clothes made him acutely aware of how much weight he'd lost. He was a bag of bones. Clara combed his hair rather bizarrely over the shaved patch. He did his best to carry off his farewells to the hospital staff with aplomb.

Mike drove them the few blocks to 75th Street. The cop on the beat stood nearby to hold the criminal classes in check. He was bundled into the house under the curious stares of a few passersby. Fortress doors closed behind him. He breathed pure conditioned air. Alice and the others made a fuss over him. He went up to his handsome living room and stood for a few minutes looking around at his possessions, thinking of the house on the water, of garden vistas descending to the jetty and the little boat bobbing at the end of it, of moving freely indoors and out breathing real air and careless of clothing, feeling a presence in whom all his thoughts and hopes and desires were concentrated. *Come to me, Tommy. Please find out. Oh, Christ, come to me.*

He made the library his headquarters, and a new life began. He felt almost well enough to go about his business normally, but not quite. He was still under heavy medication. Clara administered numerous doses according to the doctor's orders without knowing what they were for. She noticed that his mood altered drastically from hour to hour. He was frequently bright and lively but as just frequently drifted into absentminded lethargy. At least he never seemed deeply depressed.

The doctors had told her that it was important for him to regain some weight, and she gave a great deal of attention to his meals. His favorite foods were heaped before him, and he ate well, but it had no immediate effect. His California tan had turned yellow, and the operation had altered the balance of his face. One eye drooped perceptibly so that by contrast the other seemed to have a pronounced upward slant. The loss of weight was beginning to give him a wizened look.

After he had been home for five days, he noticed that his eyes were playing tricks on him. They didn't focus properly for minutes at a time, so that when he reached for something, his hand went through it. He also felt several unfamiliar sharp stabs of pain in his chest and shoulders during the day. He knew he was probably hypersensitive to any new symptoms, but he told Clara about it. She reported to her cousin.

"It may be happening faster than we expected," he said. "You better bring him in and let us have a look at him in the morning. I doubt if it's anything to worry about for the moment, but keep those pills handy. They'll make a big difference when the time comes."

Clara joined him in the library for their usual drinks before dinner, dressed as carefully as if she were going out. She knew he took pride in her appearance. He was wearing one of his expensive dressing gowns with folds of scarf arranged carefully around his neck. Emile brought ice and checked the bar cabinet and left them.

"We're going to get the last of those bandages off you tomorrow," she said. "Clarence wants to have a look at you."

"He has peculiar tastes." He smiled at her over his glass, the ghost of an imp lurking in the corners of his mouth. "I'm going to die, Clarry. We both know it. Don't you think we might have more fun if we just admit it?"

"You're not," she asserted vehemently. "Not this way. I won't let you. We're all going to die someday."

"Exactly. Some of us sooner than others. I wish you wouldn't mind so much. I'm sorry to drop off so soon, but there's really a great deal to be said for it. I'll go out in a blaze of glory. The award. The cover of *Time*. What more could I want? For a while in California, I thought I might be getting into a whole new thing. I had some exciting ideas. I know now I'll never have the strength for anything new. I'll go through another operation to show what a good sport I am. Let them have an eye if they want one. Then I'd like to pack a trunk of painkillers and take off for places where they don't have any doctors. Let's go to all the places I've never been. Exotic islands. Lazy lagoons. I'll decay elegantly amid rotting tropical vegetation."

She laughed dismissively. "You're too absurd. A trip sounds lovely. We'll go as soon as the doctors say we can. There's no reason to assume there's going to be another operation." She would find some way of making him want to live. She had always saved him. She had saved him from David. She had saved him from Mark. She had saved him from destroying his career in Hollywood. She would save his life. He had always been idolized by others. Only she knew the flaws and fissures that might have brought the idol crashing to the dust. She would continue to shore him up. "You'll want to be here for the opening of the new play, won't you?" she asked.

He put his drink down and looked at her thoughtfully. "I'm not sure. Tom's the last person I want to know about this. If he should find out and turns up in the course of time, I'll want to see him. You understand that, don't you, Clarry?"

"Of course," she said. "Why shouldn't you?" Her curiosity about Tom Jennings was satisfied. Walter was protecting him. He didn't trust their relationship to survive the knowledge of his condition. She accepted his faith in her as a tribute to the strength she had always offered him.

He picked up his glass and drank, and a touch of his old jauntiness returned. "I'm glad I'm ending with this play. It's going to be a sensation. It may not run long, but they'll know I haven't lost my touch. It's the best thing I've done since I was really picking them."

David called at noon the next day soon after Walter had returned from his visit to the hospital. He took the call in the library.

"He's gone," David announced dramatically but hurried on. "Don't worry. It's all right. I think I've got the whole story. He didn't turn up for rehearsals yesterday afternoon. I've told them to let me know if anything unusual turns up, especially anything to do with Tom. They tried to call him at home and got no answer. I called a guy who knows him and asked him to go right out to the house—you can imagine what I was thinking..."

"For God's sake, it wasn't anything like that?"

"No, I tell you. Everything's all right. This friend of mine found a woman there who works for him. She said he'd packed an hour or so earlier and had told her that he might be gone for some time. She was closing up the house. I checked the airports. He took an evening plane for New York."

Walter closed his eyes and gripped the phone until his hand ached. He breathed deeply to control the beating of his heart. "Is that all? What do you suppose it means?"

"I don't know, honey," David said. "All that matters is that anybody who's planning to do themselves mischief doesn't go off on a trip. They stay home."

"He hadn't told anybody he might skip rehearsals?"

"Definitely not. They even waited half an hour for him. He must've heard something during the break and decided to take off."

"Heard what?"

"How do I know? It might have nothing to do with you. Maybe there's somebody in New York he has to see. Maybe he's going to Europe. Right in the middle of rehearsals of a play that means a lot to him. Your guess is as good as mine."

"OK, David. Let me know immediately if you hear anything more."

He dropped the phone and sprang up and went to the drinks cabinet. His hands shook while he poured himself a whisky. He knew as well as David why he had come, but he still had to leave it all to Tom. There was a faint chance that something else had brought him. He lift-

448

ed the glass in a shaking hand and drank. He bowed his head and closed his eyes to fight back tears of gratitude. *Oh, Christ, Tommy. You've found out. You've come.*

Clara was in her bedroom when she went over the telephone messages that had come in while they were at the hospital that morning. She had been prepared for it, but she was surprised to see that he was in the city. "Please call Thomas Jennings immediately. Hotel Gladwyn." She went to the phone and repeated her instructions to Alice that nobody except David was to be put through to Walter without checking first with her. She found Walter in an oddly elated mood at lunch, but she was used to his ups and downs. He even tried to construe his interview with Clarence as being favorable. It was the first sign he had given that he still had hopes of recovery.

When she went over the mail the next morning, her attention to postmarks almost made her miss the handwriting. She was about to drop the envelope onto the pile she would pass on to Walter when she caught herself and looked at it again. It was unmistakable. She turned the envelope over. It was plain, with no return address. She slit the envelope with a letter opener and pulled out a single sheet of Hotel Gladwyn stationery. She read it.

Darling,

I know now. I understand, but you were wrong. We belong to each other, all of us, remember. I knew your letter was nonsense. You may be a theater man, but you'll never make a writer.

I've come to take you back as soon as you can go. If it's going to be some time, I'll find a place here. I'm happy again just being near you. I have a feeling that I'm being kept from you. I don't blame her, but it won't work. I know you want me with you. I can't be anywhere else. If I don't hear from you by this evening, the next crash you hear will be me breaking down your front door.

Our Tommy

She tore the sheet into a number of pieces with her calm, competent hands and dropped them into the wastebasket. She called the protection service and asked for special surveillance of the house for the next few days. If anybody was seen loitering in front of the door, he was to be cleared off. She called down to Alice and told her to tell everyone to pay particular attention to the viewing screen before opening the door. Nobody was to be admitted without her specific instructions. If he persisted, she would call him and tell him Walter didn't want to see him.

She found Walter distracted during the day, but he talked again about the chances of his not having to have another operation. They were sitting over a game of chess in the late afternoon when Emile brought them a telegram. She rose and took it, moving out of Walter's reach, immediately on her guard. She opened it and glanced through it and shrugged. She turned back and handed it to him.

"I can't make head or tail of it. Do you have another production up your sleeve, dearest? It gave me a turn for a minute. I thought Clifton was returning to haunt us."

Walter's eyes caught the first word printed on the impersonal form. His hands began to tremble violently, and the paper slipped into his lap. He shoved his hands into the pockets of his dressing gown to conceal his agitation. His breath choked in his throat, somewhere between laughter and tears. His whole body contracted with an effort at control.

"What is it, dearest?" Clara was standing over him.

He shook his head. His eagerness to read the telegram helped him over the seizure. "It's just that damned pain." His voice was almost normal. His eyes took in the message lying in his lap.

"It looks bad. Is it passing?"

"Sure. I'm OK now." He picked up the telegram and studied it.


Eaglet production available. Please notify terms immediately. Glad to win.

                                                                Webb

450

Clifton Webb. Mr. Belvedere. He'd called Tom Mr. Belvedere all one day. It had been a great joke. He puzzled for a moment over the last phrase and then remembered the name of his hotel and understood.

"Does it make sense to you, dearest?"

Clara's voice reached him though layers of relief and apprehension and joy. The enigmatic wire made him feel a need for secrecy. "I think it's from Josh. There was some elaborate bet. I've forgotten exactly. I think it was Josh. Maybe it was Hal. I'll make some calls tomorrow and find out." He folded the wire and put it in his pocket and kept his hand on it, a talisman.

Clara was seated opposite him again. "Whose move was it?"

He pretended to study the board. He wanted to appear relaxed and unhurried. "Yours. Maybe we better finish later. I always feel tired after those pains. I think I'll lie down for a minute before it's time for drinks."

"Of course, dearest. I'm sorry."

He took his time rising and leaving the room. Once out of it, he hurried up to his bedroom and locked himself in. He wanted to shout with joy. He grabbed the phone and asked for the Gladwyn Hotel. His legs began to tremble while he waited, and he sank onto the edge of the bed. The call was answered, and he managed to ask for Mr. Jennings before his breath caught, and he willed him to be there. There was buzzing on the line.

"Hello," Tom said.

"Oh, Christ," he groaned.

"Oh, darling. Oh, Jesus."

"Yeah."

"Oh, god, darling, it's you."

"It's you, Tommy. Oh, God, I've waited so—"

"Are you all right? You sound funny."

"I'm crying."

"Me too."

"Tommy, Tommy."

"Yeah. I know."

"Do you? Do you know the whole sad story?"

451

"Yeah. I know that too."

"How did you find out?"

"I don't know why it took me so long. I suddenly had a hunch the other day. I called Newton–you know, the doctor–and pretended I knew. He spilled the beans."

"I thought you were here. I've been waiting for days."

"Didn't you get my messages or my note?"

"No. Nothing."

"I thought so."

"Was that the point of the nutty wire?"

"I had to get through to you somehow," Tom explained. "I thought of asking David to tell you I was here, but I was afraid he might be in on some sort of plot too."

"You mean, Clara knows you're here?"

"She must. You should've got my note this morning."

"What did it say, baby?"

"Just that I've come to take you away. Or stay here. Whichever makes sense."

"I'm a wreck, Tommy."

"A beautiful ruin?"

"That's only half accurate."

"Would you care what I looked like?"

"No, but I don't want you to get a shock." There was no reply. "Tommy?"

"Yes, I'm crying, that's all. I love you, darling, the way you are, the way you're going to be, for however long we have."

"What're we going to do, Tommy?" Walter pleaded. "I didn't want you to know. I didn't want this to–"

"I understand what you've been thinking, but it can't work that way. We're the same person, darling. You know that."

"I've got to think. We've got to talk."

"Sure. We'll be together. You need me, darling. I need you. That's the way it is."

"Tommy. Tom Jennings. My Tommy. I love you, darling."

"I never had any doubt about that."

"Thank you, baby. It killed me to think you might. Oh, Christ, I can't stand doing this to you."

"It is sort of a dirty trick, but that's the way you are. Getting sick and scaring a guy to death. I suppose you wanted to find out if I really cared."

"It was an attention getter. You must admit that. Oh, God, Tommy. Will we really be together? Don't decide anything till you see me. You don't know all the details. You'll come tomorrow?"

"Not right away?"

"You'd have to see her. They've got me pretty hemmed in. To tell you the truth, I don't think I could stand it. I was waiting for you. That telegram was just about all my shattered nerves could take. The way I feel now, I'd just hang on to you and cry my goddamned eyes out. Give me till morning to pull myself together."

"Sure, darling. I told you in that note that I'm happy. It's true. The last few weeks have been rough. I'm happy again. I've never been happier in my life."

"Same here, Tommy. Maybe I'll decide to live after all."

"You're damn right you will. We're together. We're going to keep it that way."

"Yeah. Listen. Come at 10. I'm usually in pretty good shape by then. I'll make sure you get in, even if I have to stand out on the stoop."

"Get a good rest. I'm going to be all over you. You'll need your strength. Your shoulder's a mess, isn't it? Newton's been keeping in touch with the guys here. I can't wait to see it and kiss it and fall in love with it. A whole new kooky sex kick."

"Jesus, Tommy. You've just worked a miracle. My cock has arisen from the dead." He heard himself laughing. He heard Tom laughing. He'd forgotten what simple loving fun was like.

"Keep it that way till tomorrow. I'll tell you one thing. However we work it, I'm not spending another night alone. If you don't want me, I'll find somebody who does."

"Just try. I'll come over and shoot you dead. Good night, Tommy."

"Good night, darling."

"You didn't believe my letter?"

"Not for a second."

"I tried, baby."

"I know."

"Would you've believed anything I said?"

"No, we belong to each other."

"Oh, God."

"That's it."

"Yes, I guess it is." Walter hung up slowly. He rose and wandered around the room. He stopped in front of a mirror. His hair was growing out so that it wasn't very noticeable. Had Tom said something about Dorian Gray? It was happening. His neck looked slightly bent. His eyes were at odd angles. He looked his age. Would he care what Tom looked like? No. He could imagine loving him in different ways if he were disfigured. Tom was here. He had tried to spare him. Now he would take whatever comfort he was prepared to give.

What would he say to Clara? He should give her hell about the messages, but he decided not to mention them. He didn't want to make her feel guilty. She would only take it out on Tom somehow. At least, there was no need for secrecy.

"Feel better?" she asked as he rejoined her in the library. "I've waited for you before I had a drink. I'm sure we both want one." She went to the cabinet.

"I've just talked to Tom Jennings. He's here. That wire was one of his jokes. It took me a few minutes to figure it out. I'm not at my most brilliant these days."

"So he *is* here," she said with her back turned to him, handling bottles and glasses. "There was a message—yesterday, I suppose—with a rather garbled name, like Lewing or Jewing. It crossed my mind that it might be Jennings. I meant to check downstairs but forgot. Isn't he supposed to be with his show on the Coast?"

"I'm sure he is. I didn't get around to asking him how long he's staying, but he'll certainly have to get back for the final rehearsals. He's coming to see me tomorrow morning. I'll want to have a private talk with him. I think I'll ask him to stay with us. There's no reason for him to pay for a hotel."

She brought him a drink. "Do you think that's a good idea, dearest?"

"How do we know what's a good idea any more, Clarry? You and I are friends, aren't we? We love each other. There's room in our life for others. I can use all the love I can get. I know you'll like him."

"That may be, but shouldn't I have a chance to find out? You say you're not at your most brilliant, but you're surely aware that there's been a great deal of talk about you and Tom Jennings in the last few months."

"Who cares? I want to live, Clara," he cried. He was shocked at the depths of despair his voice revealed. He tried to go on more calmly. "I...we..." He wanted to tell her that he was in love, but the words stuck in his throat. He was suddenly on the edge of total breakdown. Tom offered him happiness, and he faced death. Tom brought him love and passion and light, and he had known all along that he could repay him only with suffering. He mustn't break down. He might never be able to put himself together again. He stumbled to a chair and got rid of his glass as he felt everything in him splinter and crack. He let out an animal howl. He rocked in the chair and lifted his head and shouted and sobbed with helpless despair.

Clara stood very straight, looking down at him. Her knuckles were white on her glass. The love affair wasn't over. She could despise him, but her heart bled for him. He looked so old and frail and pitiful, racked by his youthful love. She thought of him long ago standing naked in front of her on a beach at night, and she wanted to weep for him, but it wasn't yet time for tears. He still needed her strength. Hadn't he looked at himself? Didn't he know what any young man, no matter how much in love, would see in him? The thought of his big sex lifting from his ravaged body horrified her. She must save him once more. She must save him from humiliation and pain. She understood at last why he didn't want to live. Love would make life a torment for him. She would save him from life.

455

She went to him and stood over him and hugged his tortured body close. He flung his arms around her and buried his face against her. She stroked his hair and soothed him, and the sounds of his agony subsided. Eventually his arms dropped from her, and he slumped back in the chair with a hand over his eyes.

"I'm sorry, Clarry," he said in a drained voice. "It's pure self-pity. I swore I wouldn't give in to it."

"You're not made of stone, dearest," she said. "You've been magnificent through all this. You have the right to let go sometimes. It's all right. We'll have you through it soon. And of course, dearest, have Tom stay here if you want."

"Thanks. It can't be for long. I'm going to make him go back to San Francisco. He mustn't lose touch with his play."

She went to the table where she had left her bag and found her compact and touched up her face. She withdrew the pillbox. She didn't think she would get into any trouble. Only Clarence knew she had them, and nobody was apt to ask questions. She would act the heartbroken widow. Act? Her heart was broken, but she would find peace with him.

He dropped his hand and lay back in the chair for a moment with his eyes closed. He gathered himself together and rose. "Let's get drunk, Clarry," he suggested with a faltering attempt at gaiety. "I haven't been drunk in years."

"What a lovely idea. We'll careen around the room and sing 'Sweet Adeline.' Here, dearest." She took his glass and dropped five pills into his hand.

"What's this? Something new?"

"You'll be starting a new treatment next week. That's part of it." She poured him a fresh drink and handed it to him and watched him pop the pills in his mouth and gulp them down. A little shiver ran down her spine.

"I'm anxious for you to meet Tom." He took his glass to the sofa and sat. She sat in a chair opposite him. "His being here will give you a few days to catch up on things. I hope he'll stay for lunch."

456

"Make whatever arrangements you like, dearest. I suppose you'll want to talk to him in here. I'll see that you're not disturbed."

"I'm tired. I mustn't let myself do things like that. It takes too much out of me."

"I'll see to it that you don't feel that way again. Tell me about his play, dearest. I don't know much about it."

He did so, thinking of Tom. A few days together here would give them a chance to feel their way toward the future. When Tom came back after the West Coast opening, he could stay here again. Whether that could become a permanent arrangement depended on whether they could feel really together in these surroundings. He was resigned to another operation. They couldn't make serious plans until that was out of the way. If Tom and Clara made friends, there would be various possibilities.

"I don't think I'll tell you how it ends," he said, completing his ré-sumé of the play. "You'll be seeing it. I don't want to spoil it for you. Give me another drink. I don't seem to know how to get drunk anymore."

She mixed him a stronger one. "That should do the trick," she said, smiling at him as she handed it to him.

He took a swallow and gasped. "Wow. That's strong. Are you keeping up with me?"

"I'm doing all right. I'm about to burst into song. Clara the Crow."

He chortled. "It's just making me feel sleepy. This is ridiculous."

"Why don't you put your feet up for a minute, dearest?"

"I guess I better. I'm…" He stretched out on the sofa and closed his eyes. Tom appeared in the center of his mind, a smile lighting his face. He would see Tom tomorrow. Tom was… His mind wandered. He was very sleepy.

She sat watching him, her hands gripping the arm of the chair. She saw his breathing grow deeper. She watched a flush mount to his cheeks. He was looking younger again. She rose and arranged a wave of hair on his brow and resumed her seat. She stared into the space in front of her, listening to his deep, regular breathing. Her mind was a blank of waiting.

457

The buzzer signaled that dinner was ready. She went to the house phone. "Mr. Makin is sleeping, Emile. You'd better hold dinner. Perhaps we'll have trays up here. We'll see."

She returned to her chair and sat watching him. His breathing was getting heavier. She would have to call Alice and tell her to come back for the night. There would be the newspapers to deal with. She watched his breath grow irregular.

He made a whimpering sound. His eyelids fluttered. His body gave a twitch. The corners of his mouth curled up in a gentle smile. Still dreaming?

She went to him and kissed him on the mouth. He was leaving her for the only rival she would allow to take him from her.

The next day the following story appeared on the front page of the late editions of *The New York Times* with a photograph under a two-column headline.

Walter Makin, the internationally celebrated theatrical producer and director, died suddenly last night after a short illness. He was 50 years old and lived at 159 East 75th Street. Mr. Makin catapulted to fame in 1940 at the age of 20 with his production of *A Light in the Forest*, a play adapted from the French. The rapid succession of his hits, all produced and directed by Mr. Makin, that followed his debut earned him the nickname of Broadway's "Boy Wonder."

Mr. Makin revolutionized all branches of the theater arts. His Theatre Today, a repertory company that he managed for five years, came closer to establishing a national theater than any other company in the history of the American theater. His first film, *Gone Is Nowhere*, which he directed in 1951, created a new trend in comedy-action pictures and is generally regarded as a classic of its kind. Many of today's leading players began their careers under Mr. Makin's direction.

458

Mr. Makin was honored last May by the entire spectrum of the performing arts with a special award for his unique contributions to his profession over the course of his long and active career. He was prevented by illness from attending the ceremony. His health recovered, and he was reported to be preparing a new production before his final illness.

Mr. Makin was born May 17, 1920, in Morristown, New Jersey. He attended the...

The story was continued on the obituary page and ran for two columns, with additional photographs, listing Walter's many productions, the notables associated with his career, and his nontheatrical activities.

The following day, the paper's obituary page carried a shorter story reporting the death by an overdose of barbiturates of the well-known young novelist Thomas Jennings.

# a
## alyson
## books

**B-BOY BLUES,** by James Earl Hardy. A seriously sexy, fiercely funny, black-on-black love story. A walk on the wild side turns into more than Mitchell Crawford ever expected. "A lusty, freewheeling first novel.... Hardy has the makings of a formidable talent." *–Kirkus Reviews*

**2ND TIME AROUND,** by James Earl Hardy. The sequel to best-seller *B-Boy Blues.* "An upbeat tale that—while confronting issues of violence, racism, and homophobia—is romantic, absolutely sensual, and downright funny." *–Publishers Weekly*

**MY BIGGEST O,** edited by Jack Hart. What was the best sex you ever had? Jack Hart asked that question of hundreds of gay men, and got some fascinating answers. Here are summaries of the most intriguing of them. Together, they provide an engaging picture of the sexual tastes of gay men.

**MY FIRST TIME,** edited by Jack Hart. Hart has compiled a fascinating collection of true, first-person stories by men from around the country, describing their first same-sex sexual encounter.

**THE DAY WE MET,** edited by Jack Hart. Hart presents true stories by gay men who provide intriguing looks at the different origins of their long-term relationships. However love first arose, these stories will be sure to delight, inform, and touch you.

**THE PRESIDENT'S SON,** by Krandall Kraus. President Marshall's son is gay. The president, who is beginning a tough battle for reelection, knows it but can't handle it. *"The President's Son*...is a delicious, oh-so-thinly veiled tale of a political empire gone insane." *–The Washington Blade*

**THE LORD WON'T MIND,** by Gordon Merrick. In this first volume of the classic trilogy, Charlie and Peter forge a love that will survive World War II and Charlie's marriage to a conniving heiress. Their story is continued in *One for the Gods* and *Forth Into Light.*

**HORMONE PIRATES OF XENOBIA** AND **DREAM STUDS OF KAMA LOKA,** by Ernest Posey. These two science-fiction novellas have it all: pages of alien sex, erotic intrigue, the adventures of lunarian superstuds, and the lusty explorations of a graduate student who takes part in his professor's kinky dream project.